Dear Reader:

It is once again my pleasure to present a novel by Cairo, one of the latest and hottest editions to the Strebor Books family. His first book, *The Kat Trap*, was so intriguing that it became an instant classic. This book is also destined to become a classic.

Bianca Rivers is sexually liberated, to say the least. Some might even call her a sex addict. Others might call her "that chick." I call her "the other side of most women on the planet." There are truly two sides to every woman; the side acceptable by society and the side that hides behind a veil of fear. Bianca has no fear. She explores life with reckless abandonment and men adore her.

Hopefully, after you read this book, you will walk away analyzing your own sexual behavior, the decisions that you make in the name of love and lust, and how everything has its consequences. Cairo has once again penned a wonderful novel and we are all highly anticipating his future works.

Thanks for supporting the authors in the Strebor family and for the continuous love and support that you have shown me over the past decade. I love and appreciate each and every one of you. To find me on the web, please go to eroticanoir. com or my social networking site at planetzane.org. You can find me on Twitter as PlanetZane, on Facebook as Zane Strebor and on Myspace as Zaneland.

Peace and Many Blessings,

Zane

Zane
Publisher
Strebor Books International
www.simonandschuster.com/streborbooks

ZANE PRESENTS

THE
MAN HANDLER

ZANE PRESENTS

THE
MAN
HANDLER

A NOVEL BY
CAIRO

SBI

STREBOR BOOKS

NEW YORK LONDON TORONTO SYDNEY

SBI

Strebor Books
P.O. Box 6505
Largo, MD 20792
http://www.streborbooks.com

ISBN 978-1-59309-276-4
LCCN 2009927606

First Strebor Books trade paperback edition October 2009

Cover design: www.mariondesigns.com
Cover photograph: © Keith Saunders/Marion Designs

10 9 8 7 6 5 4 3 2 1

Manufactured in the United States of America

For information regarding special discounts for bulk purchases,
please contact Simon & Schuster Special Sales at 1-866-506-1949
or business@simonandschuster.com

The Simon & Schuster Speakers Bureau can bring authors to your
live event. For more information or to book an event, contact the
Simon & Schuster Speakers Bureau at 1-866-248-3049 or visit our
website at www.simonspeakers.com.

This book is dedicated to the voyeurs,
the exhibitionists,
and the grown and sexy.
Indulge your sexuality and sensuality respectfully.
Enjoy the sexual revolution responsibly!

ACKNOWLEDGMENTS

I am still a work in progress. Still evolving, still growing, still learning how to be better than the day before. All praises continue to go to the Almighty for continuing to guide my steps.

To all those who continue to believe in me, thank you for the never-ending love, support and encouragement.

To the growing fans, thank you, thank you, thank you!

To the sexually liberated and the open-minded, I hope you get pleasure from reading *The Man Handler* just as much as I took pleasure in writing it. Enjoy the journey!

One luv—

Cairo

CHAPTER
ONE

Is it me, or is there something primitively erotic, sexually enticing, about the scent of lust and musk that lingers beneath a man's balls and clings to every strand of his dick hairs? Mmmm. I want to rub my face all up in it, then inhale deeply, savoring the sweet, sweaty aroma. Mmmmmmmm. The smell causes my nipples to harden, my clit to swell and pop out from under its hood, and my pussy lips to part in anticipation…waiting, wanting, needing to be pierced by the hot spear of a dark, delicious man.

Oh, how I love the feel and the taste of a stiff, thick dick. Mmmm. I'm salivating thinking about all the nasty, freaky things I can do with one right now. Suck it, slurp it, lick it, kiss it…Mmmmmmmm…gulp it down one inch at a time nice, slow, and very wet. Humph.

Umm, hold up. Before we go any further, let me officially introduce myself. My name is Bianca Rivers. And I *love* to fuck. Oh my God, if that didn't sound like an introduction for an AA/NA meeting or something. Let me try again. Hello. My name is Bianca. I'm a thirty-year-old, five-foot-eight-inch, 125-pound, cocoa-brown beauty who is happily single with an insatiable sex drive and a penchant for being on the hunt for a stiff dick.

It's too bad I haven't been successful at finding one man who can hold my interest longer than the time it takes for him to bust his nut. After the sex, I generally want nothing more to do with them until the next time I feel like riding down on their dicks. Stick and move. Stick and move. That's what I typically like to do. No need for anything else. I have no time to catch feelings for anyone. And I definitely don't want them catching any for me.

Now, just so we're clear. I have no intentions of bashing men, or having a pity party. 'Cause I'll be the first to tell you that I hate women who sit around like a bunch of hens, cackling and cawing about the woes of their lives, relentlessly complaining about their men, or men in general. So, no, I'm not going to spend my time dissing men. However, I will share my own personal experiences with them, and that will include the good, the bad and the ugly, as well as my thoughts, feelings, and views on women, which definitely won't always be nice. So if anyone can't handle that, then you might want to close up shop now and excuse yourself.

Anyway, I'm not in a relationship (by choice). No children and never been pregnant. I've never contracted any STDs (thankfully!). I live in Jersey, and again, I *love* to fuck. And the best part about being single is that I can fuck who I want, when I want, how I want, where I want, and as many times I want, without answering to anyone about my actions. See, I'm what you might call a ride-a-dick-all-night-long type of chick. But, I consider myself more of a tri-sexual than anything else. Meaning I'm into pretty much all kinds of nasty, freaky sex. As long as it doesn't involve animals, body waste— being pissed and shit on is a no-no—midgets, the elderly, disabled, disfigured, or children, then I'm down for the get down. If I like it, I may do it again. And I'm typically turned on by men who are also tri-sexual. They tend to be less inhibited, and very secure in who they are as men. And that is very appealing to me. When I first meet a man, I want to know the following: How often do you have sex, or like to have sex? Do you masturbate? If so, how often? Can I watch? Are you into sex toys? If so, what type? Ever been handcuffed or blindfolded? When was your last HIV test?

Basically, if you really want me to break it down, I'm what you might call a certified freakologist. A term I use for peeps like me who specialize in freaking a man any way the wind blows until he slumps over. I'm also a skilled dicktologist who's dedicated to the fucking, sucking, and licking of fat, black dick. Yep, that's me. Okay, all right already. I'll say it for you…I'm a dick-loving ho. You already know. And? But don't get it twisted. I'm a responsible one. Hell, my motto is: If you're gonna fuck, be responsible. Wrap up and enjoy the damn ride!

And when it comes to fucking men, I have very few rules and restrictions. Don't be fat, nasty, and crusty.

And in case someone is confused about what's fat to me: if you need a bumper jack or a two-by-four to lift up your gut, then dammit, you fat. If you look down and you can't see your dick or your toes, then, duh, fat. If you have more belly than dick, duh, fat! So buy a vowel, get a clue, and get your sloppy ass on a diet before trying to get at me.

In addition, a man must have all of his teeth (that does not mean having a bunch of brown, yellow, or rotted ones either, or a row of gold or platinum fronts). He must wash his ass daily (there's nothing worse than sucking on a man's dick, then pulling up his balls and getting a whiff of ass funk. Ugh!). He also must be drug and disease free (that means no crack, no coke, no 420/weed/trees/collard greens, no dope/smack, no poppers, no damn pills, and *nothing* that I can catch). He must be circumcised (a must! I have no time for pulling back dick skin. That is an absolute no-no), and don't be busted in the face. I don't want anyone staring in my face hurting my eyes, or making my stomach turn. You don't have to be model-fine, but please, please, don't look like a damn manatee or a gorilla either.

I know, I know. Looks aren't everything. They can't get you an education, can't pay the bills, and definitely don't guarantee intellectual conversation, but dammit, if I want to see something out of Jurassic Park, then I'll go to the zoo! You can save that "Wild Kingdom" shit for those hard-pressed, ashy chicks with the black between their flabby legs, and titties flopping and sagging down over their nasty pussies. Those types of chicks are the kind to be happy someone is willing to fuck 'em. So they'll be more than willing to spread their legs open and fuck a beast. But I'm not the one.

Oh, no, I'm not angry with men. Nor do I hate them. On the contrary, I have nothing but love for them. In my opinion, there's nothing sexier than a black man's swagger. There's something about his confidence, his aloofness, his unpredictability, his mysterious demeanor that makes my pussy drip with excitement, and keeps me wanting more. Give me a man with stamina, strength, a beautiful black dick, probing lips, magical hands, and a killer tongue and I'm in heaven. But loving him is not always an easy task. It requires too much damn work and is definitely not an option for me. They either have too much ego, too many women, or too little respect for relationships. And you never know what you're gonna get yourself into when dealing with his ass. Some are too bruised, broken, and beat down by life and fucked-up relationships. Others don't know what the hell they want, and have no investment in a committed relationship. So, thanks, but no thanks! I think I'll wax his dick, and keep him fucked to the bone with no strings, no stress, and no damn mess.

Alrighty then. Now that we've gotten that all out the way, come closer. Let me whisper a little something in your ear. You see, I've come to understand that pleas-

ing a man requires patience and a desire to learn everything that turns him on. Ask him what he likes. And I
can't stress it enough—be open-minded. Explore his
body with your hands, your lips, your mouth, your
tongue. Devour every inch of him. Trust me. All men
love to be touched. They love it when you allow your
hands to wander and roam all over their bodies when
they're thrusting deep up in you. Grabbing and squeezing his ass, running your fingertips and hands down his
back, along his spine, pulling him into you as he's
stroking his dick in you. Men like to be encouraged,
urged to serve the dick how you want it. Trust me.

Anyway, find out what excites him. I don't think a
lot of women realize that men have erogenous zones
like we do. But oftentimes, his hot spots go untouched,
or undiscovered. Personally, I liken a man's body to a
playground. There's always something to swing on,
slide down on, climb up on, bounce up and down on,
or jump on.

And in my personal experience, one of the easiest
ways to get a man's dick hard (besides talking dirty or
showing him your pussy and ass) is to kiss him. A nice,
slow, sensual, tongue-probing kiss will often get his mind
wandering and the juices flowing in no time. Before
you know it, he'll start fantasizing about having his dick
up in you.

See, when I'm with a man, I usually start off by massaging his outer ear in slow movements. I gently squeeze

or nibble on his earlobes, explore the back of his ear with my lips and tongue, blowing lightly. Women don't realize how effective this can be. The sound of your breathing and the soft moans alone will usually turn most men on. Of course this technique only works provided your breath doesn't smell like hot shit.

Anyway, then I travel to his neck, nibbling. Never sucking or biting. I have no interest in trying to mark someone else's territory since most—not all—of the men I fuck are already involved with somebody else. Now, don't go rolling your eyes or sucking your teeth. It's really so unnecessary. Anyway, as I was explaining, I use my lips and tongue to journey down and around his neck to his shoulders, planting soft kisses on them. Then I make my way to his chest. Massaging it with my hands, licking and nibbling, and twirling my tongue over and around his nipples until they become erect, and hard like miniature skittles. Mmm. Planting wet kisses in the center of his chest, down to his navel, dipping my tongue in. Then I flick my tongue over the head of his throbbing dick before running my fingertips and tongue along the inside of his thighs, kissing, licking, and nibbling up and down them until my tongue reaches his balls. Mmm. I fondle them, lightly suck and lick on them, lapping up the scent of desire that clings beneath them. Finally, I place them in my mouth, and softly start to hum, flicking them with my tongue. Then I increase the humming on his balls. Trust me. This little trick takes him to the edge every time, giving him an intense, mind-bending experience. You'll have him holding his head in his hands, biting on his bottom lip, grabbing the sheets, climbing walls.

Eventually, I give him what he wants most, what he aches for—my soft lips and hot tongue swirling around the head of his dick. I kiss and nibble on it, licking the excitement that seeps and drizzles from its slit. Oooh, mmm. I can almost taste his sweet, sticky nectar. See. When I take him all the way in my mouth, I am swallowing him in, savoring the strength of his dick. And when I feel him about to explode, I massage the fleshy area between his balls and ass, pressing on his prostate, giving him a rush of pleasure that causes him to see stars. Yes, if you didn't know, now you do. I'm the Nut Cracker, aka the Man Handler. And this, my little darlings, is my official ho report. Welcome to my world, baaaaby!

Um, wait a minute. Before I let you get too deep into whom I am and what I do, I have some questions for you: Is it really as hard as most women say it is to find a good man? Are all the good men already taken? Is there really a shortage of good, decent men in the world? Is the black man really an endangered species? Or is there simply an abundance of lonely, miserable, sex-deprived women out here?

Now, before you respond, let me start off by saying I understand that no man is gonna respect any woman who drops her drawers and throws up her legs to the first man who smiles her way. If you're an easy lay, that's all you're going to be seen as, a quick piece of ass. So don't start getting all emotional when he starts dissing you, or acts like he doesn't know you after you've swallowed his nut. Take it for what it is, a fuck. If you a ho, say you a ho. And stop all the damn fronting. Chicks kill me catching feelings when a man calls them out of their name, or tries to pass them off to one of his boys. Uh, newsflash: He nutted in your mouth, sweetie. No, he's not gonna kiss you. No, he's not gonna make you his girl. The minute you let a man run up in you, the minute you swallow his babies, you played yourself. So stop all the damn whining and begging. Do you. Get your fuck on, and keep it moving. Luckily for me, I don't have that problem. 'Cause I don't give a fuck about a man's respect. Only what's hanging between his legs!

Between you and me and yes, I'm an opinionated ho—I think the problem is that women have become so desperate to have someone in their lives, and in their beds, (out of fear of being alone) that they settle for a lot of unnecessary bullshit from men. As far as I'm concerned, women are responsible for the shit they choose to put up with from a man. There's no point complaining about his ass when (nine times out of ten) you already know, or at least have an idea of, what you're dealing with. That's not to say that there aren't some women who truly have no clue as to what their man is into, or capable of. But once the truth is revealed, they are responsible for their decision to leave or stay, or take his ass back. As far as I'm concerned, if they stay, then their dumb asses deserve to get whatever heartache and grief his trifling ass continues to bring them. If they take him back, they deserve what they get. So each of you stop the damn tears, and take the shit and piss he throws in your face like a grown-ass woman.

I often wonder how many women buy into that "It's better to have a piece of a man, than no man at all" mess. I bet there's hundreds of thousands, maybe even a few million women who embrace that distorted foolishness, causing them to shed tears, lose sleep, and fight to hold on to a man whom they love more than they love themselves; women who sacrifice and lose pieces of themselves for the sake of having a man in their lives, no matter the cost, no matter the loss. A part of me wants to feel sorry for them, wants to be able to empathize with them; but because I've never been there, I can't bring myself to develop any level of understanding as to why any woman would choose to keep a man in her life who emotionally, mentally, physically, spiritually, and (most times) financially drains her.

But for the ones who do, does this make these chicks stupid? Does it make these women victims of their own hearts? Does it mean they lack self-love? Are they bombarded with insecurities? Do they feel trapped?

I mean, really. Why in the hell would any sane, rational woman put up with that shit? Hmmm…maybe she's not sane. Perhaps that's the damn problem. Her ass is downright crazy for thinking she doesn't deserve better! Ugh! I need to go lie down. This shit has given me a damn splitting-ass headache. Later!

CHAPTER TWO

At the moment, I have three steady men (not including Garrett and Maurice) who are on call whenever and however I need 'em. I call 'em my three sex charms because I fuck 'em in threes. Three's a charm, and I keep my pussy wrapped around their dicks like a tennis bracelet. Not only are diamonds a girl's best friend, so is a thick, stiff dick. And that's exactly what all three of 'em have.

First, there's sex charm #1: Jamil. He's five-eleven, 195 pounds of lean muscle, packing a solid seven-and-a-half inches of thick beef. I met him while standing in line at Commerce Bank. He's a Gemini, moody and unpredictable. One minute he's blowing my phone up, scratching and sniffing around like a dog in heat, hounding me for some more of this pussy. The next minute, he's as cold and distant as an Alaskan polar bear. Probably because of all the stress he catches from his six baby mommas and the chick he's currently living with. By the time he shells out child support for his ten kids, he barely has enough money for himself. And he knows not to ask *me* for anything. His financial state is not my problem. I have no sympathy for his dumb ass, which is running around breeding with everything moving. And the crazy mofo's talking about he wants to have three more. Go figure. I guess he's gonna try for a baker's dozen. Humph. Whatever! The only thing he can do for me (at the moment) is eat my pussy, and serve me the damn dick.

Next is sex charm #2: Wade, a six-foot-three, 215-pound solid hunk of smooth, milk chocolate with long lashes wrapped around the most entrancing pair of hazel eyes I've ever seen on any human being. Hanging between his chiseled thighs is a thick, eight-inch dick with enormous veins running along the shaft and a big mushroom head, and attached to this beautiful chocolate dick is a set of huge, hairy balls. His dick sort of reminds me of a miniature baseball bat, narrow at the base, thick at the shaft. Just looking at him makes my pussy tingle with delight.

Wade is a college graduate and owns his own landscaping business. I'll admit, if I were ever looking for a steady piece of dick, he'd definitely be the one. Okay, well, maybe *one* of the ones. Besides the fact that he's intelligent, fine as hell, and has no children and no chicks, he eats pussy like it's the only thing on the menu, and he can fuck practically all night. That's exactly how I like it. Usually after he's finished digging my back out, I can still feel him inside of me for at least two days, and then can't fuck anyone else for another three. That's how good he wears this pussy out. The only problem: he's twenty-five. And that's entirely too damn young. For a relationship, that is.

Last, but definitely not least, is sex charm #3: Mitchell. Mitchell is six-one, two-hundred pounds, and the color of midnight with a ten-inch dick that curves to the left. And he's freakier than a mutha. The last time we were together, he poured chocolate syrup in the crack of my ass, then licked and tongue-fucked my asshole clean. I almost lost my mind. He can get it *almost* anytime he wants it. However, I won't let his freak-nasty, ass-eating self kiss me.

And of course, there's Garrett, who comes through once every two weeks or so. Well, uh, that's what he used to do. Lately, it's been every chance he can get. I'm not too sure what that's about. But he keeps coming—in more ways than one. And I keep on spreading open my legs and fucking him.

Anyway, then there's Maurice whom I fuck once or twice, sometimes three times a year due to his work, travel, and family obligations. And now there's Wendell, who is still new on my dick list. But before Jamil, Wade, and Mitchell, there were Tyrone, David, and Solomon. And before them: Reggie, Carlos, and Martin. And before them: Cedric, Eli, and Thomas.

Okay. For those of you who might not have picked up on it, I fuck my men in threes. And I usually rotate 'em in threes. Basically, I change my men about as many times as I change the oil in my car, practically every three thousand miles. Or every three months, which-ever comes first. I drain 'em, dump 'em, then move on to something fresh and new. It's the only way to go.

So, basically, I've never had an issue getting a man. Now, getting rid of his ass is sometimes another story. One we'll get to at another time.

Oh, you wanna know why I fuck 'em and rotate 'em every three months? Well, because in my experience, it takes about three months before a mofo starts trying to check for you like he's your damn man, or before he starts getting too damn comfortable and starts expecting shit from you, or thinking you want something from him, or before he starts trying to move his ass up in here. Sorry, boo-boo, I'm not having that shit under any circumstances. I don't care how good he digs my back out. A man is only good for three things: Fucking, fucking, and more fucking! Other than a stiff dick, there's nothing he can offer me. At least I'm honest about that, and I let them all know from jump what the deal is. He doesn't have to worry about me trying to get him to pay my bills, or keep my hair and nails done. I'm more than capable of doing those things for myself. And I expect him to be able to do the same for himself. *No*, you can't get a ride. *No*, you can't get a hot meal. *No*, you can't stay the night. *No*, you can't move in. *No*, you can't use my address or have your mail coming to my house. It *ain't* gonna happen. I'm not running a bed and breakfast, a motel, or a damn shelter. So lick the clit, serve the dick, and be on your merry way. *Sine qua non*, bottom line: I want his ass out of my house before sunrise. No exceptions!

Please. Say what you want. Some dudes don't seem to understand what the hell "no strings attached" means. Hello. It means, let's fuck and have a good time without you trying to crowd my space, be all up in my damn face questioning me like I owe you something, or trying to keep tabs on me. Negro, get a grip!

And I've also found that within three months, whatever drama a man has in his life will eventually find its way into yours if you're not on point. That's why it's always best to fuck 'em and dump 'em within ninety days. Come to think of it. I'm really starting to believe that there really are some things money can't buy. And, baaaaaaby, let me tell you. Hassle-free dick is one of them!

Anyway, back to my three current charms. All three of 'em have been in my bed, oops, I mean my life, for almost three months. But, like with everything else in life, eventually all good things must come to an end. Sadly, nothing stays the same. And neither does the dick. Hitting this pussy comes with an expiration date.

Okay, before I forget, I'm gonna let you in on something else. There are a few things I've learned along my sexual journey, and they are: 1) A stiff dick has no conscience. It'll fuck anything moving if it can get away with it; 2) Most men lie about the size of their dicks (which is why I carry a ruler); 3) A big dick doesn't guarantee a good fuck, and a small dick doesn't guarantee a bad one; 4) An itsy-bitsy, teeny-weenie, short,

short dick can't hit it doggie-style; 5) A man with good dick isn't necessarily a good man; 6) You can't judge the size of a man's dick by his shoe size, hand size, or by the size of his nose. Those physical features don't mean shit; and 7) Old dick is no different from young dick. It may look different, but with the lights out, it's still dick. It's the man attached to the dick that's different.

I've also learned that most men lie about themselves, and about what it is they really want from you. They'll say whatever they think you want to hear to get whatever it is they want from you. Because a man calls you all the time doesn't mean he can be trusted. Because he comes through to fuck you all the time doesn't mean he's your man, or that he wants to love you. And it definitely doesn't mean he wants to get to know you better. It usually means he's only interested in *you* wetting his dick. So don't get caught up in trying to make it out to be more than what it is, a fuck.

And I've also discovered that most men think sucking on your titties and slapping you on the ass is foreplay. Or that a few tongue laps around the clit is all it takes to have you begging for the dick. Well, that may work for some women. But a woman like me needs a bit more to get it going. See, for me, great sex begins with great foreplay. And great foreplay begins with seduction. Stimulate the mind, arouse the senses, tantalize and tease the body, or find yourself on the receiving end of a miserably lousy fuck.

However, always keep in mind this tidbit: The thrill of seduction sometimes lies in the chase rather than the conquest. In layman's terms: Sometimes it's best not to fuck 'em. Masturbate to your fantasies and keep it moving.

Anyway, I say all this to say that some men get so caught up in solely fucking that they don't even consider whether you're enjoying it. I mean, damn. I don't mind being fucked when that's what I'm asking for. But don't be a selfish fuck. I mean, really. How tired is that? But some men really don't give a fuck about it being good for you too. As long as it feels good to them, as long as they can get their shit off, to hell with making sure we get ours. But I'm not the one. If he's popping a nut, dammit, so am I. Trust me. And that's exactly why I have a sign hanging over my bed that reads: "My bed, my pussy, my way! Either fuck me the way I want, or fuck off!" And I make sure every man who enters this bedroom reads it out loud. And if he can't read, then I read it for his illiterate ass.

Make no mistake. Be a lazy fuck if you want, and find yourself tossed out with a hard dick, depending on my mood. If I am extremely horny or feeling generous, then I will make him stop, roll him over on his back, straddle him, slide down on his dick, and ride him like there's no tomorrow, then throw him out. And that's exactly what I did to Benson's punk ass three nights ago. He's thirty-five, five feet, 185 pounds, with nine and a half inches of dick. And he claims he doesn't have a woman. But I know he's lying. Shit. Dude doesn't have to lie to me. What the hell do I care? I don't want him. The only thing I want is to be fucked right. Fuck me the way *I* want, or you get dismissed. And that's what it is. Ugh! Every time I think about it, it makes me want to scream. How the fuck you think you gonna lay up in my bed and not feed my pussy right?

Anyway, I leaned forward with my titties sweeping back and forth across his chest as I pounced and galloped up and down on his dick, fucking him until his eyes rolled back in his head. Let me tell you how I had him moaning and calling out my name, telling me how good this pussy is. My juicy hole slurped all over his dick, sucking the nut out of him. And when I was done, I rolled over onto my back and without giving him a second glance, I told him to "Get out!" And you want to know what this mofo had the nerve to do? He looked at me like I was crazy. He didn't say it, and I didn't give him a chance to. That look was all I needed.

"No, negro," I snapped, "you the crazy one, tryna half fuck me! Now see yourself out, 'cause your services are no longer needed."

Dude grabbed his shirt, hastily putting on his clothes, then walked out the bedroom. "Fuckin' bitch," I heard him mumble as he stomped his way out into the hallway, then down the stairs and out the door, slamming it so hard that the windows upstairs rattled. Like I gave a fuck! Yeah, I had probably bruised his ego, okay, and? Humph, some men are like spoiled-assed babies, pouting and whining when their little feelings get hurt. Whatever!

See, that's the problem with a lot of these big-dick niggas, which is why I sometimes wonder if dick size really matters, or is it really all about the motion of the ocean? Well, I guess it does matter depending on what you're in the mood for. Truth be told, I've had men as long as eleven and a half inches and as thick as a cucumber, some as short as six inches and as thick as a beer can, and others in between and as thin as a pencil. And what I've found is that the ones who fall short in the length department tend to make up for it in other areas, like eating the pussy until your uterus shakes. Most of 'em definitely have a crazy tongue game. And most (not all) men with a long, thick dick—like Benson's sorry ass—tend to be lazy with it. Mostly due to the fact that they get so much attention from dick-crazed women that they think they don't have to put in any work or make any effort to ensure you get yours too. They either want to lay back and expect you to do all the damn work, or they cum quicker than a rabbit. Ugh! There's nothing more distressing than a big-dick mofo with a whacked-ass sex game.

And the ones who know exactly how to work the hell out of it, giving you blood-curdling orgasms, have been gassed up by women (and I have been guilty of doing it too) to believe that they're God's gift to women based on the size of their dick. But I'll admit, engaging in sex with a big dick can definitely be rather intoxicating, if its owner is on point. Unfortunately, this particular night with Benson, I was fucking gypped!

Anyway, in terms of dick size, I suspect it's those chicks with the four-finger and fist pussies constantly complaining about the size of a man's dick. A man can't even finger-pop her coochie without her snatch sucking in his whole damn hand. Their holes are so beat up and stretched out the frame that fucking them with an average-size dick would be like trying to fuck the Atlantic Ocean. Humph.

Now, to be perfectly honest with you, when a man is up inside of me, I do need to feel him knocking these walls around. But he doesn't always have to knock the bottom out. Give me a thick dick with a whole lot of motion and I'm good to go. And if I'm going to suck a dick, then it needs to fill my wide mouth, and not feel like I'm sucking on a damn Tic-Tac. And if I'm going to jerk a dick off I want to be able to use both of my hands—not a set of tweezers, if you know what I mean.

Anyway, I believe the reason my snatch snaps back, and grips a dick with ease is because I alternate the dick. I don't stick with one dick type. I fuck 'em all. And no matter how many dicks I ride, it's because of that fact that I'm able to maintain this five-star pussy. Think what you like, I'm telling you what I know.

Oh, the power of dick…how it can have a chick lose her mind over *it*. How *it* can force a woman to forget everything that is rational, and pure, and have her caught up in the drama of chasing *it* down, fighting over *it*, and having babies by *it*, knowing damn well the man attached to *it* is not gonna take care of her or them little snotty-nosed crumb snatchers. I had a dude I was once fucking actually say: "A bitch will know that I'm fucking other chicks and still give me the keys to her car, let me lay up in her spot, and even hit me with money outta her bank accounts, all because I rammed my big dick up in her guts and fucked the shit outta her dumb ass."

I simply stared at him, and could do nothing but shake my head because I knew what he spoke held truth. Then he added, "If I fuck you and see any signs of weakness or stupidity over how good I've thrashed your back out, then I'm gonna run your dumb ass straight through the mud. And that's real talk."

Well, all I can say is this: I'm so damn glad I've never succumbed to such madness. And I don't really feel sorry for these chicks who have this "knowledge" and still allow themselves to get played. Shame on 'em. And to add to the craziness, I have to shake my head at the men who measure their manhood by the length of their dicks, and the number of women they fuck, use, or have fighting over them.

I don't even know why I got on this topic 'cause the

more I think about it, the more disgusted I find myself getting with these stupid-assed, dick-whipped, scatter-brained women out here with their ridiculous antics over what's hanging between a man's legs. It's obvious there's a whole lot of strength behind the thrust of a cock. 'Cause, baby, dick, like good pussy, will flat out have a chick doing some crazy shit if she lets it control her. She becomes possessed by the dick. And before you know it she has turned into a weak-minded, emotionally unstable bitch—even if only for a moment. I'm seeing more and more women doing dumb shit behind a damn piece of dick. Dick will have a woman walking out on her husband, abandoning her children. It will have her lying and stealing and pushing drugs. Dick will have her dismissing all of her friends. It will have her selling her pussy. Dick will have her risking her life and health. It will have her begging and crying, and fighting other women, knocking on doors, and playing childish-ass phone games. It will have her plotting and scheming to have someone else's man. Ugh! And it will have her dumb ass losing everything she owns because she has allowed it to fuck her silly ass into stupidity. Humph. As bad as I don't want to admit it, dick is dangerous! And I have one thing to say: All hail to the Almighty King Ding-a-ling!

CHAPTER
THREE

"Hello?" I answer groggily.

"Hey, baby. You up?" the voice on the other end asks in a seductive whisper.

I rub my eyes and glance over at the digital clock on my nightstand. I squint to make sure I'm not hallucinating. 3:15 a.m. My eyes widen. *What in the hell?!* "Please tell me you have lost your damn mind," I snap through clenched teeth, "calling me this time of the morning when I have to be up for work in another three hours."

"Damn, baby, I ain't mean to wake you," he says, almost sounding apologetic. But I know enough to know that this mofo isn't sorry about shit. "I thought you might be up thinking about this dick."

He chuckles.

I roll my eyes, letting out a disgusted sigh.

Now had this been six or seven months ago, I would have graciously accepted his call with the promise of wetting his dick up nice and slow. And with Vince, the one thing I was always guaranteed was a dose of mouthwatering, powerhouse dick. But that was then, and this is now.

"Oh, really?" I sarcastically inquire, sitting up in bed. I am pissed that he has awakened me from a delicious, pussy-pleasing dream—one that has left me sopping wet. I turn on the night lamp, sighing. "Well, I'm not! So why are you calling me so early?"

"You've been on my mind."

"Ohhhhkaaaay. And you had to call at me this hour to let me know this, right?"

"Yeah, something like that."

I suck my teeth. "Since when?"

"C'mon, baby," he says, lowering his voice. "Don't play. You know how I feel 'bout you. I got you on the brain like crazy. I've been real fucked up lately, missing you and shit."

Now a lonely, simple-minded bitch would fall head-first for this line of bullshit he's dishing out. And before you knew it, he'd be slamming his dick in her ass, twisting her guts out. But I'm not the one.

"Humph," I grunt. "That's a shame. I haven't talked to you in months. Now all of a sudden, you got me renting space in your head."

"Yeah, something like that," he says. "I still don't dig how shit went down with us. You dissed a brotha, setting egg timers 'n shit, talkin' 'bout my time expired. What kinda shit was that? You was on some real foul shit, for real, for real. But just like this big-ass dick, it's all good."

I chuckle to myself, remembering the *ding* of the egg timer alerting me that his fifteen minutes of tongue-fucking me was up. I had already told him prior to his coming over that he was only getting fifteen minutes of pussy because I had already recruited someone else to take his spot. The nigga thought I was bullshitting. Had he been smart, he would have licked my cat for five minutes, then used the other ten to stroke it with his dick, but he didn't. And when the bell went off, I politely pushed his head and face from outta the center of my crotch and told him to get out. Poor thing looked at me with his eyes popped wide open and my creamy pussy juice smeared all over his face and lips, looking like a damn glazed fool.

"Whaaat?!?!" he had snapped. "You buggin', right?"

"Does it look like I'm bugging?" I asked, slipping on my robe and turning off the stereo. The party was over.

He grabbed his erect dick and wildly shook it. "Yo, you see how hard this shit is? You need to stop poppin' all that ying yang and get up on this dick."

I laughed, flipping open my cell. I had my finger on the speed dial button for my brother, who would have come through with his boys in blue and locked Vince's pathetic ass up.

"Nigga," I warned, "you got five minutes to get your shit on and get out."

"I ain't going no-fuckin'-where until we fuck, or I get this dick sucked or something."

"You can leave willingly, or you can leave in handcuffs. Either way, you're getting the hell up outta here."

I swung open the bedroom door and stood defiantly, waiting for him to get the hell out of my bedroom. He huffed and puffed and mumbled inaudible shit under his breath, but it didn't matter to me. I had other plans that didn't include him.

When he finally got the hint that there wasn't going to be shit else popping off between us, he got up and got dressed, then stomped down the stairs. I followed behind, graciously opening the front door for his ass.

He stared at me, clenching his jaw muscles. "Yo, that's real fucked up. You on some ole other shit, for real, for real. But it's all good. I ain't beat. You'll be blowing up my shit"—he grabbed at his crotch area—"tryna get at this dick again."

"Don't hold your breath," I firmly stated, holding the door open for him. "The one thing I never do, boo, is go back to dick I've dismissed."

"Yeah, whatever," he snapped, brushing past me. "Fucking bitch! I don't know why I fucked with your ho ass any damn way."

I laughed at his ass. "But I'm a damn good one, remember that. Got your silly ass feenin' for this tight pussy, don't I? Had you tryna suck the nut outta this ho pussy, didn't I? How many times you had your tongue buried up in this ho's ass, huh, nigga? Let's talk about how many times you begged me to let you slide your dick up in this sweet, juicy ho box raw. Nigga, you fucked with my ho ass 'cause I rode your tongue and dick down into the mattress, and had your dumb ass stuttering."

He glared at me, but said nothing.

"Unh-huh, just what I thought. Yeah, I'm a ho, baby. But you can best believe it'll be a long, cold day in hell before you ever sniff this pussy again."

I slammed the door on him, then peered out the window and watched him get into his burgundy Acura coupe and peel out of the driveway, burning rubber in the process. That was months ago. And now he has the nerve to ring my line like everything's sweet. My, my, my…how the chickens come home to roost.

"Mmm-hmm," I finally say, flicking imaginary dirt from under my fingernail. "So, why are you really calling me?"

"I wanna swing through on my way to work to see you. I wanna lay in bed with you and hold you in my arms."

"Wait a minute. You mean to tell me you want to lay up in a ho's bed and hold her in your arms. Now, ain't this some shit?"

"Oh, here you go; you still on that bullshit?"

"Actually, I'm not," I state flatly. "I'm merely making a statement."

"Damn, baby. Listen. I was only talking out the side of my neck. You had me real heated, so I was saying shit to hurt you."

This nigga can't be the brightest star if he thinks calling me a ho was supposed to hurt my feelings. The word *ho* holds no power over me, so calling me one can't hurt me. I embrace my ho-ism wholeheartedly, with pride and grace.

I laugh. "OhmyGod, you are so fucking hilarious."

"Why I gotta be hilarious? I'm being dead ass."

"I'm a ho, remember?"

"Why can't I only wanna see you?" he asked, igging my remark. "Why I gotta be on some extra shit?"

"'Cause you are," I answer, still laughing. "Vinnie, baby, do you really think I'm buying that 'I only wanna see you' mess? No, nigga," I say. "You calling 'cause you tryna come through and get that dick wet. You don't miss me. It's this sweet, tight pussy being wrapped around your dick you miss."

He laughs. "So what's wrong with a brotha missing some good-ass pussy?"

"Nothing," I state.

"Then what's the problem?"

"There is no problem. Not for me, that is. But, as for you, this pussy is no longer on the menu, boo-boo. So you shit outta luck."

"Damn, so it's like that? I remember a time when you couldn't get enough of this long, black dick. Let me come through and remind you of how good this dick used to feel up in you."

Despite myself, I smile—allowing my mind to travel down memory lane, remembering the first time we fucked. Baby, let me tell you. This man did me right. I had gone to Atlantic City—by myself, of course—to chill. I had rented a suite, grabbed something to eat, then went down to the casino to do a little gambling.

When I tell you it was heads everywhere, Bally's was jumping!

Anyway, I didn't win shit on the slots, but I damn sure hit the jackpot when I brought back up to my room a six-foot-two, one-hundred-and-eighty pound, half-black and half-Italian nigga from Brooklyn. And, yes, I fucked him on the damn spot. And…oh my *Gawd!* That's all I can say. Dude tried to dig another hole into this pussy, you hear me? And when he ate me out, he ate this pussy like it was about to be his last night on earth. I'm telling you, the way he darted his tongue in and out of my slit, licking and kissing, and blowing all over my clit, then burying his thick tongue deep inside of me, I thought my walls were going to collapse, the way he made my insides shake. The man had a wicked head game, and almost had me screaming out his name— something I had no intentions of doing. But I damn sure begged him for some of that thick, ten-inch dick. He had my pussy so overheated that I needed it stoked, needed it stroked, needed it fucked deep, and hard, and fast, and all damn night long. His dick sliced into my pussy like a hot knife, causing my walls to melt around his meaty cock. By the time we finished fucking, the sun was coming up and my pussy was beat up real good and well served.

Oh, yes, Vince slayed this pussy something fierce. But he also got on my last damn nerve with his negative-ass, paranoid thinking 'bout the white man trying to bring him down and keep him down. If he lost a job, it was because they were racists. Had nothing to do with the fact that he was still on his ninety-day probation period and was late more than nine times in one month and had been warned another lateness would result in termination. Had nothing to do with him coming to work hung over, or sexually harassing some of the chicks at the job.

In his head, someone was always conspiring against his nutty ass. The man never took any responsibility for any of his choices. Everything that ever happened to him was somebody else's fault. When his girl put him out and changed the locks on the door, it was because she was fucking someone else. Not because she got tired of his ass coming and going and doing what the hell he wanted. Not because his ass wanted to lie around and be taken care of, and she got sick of it. Oh, no…he had nothing to do with it. OhmyGod, every time I was with his ass, he had one complaint after another. I mean, damn! Whenever he opened his mouth, I would start to hear violins playing. It got to the point I couldn't even fuck his ass in peace. So you know the mofo had to go. When your bullshit starts disrupting my nut, it's a wrap.

"So, dig…you letting me come through or what?" he asks, snapping me back to the present, and the reason why I dismissed his ass in the first place.

Instead of hanging up on him, I decide to toy with

him. "So, what you saying, big daddy?" I coo. "You wanna bang up this pussy like old times. You wanna make my pussy nut, hunh, big daddy?"

He dips his voice another octave; speaks in a low, seductive whisper. "Yeah, baby. You know that's what I'm tryna do. Let daddy come get up in that fat pussy, baby."

I lie back in bed and decide to seize the moment. A girl like me believes she should never pass up an opportunity to pleasure herself at an unknowing man's expense. I spread open my legs and place my left hand over my pussy, massaging my neatly trimmed mound. I glide my hand to my clit, lightly brush it with my fingertips, then slip a finger inside my hole.

"You wanna slide your long dick down in my deep, wet throat and face-fuck me like old times, hunh, daddy?"

"Damn, girl, why you fucking with me? You got my dick hard as hell, baby."

"Mmmm. You want me to drop down low and suck that hard dick balls-deep, don't you, daddy? Edge it. Lick your balls...stick my tongue in your ass. Give you a long, hot, slow cock-sucking until your nut explodes in my mouth and down my throat. Is that what you want?"

"Oh, shit yeah," he says. "You gonna let me get some pussy or what?"

I slip another finger inside my pussy and massage the opening of my walls, rotating and twisting and pumping until my fingers become warm, creamy-coated sticks of pleasure. My voice catches in the back of my throat as I feel an orgasm swirling. "Tell me…what…you wanna do…to this…pussy…if I let you come through?" I say, moaning as I pull my fingers out of my slippery slit and suck the sweet, sticky elixir, then plunge each finger back in.

"I'ma ram this fat dick up in you, and fuck you nice and slow and deep. Then I'ma flip you over onto your stomach and hit that pussy from the back, spreading ya ass checks open so I can watch ya fat juicy cunt lips wrap around my dick as I stick my finger in that pretty brown asshole…"

Not with them fingernails, I think, remembering the fact that he had nails a bit too long for my liking. They weren't homo long, but they were long enough to scratch up the inside of my walls, or to see dirt up underneath them, and for *me*, that is a no-no.

I frown, but say nothing.

"…Then I'ma pull out, and slap ya ass with my dick, before I eat that sweet, wet pussy from the back. Damn, baby…I wanna fuck," he says, practically panting.

For some reason, I find myself recalling the time I got my first glimpse of two naked bodies. I was seven. I remember sneaking down to our basement and watching my oldest brother, Tyrell, lying on top of his girlfriend, humping and grinding into her, and her moaning. I stood there crouched down low, watching them in amazement. Every day after school, I'd sneak downstairs to watch, listen, and learn. And every day, they did something new that excited me, like him putting his face between her legs and licking her pussy, and her moaning; or him moaning while she had her mouth on his dick. I watched them in delight for almost the whole school year until one day my brother Terrance caught me and spanked my ass for "spying" as he called it.

He threatened to beat me again if I told our parents what I saw. Little did he know, I'd been spying and keeping it to myself for months. Keeping secrets was a game to me. Although I didn't quite understand what they were doing, I knew it was something that shouldn't have been done, and I knew enough not to repeat what I saw.

Every time I watched, I took mental snapshots of everything he did to her, and she to him, tucking it all in the back of my mind. And every now and then, I'd close my eyes and replay the images and sounds in my head. It was then that my imagination began to grow wings and take flight. I wanted to do what they did. I wanted someone to hump on me, and make me moan too. And that's where it all began.

I purse my lips, contemplate. *Do I really feel like fucking him?* I remind myself of how good the dick was. Hell, it was better than good…it was great! But truth be told, when we were fucking, I could only ride his dick with him on his back, or take the dick doggie-style, because he had a back full of pimples and blackheads that I couldn't stand to feel or see. Running your hands along his lumpy-ass back was like trying to read Braille.

To fuck or not to fuck…that is the question.

I dip my two fingers back into my sugar well, then pull them out and suck my juices off. Mmmm-hmm, delicious! I smack my lips then say, "Vince, sweetie…"

"Yeah. What's good, baby?"

"Thanks for the nut."

"Say what?"

"I said, thanks for getting me off."

"Wait a minute. You're telling me you were playing with yourself this whole time, and came?"

"I sure was," I say, moaning. "Had my fingers all up in my hot pussy, and all over my slippery clit. And, yes, I came all over myself." I stick my fingers back into my mouth, and start making loud sucking sounds. "Mmmm Mmmm…finger licking good," I tease.

"Damn, that's wassup, baby. I always loved it when you got that pussy nice and wet for me. Mmmph, fuck! I can't wait to slide this dick up in that fat, juicy—"

I laugh.

"What's so funny?"

"You, boo," I say.

"I ain't laughing," he replies, sounding annoyed.

"Well, I am. You gotta lot of nerve to think you can call me out the blue, and I'm supposed to welcome you with open legs and a wet pussy. Nigga, make no mistake. You won't be sliding a damn thing up in this sweet snatch. Not tonight; not ever again."

"So, what you saying…I can't come through?"

I pull the cell from my ear, turning my lips up at his dumb ass. *What the fuck?!* It baffles me how some men really think because they're packing dick and tapped a chick's ass up and dug her back out a few times that he can hit it anytime he wants it 'cause he's *that* nigga. That may be the case for some chicks, but it definitely doesn't apply to me.

"Uh, basically," I say, placing the phone back up against my ear.

"Damn, that's fucked up. You got me over here with my shit all bricked up."

"Oh, well. You'll be alright."

"So, it's like that, huh? You really gonna do me like that. Leave a nigga hangin'?"

"Yep."

"You real fucked up."

"And so is your crusty-ass back," I snidely reply.

"Oh, you got jokes, right?"

"You don't hear me laughing," I say. "I've already had your dick, and if you recall correctly, I done fucked it every which way imaginable. So there really is nothing else you can do for me."

"You can be a real bitch, you know that, right?"

"Yes, I know. And don't forget to add *ho* to your list."

"Check this—"

"Good night, Vinnie," I say, cutting him off. "And while you're at it, do us both a favor—lose my number. Oh, and by the way, thanks again for the nut."

Before he can open his mouth to say anything else, I end the call. I turn off the light, then turn over on my side—sticky and exhausted—and drift back to sleep, chasing the remainder of my dream.

CHAPTER
FOUR

You know, I'm sitting here thinking that I'd better make a few things clear so that we're all on the same page before you start passing judgment on me or trying to label me as some wounded trollop. See, the reason I fuck the way I do has nothing to do with some deeply rooted, unresolved psychological and emotional bullshit. Please don't get caught up in that textbook hype. My upbringing doesn't have a damn thing to do with my hunger for dick. This is who I am, and this is who I choose to be. I refuse to live my life in a box constructed (and confined) by the thoughts, beliefs, or feelings of others. So if I choose to suck or fuck a dick every hour on the damn hour, that's my business. Honestly, in the grand scheme of things, with the recession, the collapse of the stock and housing markets, and all the killings and crooked shit going on in the world, is my fucking really that big of a deal?

I mean, *really*. I don't want or need anyone trying to psychoanalyze me. No, I was never sexually, physically, or emotionally abused by anyone. I was never neglected or deprived. Nor am I the product of a dysfunctional family. So there are no wounds to heal. My father didn't beat up on my mother, run out on her, abuse substances, or abandon me. I come from a very loving, two-parent household. Both of my parents were hard workers who now live in San Diego. My mother is a retired elementary school teacher, and my father is a retired police officer. I am the youngest of seven, and the only girl. And none of us ever wanted for anything, especially me. So let's be clear. There's nothing wrong with my self-esteem, and I'm not scarred from some traumatic experience.

I fuck because it's something that I enjoy doing. Some people find pleasure in reading a good book. Some people gamble. Some people shop. Some people drink and use drugs. Well, I take pleasure in the feel of a stiff dick. And ain't a damn thing wrong with it. We all have our vices, and fucking is mine.

See, the difference between me and most chicks who randomly fuck and suck niggas: I know what I am. I don't try to hide it, or make any excuses for it. I am what I am. I am a grown-ass woman. I am adventurous, uninhibited, spontaneous, and unrepressed. Hello. I am a nymph. I *love* dick! And I do what I wanna do because I can.

And make no mistake; there's absolutely no shame in my game. I am my pussy, and my pussy is me. Sweet, juicy, tight, and finger-licking good! Intoxicating, addicting, mystifying. My pussy beats to its own pulse. And it craves dick. Hell, I crave dick! I love a man who can match me stroke for stroke, a man who can serve me the dick inch by inch, a man who can make my toes curl, my eyes roll up in the back of my head, and have me speaking in tongues. Oh, yes…that's the kind of man I love. And that's exactly the kind of man currently hovering over me, sliding his thick dick with its huge mushroom head deep into my slickness.

Face contorted, hips bucking and grinding, lips smacking, tongues licking and lapping and flicking against each other. Oh, he's fucking me so damn good. His name is Garrett. Six-four, two hundred and thirty solid pounds of muscled man dipped in smooth, milk chocolate with a thick, eight-inch dick that points upward. He also has a beautiful smile and mesmerizing brown eyes that have a way of piercing deep into my soul. If this were a perfect world, if my heart was open and unhardened, I could probably fall in love with him.

However, I am at a point in my life where I'm living for the moment. I have no expectations of anyone (particularly men), and I don't want anyone having any of me. Expectations open the door for disappointments and misunderstandings. And I'm not interested in either. So I like to keep it simple. Just fuck and go.

Oh, no, boo-boo. Please don't ever think I'm some lonely, lost, confused woman. Never that! And, yes, I fuck without any emotional connection to these men. Not that I'm not capable of loving or afraid of loving 'cause I've been there, done that. But right now, love is the last thing on my mind. Most of the men I fuck are emotionally unavailable anyway, so why would I want anything more than a stiff dick and long tongue from 'em? So, yes, I am very detached when it comes to fucking and men. Some may call it empty, meaningless sex. That's cool with me. As long as I'm keeping my pussy well fucked and wet, what the hell does love have to do with anything?

Garrett slowly pulls his dick out, then plunges it back in. "Mmmph…" He pulls out again, plunges back in, then pulls out again, leaving the head in. He tip drills me, tickling the opening of my pussy, teasing it. "Mmmph…Put your dick in…put your dick in…put your dick in…" I chant, reaching for him, trying to pull him into me. He grabs me by the wrists and slams them back onto the bed up over my head, pinning them down. I buck my hips, desperate to feed all of my pussy with his thickness. "Stop teasing me, Garrett," I warn, practically begging.

"Is this what you want?" he asks, slamming his dick back into me, then going into a nice, slow grind before picking up his pace.

"Uh," I moan. My lust-swollen clit flutters as the thickness of Garrett's eight-inch dick strokes against it while he pumps it in and out of me, stretching and smashing against my pussy walls.

"You like that dick?" he asks, letting my wrists go, then reaching up under me and palming my ass.

"Ummph," I moan again, grabbing him by his firm

ass, digging my nails into him, and pulling him deeper into me. I have my left leg wrapped around his waist and my right leg up over his shoulder. "Oh, yes…fuck me. Oh, shit, the dick is so good."

Now, between you and me, what I like about fucking Garrett is, I don't have to pretend that the dick is good. It *is* good. No scratch that, this nigga's dick is the closest thing to heaven. It's fucking D-I-V-I-N-E. Anytime he comes through and serves me, it's *always* on point and I'm guaranteed a fantabulous fuck session. Lord knows I can't stand a lazy-dick man. And there's nothing worse than a can't-heat-the-pussy-up-right-clumsy-fuck nigga, poking and stabbing at nothing. Ugh! What a bore, and a damn waste! And trust me, I have had my share of men who can't fuck the pussy, can't eat the pussy, and can't make the pussy do what it do. That shit burns me the hell up. Those are the ones who never get invited back between my legs. So this is probably one of the reasons I keep Garrett around. Okay, besides the fact that he's also extremely fine.

He grunts and lifts up on his hands in push-up position as he pounds in and out of me, beating my pussy like it stole something from him. "Aaah, shit, this pussy's good," he says, bringing me back to the reason why I'm lying on my back with my legs wrapped around his body.

A slight smile spreads across my face as I watch Garrett toss back his head, closing his eyes and biting down on his bottom lip. Sweat drips from his face, rolls down the center of his chest, and drips down on me. I reach up and roll his nipples between my fingers, then lightly pinch them. My pussy sloshes a bucket of sweet, creamy cum all over his dick.

"Oh, fuck. Damn, baby," he moans.

"You like this pussy?" I ask, pulling him into me by the back of his neck, then slipping my tongue deep into his mouth. We kiss for about twenty tongue-probing seconds before he pulls back for air, trying to steady his balance. Without much effort, I clench and unclench my pussy, gripping and releasing his dick, causing a popping sound every time he rams it in and out of me.

"Hell yeah," he moans, gripping my hips tighter. "Damn, I love this pussy." He says what I already know. But I ask because I like hearing the obvious. Truth be told, I haven't fucked a man yet who hasn't loved the feel of this sweet valley, who hasn't craved to have his dick wet by its cream, or who hasn't begged for more. And usually, I give them exactly what it is they desire.

"Yeah, daddy, just like that. Oh, yes…hit that pussy," I urge, arching my back and digging the back of my head into my goose-filled pillow. I feel an orgasm building inside of me, pushing against the walls of my uterus. I love the way his dick stretches me open. "Oooh, uh…"

You want to know one of the things I love about men: their balls. My mouth starts to water thinking about 'em. If a man's hanging low, that's always a plus. I love a man with big, heavy balls that hang. I call 'em nut clackers. Mmmm. There's something about seeing his balls swinging and smacking between his legs while he's standing with his legs spread apart, dipping his knees, pumping his dick in his hands at full speed. That shit turns me on. Especially when I'm lying back playing in my pussy while watching him jack off. Mmmm. And don't let his balls slap up against my pussy while he's slamming his dick in and out of me. Oh, Lawd! That's enough to have me scream out his name (or someone else's, which I've done more than once) to the high heavens in twenty-seven different languages, and fuck him limp.

And I love sucking all over them. Hairy, smooth, it makes me no never mind. As long as they're clean, I'm going to gargle with them. However, with smooth balls, I don't have to worry about coughing up hair balls or picking hair from between my teeth.

Make no mistake, I don't discriminate. I'm an equal opportunist. I don't care if you're involved, single, lonely, or confused. But don't be married! As far as I'm concerned, a married man is off limits. I don't believe in fucking someone else's husband 'cause I wouldn't want it done to me. Some things should be valued and kept sacred. The institution of marriage is one of those rare things I do respect. So doing a man rocking a wedding band is an absolute no-no. However, anyone else is fair game. I'll fuck him, and suck him straight into a damn coma, then send him on his way with no questions asked. I only expect him to be able to pump the hips, slam the dick, and get it up for more than one round. If his sex game is really on point, he's almost guaranteed to smash it again.

"…uh…oh…mmmph…pull your dick out and eat my pussy, baby," I say in a deep, throaty moan. It is a request that sounds more like a command. Although his dick feels so damn good inside of me, my clit wants, no, needs to feel his warm tongue. I need to bust my nut all over it, then suck my creamy juice off his lips and tongue as he slides his dick back up into me. This is what I want; this is what I need. He eagerly obliges, making his way down between my legs, then kissing the hood of my clit before pulling it back to greet it with his tongue. I let out another moan. "Oh, yes, Garrett. Oh, yes, baby…lick that clit, baby."

Now, I don't know about you, but for me, there's something sexy about seeing a man's lips glistening with my pussy juice that really turns me on. That's what I'm thinking while Garret is between my legs with his tongue darting in and out of me while placing his mouth over my dripping-wet pussy so he can drink, lick, and slurp the warm, sticky treat that gushes out of me. Each time I cum, the orgasms are more intense, causing my whole body to shake. "Oh, yes…oooh, yes…Fuck me with that tongue, baby…"

I can't front, Garrett has me going. I'm not sure if it's because I haven't had sex in over a week and I'm extremely horny, or if I miss having his tongue in my pussy. I wrap both legs around his shoulders, pull him in deeper, and smother his face in between my legs, allowing him to continue sucking and licking on my clit while dipping his thick fingers in and out of my hot hole. My creamy pussy pulls at his fingers, greedily gripping them as he presses his tongue against my throbbing, swollen clit. Just before my next wave of orgasms comes, he lifts me up, flips me over, then in one swift motion glides his thick, rock-hard dick inside the back of my pussy and pounds deep, fast, and hard, slapping me on the ass until I am creaming all over his dick again. He thrusts his body up into me and gyrates and jerks, pounding away. Sweat drips onto my back.

"Aaah, shit…fuck…uh…Damn, this pussy's good," he grunts before abruptly pulling his dick out of me. I can still feel the pressure of his dick inside of me. My pussy is pulsing and I wind my hips, craning my neck over my shoulder to see what he is doing, why he has left my pussy vacant and aching to be refilled. He abruptly yanks off the condom and starts jerking his dick. "I'ma bust this nut all on this pretty, fat ass of yours," he says, slapping his dick across my ass. "Pull open ya ass for me." I do, and he begins rubbing the length of his cock across my asshole, back and forth, then slapping it several times, causing it to pucker as he beats it with his heavy stick. I moan. "Yeah, baby, look at that pretty asshole. Next time you gonna let me fuck you in that ass, right?"

I moan again. He takes that to mean yes, and I don't

tell him otherwise. I keep moaning until he backs up and shoots his hot, creamy nut straight in the center of my ass and onto my lower back.

"Aaaahhh, fuck," he moans, still jerking his dick and flicking the last droplets of his cum on my ass. Then he takes his dick and starts to smear his nut into my skin and around the center of my hole, coating it. I moan, rubbing my clit.

"I want some more," I whine, turning around and taking his still-hard dick in my hands and stroking it. I kiss the head, then flick my tongue across the eye of his dick, hoping to get a taste of his milk.

"Damn, girl, you know how to keep this dick happy," he says, as I lift his dick up and pull his balls into my mouth one at a time, slowly sucking them while jacking him off. My mouth waters and wets his heavy sack as he leans in and gently tweaks and rolls my nipples between his fingers, then pinches them firmly.

I glance over at the digital clock on my nightstand and notice it reads 11:43 p.m. We've been fucking for over an hour and I know it is a matter of time before it has to end. Garrett doesn't have to be at work until eight in the morning, so technically, we could go a few more rounds, but knowing him, he'll want to get home to get a few hours of sleep. Hell, it's fine with me since I have to be at work in the morning myself. Interestingly, Garrett is the only man I fuck—oh, and Maurice—whom I allow to shower after a night of hot, sweaty sex; whom I willingly kiss; and whom I don't keep on a time clock. He can usually come through and get his dick wet any time our schedules coincide, whether it's day or night. The others…well, they come when I say it's cool to come through, which is usually after the sun goes down, and before the sun comes up. And that usually works out best for them since most of them have to get home to their girls 'n shit, or to whatever else it is that keeps them occupied. I don't ask, they don't tell, and I don't care.

I continue stroking his dick, waiting, wishing for another drop of his nectar. *There it is*, I think, licking my lips in anticipation. I kiss the tip, then lick the clear sweetness that leaks from the slit. I allow my tongue to glide across the thick vein that runs along its shaft. He moans as I slowly roll my tongue around the head before wrapping my soft lips around it and sucking on it, pulling it deep into my warm mouth. Drool drips from the corners of my mouth as I bob my head back and forth. I look up and see that his eyes are now rolling back up into his head as I suck and slurp and gulp down every inch of him.

"Oh, fuck…oh, shit…Damn, girl," he grunts, grabbing me by the back of the head with his right hand. He wraps his hand in my hair. I suck him slowly, then pick up the pace and start making popping and smacking noises while moaning and gently pulling at his balls, massaging them, squeezing them, milking them. "Uh, you about to make me cum," he announces in a deep, groggy whisper. I can feel his dick throbbing as I suck and his balls are starting to draw up, which lets me know he's on the brink of splattering a hot one. I increase my suction around the head of his dick, then use my hands and grip the base of his dick tightly and start stroking it in long, fast motions. Garrett's body begins to rock and tremble as he becomes enthralled in the throes of passion caused by my sensual tongue and loving mouth. "Aaah, fuck…I'm about to nut, baby." I reach up and start pulling on his nipples, which causes him to shudder and moan. "Oh, shit…I'm coming, baby." His body jerks and within moments, he pulls out of my mouth, backs up, and aims his dick at me, shooting his hot cream all over my chest and neck. He pants and jerks a few more times, milking out the last bit of his nut, before dramatically collapsing over onto the bed beside me. "Whew," he says, trying to catch his breath. "You wear me out."

I cut my eyes at him, grinning. "Which is why you keep coming back for more," I state, getting up out of the bed. His sticky nut runs down my titties and over my hard nipples. Now, if he were my man, I would have both nipples in my mouth, lapping up all of his sweet man milk. But he's not, and probably never will be, so his nut goes wasted. If Garrett were one of them really kinky, tri-sexual men I was telling you about, I'd cradle him in my arms and feed him my cum-drenched titties and have him suck his nut off them. I'd nurse him like a newborn baby. Oh, well.

"Partially," he says, leaning up on his forearms and looking at me. He tilts his head, studies me.

"And the other part?" I ask, matching his gaze. I'm not sure if what he is going to tell me is something I really want to hear, or know. But I ask anyway.

He senses this and simply says, "Let's leave it at partially, for now."

There's something about the way in which he says *for now* that makes me uncomfortable. Between you and me, I am relieved. Garrett and I have been fucking off and on for almost three years now, and I'd hate for it to have to end because of some extra shit he's now trying to bring into it.

I smile. "Well, I'm glad I can keep you and that fat dick of yours fucked and sucked down to the bone."

"That you do, baby," he replies finally, pulling himself out of the bed. He grabs his dick and shakes it. "You definitely know how to keep me and my man here feeling good."

I suck my teeth, rolling my eyes up in my head. "Whatever," I snap, swinging my hips and bouncing my ass into the bathroom. I turn on the shower, then get in. I stand under the pulsing showerhead with my head back, rolling my neck. I close my eyes and allow the water to beat against my body before taking the shower head in my hand and positioning it between my legs. I brace myself up against the wall, steady my right foot up on the ledge, then spread open my pussy lips and allow the water to beat against my clit. I let out a soft moan as my pussy opens and closes in its attempt to catch beads of water.

I think about my encounter with Garrett, rub the space that held his dick moments ago, and find myself asking the question: If a man had to use one word to describe a woman's pussy, what would it be? I toy with the question for a moment. I mean, honestly. Every woman wants to believe she has a tighter, wetter, sweeter pussy than any other. She wants to believe her pussy can out-fuck the next chick's. But at the end of the day, what does the man fucking her really think about what's between her legs?

Hmmm...I wonder if any woman has ever given thought to that. I mean, would his one-word description of her pussy be *smelly*, like rancid meat or sweet, rotting fruit? Would it be *cavernous*, because it's huge, dark, and damp? How about *deep* like an ocean? Would it be *addictive* like crack? Would it be *worn* like the heel of an old shoe? Would it be *juicy* like a ripened peach? Would it be *dry* like the Sahara desert, or *gritty* like sandpaper? Maybe *tight* like a Venus fly trap. Or *aged* like fermented grapes or blue cheese. Perhaps *sweet* like cotton candy. What about *sour* like curdled milk? Or maybe it would it be *sticky* like molasses. Would it be *wet* like a gushing waterfall? Would it be *hot* like an inferno? Maybe *rank* like it's covered with sweat and crusty pussy and cum juices. Humph. Or perhaps straight *rotten* like the back of a garbage truck?

The numerous descriptions cause me to chuckle to myself. *Humph, can you imagine?* I think. Then, for some reason, I find myself wondering how many women actually look at their pussies. I mean really look at them. Lie back, spread open their legs, pull open their lips and use a mirror to look up into their treasures. I don't know about anyone else, but I look at my pussy regularly, at least once a week. Hell, I have a pretty snatch, if I do say so myself. Every man who has ever seen it always tells me how pretty (and tasty) it is. It's all one color on the outside, a golden brown, and a deep shade of pink in the center. And my lips are puffy and don't flap over like elephant ears, which are not a good look, in my opinion. Anyway, although I don't make it a habit to look at another woman's twat, I have seen a few that weren't too appetizing or appealing and I have been told by men that some chicks have the ugliest holes imaginable. Humph. Well, I'm glad I don't have that issue. 'Cause not only does it look good, it tastes good, and feels even better. There you have it!

Bottom line: No matter what her hole looks like, I believe all women should love their pussies. Admire their pussies. Be proud of their pussies. Never forsake their pussies. Never be afraid to look at their pussies. And most importantly, be in control of their pussies.

No one should ever rob a woman of her freedom (of her right) to deny someone access to her pussy. Yes, dammit! Women from all walks of life should unite in their femininity, celebrate their womanhood, and behold the essence of their pussies. We are women. We are one. We are good pussy.

I am so deep in my musings over pussy that I don't even hear Garrett step into the shower until his voice slices into my thoughts. I return the shower head to its resting place.

"You know I enjoy spending time with you," he says, taking his strong hands and massaging my shoulders, then replacing his hands with kisses. I hand him my washcloth and the bar of soap so that he can wash my back.

I take a deep breath, hold it in, then slowly release it under the stream of warm water beating against my face. I turn to face him and begin washing the front of his body without saying a word—starting with his chiseled chest, massaging his nipples, before trailing down to his smooth abs lined by fine hair around his navel. He stands in front of me, allowing my hands to explore his body. He licks his lips as I make my way down to his semi-hard dick. I take it in my soapy hands and lather it up, stroking it until he hardens and thickens. When it swells to its capacity, I rub it between the palms of both of my hands as if I'm rubbing two sticks together, then slide my slippery hands up and down the length of it, twisting and turning my hand over the head of his dick like I'm turning a doorknob.

He moans. "Damn, baby…oh, shit…"

I keep my eyes locked on his, giving him a variety of handwork. From stroking his dick from the top to the bottom with one hand, then releasing, bringing my other hand to the top, then repeating, alternating with both hands; to grabbing his balls with one hand and lightly pulling as I stroke him with the other. This gets him off all the time.

"Aaah, fuck…oh, shiiiiit," he moans again.

His eyes open and close, then roll in the back of his head.

"That's right, daddy, give me that dick milk," I coo. "Bust that big nut in my hand."

He leans in and brushes his lips against mine, then kisses me softly on them. "Why you fucking with me?" he asks, dipping at the knees.

"Is that what you think I'm doing?" The way he is looking at me is making my temperature rise. I can feel my boiling juices trickling down my inner thighs.

"You know what you're doing, girl," he says.

I smile, knowing if there was a condom in here with us, he would have ripped it open, rolled it over his dick, then turned me around, slammed me up against the wet tile, and relentlessly fucked me from the back. Garrett is the type of man who can't stand having his dick hard and not being able to bury it inside of me. Stroking and sucking his dick is good, but he's the kind of man who will eventually want the pussy. It's sweet, hot, and tasty, and he's gonna want it to wet his dick. But he knows there's a line that doesn't ever get crossed, and that's him fucking me without a condom. Since there are no condoms around us, he will settle for a soapy hand job. Although I enjoy living on the edge, I will not compromise my health by playing Russian roulette with him or any other man. Now, some may say that that's what I'm already doing with the number of men I fuck. They're entitled to their opinions. But I consider it doing what I enjoy doing responsibly. So we can agree to disagree.

Anyway, I suppose if I ever did decide to have a man (of my own) in my life, the one advantage would be not having to use a condom. 'Cause, honestly, I don't like using them. But like I said, I refuse to jeopardize my health by fucking without one. So if he ain't strapped with a Durex, then there's no sex. That's the only condom that feels like he's using nothing. I will say, it sure would be nice to get fucked in the ass the way I like. Straight up raw. I love to feel a man nut in my asshole. There's something about feeling his dick throbbing inside of me as his cum is spurting out and into my tight hole, filling it up with his thick, hot cream, then it starts oozing out as I use my muscles to push it back out. Mmm. I can almost feel it running down the crack of my ass as I speak. Oooh, baby, and to be able to swallow a man's gooey nut would be a delicious treat. Yep. It sure would. The thought of a nigga's hot love custard hitting the back of my throat has my mouth drooling.

However, the way so many men are out here creeping on their wives and girls, it'd be my luck that my man would end up being one of those cheating-ass niggas like the ones I already fuck. And the risk of him getting sloppy and bringing me something home…oh, hell no! I'd rather be fucking who I want, and know I have to protect myself, than have a man I *think* I can trust, who I believe is respecting our relationship, and he's out behind my back sticking his dick in the next chick.

So tell me. Who's the one really at risk, them or me?

Garrett kisses me again, bringing me back to the reason I'm holding his dick in my hand. "I love this big dick," I tell him, stroking his dick—and his ego—faster, and harder, kneading it and twisting my hands over the head of it. "It feels so good in my hands."

"Oh yeah, you love that dick, baby?"

"Mmm-hmm," I moan. "Bust that nut for me."

"Yeah, you want this nut…you want this nut, huh? Huh?" I spread open my legs as he reaches over and slides his hand between my thighs. His fingers find their way to my treasure chest and toy with its opening, causing my pussy to clamp around each finger. I increase my strokes on his dick as he increases his strokes against my clit and inside of me. Within a matter of moments we are each shuddering and exploding into the other's hands.

"What you trying to do to me?" he asks, kissing me on the lips again.

Now between you and me, this kissing between us has really gotten out of hand. And I am still trying to figure out how in the hell what Garrett and I share— umm, let me see—how it has evolved from strictly fucking to fucking and kissing. But it has. That wasn't supposed to be a part of the equation, but somehow over the last year it has found its way into it; probably because of him being in my bed as many times as he has over the last three years. It seemed to happen all of a sudden. Come to think about it, I allow Maurice to kiss me as well, most likely for the same reason. Hmmm, then there's Wade who tongues me down too.

I shrug, half-smiling. "Nothing you don't want me to," I offer, turning around to face the shower head. I rewash myself, then step out of the shower, leaving Garrett to finish his shower.

Twenty minutes later, I am sitting downstairs on the sofa in my silk robe, waiting for Garrett to come downstairs. When he does, I get up and walk him toward the front door. "As always," I say, opening the door, "thanks for the dick."

He smiles. "It's all yours anytime you want it."

Of course it is, I think, returning the smile. I know I

can fuck Garrett seven days a week, twenty-four hours a day if I wanted to. But I don't. However, lately, it seems like I've been riding his dick at least two, sometimes three times a month, if not more. "It was good seeing you," I say, dismissing his comment.

"It was good seeing you too, baby," he says, stepping into me and kissing me on the forehead. "I'll call you later. Maybe—"

I reach up on my tippy-toes and shove my tongue in his mouth to cut off what he is about to say: "Maybe I can come by later on tomorrow."

"No, I don't think so" will end up being my response if he says it, so I kiss him before he has the chance to. As much as I enjoy spending time with Garrett, I only want to see him once in a while, meaning once every few months. Seeing me more than once in the same week starts to look like something more than what it is and I'm not interested.

"Call me," I finally say, stepping back from him, then opening the door wider. It is his cue to bounce, and he takes it.

"Good night, baby," he says, walking out the door.

"Good night," I say, shutting the door behind him. I press my back up against it, then close my eyes, hoping Garrett isn't crazy enough to start catching feelings.

CHAPTER
FIVE

Question: Have you ever wondered what's really in a man's nut? I read somewhere that a man's cum is ten percent sperm, and the rest is enzymes, vitamin C, calcium, protein, sodium, zinc, citric acid, and fructose. Hmmm…now, if this is true, then I'd say this is the makings of a wonderful, rich protein shake. Imagine a thick, gooey, hot, and creamy nut first thing in the morning, sliding down your throat. Hmmm…delicious! What a way to start your day. Wouldn't you agree?

Oh well, it's been so long since I've swallowed a nut. I'd probably throw it back up if I even tried to. Speaking of cum, how many women do you think enjoy having a man crack his nut on her face? Hmmm. That would make for an interesting survey. Well, I tried it once, about six years ago. I was on my knees feverishly sucking the hell out of an ex-boyfriend's dick when he asked me if he could nut on my face. He got to stroking and yanking and pumping his dick in his hand, and talking real dirty. The sight of the head of his dick sliding in and out of his hand sent a fire through me. I begged him for that nut, waited with anticipation to feel his cream on my face. He deepened his strokes, slowed his rhythm, and a blast of white gook shot out of the slit of his dick straight into my damn eye. Ugh! It was so hot and thick. I screamed, thinking the fool had blinded me. I got up scrambling, tripping over shit trying to get to the bathroom to wipe my eye. Seemed like I smeared it deeper into my eye and made it worse. My vision was cloudy for almost two hours afterward. I was so damn disgusted. The idea of having cum dangling from my nose, on my eyelashes, or in my eye isn't exactly an exciting thought. So, no thank you. He can shoot his load on my back, on my stomach, my titties, or my ass. And if he's my man—something I haven't had in a very long time—I want him to pull out and nut on my pussy, then smear it with his dick all over my clit. Or he can bust deep in my ass. Then again, he can pull out and let me suck it out of him. Mmmm. There's nothing tastier than a dick soaked in pussy juice.

For some reason, I am having a flashback moment. I am remembering years ago riding the Greyhound bus late at night to D.C. from New York to visit my brother Terrance at Howard for their homecoming. I was like seventeen, and this older dude was sitting in the back row of the bus with me, drinking a forty ounce. I don't remember exactly how we started talking, but by the time we had crossed the Delaware Memorial Bridge, I had his long dick in my hand and was jerking him off. I didn't ask him his name, and didn't give him mine. The only thing I wanted to know was how thick and hot his cum was. I remember pulling out my bottle of baby oil, pouring it all over his dick and in my hands, then rubbing his dick between the palms of my hand as if I were rubbing two sticks together. In swift, deep motions, I went up and down the shaft of his dick, stroking him from the top to the bottom, then releasing, bringing my other hand to the top of his dick, then repeating, alternating with both hands. He begged me to suck it, so I flicked my tongue over the head, just enough to tease him. And, before his dick was about to spit, it swelled to maximum capacity, then spurted out a hot, thick nut. I knew then I was at a point of no return. I was hooked on dick cream.

Anyway, Tyrese is here, standing in the middle of my bedroom floor, with his dick in his hand, stroking it for me. I lean back on my left forearm, spread open my legs, and rub my clit over my thong. Me'shell Ndegeocello's "Trust"—from the album *Cookie: The Anthropological Mixtape*—is playing in the background. The title is so unfitting for his cheating-ass since he can't be trusted, but the words say what I want. "*…Lay me down…Spread my legs…tell me…what's it like…inside me…Let me stroke you with my warmth…make you cum…*"

The song is sexy, and sitting here watching him stroke his fat dick makes my pussy cry out for a taste of passion. I gesture with my index finger for him to come to me. He slowly moves toward me. I smile, taking in his nude body. The male anatomy deeply fascinates me. Every man I'm with, I make it a point to examine every part, every inch, of his body. I love making him strip down and prance around naked. Without him even knowing it, I am taking him all in from head to toe. And I'm always amazed at the different shapes, sizes, and colors of dicks there are. There is also a wide variety of balls. Loose balls, tight balls, hairy balls, hairless balls, and those extra-long, bull balls. Mmmmm. The thought of a man's dick and balls gets me hot. I can play in my pussy and imagine all the different types of dick attached to a man's body, and cum all over my fingers. I think this is why I constantly crave variety. This is why I lust for dick.

But please don't get it twisted. My fascination with watching a man undress himself and taking in all of his nakedness is also about being able to see whether or not he has any abnormalities, scars, blemishes, bruises, discolorations, lesions, leakage, etc. When I take his dick in my hands and slowly stroke him into a throbbing erection, I'm not only doing it to bring him pleasure; I'm doing it as part of my cock inspection. Hell, I need to be up close and damn personal with his dick to see what's really good before I go any further.

This is Tyrese's fifth time being here, and I still inspect the dick to make sure there are no changes from the last time he was here. He steps up in front of me.

His dick is thick and rigid and heavy and excited, its tip already leaking sweet, sticky strands of pre-cum. I get off the bed, sink down to my knees on the floor, and take it into my hands, squeeze it at the base, then lift up his balls and gently squeeze and bounce them in the palm of my hand. Then I run my thumb over the slit of his dick, rubbing his lust over the head. Once again, he passes my inspection.

"You like playing with daddy's big dick, don't you?"

"Mmm-hmm," I moan, licking my lips. Now, I don't actually consider his dick big, but I indulge him nonetheless. I mean it is fat and all, but measuring in at seven-and-a-half inches doesn't exactly qualify as "big" in my book. Nevertheless, it is meaty, and definitely a beautiful, mouthwatering piece. I look up at him, then kiss and bury my face into his groin. The coarseness of his pubic hairs tickles my nose. I inhale his scent, taking in his manliness. I cup his balls, kiss them, then slowly lick them, wetting them with my spit. I use my free hand to play with my clit.

"Yeah, that's right, baby. Wet daddy's balls up. Mmm… Oh, shit."

I replace my tongue with my fingers and fondle his balls, tracing a slow sensual path over and behind the heavy sacs. In my head, I'm pretending to be Tyrese's personal dick sucker: soothing him, relieving him, sucking away his stress, enveloping and riding his dick with wet lips and a warm tongue, flicking, tickling, and probing all around and over it. Swallowing him down into a deep, pulsing throat, contracting around every inch of his dick like a boa constrictor, squeezing his thick dick in a vice-like grip until it spasms, convulses, and erupts a tidal wave of hot foaming cum. Mmmmm. My imagination causes me to let out another deep moan.

"You want me to wet this dick up?" I ask, looking up at him in between licks along the shaft of his hot dick. The eye of his dick continues to leak a stream of clear, sticky nectar. I will myself not to run my tongue over it, but, despite myself, I give in to temptation and lap at its slit, savoring the stream of sweetness.

"Yeah, I want a wet, sloppy dick suck, baby." He reaches for my breasts and fondles them. Pinching my nipples, he causes the milk from my pussy to explode onto my fingers and run down my hand.

"Go lie down in the middle of the bed," I order him. I get up from my knees and suck my cum-soaked fingers as I watch Tyrese walk over to the bed. I take in the back of his heart-shaped calves, admire his muscled thighs, and amazing ass.

Tyrese stretches out in the center of my bed, waiting to get his dick wet. He sneaks his ass over to get piped every chance he gets—when I allow it—because his girl is scared to suck his dick. Matter of fact, she doesn't even like sucking it, and when she does, it's only for a few minutes, before she complains about her jaws being tired. The last time she did it, he claims she ended up throwing up all over his dick. Humph. Lame-ass! That shit is so fucking whack! Who in the hell doesn't suck dick in the twenty-first century? Humph.

Well, obviously, that bitch sure as hell doesn't. So, every now and again, when I feel up to it, I suck him all the way down to the base while licking his balls and let him get his nut, then send him back home to his non-dick-sucking whack-ass "wifey" with my pussy juice smeared all over his face and thick lips.

Tyrese strokes his dick as he watches me suck on my fingers. Now listen up. The key to sucking a man's dick is seducing him mentally first, then sucking him like you love him. Fuck his mind, make love to his dick. Stroke his ego, and worship the dick. That's my strategy. And it generally works. Every time he sees you or hears your voice, he'll think about how good you sucked down his cock. In the still of the night, when he's lying next to his woman, his dick will brick up thinking about your head game. He'll be wondering when (and how) he can get you to wrap out soft lips around his shit again. Trust doing it at all, as in his chick isn't doing to suck him again once he's Tyrese's bottomless throat.

daddy, just like that. Stroke that fat cock for

"You like watching me stroke this big dick, don't you? You want me to slam this fat dick in your pussy?"

"Yessss, daddy," I coo, turning around and pulling open my ass cheeks, giving him a rear view of my pussy. "Look how wet you got this pussy." I reach between my legs and slide two fingers into my love nest, winding and thrusting my hips. I glance over my shoulder to see him stroking his cock a mile a minute. "I'ma suck that dick so good. Ooh, I can't wait to suck that big dick," I tell him, turning back to face him, slowly making my way over to the bed. "I want you to wrap your hands around my head and shove it all the way down my throat. I want you to pump and grind your cock down in my throat. Fuck my hot throat like it's a pussy. I want you to watch your dick get lost in and out of my neck. Can you do that, daddy?"

The more I talk the harder and thicker his dick gets, and the wetter my pussy gets. I'm working him up, but I am also working myself up as I imagine him pressing the inside of his muscular thighs on either side of my head, slow-fucking my face, spreading open my throat, stretching my neck, sliding his dick in and out and it getting all my spit. I pinch my clit and let out a moan.

"Aaah, shit," he moans dick. Stop playing and come shit."

"Oh, you ready to have this throat w... k this

your dick, huh?" I ask as I climb up on the bed, then crawl between his legs. I take his dick in my hands, squeeze it at the base, kiss the tip, slide my lips back and forth, then up and down along the shaft, then slap the center of my wet lips with it. I allow it to make smacking sounds against my lips for several minutes until my mouth overflows with saliva, and then...I slowly slide his dick into my mouth.

He moans.

Now I don't know about you, but I love to hear a man moan. And I love it when he talks dirty to me, pulls my hair, grabs me by the back of the head and face fucks, skull fucks, or whatever else you want to call it when I'm sucking his dick. Oooh, baby. You want to see how fast my panties get soaked, do all the above and it's on.

"You like that?" I ask, slipping his dick out of my mouth, then sliding it back in.

He moans again. "Yeah, baby. I love them lips on this dick. Ah, shit."

I decide it's time to shift my position so that I can really get this neck stretched. I pull up off his dick.

"Yo, that's good. Why you stop?" he asks, sounding all desperate and confused and whatnot.

"I'm changing positions so I can really get at your cock," I say, turning around so that I am lying across the bed. "Stand up over me," I tell him, resting my neck on the edge of the bed so that my head is hanging upside down. Okay, now pay attention. This is where it starts to get fun. Tyrese jumps out of bed with his stiff dick swaying side to side like a sword preparing for battle. He hovers over me with his dick twitching. It bounces in anticipation of what's to come. I grab his dick, open my mouth, extend the tip of my tongue past my bottom lip (this helps flatten the tongue), then guide the head in, forcing the back of my throat open as if I'm yawning (this creates a larger opening for the dick).

"Oh, shit," he moans, trying to push more of his dick in. But I am the one in control, and he knows this. I've learned that an overzealous man will try to ram his cock down in your windpipe if you let him. And I'm not the one, which is why my hand stays on it to guide it at my pace. Not his. I tighten my grip on his dick, then take a deep breath and slowly slide the length of his cock all the way into my mouth, along my tongue. I remember the first few times I tried this, I felt the urge to gag, but I would stop, leave the dick where it was for a few minutes, then pull it out. I kept repeating that until I finally mastered taking it all and was able to swallow the whole dick as I was doing now. Now you'll have to excuse me; it's going to be a bit complicated trying to talk with a mouth full of dick so sit and watch. Gurgling sounds come from the back of my throat. He has his groin pressed up against my nose, grinding himself into my mouth. "Ah, fuck…damn, you can suck some dick."

I reach out and grab Tyrese's ass, pulling him deeper into my throat. I remember to breathe through my nose so that I don't choke to death. Tyrese is skull-fucking me lovely, and I am wetting his cock with my wet throat and the spit that dribbles out of the sides of my mouth. He reaches over me and slides his hand back and forth over my pussy, then presses on my clit and strokes it. I thrust my hips up, and a moan escapes me as he slides two fingers into me and finger-pops my juicy fruit.

"Oh, fuck," he grunts. "Aah, shit...I'm getting ready to cum..." He's riding my face like his cock is on fire and he's trying to get my throat to put out the flames. "Oh, shit...uhh...fuck..."

Now, listen...I'm not promoting it (safe sex is first), but it's probably a better idea to deep throat a man raw, or make sure the rubber is extremely lubricated to avoid getting a condom lodged in your throat. That is not a good look, okay? However, if you do him raw, I can almost assure you he is going to want to bust his baby batter down in your throat. Believe that. But with so much shit out here, I encourage not giving it raw to just anyone. They really have some wonderful flavored condoms that make it really cute to stay on your knees gulping down a dick.

But for the cum lover in you who might be afraid of the taste or throwing up, lean your head all the way back as far as you can, get the head of his dick as far down your throat as you can, and when he pumps that thick, hot cream down in your throat it'll slide down nice and easy. It'll be finger-licking good. Trust me. It turns a man on when you guzzle it all down. Yep, right down to the last damn drop. From my lips to his dick...enjoy the journey!

CHAPTER
SIX

It's only ten o'clock in the morning, and I'm already sitting here at my desk, disgusted. It's bad enough I don't even feel like being here today. It started at eight-thirty when I was standing in line at Commerce—oops, I mean, TD—Bank, trying to make a deposit. The line was long as hell and they only had two tellers working. Something had told me to go through the drive-thru but against my better judgment, I hadn't. So I'm patiently waiting for the line to move along when this chick in back of me starts talking to two other chicks, telling them how her man had gotten a suite at the Borgata in Atlantic City and how he had rocked her socks off with his love making. And how she felt he was "the one." She was giving her audience an earful of juicy tidbits. I glanced back a few times. By the way they were staring at her, I could tell they were clinging to her every word, practically salivating. I bet these new Gucci heels that one of them hoes wished she were in her place. I had to shake my damn head. Some women really don't know when not to run their mouths when it comes to their men and their relationships. Only a careless bitch is going to brag about what her man does for her financially, sexually, or otherwise.

I'm telling you, by the time I walked up out of that bank, not only did I know that chick's whole life, I had a banging-ass headache.

Humph, so that was the start of my day, along with popping two Excedrin. Then I come up in here and have to be surrounded by a bunch of nosey-assed, phony women. Some days I can deal with it, but not today. I'm not sure if it's because I'm tired from being up fucking most of the night, then waking up and masturbating myself back to sleep; or if it's that I'm in need of a change, or maybe a damn vacation. Whatever it is, I'm beat today.

Between you and me, I can't stand working around a bunch of bitches. Okay, maybe I shouldn't keep using that word to address women, but...dammit, say what you want, that's exactly what the hell some of these woman I work with are. I mean, downright petty and jealous. Someone is always talking about somebody else instead of focusing on themselves. And if they're not gossiping about, or lying on, somebody, they're around here trying to figure out who's fucking whose man. I mean, really. Give me a damn break. It isn't that serious.

Then you have the ones who come up in here and blab all of their business, letting everyone in earshot know what they did, who they did it with, and where they did it. Humph. Or they're sharing their sob stories about their men, disclosing all their family secrets, or bragging about what they have. Then they got the nerve to get pissed when they find out someone is talking about them. I'm like, "Bitch, are you serious? If you learned to keep your damn mouth shut, maybe you wouldn't have to worry about someone putting your shit on blast."

I tell you, it's sickening. This is exactly why I don't fuck with any of these hoes in this building. They all know not to come to me with none of that shit 'cause I don't want to hear nothing that comes out of any of these mountain coons' mouths. You'd think working in a so-called professional environment would thwart the pettiness and cattiness. Not! Some of these bitches are worse than someone with less education, or experience. Always backstabbing, and undermining someone who they think is a threat. And the gossip mill is constantly churning. Education definitely has nothing to do with being an ignorant-ass, trouble making bitch.

I can't be so bothered. I come to work, do my job, and keep it moving. And it kills 'em, 'cause they don't know shit about me. Other than that, I own my own home, drive a Mercedes CL550, and wear designer shit to work every day of the week. They don't know jack, and that's exactly how I'm going to keep it. No, I don't want to go out for drinks after work. No, I don't want to do lunch with your fake ass. No, I don't want to know shit about your personal life because I'm not telling you shit about mine. No, your nosey-ass can't stop by my home to see how I'm living. So beat it!

Of course word around the building is that I think I'm better than everybody else. Hmmm, what's the word they use? Oh, yeah…*stuck-up*! Well, that works for me. 'Cause I love having a stiff dick "stuck up" in me. So say what you want. I've never cared about what someone else thought about me any damn way. Other than a hello, and maybe an occasional lunch gathering, I stay as far the hell away as I can from all of 'em. Well, okay, with the exception of Nahdirah, whom I marginally consider a friend—and I'm using the term *friend* loosely—I have very little patience or tolerance for any of 'em. Nahdirah's ass is starting to wear my nerves thin as well.

I'm sorry, but I will never be able to wrap my mind around the thought of people who run their mouths about everything. What's done behind closed doors should *stay* behind closed doors. I'm a firm believer that what you do in your personal life is your business. If you wish to share, then do. But don't get upset when these same people you confide in turn around and make you the brunt of their jokes, or the topic of their discussions. You can call me what you want, it's fine with me. I'm here to work, not be friends or swap war stories. I keep trying to tell Nahdirah's dumb ass to stop running her damn mouth so much around here. I told her twice already that these hating-ass hoes are jealous and conniving, and to feed them with a long-handled spoon. But what does she do? She sits up in the damn break room, first thing this morning, and gives them the 4-1-1 on what she and her man, Jake, did over the weekend. I came in on the tail end of her conversation when she spotted me walking through the door and started waving for me to come over.

I silently rolled my eyes when I saw whom she was sitting with at the table. Cheryl, the perfect example of a *bitch*. Cheryl is every bit of fifty-five and the chick walks around acting like she's still in high school, wearing a head full of front-laced weave, with a gym body wrapped in teenie-tiny skirts and little-assed blouses, her double D titties all bunched together in 'em like that shit is sexy, and click-clacking her damn gum all over the place. Fucking ghetto! Granted, she does have a beautiful face on which she packs a bunch of makeup. And she also has a nice shape for a woman her age. Actually, she puts some chicks half her age to shame, which is why I can understand why she likes to flounce around here acting like she's the Queen of Seduction or some shit.

Don't get me wrong, I am all for a woman feeling good about herself and being comfortable in the skin that she's in. And I'm all for a woman feeling and dressing sexy, but there's a time and a place for everything. Contrary to popular belief, there is nothing—and I do mean *nothing*—sexy about a bitch coming to an office environment in hooker pumps and spandex pants so tight that the whole building can see your pussy lips, or a skirt so short you can see your bald snatch when you sit down. This trick is old enough to be my mother. Hell, she's a grandmother of three. And this is how she represents herself—like a two-dollar trollop. Say what you want. It's tacky and downright disgusting, if you ask me. And that's exactly how this tactless, classless chick comes to work every day!

So anyway, when I finally do make my way over to the table after purchasing a cup of green tea and a cinnamon bagel, I act like the office hooch is invisible, which I know pisses her off since she loves being the center of attention. The other two chicks sitting there with them must have been temps or something 'cause I'd never seen them before. I ignored them as well. I'm not the phony type. If I don't like you, or dig your energy, I'm not fucking with you. And that's what it is. And all three of them bitches reeked of negativity.

"What's up, Nahdirah?" I asked, glancing at my watch. I had only been in the building twenty minutes and still needed to log on to my computer.

"Not a damn thing, girl," she said, brushing a strand of hair from out of her face, then sweeping it behind her ear. "What's been up with you? I haven't seen you in a while."

"Oh, Nahdirah is the only person you see sitting over here?" the hooch asked with 'tude.

"She's the only one I choose to speak to," I flatly stated, shifting my focus back to Nahdirah.

"Whatever," she huffed, giving me a flick of her wrist.

I ignored her, keeping my eyes locked on Nahdirah. "I've been keeping it real low key," I said to her while taking a look around the break room to see who was in there. I rolled my eyes when I spotted Marcella, another two-faced bitch, sitting over in the corner with this dude Clinton from downstairs in the finance department. Apparently, they'd become an item of sorts over the last few months. They were huddled up, whispering and giggling like they were conspiring about something. Truth be told, they probably were. *Hmm, what's he make…man number four in six months?* I think, shifting my attention back to Nahdirah. "You know I don't play the front too much. What's been up with you?"

"Nothing much," she replied. "Same ole, same ole. I was sitting here telling Cheryl how Jake took me into the city over the weekend to see *The Color Purple*. Girrrl, if you haven't seen it, you must. Anyway, I thought we were only going in for the day, but Jake surprised me by getting a room at the Marriott. He had a bottle of champagne and a fruit basket, along with roses, there waiting for me. Chile, I was so damn shocked 'cause you know he never takes the initiative to do anything romantic." I stood there, trying hard not to suck my teeth or roll my eyes. I glanced over at Miss Hooch and saw her soaking in everything.

"I was telling Cheryl that Jake even ate my kitty-cat, something he hardly *ever* does. He ate me so good I almost passed out." She laughed. "Oh my God, he did things to me this weekend that I would have never expected. I swear that man is a freak."

"Girl, I know that's right," the hooch said, slapping her five. "So, ole boy turned you out, huh? Humph, I know he did you lovely."

Nahdirah nodded, then said, "Mmm-hmm. He rocked my box all weekend long. It had been so long since he handled me like that, I was starting to think maybe he was fucking someone else. But this weekend, he cleared all that up with one deep stroke of his big dick." She shook in her seat, like she had the shivers. "Ooh, he did me so good…"

Okay, that was it for me. I abruptly excused myself. I didn't want to hear or know anything else. I carried my cup of tea and bagel right on up out of there, taking the elevator up to my floor, then going into my office, and shutting the door behind me.

Ugh! Learn to keep your motherfucking mouth *shut!* Why the hell would a woman sit around and share the most intimate details of her relationship with a bunch of other women? You best believe there is gonna always be at least one dick-thirsty chick in the group who is gonna be absorbing every little morsel of information, soaking it all in like a sponge. She'll disguise her scheming-ass ways with fake concern, trying to be the friend you can always lean on. And the first chance she gets to slither her ass into your man's space, she's gonna try her best to fuck him. Or at the very least, suck his dick down to the gristle.

I call this type of bitch the dick-thirsty chick, 'cause she's the type of drooling-ass broad who's going to sweat a dude to no end, practically throwing herself at his feet, begging for the dick. First it'll be real subtle. Every time she's around him, she'll start complimenting him about his looks or the way his cologne smells. She'll comment about how lucky his wife is, and how she wishes she had a man like him. She might even start wearing tighter, more provocative clothing, or a little extra makeup to get his attention. Most men will eat up all this attention. Some will let her attempts to woo him go over his head. Others will flat out check her ass, and let his woman know (not many, though). But some, yes, definitely will give in to her relentless ass.

Trust and believe, if he doesn't bite soon, if he keeps brushing off her advances or doesn't recognize her ploy to get into his wallet and his boxers, this snake bitch will start to get frustrated. Or she'll become more obsessed, more desperate. Being ignored only adds fuel to her fire. She'll become more direct. She may be bold enough to offer him some pussy. Ssssh, nobody has to know. She'll promise to suck the shit out of his ass just to get his nut. This greasy bitch will try to get at a man right in front of his woman with no regard for his relationship. She's a brazen freak with no damn boundaries. She's also a borderline whore, if you ask me. And of course, this is the world according to a ho. Anyway, she sees him as a challenge. She craves him. And will stop at nothing until she gets him. I'd like to get my hands on an intercom, speaker, bullhorn, or whatever, and say to all these simple-ass women who trust every bitch who's in their social circle: "Dear, there's no other way to say it. Stop broadcasting your damn business. There's a conniving, home-wrecking bitch among you. She's envious. She's jealous. And she's gonna fuck your man. So pay attention, and beware!"

Okay, if you haven't figured it out—yes, I have a problem with scheming-ass women (well, bitches!) trying to get at someone else's man, but I have a bigger problem with the chick who constantly runs her damn mouth, giving these tramps all the ammunition they need. I mean, really...what the fuck! Oh, please. I know, I know. I've heard it all before. We shouldn't blame the other woman because it's the man. Well I think sometimes that's a bunch of bullshit. Especially when you think the people in your personal space are people you can (or should be able to) trust. That bitch is as much at fault as he is. I mean, damn, I may be a ho, but I'm not (nor will I ever be) a trifling one. I would never stoop to fucking someone whom I say is my friend's, or family's, man. A chick I don't know, or don't want to know, yes, I will borrow her man's dick and return him to her happily fucked. But not someone I know. I'm sorry. There has to be some dick that's off limits. There needs to be more honor among hoes, don't you think?

Oh, please! Don't even go there. I know what you're thinking. You're trying to figure out what makes me any different from the women I'm talking about. Well, for starters, I don't hang around a bunch of chicks, or gossip with them. I'm not impressed by what some other chick's man is doing for her, or to her. Nor do I need to sit around, plotting on how I can have what she's getting at home. There are too many men out here more than willing to give up the dick (even step out on their chicks) without me needing (or having) to sleepwalk him. Besides, I don't want another woman's man any damn way. Like I've already said, I only wanna fuck him, then send him home.

Okay, you know what…before things get out of hand between us, I'd better clear up a few things. I know some of you will never, ever, comprehend how I'm any different from the home-wreckers, mistresses, and whores. I really don't care. But I'm going to enlighten you, anyway. So let me break it down for you, something I should have done from the gate.

See, the Other Woman, which I will never be, is the dizzy chick who is claiming another woman's man as her own. In her cluttered mind, she shares a special type of relationship with him. In her own sick, twisted way, she feels deeply connected to him. She's the chick who doesn't involve herself with other men 'cause she's faithful to *her* man, you know, the one she's sharing with the wife or girlfriend. She may or may not be interested in actually breaking up his home, but there is a part of her that fantasizes about building—and having—a life with him. Whether she admits it or not, she wants him for herself. But knowing that dream may never come true, she settles (or accepts) the role of his mistress and gladly embraces those moments when *her* man can sneak away from the wife and kids for more than a few hours or a night. Unless she works with him, she may not see him regularly, but they will talk on the phone, email, or text daily. She lives and breathes for his calls. And for the most part, she's okay with hearing him whisper sweet nothings into her ear about how much he misses her, needs to see her, wants to be with her. She plans her whole life around him. And using the excuse of a business trip, she's happily in tow, wrapped in her lover's arms like she is the real first lady. Oh, joy!

Now the Jump-off is exactly that. A chick who jumps on and off the dick. She's not interested in taking him from his woman; she doesn't want to have his babies or meet his family. She only wants to borrow him for his dick, then send him on his way, nothing more, nothing less. If she's strong-willed, she'll never allow emotions to get in the way of her need for a good fuck buddy. Hell, most of the time, she's in a relationship herself, and it's usually with someone who can't seem to handle her in the bedroom. So she seeks out extracurricular sexual activity. Yes, she's using him. But he's using her as well. Both parties get what they want without hassle, so it's a win-win situation. Unfortunately, most jump-offs get dick-whipped, then start disrupting the rules of engagement with the "why-can't-you-leave-her-for-me" bullshit. And before you know it, they submissively fall into the "other woman" category, or leave their own men for their fuck buddies.

The Ho (which is what I am) doesn't usually have a man, and doesn't necessarily want one. She only wants to fuck. Typically, she fucks more than one dude at any given time. She might even let him bring a friend along, but she's not going to let him or anyone else disrespect her. She's usually mad cool, very discreet, and extremely private. She's typically well liked, and knows how to fuck a dick. And dude may or may not put all her business out on blast.

But the Whore, aka the Slut, or Smut...forget it. This bird is downright nasty and trifling. Her name is all out on the streets. She's the chick who will fuck and suck almost anybody, anywhere, anytime, anyplace. She likes it all, and usually gets passed around like a forty-ounce and a blunt. Nut, nut, pass. Nut, nut, nut, pass. She'll let a nigga bust in her face, make her swallow his cum, allow a group of niggas to circle jerk on her, fuck her in the ass, double-fuck her—you know, slam a dick in her ass and pussy at the same time, fist fuck her, spit on her, piss on her. You name it, she's gonna let them do it to her. And then she wonders why she can't get a man. Hell, a prostitute has better luck at getting a man than the whore does. 'Cause at least with a prostitute, fucking is a paid event. It may not necessarily be something she likes, but it's a means to an end. However, a whore gets pleasure from solely being on her back or on her knees for free. And she has the worked-over, stretched-out snatch to prove it.

Now, I am sure there will be some who will want to argue with me about what I'm saying, but who gives a damn! This is the world according to a ho. It doesn't really matter what anyone else thinks about it. It is strictly *my* opinion. This is going to have to be another area in which we agree to disagree. So, if you'll excuse me, I have a ton of emails to get to and a desk load of work to finish before I get the hell up out of here today. We can catch up later. Until then…peace, love, and happy fucking!

CHAPTER
SEVEN

I guess even after I've broken the shit down for you, some of you are still scratching and shaking your heads, wondering what type of woman would willingly spread her legs and knowingly fuck another woman's man. What kind of woman would stoop so low that she'd purposefully disrespect another woman's relationship? Well, I'll tell you again who she is. She's unscrupulous, scandalous, devious, and merciless. She's the harlot, the whore, the slut, the tramp, the trick, the skeezer, the strumpet, the skank, the jezebel, the ho; she is your neighbor, your friend, your sister, your mother, your aunt, your cousin, your coworker, your enemy. She is the type of woman who doesn't give a fuck about you or your relationship. That is the type of woman who will fuck your man.

You fear her? So you should. Your man has been in her bed; she may have been in yours. He has licked her in places that should have been reserved for only you, has fucked her in every position imaginable, has tasted her, explored her, enjoyed her, then has come home to you. She has hooked him by the balls and has conquered him. She stands boldly in your face or silently behind your back, smiling, lending you a shoulder to cry on, lurking in your shadows, anticipating the moment when your man becomes weak, when she crumbles his resolve, then fucks him relentlessly.

So before I move on, I have one thing to say: Listen up! For all you chicks without a clue, no man wants a woman who can't suck dick, can't take dick, and is downright scared of dick. And he damn sure doesn't want a dry, lazy pussy. You'd better learn to drop it like it's hot, and make that shit do what it do: Snap, crackle, and pop! 'Cause if you don't, it'll be a freak like me who'll turn his ass out.

And for the love of sweet, black dick, women, keep the kat house clean and the hairs clipped and trimmed. Having a wild, musty, damp jungle between your legs is not chic. You don't know how many of your men I've heard complain about how nasty some of your snatches are. Or that your sorry ass has on mismatched panties and bras. The only thing I can do is shake my head. See, that's exactly what a man gets when he deals with you low-budget, Conway, Dots, and Walgreens bitches. 'Cause it's a two-dollar ho who doesn't care about her pussy hairs being wrapped around the edges of her panties or nothing matching. But a classy chick or a chick who takes pride in her look and hygiene (even if she's a ho) is always going to step out of her clothes with her pussy on point and a sexy, color-coordinated set of undergarments. Believe that.

Well, since I'm on a roll, here's something else to

think about: When it comes to women and sex, men want the whole package in a woman. Otherwise they're most likely going to go out looking for everything she lacks in someone else. So if your head game is serious but your sex is whack, your man is going to be looking to fuck someone who can slay the dick. If your sex game is tight, but your slob job is weak, he's going to be out looking for someone who can handle a skull-fucking. Bottom line: In order to be a *great* fuck, you have to be good at everything, or damn near close to it. You need to know how to be a classy chick in the streets, and a slutty freak in the sheets. Of course, some will dispute this, and that's fine and dandy. Again, this is the opinion of a certified ho who has probably fucked enough men to know what it is they want and don't want—whether they'll openly admit it or not.

Since I'm sharing, I might as well tell you some of the many things men love about me, the things that keep them coming back for more. Men love it when I get on all fours and slowly crawl toward them real sexy-like, with a come-hither look, enticing them, urging them to lie back and allow me to indulge their fantasies. They love it when I lick my lips, whine, and beg them for the dick. They love it when I make my fat, perfectly round ass dance for them, one cheek at a time, clapping and popping. They love it when I taunt them and tease them, slowly, sensually, rotating my hips and thrusting my pelvis at them. Or when I wildly toss my hair, pout my lips, and swing my hips toward them. They love it when I narrow my eyes into seductive slits and sensually suck on my fingers, or when I peel the skin off a banana, then swallow it whole, pretending it's their dick going deep down in my throat. They love it when I use my warm tongue to lick all over their balls. Men love it when I moan and make slurping noises while sucking their dicks. They love it when I bend my knees and slowly spread open my legs, teasingly pulling open my pussy while licking my lips. They love it when I whisper and whimper for them to "fuck this pussy;" when I tell 'em in low, chant-like groans to "make my pussy cum."

These sexual gestures cause their dicks to swell and ache in anticipation of what they want the most: to taste this sweet, wet pussy and to feel their dicks engulfed in its warmth. Some of you should try it sometimes. It might keep some of your men from straying.

You see, while I'm fucking a man, I make him believe that I care about his needs and wants, even if there's no truth to it. I stroke his ego, and do whatever it takes to make him feel important; to make him feel special. For that moment, I become his healer. I release him from his frustrations. I unlock his imagination and take him places mentally and sexually where most women dare not venture. I give him the illusion that he is in control. But we both know it is the vise-like, suction grip of my thick pussy that forces him to weaken at the knees and bust his nut against his will. And when I'm done with his ass, he leaves out of here with a smile on his face, feeling like he can conquer the world.

Men also love the fact that I'm positive, confident, beautiful, and extremely comfortable in the skin that I'm in. They love it that I know what I want and how I want it, and that I'm not afraid to demand what I want. They love it when I tell them to fuck me from the back, to pull me by the hair, and slap me on the ass. They love it when I tell them to talk dirty to me. When I taunt them, incite them, to fuck me harder. When I look over my shoulder and gaze at them, licking my lips. They love it when I slam my pussy back at them and say, "What, is that all you got?! When you gonna fuck me? When you gonna make me feel the dick, nigga? When you gonna bang this pussy up, huh? Why you teasing me? When you gonna put it in and give me the dick, huh?"

Oh, it drives them over the edge when I challenge their ability to fuck, when I make 'em feel like they're not slaying the pussy right. All the while, I'm smiling inside, watching their faces contort with pleasure, purpose, and exhaustion all at once.

Yes, men love it when I make them work for the pussy, when I make 'em work for that nut. No matter how many times I make a man feel chumped, he wants more, he needs more, he craves more. By the time I'm done fucking him, he walks out of here feeling like a champion of the pussy, no matter how much of an illusion it is.

Not to brag or anything, but I've been told by all the men I'm fucking, or have fucked, that my pussy is "da bomb." They love how hot it gets, how wet it gets, and how tight it grips. So that should explain the line of men wrapped around the corner trying to get a ride in this pussy.

I also believe that who I am as a woman is what drives men crazy. Men are usually already turned on by my physical beauty way before I ever spread open my legs and pull them into my love cove. I seduce them mentally. So by the time I give them a taste of what's between my legs, they've already worked themselves into a sexual frenzy. The fact that I make it my job to help men realize (and oftentimes maximize) their "fucking" potential—or at the very least, expose them to new experiences—is a big part of why they keep wanting more.

I am not the least bit surprised when my doorbell rings at almost midnight, and I open the door to find Mitchell standing there with a silly-ass smirk on his face. I can tell by the glassy look in his eyes that he's been drinking. Wrong answer!

Besides, the last time he was supposed to come through, his sorry ass was a no-show, no-call. But it was all good. I sweat no man. Believe that. As far as I'm concerned, what one man is unable to do, another will. And when all else fails, I keep my bullet and a vibrator on standby, charged and ready to take the edge off.

I sigh, swinging the door open. "Why are you here?" I ask, holding the door and blocking the doorway to keep him from coming in.

"Damn, baby, a nigga can't get a hello? You gonna let me in or what?"

"No, I'm not letting you in," I say, rolling my eyes. "You were supposed to come through two weeks ago when I called your tired ass. But you didn't, so you're shit out of luck. Go ring someone else's bell."

"C'mon, baby," he whines. "Why you gotta be hard on a brotha. Ole girl's been on her bullshit lately 'bout me hanging out...you already know my situation."

I glare at him. "Nigga, you have me confused. I don't give a fuck about your situation. You only get one time to stand this pussy and ass up; then you'll never get another sniff of it again. I mean that. And you knew this from the gate. I have no time for any of the lame excuses, and there's no need to give any because you ain't my man, and will never be. The rule is and has always been you come when expected, not when you feel like it, or you get the ax. I don't care how good the dick or the tongue is. There are no rain checks. And I'm not offering up no drive-thru pussy where you can place your order whenever you get around to it. So your black ass has been scratched off the list." I let out a disgusted grunt. "Then you have the nerve to ring my damn doorbell this time of night like you got it like that."

"Listen, baby," he says, trying to get up in my face. "I had to wait until my girl took her ass to bed before

I could sneak out. I'm sorry 'bout the other week. I know I shoulda called, but I got caught up. I'm here now and I promise to make it up to you. But I only got thirty minutes or so, so instead of you standing here wasting most of it, stop playing games and let me in."

"Um, excuse me," I say, putting my hand up to stop him from getting too close. I feel myself about ready to scream on his ass. "I'm hardly playing games with you. I'm being real as hell. Now, what the fuck you think you gonna do with me, or for me, in thirty damn minutes?"

"Eat that pussy, baby," he boldly replies, gliding his tongue across his bottom lip. "I've missed all that sweet, juicy pussy."

Now under different conditions, I would have eagerly swung open the door and let his happy ass in without blinking an eye 'cause Lord knows he can eat the hell out of some pussy. But thirty minutes? He can't be fucking serious. Besides, my mind is already made up. Like everyone else I choose to fuck, he knows the house rule. Call first. No exceptions. I don't do walk-ins. This pussy is by appointment only. What the hell is wrong with these mofos, thinking they can waltz in and out of here like they got it like that? Just because I'm fucking you on a regular doesn't give you any special privileges. See, that's why I like one-night stands. Everyone plays their position without all the damn extras. There are no expectations. No questions asked. I get what I want.

They get what they want. I go about my business. They go about theirs. And we're all happily fucked.

I twist my lips up. "Humph, so you've missed this deep, wet pussy, huh?" I ask, fucking with him.

"Don't play, girl," he says, grabbing at his dick. He has on a pair of sweats and I can tell he isn't wearing any underwear. "You know what time it is." He glances down at his hardening dick as he stretches it through the fabric of his sweats.

"Yeah, I know what time it is," I respond, smirking. "It's too bad you don't." He tries to come in, and I quickly push him backward with the palm of my hand. "Oh, hell no," I snap. "You done banged your damn head. If you think you gonna come up in here and get some pussy, you are out of your retarded-ass mind."

"Look," he starts, "I ain't come here to beef. I'm sorry I haven't called. And you feel neglected. But like I said, shit's been hectic. You know I'm always thinking 'bout you. It's just that sometimes my girl is on my back 'n shit so I gotta stay close to home to keep the peace."

"Beefing? Nigga, I have no emotional ties to you to beef with you. So who said anything about me feeling neglected?"

"You didn't have to. That's the only thing that explains your shitty attitude."

"Nigga, please," I say, laughing. "You are not my man, nor will you ever be. So trust me, the last thing I have is an attitude. But for you to think you can roll up over here with a stiff dick in your hand and I'm supposed to drop down and wet it for you is a bit much."

"It's not like that," he says. "I'm not here for you to wet this dick. I can get it wet at home, if I want."

"Oh okay," I say, rolling my eyes. "So, then, why are you here, again?"

"I told you. I wanna plant this tongue up in that tight pussy. But you on some other shit, tryna beef 'n shit."

"Mitchell, the last thing I'm doing is beefing with you. I don't beef with nobody else's man, baby, trust me. I dismiss 'em."

"So, then why am I standing out here going back 'n forth with you instead of being inside wetting that clit up?"

I tilt my head, smiling. I love it when men think that they are the masters of the sex game, and are the ones to plot on the pussy instead of it being the other way around.

We know that it is really the woman who chooses the man. She knows the minute a man walks into the room whether or not she wants to fuck him, marry him, or strictly be friends. She has already sized him up; already checked out the competition or lack thereof. And has already made up her mind how she wants to proceed. To fuck, or not to fuck! Too bad most men missed or overlooked the memo. It would probably cut down on a lot of unnecessary foolishness.

I blink, blink again. I sift through the series of questions I typically ask a man before I ever fuck him, and wonder if I might have missed a few with Mitchell prior to squatting over his face and lowering my sweet pussy down on his mouth. I recall each question I asked him, and his responses: Do you eat pussy? *Yes.* Eat ass? *Yes.* Love your dick and balls sucked? *Hell yeah!* Are you circumcised? *Yes.* Can you fuck more than one round? *Yes. Well, most times.* Ever fuck a chick in the ass? *Nah, not yet, but can't wait to try.* Can you give it to me freaky and nasty? *Most definitely.*

Truth be told, when I ask these questions, if the answer is "no" to more than three, there's no further discussion. If he answers "yes" to at least three, then I might take his number, depending on what he looks like. But, if he answers "yes" to all seven, then nine times out of ten, I'm going to fuck him on the spot, or at least within the first two weeks, depending on when my last dose of dick was. In Mitchell's case, I fucked his tongue on the spot because that's what I wanted from him. To eat this pussy like it was going to be his last meal on earth. And that's what he did.

Speaking of which, when a man eats my pussy, I typically prefer the sixty-eight because it gives him full access to my pussy and asshole. I also like it when he lies on the bed with his head back over the edge and I straddle his face and smear my pussy all over his lips, which is how Mitchell usually loves to eat me.

However, there are other times when I enjoy the

standing sixty-nine. This is another position in which Mitchell is skilled at delivering his tongue game. It always gets me off quick. There's something about being hung upside down, swallowing a dick, that drives me wild. Although I did have a bad experience a few years ago when the mofo I was serving got the shakes and his knees buckled. Next thing I knew, I had hit the floor. The fool dropped me on my damn head. I had a head-ache for days behind that. Needless to say, I never fucked or sucked him again after that.

But tonight, standing here remembering how wicked Mitchell's head game is does nothing for me. My clit doesn't jump at the thought of having him between my legs, so I know for certain he will not get in. Period! At this very moment, he disgusts me. And I am certain he is officially axed from the fuck squad.

"Uh," I finally answer, looking him dead in the eyes, "because the last time I checked I paid the mortgage here, and I let who I want up in here, when I want them up in here. And tonight, you are not welcomed. So I suggest you take your hectic ass back home to your little wifey and wet her, 'cause this pussy is not available to you, not tonight or any other night. I suggest you call first the next time you catch yourself trying to creep."

He stares at me with a dumb-ass look on his face. He stands there for a few minutes just looking at me, then swipes his big hand over his mouth, and pulls at his chin hairs, realizing what I'm saying. "Oh, shit. You really not gonna let me in, huh?"

Oh my God, this nigga is dumber than I thought. "No. Now have a good night." I shut the door in his face, leaving him standing out in the night air. He rings the doorbell again. I shut off the porch light, then the lights in the living room.

"Fuck it, then," I hear him say as he stomps down the sidewalk to his car. "Crazy bitch!" I watch him from the window and laugh at his ass as he slams his car door and speeds off. *Niggas*, I think, closing my curtains and making my way upstairs to my bedroom.

Ugh, let me tell you something else about men before I go to bed. Most men don't appreciate any damn thing they obtain too easily. Believe that. If you want to keep them interested, then you have to stimulate them mentally and learn to give them a challenge. Trust me. Men love a challenge. If you give in to their temper tantrums when they don't get their way, or their threats to move on to the next chick, then they've won. You've opened the door to being manipulated into doing any and every-damn-thing they want. The more they want, the more they're going to demand. The more you give, the more they're going to take. And once they know you can be manipulated, they know they have you wrapped around their finger. And guess what? At the end of the day, they're not going to have one ounce of respect for your ass.

However, if you're a woman who is like me, a chick who's simply doing her thing, a chick whose only interest in a man is to fuck him, suck him, and send him on his merry motherfucking way, then you can truly not care less about what he thinks about you when it's all said and done. He ain't playing you, and he ain't manipulating you into doing jack you don't already want to do. I have messed plenty of niggas' heads up by fucking them, then dismissing them all in one breath. I've even gone as far as acting like I don't know 'em when I run into 'em on the street.

I remove my clothes, then go into the bathroom to wash my face and brush my teeth. When I am done, I pull my hair back, stare at my reflection for a minute, then shut off the light. I climb into bed, wondering what would happen if every woman in the world went on a pussy strike. Basically shut down all fucking and sucking for one year. Oh, hell no! That's too damn long. Okay, maybe for sixty days. Well, maybe for a month. Okay, okay, let's start out with two weeks. Anyway, what would men do?

Perhaps masturbate until they got dick burns on the palms of their hands. Or go on a raping spree. 'Cause most men can't live without pussy. Not for long. So the clincher would be that every woman would be strapped and loaded, and if a mofo tried to bum rush her for some pussy, he'd be shot on the spot, or at the very least be pistol whipped and castrated. The mere thought is quite entertaining. I think men would literally lose their damn minds if they couldn't get their dicks wet. If women had the will to shut their legs, seal off the pussy, and let a nigga know who really has the control, he'd act like he had some damn sense. Imagine that.

The thought cracks me the hell up for almost two minutes. But then reality sets in and I suck my teeth, knowing it'll never happen in this lifetime 'cause there are a lot of women who'll cut a chick for some dick, who can't live without the dick. *Humph*, I think, cutting off the lamp on my nightstand, *women better start realizing the power of that wet box between their legs, and learn how to fuck a man into submission.*

CHAPTER
EIGHT

I t's 9:15 in the morning, and I am sitting bored shit-
less in a mandatory staff meeting. Shari Flemmings,
who works in Human Resources, and Mark Lennon,
the executive director of operations, are standing in
front of us, talking. Actually, Mark is the one doing all
the talking. Shari's standing there looking like a damn
porcelain doll with all that foundation on her face,
nodding every so often as he discusses the upcoming
strategic planning the organization will be having over
the next few months. Today, for some reason, she seems
a bit scattered, nervous almost, and I'm trying to figure
out why she's so distracted. I'm sitting in my seat wondering why this chick is even standing up here while he
is talking about this process. Although I've hardly had
much interaction with her, I've always thought she
was a well-put-together woman, not to mention being
a sistah! Girlfriend is always articulate and to the point
when she speaks. But today she is different. I can't put
my finger on it as I watch her eyes dance around the
room like tennis balls.

Mark, a very handsome, *very* rich white man, in his
late thirties, with sandy brown hair, green eyes, and a
lean runner's body, goes into this long, drawn-out ex-

planation of why the board of directors feels now is the time to do an assessment and evaluation of the organization as a whole.

"Throughout this process," he says, looking around the room, "we will be taking a look at all of our existing services provided in each department within the company, seeing how we can enhance them and provide more effective ways of meeting our clients' needs. We will also be taking a look at those departments that are not being utilized to their full potential, seeing how we can strengthen them…"

My God, as good-looking as his ass is, that nasal voice of his is giving me a headache. I look around the huge conference room, watching the faces and actions of everyone assembled there. I spot Miss Hooch over in the corner, staring out the window. Nahdirah is sitting two seats over from me, writing something on her notepad. Definitely not notes. *Her ass is probably doodling*, I think, shaking my head. On my left is Everett Wells, one of the computer techs who works on the second floor. He sort of reminds me of the actor Sean Blakemore. I keep my face forward and occasionally cut my eye at him, smiling to myself. There's only one word to describe this six-foot-two, two-hundred-and-something-pound, chiseled, chocolate delight, and that is *delicious!* Mmmph. Under different circumstances, this man could get it. You best believe if I were the type to fraternize in the workplace, he'd be the first one on my list of people to fuck. Just by the way he walks, the way he sits, the way his slacks hang in the front, tells me he is most likely one of them Mandingo dick mofos, or he has some really extra-large balls. However, since I do not, nor will I ever shit where I eat, I ignore his advances and invitations to dinner, "or whatever." But that doesn't mean I haven't already fucked him in my mind.

The scent of his cologne forces me to inhale deeply. I try to figure out the fragrance. *Sean John? Unforgivable?* I think, shifting in my seat. I feel his eyes on me, but I ignore the tingling sensation his gaze causes against my flesh. Right at this moment, I wish he wasn't sitting so close to me. I wish he wasn't someone who worked in the same building as me. Wish he didn't take up space in my many fantasies. I know he smells my lust, know he wants to get my attention. I cross my legs, pinch off the desire to have his tongue lost between my thighs, and focus on Mr. Lennon.

"…This is a very exciting time for us as we approach another decade of being one of the most innovative, cutting-edge technological companies in the country. And with your help, I am hoping that we can continue to raise the bar…"

I am watching Mr. Lennon's mouth move, but I am not hearing words. The only thing I hear are soft moans floating throughout the room. I am not seeing him standing in front of us wearing his signature Brooks

Brothers pin-striped suit and crisp, white monogrammed dress shirt, or his Bally wing-tip shoes. He is naked with his soft dick in his thick hand, slowly stroking it. His cock is nowhere near its potential and it is already long and fat. I bite down on my bottom lip, twist in my seat.

Don't ask me where all this craziness is coming from. But the notion starts to take root and spread like a wild fire. My fleeting fantasy of being fucked by a white man with a big, thick cock starts to come into full view. Uh… hmm…ooh. Don't get me wrong, there's nothing more delicious than a juicy black dick, but…hmmm, a taste of vanilla could also be oh, so sweet.

Yes, I've crossed over once. It was two years ago while I was down in Atlantic City. Once again I had gone there to gamble, but ended up in a hotel room with my legs wide open. Anyway, when I tell you this white man was beautiful, I mean he was capital B-E-A-U-T-I-F-U-L! He had an olive complexion, dark curly hair, big brown eyes, thick lashes to die for, and a chiseled, fresh-from-the-gym body. Truth be told, I had never wanted to do a white man until him.

Anyway, I was at the Pier Shops in Caesar's doing what I do best, shopping, when I spotted him in the Bottega Veneta store. He smiled. I smiled. He said hello. I said hello, then continued about my business. Dude kept staring at me and smiling. So you know me. I asked him if he knew me from somewhere. Of course he didn't, but I asked anyway. We got to talking, then one thing led to another and he finally asked me if I wanted to go upstairs to one of the restaurants for a drink and grab a bite to eat. I was like, sure.

Well, long story short, after a few drinks, he invited me up to his room. I only agreed after he said he wasn't married and answered *yes* to every one of my damn questions. So I got to his room and we started kissing and grinding. Before I knew it, my pussy started dripping, and Mr. Sexy Vanilla Man was doing a strip tease for me. This mofo had a damn eight-pack and a big-ass bulge in his white Calvin Klein underwear that made my pussy tremble. A bitch was ready to pounce down on that juicy stick.

Well, the clincher was, he only wanted me to get my panties real wet with my pussy juice, then take them off so he could sniff and suck them while I watched him jerk off. I thought it was a bit bizarre, but hey…I aim to please. So I got my snatch real wet and juicy for him, then took my panties off and wiped my pussy with them. I handed them to him, then sat back on the bed and watched him lick, sniff and suck the juice from my panties while he stroked his thick white dick (eight and a half inches, I might add).

Oh, I wanted him inside me so damn bad, I started shaking. But his only focus was on sucking my pussy-stained panties. So I played in my pussy, talked real nasty to him, then came all over my fingers when he wrapped my panties around his dick, jerked himself off, then nutted all in the crotch of my panties. Well, that little experience did nothing for my cock-hungry pussy. I needed the thrust of a dick inside me. I am so glad I had packed my thick six-inch friend in my bag because it was exactly what I needed to take the edge off. I fucked myself while he watched me, as he continued pulling and tugging at his semi-hard dick. Surprisingly, his dick got hard again, and before I knew it, we were both moaning and cumming at the same time.

I laid back, kept my legs spread apart with my dildo still stuck inside of me and watched him as he wiped his nut in my panties again, sniffed them, then asked me if he could keep them. Hell, why not. It wasn't like I planned on putting them back on anyway. And, then, for the grand finale, Mr. Panty Eater walked over to me, pulled the dildo out of my sopping wet pussy, and sucked the juices off it. Well, I'll be damn! I was floored, to say the least. So, there you have it. My first live experience with a white man!

And now, as I sit here, I am entertaining lusty thoughts of fucking another one. Mr. Lennon's freshly shaven, salon-tanned face is attached to my daydream. In my mind, I'm getting off on the contrast of my beautiful brown flesh against his stark whiteness as he plays with my titties, kissing and sucking and licking all over my nipples as though they're dipped in the world's finest chocolate. His lips begin to plant wet kisses down my stomach, dipping his tongue into my navel, then pulling my legs up over his shoulders as he sticks his tongue into my pussy while he continues playing with my nipples, gently pulling and rolling and twirling them, while rapidly flicking his tongue against my clit, teasing my pussy. Mmmm, it starts to feel so good, and I begin to beg him to stop teasing me, beg him to let me feel his throbbing dick inside of me. But he doesn't. He continues to torture me with his tongue until my pussy walls are quivering for the thrust of his dick.

Finally, when he has my pussy sopping wet, he slides his dick into my hot canal, slowly, inch by inch, then pulls out to the tip. He does this several times, taunting me. My pussy is on fire! I am screaming for the dick! Literally begging for the dick. And he gives me exactly what I want as he slides his dick back in, pushes deep into me, then pulls out again.

Push.

I moan.

Pull.

I grab for him.

Push.

I moan again.

He pulls out again. Tip-drills me. Slow-fucks the inner walls of my pussy until it begins to quiver.

There's an erotic sexual energy building up between us, and its intensity is driving me crazy with desire. He feels it too—this mounting, uncontrollable surge of animalistic pleasure. He slams his dick back into me and begins pounding my pussy, burying his dick deep inside of me, hitting the bottom of my well.

I tell him: "Fuck this sweet black pussy…hmmm, give me that big white dick. Oh, yes! Fuck me."

And he's saying: "Damn, you got some good pussy. Wet this big white dick with that sweet juice. Yeah, that's it, grab that big dick! Oh, shit! You like this big cock?"

I am moaning. He's groaning. I lean on my elbows and watch his dick glide in and out of my slippery love nest, slick and glistening from my wetness. He goes deeper and deeper and deeper, getting lost inside of me, then he pulls out and allows the head of his dick to brush up against my clit, before slapping it with his heavy dick. My dripping pussy opens and closes, waiting with anticipation. But instead of feeding my pussy with his dick, he goes back down on me and laps my clit and pussy, sucking out my sweet, sticky cream. He tongue-fucks me for what seems like forever, then lifts up and rams his dick back into me, alternating between dick-fucking and tongue-fucking me. I am grunting and groaning and moaning and screaming as I climax and nut all over his dick and tongue.

Suddenly, he flips me over and begins to dig me out doggie-style, nice and slow. Mmmm, he leans into my ear and talks real nasty, slapping my soft ass. Oh, how his dick is stretching me, making my sugar walls shake with pleasure. His thrusts become deeper and faster and harder until my pussy squirts a creamy juice all over his cock. When the heat from his balls reaches its boiling point, he pulls out, yanks off the condom, then splashes a bucket of hot cum all over my ass and back. Mmmm.

Without thought, I shift in my seat, uncrossing, then crossing my legs again to ease the tingling sensation between my thighs.

"…Does anyone have any questions?" I hear him asking, snapping me out of my trance. I feel a dampness clinging between my legs. At some point during Mr. Lennon's speech I have cum in my panties. I am thankful I'm wearing a panty-liner. I glance around the room, taking in the faces of those present. When no one raises their hand or stands, he remains planted in his spot, waiting. But no one is interested in prolonging this meeting. He finally realizes this. "Well, I guess that's it for now. We'll keep you posted as things progress. I'll be meeting with all department heads in the coming weeks. Thanks for your time. This meeting is adjourned."

Before I can make a mad dash to the ladies' room to remove my wet liner, which now feels like it is sticking to my pussy lips, Everett's voice drifts toward me, stopping me in my tracks. *Shit!* "Bianca," he says, quickly walking over to me. He smiles. *Fuck! I don't need this right now*, I think, forcing a smile of my own.

"Oh hey, Everett," I say, turning around and willing my eyes to stay on his instead of allowing them to roam his manly body. "How are you?"

"I'm good," he says. "But I'd be even better if you'd stop running from me and let me take you out."

I playfully roll my eyes, sucking my teeth. "Running, Me?" I ask coyly, looking around the room. I laugh. "Oh, you've got me confused. I'm not running from you. I'm keeping my interaction with you strictly professional. There's a difference."

"Is that so? Are you heading back to your office?"

"Yes, Everett," I say, feeling myself getting lightheaded from his cologne, and from the lack of dick in my life this week. I envision myself on my knees wearing nothing but a red G-string and my six-inch red Christian Louboutin pumps, being fucked doggie-style by him. I imagine that he knows I like it when a man yanks my string to the side and slides his dick in. And he gives it to me precisely how I like it, pumping deep inside of me while pulling the string and letting it pop against my soft ass. I'm throwing my ass up on his dick, taking it all in, allowing him to feed my cum-soaked pussy every inch of his goodness. I swallow hard, blink away the image, and make a mental note to schedule a tune-up.

"Good. I'll walk with you to the elevators." He lowers his voice. "So, when you gonna let me take you out?" he asks as we slowly stroll out of the conference room. "You know I'm gonna keep asking you until I get a 'yes' from you."

"There'll be no 'yes.' I told you before, I don't mix

pleasure with business, so you're wasting your breath and your time."

"Yeah, yeah, yeah, I heard all that before." He moves in closer. "Listen, I know you're all private and all. But I can assure you, it'll be discreet."

"Nope," I say, shaking my head. "Not interested."

"Okay, then how 'bout we get together for a business dinner, two colleagues merely unwinding after a long day at the office?"

I laugh, shaking my head. This man doesn't give up, and I like that about him. His persistence is appealing. Too bad it doesn't change my mind about workplace dating.

In the six years I've been here, I have seen at least ten colleagues get involved with coworkers, and none of those situations have worked out. If anything, it made their working conditions practically unbearable 'cause everybody and their mother knew their business. A chick who was fucking one of the graphic designers ended up losing her job because she couldn't bring her ass to work like she was supposed to because she was too depressed over their break-up. Give me a damn break! I'm sorry, but there is no damn way I'm going to lose a job over some nigga and his dick. Anyway, workplace romances can get too messy and complicated for me, and I'm not the one.

"We don't work in the same department, so what would we need to talk about?" I ask. There's a large crowd of people waiting to get on one of the three elevators on each side of the hallway.

"Here," he says, gently taking me by the arm and ushering me past the crowd. "Let's catch the ones on the other end of the building." I follow along. "Anyway, I'm sure we can figure something out."

"Yeah, I'm sure we could. But if it's only you and me out to dinner, then it's a date. And I'm not up for dating, especially not someone I *work* with."

"But we don't *work* in the same department; your words, not mine. So what's the harm? It's only an innocent dinner between two adults, trying to get to know each other."

"Nice try, but no cigar," I say, catching sight of Nahdirah talking to another one of these phony bitches up in here.

He tosses his arms open in mock defeat, flashing a beautiful, ultra-white smile as we step into the elevator. "Can't knock a brotha for trying," he says, shaking his head. "You win for now."

"I didn't know this was a game."

"It's not," he states, eye-fucking me. He steps into my space. He lowers his voice. "You're the one tryna make it one."

"Hardly," I say, stepping back from him. I can tell he's not used to women brushing him off so easily. He's probably used to them falling at his feet, worshipping him. I'm certain the only reason he continues to push the issue of me going out with him is because I'm one of the few women in this building who hasn't taken him up on his offer. Yes, I've played in my pussy while imagining what it would be like riding his dick, but there'll be no office rendezvous. "I'm sure you have enough women already on your fan club roster you can call up for a dinner date."

"Yeah, I could," he says, laughing. "But they ain't you."

The elevator door opens. "And they'll never be," I say, stepping off. I turn to face him as the door starts to close. "Thanks for the ride." He opens his mouth to say something, but the doors shut in his face.

I finally make it to the bathroom and rush to an empty stall to remove my liner. I reach into my bag, pull out a small container of wet wipes, then pull up my skirt and pull down my panties. I wipe my pussy. Now, I don't know about you, but I use wet wipes after every piss and shit. I am a stickler for keeping a baby-fresh snatch and ass, no matter what time of day it is. I place a dry liner in the center of my underwear, then pull 'em up. I wash and dry my hands, then reach into my bag and pull out my designer make-up case, pulling out my supplies: lip liner and lip gloss. I've never been one for a bunch of make up because I don't need it, but I'm telling you, I love the Queen Collection by Cover Girl. It keeps me looking flawless all day, every day.

Nahdirah walks into the bathroom as I am gliding a coat of pearled peach lip gloss over my succulent lips.

"Hey, girl," she says, coming up to the sink next to me to wash her hands. "What'd you think about that meeting downstairs?"

"Well, if they are really going to look at each department like they say they are, then I think some of us are about to be on the unemployment line." I didn't want to sound like the prophet of doom or anything, but companies are downsizing all over the country, so I wouldn't be the least bit surprised. I really hope my ass won't be one of the ones scrambling for another job.

"Let's hope not," she says, drying her hands. "I have almost ten years here, and the last thing I wanna be doing is looking for another job."

"I know that's right," I say.

"I saw you over there talking to Everett's fine ass. He still tryna take you out?"

I shrug, fixing a few loose strands of hair. "Girl, I don't know what he's trying to do."

"Oh, please. Even a blind man can see he has it bad for you. He practically salivates and pants every time he sees you."

That's because he's a two-legged dog. I roll my eyes, heading toward the door. "Well, he can keep wagging and salivating all he wants. I'm not interested."

She follows behind me. "You on your way to your office?"

"Yep," I state, silently hoping she's not going to come sit up in my space and beat me in the head with stories about her and her man, or any of the dumb-ass bitches around here—not today. Unfortunately, I can't be so lucky.

"Good, I'll walk with you."

Fucking great!

"Me, Samantha, and Regina are going to the Cheese-cake Factory for lunch today; you wanna go?"

I shoot her a look, opening my office door. "No, thanks," I say, closing the door behind us. "You know I'm not beat for going out to eat with any of these chicks around here."

She grunts, plopping down into one of the leather chairs. "Humph. I know, I know. I thought I'd ask anyway. I don't know how you can come to work every day and not have one friend here, other than me. You know, most of the women here aren't as bad as you think they are."

I sit in the chair across from her. "Well, that may be true. But I'm not interested in finding out. I've never been one for being overly friendly with a bunch of chicks, and I don't think I need to start now. The little I know about them, and the little they know about me, is perfectly fine with me."

"Okay, anywaaaaay," she says, quickly changing the subject, "why won't you go out with that fine hunk of man upstairs?"

"Who you talking about? Everett?"

"Uh, yeah…you know who I'm talking about."

"Because I'm not interested."

"And why not?"

"Because I'm not," I insist, slowly getting annoyed that this nosey bitch is trying to press the issue.

"Well, there has to be a reason," she pushes. "So, what is it?"

"For the thousandth time, I don't believe in dating anyone I work with, or around, or who works for the same company as me. That is a no-no for me."

"Why?"

I sigh. *Oh my God*, I think, shifting in my seat, *this bitch is going to have me curse her out.* I stare at her, trying to figure out what part of the "I'm not interested" she doesn't get. "I really think it's bad business to get too personal with someone you work with. When shit doesn't work, then someone ends up feeling some kind of way, which creates a bunch of drama for you, or makes it unbearable to work in the same place. Most of the time, it just doesn't work."

"That's not true. Look at Sabrina and Nathan. They've been together almost eight years."

I blink, blink again.

Nathan hasn't worked here in almost three years because of all the drama that came with his workplace romance with Sabrina's dumb ass, which is exactly my point. So what the fuck is this dumb bitch talking about? Go figure! Anyway, Sabrina is another office tramp who is always trying to keep shit stirred up. I can't stand her. She's the same bitch whose man I fucked right under her damn nose. She's always talking about what her man would never do, how she has him wrapped around her finger, blah, blah, blah. Bitches like her need to wake the fuck up with that dumb shit. You don't know what the fuck your man wouldn't do. Trust me. And because I don't like her bogus ass, I slipped him my cell number last year at our tired-ass holiday party (the one I was forced to attend because the president and his cronies were attending). Nathan, along with a few other chicks' men, was checking me out on the sly the whole night. All while Sabrina's all hugged up on him, laughing and smiling like she was the happiest woman in the world, her so-called "perfect man" was ogling me.

Obviously, he didn't share her sentiments because if he had, he wouldn't have called me, and he damn sure wouldn't have been fucking me as if my pussy was his life support, begging me for more. He moaned and groaned louder than me. He whispered and whimpered, and mumbled shit I didn't understand. And he got on my damn nerves so bad with all his screaming about how good the pussy was and yelling out my name, that I literally shoved my damn panties in his mouth to shut him the hell up so I could concentrate. And, yes, I fucked him again because I could. Definitely not because the dick was all that. It was a nice, sturdy eight inches but his balls were about the size of cashews. He had about as much rhythm as a paraplegic. And this was that bitch's door prize. Go figure! Now whenever I look at her dumb ass, I chuckle to myself.

"Nathan is a dog, and you know it. How many times did Sabrina come to work all stressed out, looking like a damn Raggedy Ann doll 'cause she had caught him screwing some chick from the job? He fucked at least four chicks, black and white, on at least three floors in this building. She worked herself up so much over his sorry ass that her damn hair started falling out. So, *please*, let's not use them as an example to state your case."

"Okay, then. Look at me and Jake. We dated and worked together. And now, here we are, almost four years later, still going strong."

"And how many times before you started going strong did you come to work worrying about what he was doing, what someone was saying, or finding out who else he had fucked? Every week you were catching attitudes with chicks you saw all up in his face 'cause you didn't trust his ass."

A few times this bitch was about to get her ass beat in the parking lot, but I won't remind her of that. We work with a bunch of Union and Essex County switch-blade bitches, and trust me when I tell you, a few of them are fucking nutty as hell. Nahdirah almost caught it several times, fucking with Jake's ass.

She waves me off. "Oh, please. That was in the be-ginning of our relationship. I am so over that now."

"Oh, really? Is that before or after he left this place? Or before or after baby number two? 'Cause you know like I know, if he was still working here, you'd be going through the same shit."

"Now, I didn't say messing with someone you work with doesn't come with a set of challenges. 'Cause it does, but it can still work. Besides, Jake and I have both grown since then. And my boo is all about me."

"And how do you know that?"

She places her hand on her hip, raising up in her seat. "Do you know something I don't? 'Cause if so, then fill me in."

"No, I'm only asking the question." *I must have hit a nerve*, I think, smiling. These women crack me the hell up. This bitch is sitting in front of a certified dick-loving ho. I know for a fact that if I wanted to fuck her man—not that I do or would 'cause he isn't my flavor— I could ride his dick, or have his tongue shoved in my asshole in the blink of an eye. There's no question in my mind. It's all in his eyes. Every time dude is around me—which isn't that often now that he no longer works here—he looks at me like he's trying to undress me with his eyes. And then he has this habit of licking his lips, looking me up and down when he speaks to me, drooling—and basically eye fucking me!

"Well, like I said, there's nothing wrong with dating someone you work with."

She fails to answer the question, and I won't press.

The bitch obviously doesn't know how Jake really feels. Women kill me, putting their men up on pedestals, and men kill me, too. No one can predict what another human being will or won't do. You can only hope they do what's right, and not only when they believe someone is watching them. But we all know there are so many who don't, and won't. "Yeah, okay, if you say so. And how many women here had Jake before you did?"

She shrugs. "I don't know. A few, I guess."

"A few?" I repeat, laughing. "Nahdirah, get real. Jake was worse than Nathan, and you know it."

"Okay," she says, getting defensive, "and?"

"And how long did the two of you date before you got into a relationship with him?"

"A few months; why?"

"And what did you really know about him?"

I can tell her mind's scrambling to come up with an answer, one that will hold truth. The dumbfounded look on her face tells me she can't locate one that makes any sense to her, or me. "Well, we were still getting to know each other," she offers.

I roll my eyes. "And during that time of 'getting to know each other,' did you ever ask him how many of his coworkers he screwed?"

She looks at me like I have said something stupid. But girlfriend forgets I know they were only dating three weeks before her ass got knocked up by him, so that says to me the only thing she was getting to know was his dick. The whole time her ass was pregnant, she stressed because bitches were flaunting the fact that they had fucked him first, or were still getting a ride on his chocolate joystick. Not to mention, his other baby's momma, who works down in the mailroom, was causing havoc in his life because he was fucking "that ugly bitch in promotions." But, of course, girlfriend had no clue that he had two other children until after it was too late.

"Why? We all have a past, so why do you feel the need to always bring shit up and be so damn negative all the time? Why can't you leave shit alone?"

I blink, blink again.

Poor thing, she truly doesn't get it. That's exactly why men and women have problems in their relationships, 'cause they don't fucking ask questions. I roll my eyes and shake my head. Like I told you before, I use the term *friend* loosely with this chick. If anything, it's more of a friendly working relationship than anything else. 'Cause ain't no fucking way I'd ever be *real* friends with a ditsy bitch like her.

I glance at my watch; it's almost noon. I'm done with her ass. She's exhausted all the time she's going to get out of me today. I don't have the strength or the energy to continue on with her.

I sigh. "You're absolutely right. We all have a past." I get up from my seat, walking over to my desk. "Well, I don't know about you, but I have a ton of reports to get done. So I better get to 'em."

I busy myself at my desk, shuffling papers, pretending to be reading shit I have no interest in. She gets up from her seat. "Yeah, girl, I'd better get going. I gotta meet Samantha and them downstairs in a few, anyway."

"Have fun," I say, not looking up.

"I'll stop by later."

"Oh, okay," I say, raising my eyes from the monthly projection report. "Enjoy the rest of your day."

"You too," she says, pausing before leaving. I can tell she wants to say something more, but can't quite find the words. A few seconds go by.

I tilt my head, turning my hands palms up. "Umm, is there something else?"

She slowly shakes her head, pursing her lips. She has decided not to strain her brain, and I'm thankful. I watch her make her way to the door. When she is gone, I shake my head. "There's no fucking way I'm ever dating anyone from this place," I say to myself. "I don't care how fine he is. Besides, most people don't know what the hell *dating* means any damn way."

Now help me understand something. Is it me, or am I the only one who got the memo on dating? I mean, damn! In my opinion, *dating* means you can go out with Fred on Thursday, go clubbing with Leon on Friday, have drinks and a movie with Stan on Saturday, and fuck all three of 'em on Sunday if you so choose. Not that you have to, or should be expected to. However, if you feel the urge to ride the dick to see what they have to offer, then you do exactly that. Just be responsible. And don't expect it to be no more than what it was, a fuck.

Unless I'm missing something, dating does not equal relationship. Dating is a filtering, get-to-know-you process. It helps you weed out the men who are full of shit. Dating is asking questions. It's one big interview, in my opinion. But, of course, no one dates anymore. It's straight fucking, then right into moving him in. Talk about stupid!

Then when shit starts coming up missing in the house, or he starts staying out late or not coming home at all, or has trouble keeping a job, or wants to lie around the house in his boxers, scratching his balls and playing Xbox all damn day, you want to bitch and complain about it. Uh, duh, dumb ass, that's what your ass gets when you don't take the time out to learn a man before jumping straight into a relationship with him. Oh, don't think that doesn't go for men too. They get caught up in a big butt and smile attached to some good pussy, then before you know it, they're complaining about her ass too.

Whatever! All I know is you get what you get when you don't take the time to look for what you really want, and don't ask questions. You know, maybe it's me. But some of these fucking people today are really pathetic.

Humph. Well, since I'm already disgusted, I might as well go in for the kill and send out this special pub-

lic service announcement to these dizzy-ass chicks—
better known as the birds—swooping around the room.
Listen, sweetie. I hate to be the one to tell you, but
most dudes ain't tryna wife you. They only want to
fuck your low-budget ass every which way.

Besides giving you a stiff dick, don't think he's really
going to lace you with much. He already knows that all
he has to do is buy you a bottle of Hennessy, some Alizé,
and come through with some smoke (trees, collard
greens, or whatever else the pot heads call it) and you're
going to let him smash your insides out all night. And
if he's feeling generous, he'll hit you with a fresh pair
of kicks, or slide you a few dollars to get your hair and
nails done. You might even be able to get a few more
dollars (a hundred at most) out of him. Yeah, he might
even splurge on a standard room at the Hilton or
Sheraton for you. Hell, he knows it's a step up from
the Motel 6s and the backseats of cars you're used to.
He knows it doesn't take much to excite you. You love
his company and the fact that someone like him is paying you some attention. He already knows you think
he's the best thing that has ever come your way and
that you're not trying to let him go. He might even tell
you he's "feelin" you. But, *you* best believe you aren't
ever going to be his main girl, even if he is splashing
off raw inside of you. At the end of the day, you just a
bird to him. And when he bounces from your nest, he's
shaking off the feathers and going home to his main
chick. Believe that!

CHAPTER
NINE

I *love* New York, damn it! Yesterday I went to the Harlem Book Festival and it was packed. There was so much positive energy flowing. There were a ton of well-known and up-and-coming authors pushing their books. I finally got the chance to meet Anna J. She's the freaky chick who wrote that book *My Woman, His Wife*. She was actually pretty cool, and I loved her sense of humor. Now you know I had to ask her if she was down with any of that stuff she wrote in her book. She laughed, then leaned in and whispered, "Girlfriend, I'm strictly about the dick; there's nothing a chick can do for me." Well, now, that's what I'm talking 'bout. She's all right with me.

Not only did I get autographed books, I took a ton of pictures. I also had the chance to meet some of the authors whose books I've read. And, baaaaby, let me tell you. There were some fine-ass men out there, showing body. Whew, dick for days! We are really some beautiful people. And it was really nice to see us all together without drama. Plus, the weather was beautiful!

Humph. Who said black folks don't read?

Anyway, I got home around eight-thirty, then had the nerve to go to a club in Woodbridge called Studio

9. This big-time promoter from Newark was having a party there. I've been there twice, and each time I've had a great time. It's always packed, and the music is enough to make my body hot. And the men are always plentiful. So I decided to get fly, and do the damn thing—by myself. I will never understand why a chick would hang out with a bunch of other chicks like a pack of wolves, competing for the attention and some-times temporary affection of a man. I can see maybe two chicks going out on the town together. Even that would be a bit much for *me* since I like doing my dirt solo. But hanging with four, five, and six bitches, humph. You know like I know that if there are five chicks in a bunch, at least three of 'em are on the prowl for some dick, hunting for someone to take home who will fuck them relentlessly. Nine times out of ten, of the three hoes in the group, two of 'em got their eye on the same nigga. Please. Who has time for that shit?

Anyway, I got my dance on, took a few numbers, then was ready to go on my way. But of course, things don't always go according to plan, which is not always a bad thing. Interestingly, I wasn't really out on cock patrol or looking to get into anything last night. I wanted to finger-pop a bit, then bring it back to the house. But as I was walking toward my car, this brotha leaned his head out of the passenger's window of a sleek, black S600, and said, "Yo, ma, damn you fine. Let me holla at you."

Now I started to ignore him and keep it moving, but

when I cut my eyes over at him, I noticed how sexy he was, so I told him if he wanted to speak to me, he needed to step out of the car and come over to me like a grown-ass man instead of some little boy. And that's exactly what he did. I immediately sized him up. The dude was fine, and definitely young. But who cares? He had a grown-man swagger I found appealing. If he wanted to play with matches, then I'd be more than happy to set his ass on fire.

The minute he stepped up in my space, I asked him how I could help him. And he said I could help him by giving him my name and number. I smiled and told him to walk me to my car. He did. As we walked, I learned he was twenty (just like I thought, barely legal), from Hartford, but was resting in Elizabeth. When we got to my car, I told him he'd better get back to his ride before they left him. He gave me a look, then made it clear that nothing moved unless he moved. That made my pussy jump. I smiled.

"You ever been with an older woman?"

"Yeah," he boasted. "I don't rock with no one under twenty-five. Chicks my age bore me."

"Is that so? Well, I'm thirty. Think you can handle that?"

"No doubt, baby."

"You ever fuck a chick in her ass?" I boldly asked.

He didn't flinch. "Nah, not yet. I haven't met a chick who wasn't scared to let me."

"I love it when a man fucks me in the ass," I said, getting right to the point. "It makes my pussy wet and creamy. Once you get a taste of a nice, tight ass wrapped around your dick, you'll think you were in heaven."

"Damn, you a real live freak, I see."

"I like to get my fuck on. You got a problem with that?"

"Nah, baby. Do you?" He rubbed his chin, then pulled at his neatly trimmed goatee. He licked his lips. "So you like taking dick in the ass?"

"I love it," I said. "It makes me cum like a fountain whenever I have a nice big dick deep in my ass, and fingers fucking my pussy. Do you have a big dick?"

He grinned, stepping in closer. "Is ten inches big enough for you?"

"Is it thick?"

"Like a cucumber. And it shoots more than one round."

"Well, check this out," I said, all sexy-like. "I need my pussy and ass licked. And I'm looking for a nigga who ain't scared to put the work in. Then when I'm done cumming all over his face and lips, I want dude to lie back, close his eyes, and let me use my mouth and tongue to suck and lick his balls, then milk the nut out of his dick. And for the record, I got a fat, puffy pussy with thick lips and a big clit. And I like it when, after a man finishes slurping, licking, and sucking all over it, he turns me over, spreads open my fat ass cheeks, then eats my ass out the way a freaky, nasty-ass man is supposed to." Then I told him I would fuck and suck his ding-a-ling into a damn sling. You know, straight house him until his dick cramped up.

Let me tell you. By the time I had finished, I had him drooling.

"So, you still tryna holla?"

"Hell, yeah. Shit. Let's go get a room."

I laughed. "Slow down, tiger. Not tonight."

"Oh, you playin' games, right?"

"Baby boy, I don't play games. I live life. And I fuck on my terms."

"You got a name?"

"It's Janaye. And yours?"

"Quincy, but all my peeps call me Q."

He was not only intrigued, but turned the hell on. I could tell his dick was harder than steel by the way he shoved his hands down in his pockets and kept shifting from one leg to the other. He pulled his dick to the side, trying his hardest to keep it in check. I smiled, then leaned in closer and asked him if he was willing to release his inhibitions, to relax his mind, and allow me to take him to higher ground.

When he said, "Hell yeah," I discreetly ran my hand along the front of his jeans, squeezed his dick, then whispered my pre-paid cell number into his ear. I opened my car door, then slid in. I rolled my window down, blew him a kiss, and slowly pulled out of the parking lot. Now between you and me, if he's able to remember my number and calls, I'm going to fuck his young ass sideways. If not, oh well.

Well, gotta go. I'm exhausted from my weekend, so I need to get my ass in the bed. Tomorrow it's back to work, and I need to have my mind right in order to deal with them folks. Ugh, I really fucking hate Mondays. Oh, well. Good night. Until the next time…happy fucking and sucking!

CHAPTER
TEN

L et me ask you something: Do you think if a man allows you to insert a finger into his ass and he *really* enjoys it, he might have bisexual or gay tendencies? How many men do you think have allowed their partners to finger-fuck 'em, then felt guilty afterward? He's afraid of how she's looking at him, worrying about what she's thinking, or whether she's going to tell the world their bedroom secret.

Well, if I had to answer the first question, I'd say, "Personally, I don't think so." There is nothing wrong with massaging a man's prostate and giving him that ultimate nut. Now, uh, if he's asking you to strap on a dildo and fuck him deep, then I'd say, "Proceed with caution, and keep your eyes and ears open." But it still doesn't mean he's sexually attracted to men. Honestly, if a man wanted me to fuck him, I would. I'd slap that ass, strap on a long, thick dildo, and dick him down like no tomorrow, then suck his dick when I'm done tearing his asshole out the frame. I'd do him exactly like some of them do us. Rough and dirty.

"Yeah, take this dick, nigga. You like Mommy's big black dick? You want Mommy to nut up in that ass?

Whose ass is this? That's right, back that hairy ass up on this dick...this ass is mine, nigga...damn, you got some good, tight ass...don't let me find out you givin' this ass to some other bitch."

And the whole time, I'd alternate slapping both of his ass cheeks. The thought has me cracking the fuck up. Yep, I sure would strap it up, and tap it up. I'd fuck him silly. Then afterward, I'd give him some of Mommy's hot, wet pussy and let him know he's still a damn man. At the end of the day, I wouldn't think it meant he was gay or had bisexual tendencies. You can only be gay or bisexual if there's a sexual attraction to the same sex, right?

Anyway, my answer to the second question is, "I think men who are very insecure in whom they are as men, or have secretly questioned their sexual identities are the ones who start tripping." If they're really secure in their sexuality and their women feel secure about who they are as men (and partners), then I don't think there should be any guilt or concern. I see it as two open-minded adults satisfying each other sexually. However, a woman still needs to keep her mouth shut about what is jumping off in the bedroom. Just because she may think there's nothing wrong with it, doesn't mean her girls won't. They'll be looking at both of them sideways, snickering behind their backs. Or if a woman does think there's something wrong with her man liking anal play and she discusses it with her so-called friends, trust and believe they're gonna have a lot to say about that. They'll get all up in her ear and head. Then by the end of the night—after three bottles of wine, or a few shots of Henny—they'll have her ass thinking her man is a full-fledged drag queen. Then her drunk ass will go home and curse him out and accuse him of fucking men. And before you know it, he's done packed his shit and left her ass. Then two weeks later, guess who'll be fucking her man? You got it! It'll be one of the same bitches who sat up in her face and gassed her ass all up. So she should definitely keep her mouth closed about it. Of course, this is the opinion of a ho. So what do I know?

Well, for starters, I know—and I will keep repeating myself on this—I can't stand a person who flaps their lips like wings, yapping all of the goings-on behind closed doors. That to me is a damn no-no, especially if this is someone you plan on seeing again or becoming romantically involved with. Now if it's a one-time fuck, then do you. Other than that, keep your fucking mouth shut!

I also know that most men want a woman who knows how to get freaky with it. Yeah, they want a conservative, mild-mannered chick in public, but behind closed doors, men crave a woman who can, I repeat, fuck a dick, suck a dick, and ain't scared of a dick. They want her to be open enough to experiment, to role-play, to share all of their freaky little secrets.

I sigh, deciding that in addition to the questions I

already ask men I meet, I'm going to add some others to the list: You ever had a chick lick your asshole? Or stick her finger in your butt while she's sucking your dick? (If he says no, I'll ask him if he's willing to try it. This will give me an idea of exactly how far he'll go sexually.) Are you secure in your sexuality? Are you willing to step outside of your comfort zone and really get freaky with it? Ever been with another man? If not, have you ever wondered what it would be like? Would you ever consider trying it if the opportunity presented itself, provided it would be kept private and discreet? This is what I need to know. Of course, I don't expect him to be honest about that last question, but I'll ask it anyway just to watch his facial expression and body language. Let's be real, men who like it in the ass would never admit to it, not to a woman, for fear of being dissed. He might secretly masturbate while thinking about it, but he would never actually confess to it.

I want men to know that all their nasty little secrets are safe with me. My lair is a place where a man can explore his deepest, darkest sexual fantasies without judgment. Without sideways glances. Without being emasculated. Behind these closed doors, I allow a man to be as freaky as he wants to be. Hell, as I already mentioned, I'm willing to strap on a dildo and do him in his ass while jerking him off if that's what he's into. I aim to please.

Not that whether he's honest or not really matters

'cause if I want to fuck him, I'm going to do it anyway. He'd just have to double-wrap his dick, then keep it moving. Hell, there're many women fucking men who have no idea who or what the hell the guys are doing at the end of the day, so what damn difference does it really make?

Well, knowing gives us choices. Not knowing puts us at greater risk. But either way, one should always, always practice safe sex; especially when he's not your damn husband or man. But, then again, even then, you still don't know. Do you?

My cell phone rings. I glance at the number, rolling my eyes. It's Barry. "Hello," I say into the receiver.

"Hey, stranger," he says. His rich baritone voice drips with sex appeal. "What you been up to?"

"Not much," I offer, sitting on the edge of my bed. I close my eyes, envisioning his naked body sprawled out in the center of my bed. "What's been going on with you?"

"Same shit. I wanna see you tonight." He's talking all low 'n shit on his cell while his wife is in the other room getting their kids ready for bed. He tells me how he can't stop thinking 'bout how good this pussy feels wrapped around his dick. And how bad he wants some more. Well, of course he does! They all do.

I sigh. Let me tell you a little bit about Barry. He's a six-foot-four, two-hundred-thirty-pound, wanna-be Rasta whom I met in New Orleans at the Essence Festival last year. He has six children with four different baby mamas. And yes, I fucked him on the spot. Once I learned he was from East Orange, I made it my business to fuck him again, and again, and again until I had enough of his cum-cannon. The last time I fucked him was almost four months ago. It took me almost two days to recover from him rocking my pussy inside out.

"Aww, I wish you would have called me earlier," I lie.

Between you and me, I have no interest in allowing this man up in my pussy again. One, he's packing extremely too much damn dick to be trying to fuck me on the regular.

That eleven-and-a-half-inch, dark-chocolate pole is about the size of a damn arm. And I'm sorry, say what you want, but I'm not the one. In my opinion, a big dick like his has to be taken in very small doses, like once every three to six months. There's no way I want him plunging in and out of me—not today, or any other day. I'm a firm believer that any woman who lives for a big-ass dick on a regular has got to have a pussy as wide and nasty as the Hudson River. Ugh! There's nothing worse than an overworked, over-fucked, sloppy, stretched-out hole.

Two, he blazes trees like a damned forest fire. Can't seem to focus or function without it. The shit seems to reek from his pores when he sweats. I don't know 'bout you, but I don't think there is anything sexy about having a nigga lying up on top of me smelling like he rolled himself up in a blunt. Sorry, getting a contact high is not my thing. Not that it's my place to judge, but this nigga is a real fiend, if you ask me. He'd rather blow two, three hundred dollars a week on weed than invest it in something more constructive. Like a set of braces for his crooked-ass teeth.

And three, Barry's one of those people I was talking about a while back who jumps into a relationship with someone without knowing them, then complains. From what he has shared with me during our few encounters, he met his chick at some strip bar; fucked her a few times; then she got pregnant. Now, the mofo was already in between places and needed a spot to lay his head, so what does he do? He moves in with her. Now, two years later, he's miserable and feels trapped. Dumb ass! That's what the hell he gets for splashing off in her without a damned condom. I'll say it again: Date, date, date before you jump into shit with someone.

"I can get out around two, if that's cool with you," he says.

Two in the fucking morning? I think in my head. *Oh, hell no! This muthafucker is one screw from crazy.* "No, it's not," I say.

"What about—"

My call waiting beeps. "Barry, hold on," I say, clicking over to retrieve the other call before he can respond. "Hello?"

"What's good, lady?"

"Hey, Ian," I say, smiling. Ian is a sexy, half-black, half-Korean cutie. He's twenty-seven, six-foot-three, and one hundred and ninety-five pounds, with nine inches of thick cut man meat! And mother-f-ing f-i-n-e. Yes, I've fucked him before. Between you and me, he's really not all that good in the pussy-eating department, but fucking...baby, let me tell you. This dude can slay some pussy. Now that he's called, I'm going to invite him deep inside these wet sugar walls and allow him to nut himself to paradise! "What's good with you?"

"This big dick," he says.

I laugh. "Is that so?"

"Don't play. You already know. So, dig, you up for some company or what?"

"Hell, yeah," I reply excitedly. "It's been a minute since I've had some of that dick."

"Oh, so you've missed this dick?"

I smile. I will tell him what he wants to hear; stroke his ego and make him feel like his is the only dick that matters. "Yes, baby," I moan. "I haven't been fucked right since the last time you knocked these walls. And that's been a minute."

"So you saying you ain't had no dick since me?"

"No, I'm not saying that. I'm saying your dick is what feels best inside me. These other niggas don't know what the hell they're doing."

In my mind's eye, I can see him nodding and smiling and patting himself on the back.

"Oh, word? That's what it is. Well, check this. I'm coming to split that asshole wide open tonight."

I smile. "You can do whatever you want, as long as you licking it first."

"No doubt," he says. "What time you want me to slide through?"

I glance at my watch. It's already seven-thirty. "Nine-thirty's good," I state.

"Bet. I'll see you then."

"Mmmm," I moan, almost forgetting about Barry on the other line. "My pussy's already wet for you."

"Exactly how I like it."

"See you at nine-thirty," I say, hanging up, then clicking back over to the other line. "Barry, sorry about that. Look, I gotta get ready to go. Call me one day next week if you can."

"Oh, word? It's like that? I was trying to stop through later on tonight."

"Umm, for one, two o'clock is too late for you come over here."

"Since when?" he asks.

I frown. "Since I have other plans, that's when."

"What, you got another nigga coming through?"

I roll my eyes. See? This is exactly why I can't be so bothered with a man. Talk about a mofo overstepping his boundaries. Give a nigga some pussy and he starts thinking he can question you and keep tabs on the pussy—even when the mofo has a woman at home. Now I have to get ugly.

"Nigga, not that I owe you any explanations, but yeah,

I got a better offer," I flatly state. "Now if you'll excuse me, I'm expecting to get my guts wrecked tonight so I need to freshen up."

"I'll be there around two," he says, dismissing what I tell him. "Have that nigga gone before I get there."

I laugh. "Fool, get a damn grip."

"Oh, you think I'm joking?"

"No," I say, still laughing. "But I do think you are a joke."

"Oh, so you think I'm a joke, huh? Well let me come through and show you exactly what kind of joke I am when I slam this dick up in you."

"Cuckoo…cuckoo…cuckoo," I chant in a singsong tone. "Can we say, 'med check,' please?"

He lowers his voice. "Oh, so you tryna to be funny, right? Why you gotta fucking play all the damn time? Can I come through or what?"

I roll my eyes. He is slowly starting to get on my last nerve. "Barry, do me a favor. Delete my damn number, *please*."

"What?" he asks.

I sigh. "Don't call me again. The dick was good while it lasted, but I'm done with it. So no, you can't come through. And no, you can't have any of this pussy—ever again. You might as well keep that dick right where it is 'cause I don't want it."

"Whoa, whoa, whoa," he says. "Hold up. Where's this coming from? A few minutes ago you were acting like it was all good between us. Now you flipping the script. What's up with that?"

I suck my teeth. "Barry, what script am I flipping? I fucking told you straight out that I was getting my back dug out tonight by another dude, and you still pressing me about coming through. Well, you can't 'cause, news flash, I'ma be riding another nigga's dick. Speaking of dick, would you like to suck his nut out of my pussy when he's finished fucking me down?"

"Yo, what kinda shit you on?" he snaps, sounding offended. "I don't fucking get down like that, so don't play me."

"What, did I hit a nerve, huh, Barry?" I lower my voice to a seductive whisper, and say, "Tell me, big daddy. Do you ever fantasize about tasting another man's hot nut? Fantasize about having it slide down in your cheating-ass throat? Mmmmmmmm, finger-licking good," I moan, then laugh.

This only pisses him off more.

"Yo, what the fuck you laughing for? I told you I ain't on none of that homo shit. I'm all man, baby...believe that."

"Oh, well. Too bad, then. 'Cause had you been willing to eat my pussy after him, I might have reconsidered letting you come through. But—"

"But nothing," he snaps. "I'm tryna come through for some pussy, and you wanna be on some fucking dumb shit."

"Nigga, please," I say, laughing again. "You can come around here if you want. But make no mistake. It won't be any of this wet pussy you get. It'll be a set of damn handcuffs, locking your crazy ass up. Now, try it if you want."

"You know what, I ain't even beat. I see you wanna play 'n shit. So, whose this nigga you fuckin'?"

Oh, no, he didn't just fucking ask me who I'm fucking. This motherfucker got the wrong one!

I take a deep breath, then asks, "Barry, where's your woman at?"

"She's upstairs, why?"

"Let me speak to her."

"Say, what?"

"I said, let me speak to her."

"Are you fuckin' buggin'?"

"No," I snap. "But *you* are for thinking you can question me or dictate to me. I'm not your dumb-ass chick. I don't answer to you, nor do I take directions from you. She puts up with your shit, not me. So don't get it twisted."

"Yeah, aiight," he huffs. "Whatever. I see you on some other shit. So I'll get up with you."

"No, sweetie, please don't." Now, I've never been the type of woman who kisses and tells, 'cause I believe what two consenting adults do is what they do. But there's a first time for everything. And make no mistake, Barry will have me blow his spot up if he doesn't bow out gracefully. "'Cause if you do, I promise you I'm going to be ringing your doorbell to have a little chat with your woman. And I don't think you want that, so let's say our goodbyes, and keep it moving."

"Yeah, whatever, bitch," he snaps, hanging up on me. Oh, well. He asked for it when he opened his mouth trying to be on some extra shit with me. I might be a *bitch*, but trust and believe, I ain't *that* bitch. The nerve of him!

Well, alrighty then. I don't know about the rest of you, but it's almost eight o'clock and I need to get ready for my company. So, until the next time…peace, love, harmony, and mouthwatering black dick!

CHAPTER
ELEVEN

The buzzing sound of my alarm clock awakens me, alerting me that it is six a.m. I reach over without opening my eyes and press the snooze button. I'm exhausted and sore from my night with Ian. I can still feel his cocoa-colored dick throbbing inside of me. I have been fucked and stretched to my limit. Have been licked and sucked and nibbled on to the point of no return. Whew…he fucked me *down!*

My nipples harden as I remember the thrust of his thick, mocha-colored cock in and out of my hot, slippery hole. How the width of his dick spread open my slick walls! How its length tickled the back of my pussy! Goosebumps form along my body and cause me to shiver as I repeat his words in my head. *I can't wait to slide my dick up in you and fuck you; can't wait to feel you grab my dick with your sweet, wet pussy. I wanna fuck you until I can't fuck no more; until your pussy is raw. Until my dick cramps and my balls shrivel.*

"Damn, baby," he whispered as he slapped his dick against my clit, beating it until it ached and throbbed, until it enlarged and filled with desire, until it caused my outer lips to quiver, "you got a pretty pussy."

He teased me until I could no longer take it. I wanted him inside of me. I was ripe and ready and needed to be fucked. I spread open my thighs as wide as they could go and reached for his taunting cock, thrusting my hips upward to guide him inside of me.

"Fuck me," I urged. "Stop teasing me, and fuuuuuck meeeeee. Give me the dick…mmmm…let me feel that dick."

He jabbed at the mouth of my pussy with the tip of his dick. Poked and stabbed at it until a fountain of warm, gushy lust spurted out from its opening, wetting his cock. He pushed himself deep inside of me, allowed himself to get lost in my wetness. I threw my right leg up over his shoulder and wrapped it around his neck, offering him all of my goodness, allowing his dick to feel all that my pussy is made of—sweet, delicious, mouthwatering pleasure.

"Aaaah, shit, baby," he moaned in my ear while stroking my walls. "This pussy is so fucking good. I wanna spend the rest of my life inside of it." I clenched my snatch around his cock, milked his thick muscle until he trembled inside of me. "Oh, fuck…Oh fuck…"

"That's right, daddy," I urged, bucking my hips up against his. "Fuck this pussy…Fuck me with that big dick…Oh, yes, fuck meeeee…"

With each thrust, I could tell his dick—like that of every man I fuck—craved more of my pussy. Could tell it ached for release into my sweet snatch, my warm mouth, and my ultra-tight asshole. And I invited him to fuck me in every hole until he shuddered and yelled out in ecstasy.

Humph…

My hand wanders lazily over my tingling pussy as I continue to replay the events in my mind. I allow my fingers to graze against my clit. Warm cunt juice is beginning to trickle out of my slit. I insert a finger, begin to stir, then the alarm clock buzzes again, disrupting my reverie. I let out a disgusted sigh, pressing the snooze button again. *So much for pleasing myself*, I think as I stretch, yawn, and roll over in bed, wanting to stay beneath the warmth of my comforter until noon. I open one eye, glancing at the clock. Thirty minutes have gone by. I let out another deep sigh, then close my eyes in hopes of catching a few more zzzs.

But sleep doesn't come. Instead, I find my thoughts shifting from Ian to the block hugger I fucked nine months ago. Don't ask me why he enters my mind after all this time, but he does. I allow myself to savor the memory. Shareef, Shareef, Shareef. My Lord…he was twenty-four, six-foot, three, and one hundred ninety pounds of lean muscle with a shiny black, ten-and-three-quarter-inch dick that curved slightly to the left. He'd been trying to get at me for over a year, and I'd always brushed him off because of his age. That particular night when I ran into him at Fantasy's, a titty bar in Keyport, he was standing there looking good and talking real sexy-like, trying to convince me to let him show me how a man's supposed to treat a woman. Asking me when I was going to let him take me out. I was flattered, but told him taking me out would be like a date, and I don't date. Please. Dating, as you already know, would mean I was trying to get to know a mofo outside of the bedroom. Imagine that. Not going to happen.

Anyway, I asked him what he'd do with a woman like me. He grinned, stepped up closer, leaned into my ear, then whispered how he could show me better than he could tell me. I immediately asked him my standard questions. He answered yes to all of 'em. Of course he would. He wanted some pussy. Needless to say, I told him when he was ready to go, to let me know so he could follow me home.

Forty minutes later, he was trailing behind me out the door. When we got here, I led him upstairs to my bedroom, and he got right down to business. Pinned me up against the wall and started kissing me. To my surprise his lips were as soft as a baby's. He jabbed his Hennessey-flavored tongue in and out of my mouth while slowly unbuttoning my blouse. When he freed my breasts from my bra, he placed his mouth on them, sucking each one like a greedy newborn hungry for its milk. He picked me up, carried me over to the bed, then laid me down and removed the rest of my clothes, then his own. His mouth and tongue traveled down my stomach into the center of my neatly trimmed bush while he massaged my titties. Homeboy rubbed his face into my mound, and I spread my legs open wider, giving him full access to the treat that awaited him. He lapped my clit with long, slow strokes, then dipped his tongue inside me, holding my pussy in his mouth, losing himself. He licked back up to my titties (sucked my nipples like they were dipped in honey), then moved up to my neck, then back down to my pussy, bathing every inch of my body with his eager, hungry tongue.

I'm not going to front. The heat from his breath and the feel of his tongue had me on fire. I wanted to feel his dick inside of me, and begged him for it. Yes, I begged for the dick. Please. This ho ain't too proud to beg, okay? And he gave it to me.

He got between my legs, rubbed the head of his dick along the slit of my pussy, then slid it inside of me. My pussy churned with excitement as his fat, black dick crashed into me, stretching my wet pussy. I started moaning and groaning, talking real fast and nasty, telling, demanding him to fuck me. He reached over, grabbed his boxers from the side of the bed, then stuffed them in my mouth. That shocked me at first (I've never had a man's underwear in my mouth), but he had me so damn hot, that it cranked my thermostat up higher. He had my pussy overheating with each thrust. Steam was everywhere. The sweet smell of my pussy filled the room.

He pushed my legs back toward my head, then shoved his dick in my hole as deep as he could. I wrapped my smooth legs around him, placing one leg over his shoulder, and the other around his hip. The way he thrust in me, I knew he wanted to make me scream out his name. Please. He'd have to put in a lot more work for that.

Finally, we shifted positions. I took his boxers out of my mouth, placed them over his head, got on my knees, then arched my back, and he slid his beef back in me. My pussy swished and swashed, squeezed and pulled at his dick. He groaned, moaned and grunted, gripping my hips, smacking my ass. I kept telling him how good his dick felt in me, begged him to give it to me harder. I watched him watching himself in the mirrors as he rode my ass with all his might, sweat dripping and face twisting. The nastier I talked, the thicker his dick got, the harder he pumped, the deeper he went. Mmmm. That young stallion fucked me good.

I roll over onto my stomach now with two fingers strumming inside my pussy, while another is stroking my clit. I pump and bounce my pelvis down on my hand, which has become an imaginary dick that widens my walls and causes me to gasp and moan in ecstasy. In my mind's eye, I am being fucked from the back. A thick, black sword is slashing into my pussy, creating a sweet mixture of pain and pleasure that shoots through the center of my being, then explodes into tiny pellets of creamy ecstasy.

When I am done cumming all over my hand and fingers, I lie still for a moment to steady my breathing. I wait a few more minutes, then roll over, kicking the white comforter and sheet off me.

Whew! All this thinking about sex and dick and fucking causes me to think about the types of music I enjoy while getting my pussy popped. Good dick. Good sex. Good music. Put the three together and something magical seems to happen. A list of some of my most favorite songs—music I like to fuck and suck a dick to— begins to play in my head, sensual melodies and tantalizing sounds that remind me of something wonderfully delicious. I mentally sift through each song, thinking, remembering, and smiling.

1). "Love You Down" by Ready for the World
(I love having my legs up and knees bent while a dick is slowly, deeply, moving in and out of me, brushing up against my clit with each stroke.)

2). "Woman's Work" by Maxwell
(I love my pussy eaten to this song!)

3). "Who Can I Run To?" By the Jones Girls
(I ain't running to a damn soul for love, but, baby, I'll run down a stiff dick.)

4). "Moments in Love" by the Art of Noise
(I love this song for deep-thrust fucking!)

5). "Remember the Rain?" by the 21st Century
(Oh, how I love the rain!)

6). "You Are My Starship" by Norman Connors

(I like closing my eyes and listening to this song while I'm riding up and down on a dick. Makes me feel like I'm riding waves.)

7). "Tender Love" by the Force M.D.'s

(I like being fucked on my side nice and slow to this song while his hand is playing with my clit.)

8). "'Cause I Love You" by Lenny Williams

(Oh my God! This song makes me want to swallow a dick whole.)

9). "Reasons" (the live version) by Earth, Wind & Fire

(Baaaby, this song makes my pussy extra wet and hot.)

10). "Silly" by Deniece Williams

(No, sweetie. Silly of you for sitting home wringing your hands while your man's face is between my legs with his tongue stuck in my pussy.)

11). "Fire & Desire" by Rick James and Teena Marie

(Oh, yes, this song calls for a slow, deep-grinding fuck.)

12). "Magic Man" by Robert Winters & Fall

(Humph…)

13). "Golden Touch" by Rose Royce

(Baby, this song was playing the first time Derek, my first love, kissed me, then bust my cherry. I cried!! Every time I hear it, it makes me think of him.)

14). "Ooh Child" by The Five Stairsteps

15). "She's Got Papers on Me" by Richard "Dimples" Fields

(As if I really care!)

16). "I Who Have Nothing" by Linda Jones

(My God, this heifer could saang! When I play this

song, it makes me want to fuck a man down into the ground, straight to his grave.)

17). "Very Special" by Debra Laws

18). "Betcha By Golly Wow" by the Stylistics

19). "Children of the Night" by the Stylistics

Before I can continue playing my song list in my head, I am once again snapped out of my reverie by the pesky, annoying sound of my alarm. I blink, staring at the clock. I can't believe that it is almost eight o'clock. I am shocked that I have been lying in bed daydreaming and reminiscing when I should already be on my way to my office.

"Fuck 'em," I say out loud, reaching for the phone. I call out from work. This is the second time I've called out because I spent all night sucking and fucking.

But between you and me, sitting at a desk today would be downright torturous. Ian tried to rip me a new asshole last night. Now I'm paying dearly for it. Ugh! I should have never let him stick that thick dick in my ass. My hole is aching something fierce! On top of that, I think I have the beginnings of what feels like hemorrhoids. My ass is on fire!! The only thing I plan on doing today is soaking in a tub of Epsom salts and applying ice to my ass to quench these damn flames. There'll be no further digging out this hole for at least a month. Believe that! Thank goodness I have two other holes that are still functional. Ugh, damn him! But, oh, baby…that dick was so damn good.

CHAPTER TWELVE

"Hey, baby."

For some reason, hearing those words, *hey baby*, the way he says it, the way it rolls off his thick tongue—low and sweet, dripping with innuendo, causes my chest to tighten. I'm not sure why, but hearing his voice today and the happiness in his tone makes me nauseous. For a brief moment, my breath gets caught in the back of my throat. I feel myself getting lightheaded as I imagine his large hands wrapped around my neck, twisting the life out of me, strangling me. Eyes bulging, gurgling sounds seeping from the back of my throat until my body goes limp. I gulp a deep breath, fighting for air, my eyes darting around the room as I attempt to break free from his grasp.

Coming to my senses, I blink the thought away.

"Garrett."

I glance at the clock. It's after eleven and I am still in bed, naked underneath the covers. I can't believe I have slept most of the morning away.

"Yeah, baby," he says thoughtfully. "I haven't spoken to you in a while so I thought I'd call to check in on you; you know, see how you were doing."

"I'm fine, thanks."

"You sound like you're still in bed."

"I am. I'm playing hooky today."

In my mind's eye, I can see him smiling, licking his lips. "You up for some company? I'd love to stop by and help reenergize you."

"No, I'm too exhausted," I reply, bursting his bubble. "Besides, didn't I see you a few days ago?"

"Yeah, and? Can't a man call a special friend to see how she's doing and want to spend more time with her?"

Friend? In the three or so years I've been fucking Garrett, I have never really placed a label on the two of us, except for maybe…fuck buddies. But, friends… uh, that would be stretching it a bit. Outside of sex, there is no exchange of information between us that is usually shared between two people who consider themselves friends. There are no secrets shared, or nights out on the town; just pure, unadulterated, sweaty fucking. So how the fuck does he come up with this *friends* shit? Humph.

"I guess so," I offer halfheartedly. "Is everything alright?"

"Yeah, everything is fine. I was thinking about you, and wanted to hear your sexy voice and let you know you were on my mind. That's all."

I roll my eyes, shaking my head. I know I should be touched by the gesture, but I'm not. The last thing I want is for him or any other man to be getting all mushy and shit on me. That is not part of the arrangement. I know, I know. I can't control how someone else feels about me. Nor can I prevent them from feeling what they feel. However, I still don't have to like it, and I definitely don't have to subscribe to it.

I inhale deeply, then slowly exhale. "Thanks," I say, trying to sound sincere. "I appreciate that."

"Do you?" he asks.

I suck my teeth. "Didn't I already say I did?"

"But did you mean it?"

"Why would you ask that?"

"C'mon, Bianca, you know, like I do, that sometimes what a person says and what they actually mean aren't always the same. So I'm gonna ask you again, did you mean it?"

"Okay, Garrett. You want the truth?"

"Yeah," he replies, sounding annoyed. "That would be nice."

"No, I didn't."

"Then why'd you say it?"

I frown. *Who the fuck does he think he is questioning me?* "Excuse me?"

"I asked you why you said it, if you didn't mean it."

"What is this, an interrogation?" I'm feeling myself becoming agitated.

"No, it's us—two people who spend time together— having a discussion, and me asking you a question for clarification."

"Oh, okay," I say.

"I don't ever want there to be any misunderstandings between us," he adds.

"Well, I said it because it felt like the right thing to do, and I didn't want to hurt your feelings."

"Baby, check this out," he says. He pauses, then continues. "You can't hurt my feelings if you keep shit real with me. I'm not gonna lie to you or mislead you, and I hope you won't either. Just because I feel a certain way, that doesn't mean I expect you to feel it too. I mean, don't get me wrong, I would like you to. But I'm smart enough to know that's not how the world moves. All I ask is that you keep shit real. Is that cool?"

"Garrett, I've always been straight up with you."

"Yeah, aiight," he says, sounding skeptical, "if you say so. Sometimes I think you got me confused with some of those little-ass, confused boys that you have swarming around you. I'm a man, baby. I know what I want. Believe that. Look, I gotta get going. I'll call you a little later, alright?"

For some reason, I feel like he's just finished checking me, and is now dismissing me. I consider giving him a good piece of my mind, letting him know that he isn't running shit with me, but…instead, I acquiesce and allow him to think he is. Hell, I am still exhausted from my night with Ian, and don't have the strength or energy to waste on Garrett with this mess. Not today. "That's up to you," I finally say.

I hear, *click*.

I know he didn't hang up on me, I think, getting out of bed and sliding my feet into my slippers. "That mother-fucker is really losing his damn mind," I say aloud as I shuffle into the bathroom to relieve myself. "And I'm crazy for letting him get away with it." When I am finished pissing, I wash my hands, then retreat back to the comforts of my bed.

I don't awake again until after one o'clock, and by the time I finally decide to get out of bed, it's already going on two in the afternoon. At almost four o'clock, I still haven't showered. I'm sitting here in my silk robe listening to my girl Syleena Johnson's CD *Chapter 3: The Flesh*. I love her!

She has this song titled "Phone Sex" that I've played three times today. Whew! I love me some nasty, freaky phone sex. Mmmph. Baby…let me tell you. There's nothing like it. How many women and men do you think get off on phone sex, or have even tried it? I personally think it helps keep things exciting.

There is so much power in mind fucking, sexually speaking that is. To create the mood, to be able to role-play fantasies, to be able to bring someone to the edge of an orgasm by taunting and sensually teasing them. Then when they're about to cum, you make 'em slow down or stop, then start back again. Bring 'em to the edge again, and again, making them stop each time they are about to nut. Torture them in sweet, delicious whispers until they can no longer take it; until they are begging you, moaning and groaning, for the real thing. My God!

For anyone who hasn't tried it, I say shame on 'em. And for those who can't get into it, I say humph. Boriiiiiing! Of course, I know there are some people who would only become sexually frustrated with phone sex, especially men. I had a man tell me he's cool with it (and with foreplay) for a while. But after thirty minutes or so, he was ready to fuck. I was like, ohhhh-kaaaaay. Click. There was no need in trying to go any further with him. No man is going to short-change me when it comes to foreplay or role-play. And any man who can't open his mind to phone sex, or lacks a creative imagination, is not for me. End of discussion.

Anywaaaaaaay, moving on, let me ask you something: Does having sexual fantasies about being with the same sex mean I'm a budding lesbian? Or does it simply mean I'm curious? 'Cause let me tell you, the last few days I have been fantasizing about having a woman eat my coochie while I'm sucking a cock. I've had fantasies in the past where it's strictly me and another chick, and I'm fucking her with a double-headed dildo. Other times, it's with me, another chick, and a dude. Chick is riding him reverse cowgirl—with her back toward him, for those of you who might not know. His legs are spread open and hers are draped over his and I'm on my knees between both of their legs, rubbing her clit, sucking his balls and licking her pussy juice as it drips down the shaft of his dick. It gets me off every time.

But as of late, my fantasies consist of me lying flat on my back with my head hanging off the bed. My legs are bent and my knees pulled up to my chest and a cute little cat licker is between my legs lapping and nipping at my clit, then tongue-fucking and sucking my pussy voraciously while a tall, dark-chocolate daddy is skull-fucking me with his fat, juicy dick, stretching my throat and slapping my forehead with his balls. Whew, baaaa-by, listen…there's nothing like a good dick-swabbing. OhmyGod, the thought gets my pussy juice boiling every damn time. And now it has me wanting to slam down on some dick, or at the very least, grind my pussy down on a pair of wet, hungry lips.

Hmmm, let's see, I think, scrolling through my cell phone contact list. *Who can I hit up for a quick fix? Who am I in the mood for tonight?*

I purse my lips, contemplating. But before I can decide on my fuck for the night, my cell rings. I don't recognize the number, but answer anyway.

"Hello?"

"Hey, baby," the voice on the other end says.

"Baby?" I repeat with attitude. "Who is this?"

"Damn, baby," he says, "you done forgot my voice that fast? It's Benson."

I frown, then let out a disgusted grunt. "Ohhhhh-kaaaaaay, and why are you calling?"

"I was hoping to—"

Oh hell no, I think, shaking my head. I cut him off before he can part his lips to finish his request to hit this pussy. "Sorry to burst your bubble, but there's no sense in hoping 'cause it's not gonna happen, boo."

"Why, you got some other plans? Did I catch you at a bad time?"

I pull the phone away from my ear and stare at it before placing it back up to my ear. "Uh, nooooo," I answer sarcastically. "I thought I told you the last time I saw you to delete my number."

"I didn't think you meant it," he states, sounding serious.

"Oh, I meant it. Along with everything else I said that night."

"Damn. I was hoping a little space and time would mend whatever ill feelings you might have had the last time we were together."

"Benson, are you delusional?"

"Hunh? Whadaya mean am I delusional?"

"Just what I asked," I say. "I want to know if you are crazy, 'cause you really must be if you think you and that lazy dick of yours will ever be invited back into this tight pussy again. After the way you half-fucked me the last time I had you in my bed, I don't think so, nigga."

Silence.

"Are you still there?" I ask.

"Yeah, I'm still here. I'm thinking before I speak. I really don't appreciate how you coming at me. Have I ever disrespected you?"

I take a deep breath. "No, not that I can recall," I admit.

"So then what makes you think you can come out your mouth all slick?"

"Let me explain something to you. Number one: I'm a grown-ass woman, and I speak to you how I want. I have no respect for a man who creeps on his woman, so get it right. Number two: When I ask—no, *tell*—a nigga to not call my fucking house again and he does anyway, then it's obvious to me that his ass doesn't understand basic English and he damn sure doesn't respect my wishes, so I have to give it to him raw and uncut. Bottom line, if you don't like how you're being talked to, then don't call my motherfucking house. You had your opportunity to get some good pussy on a regular and you blew it, so let's keep it moving."

"You know what? Fuck you…you fucking nasty, trick-ass bitch."

"No, fuck *you*," I say back, laughing. "I know you don't think you hurt my feelings with that little bullshit line. Nigga, puhleeeeeeze. You need to get your dick game up first, before you try to come for me."

"Fucking smut," he snaps.

I continue laughing. "And so is your dumb-ass mother for throwing up her rusty-ass legs and giving birth to a pathetic-ass motherfucker like you," I snap back. "Nigga, you are a fucking waste of dick. So you might as well do yourself a favor and go put a bullet in that lazy-ass cock of yours. You retarded fuck. Now, don't call my fucking number again 'cause the next time you do, I won't be so nice."

"Whatever, bitch," he snaps, hanging up on me.

I fall back on my bed, laughing my ass off until tears pour out of my eyes. These niggas crack me the hell up. I swear they do. The minute you check their asses, they wanna resort to calling you out of your name. That shit is hilarious to me. Hell. I keep shit real with 'em and their dumb asses want to start feeling some kind of way about it. Oh, well. The truth hurts. And I don't give a hot fuck whose feelings get hurt. Niggas have been dismissing and disrespecting women for centuries. It's about damn time women turn the tables and start shoveling the shit back at them. As far as I'm concerned, it's a new damn day. I'm not letting any man try to pimp me, or play me. Believe that.

Instead of dealing with a nigga tonight, I decide to take my ass a long, hot bath, climb up in bed, and masturbate. *That's exactly what I'll do*, I think, getting up and removing my clothes, *fuck myself into a delicious slumber*.

CHAPTER
THIRTEEN

O f all the people to run into first thing this morning, I have to bump right into Everett's ass, literally and figuratively. "Ooh," I shriek. He turns around. "I'm sorry. I didn't see you standing there," I say, looking up at him. I was so deep in thought, looking over some last-minute changes to one of my weekly reports, that I rammed right into him.

"Anytime," he says, offering me a mischievous grin. He steps back onto the elevator with me. "I'm glad it was you, instead of someone else." He flashes me a smile, pausing, taking me in with his eyes, considering what stands before him. Today, I am stylishly dressed in a brown and orange print wrap dress with a pair of brown four-and-a-half inch heels. My hair is in an updo with a sweeping bang that curves along the right side of my face, and I am wearing a light coat of cranberry-wine lipstick to accentuate my luscious lips. He scans my body, smiling, then continues, "I'd like to bump into you as many times as I can."

I roll my eyes, waving him off. "Yeah, I'm sure you would. Umm, I thought you were getting off."

"I was," he says, seductively licking his lips and eyeing me up and down. I try to act as if I don't notice. But his smoldering gaze is slowly causing a fire to stir between my thighs. "But I forgot something."

"Oh, really?" I inquire, pressing the button for the basement level. The door closes. "And what's that?"

"You," he says.

I roll my eyes dramatically and say, "Oh, please. How many times have you used that tired line?"

He laughs. "Including you, three. But those other two times don't count since I didn't mean it."

I smile. "Oh. And now you do?" I shift my weight from one foot to the other, glancing up at the flashing numbers of each floor, trying to keep my eyes focused on anything other than him.

He steps in closer, lowers his voice. "I mean everything I say when it comes to you, pretty baby…"

I slowly begin to fade out of this conversation. I quietly inhale, hold the air in for a few seconds, then slowly exhale. At this moment, there's a battle going on in my head. My ho voice is fucking with me, whispering shit like: "Ho, fuck him one good time; then be done with it. The nigga is practically throwing you the dick…you know you wanna wet his dick up, so stop acting all shy 'n shit. Fuck him already. You're a ho, damnit! Let's do what we do, ride that nigga's dick. Let 'im feel how good that pussy is…"

Then there's my other voice, the one that is milder, tamer, and a bit more logical in its ho thinking, saying:

"Stay focused, ho. Fucking him would be your biggest mistake. We don't shit where we eat, remember? Keep it cute, and keep it moving…"

Both of you bitches shut the fuck up, I think as Everett's baritone voice forces my attention back to him. I hear him saying, "…all you need to do is give me one night to show you."

"Big daddy," I say, allowing my eyes to linger over his body much longer than I should. "You couldn't handle me in one night."

"Try me," he says, in a tone full of dare.

In my mind's eye, I see myself yanking his black boxer briefs—assuming that's the color or kind he wears, or that he wears any at all—down to his ankles, watching his soft and surprisingly fat cock plop out. Before he can speak, I grab it at the base, then shove my open mouth around it, slowly slurping and sucking and slobbering all over it until it begins to lengthen and thicken. He looks down at me in delicious delight as his dick hardens, hitting the back of my throat. I moan, and continue to take his dick, inch by inch, into my mouth. I can tell he is turned on watching his dick disappear each time he thrusts. Streams of spit drizzle out of my mouth and roll down onto his big, heavy balls. I cup them, and begin massaging and gently tugging on them while increasing the suction of my sucking, causing a popping sound to echo around the elevator car. And then…and then…

The bell dings, and the elevator doors open. I step out, and turn to face Everett. I give him my most seductive look, and just when the doors are about to close, I blow him a kiss. He quickly sticks his hand in the doors, causing them to reopen.

"Is that a yes?" he asks, sticking his head out.

"Nope," I say, walking off, glancing over my shoulder.

"You need to stop playing with a brotha's emotions," he says jokingly, clutching his chest.

I ignore him and continue sashaying down the hall. I feel his eyes on me and purposely throw a few extra shakes in my hips, glancing over my shoulder to catch his eyes lustfully locked on my perfectly shaped ass. I shake my head, laughing. "I hope you're enjoying the view."

"You know you're wrong for saying that, right?" he says, laughing also.

"I'm sure you'll survive," I respond over my shoulder as I head toward the cafeteria.

Fifteen minutes later, I am sitting at my desk back in my office drinking a bottle of Lipton Green Tea, and going through my emails. There's one from Everett. I click on it, and wait for it to open.

It reads: *It was nice "bumping" into you. We'll have to do it again. How about later today, before, during and after lunch?*

I type back: *no, not interested!*

Five minutes later, another email comes through. *Oouch! Thanks for putting the steak knife through my heart.*

I respond: *Enjoy your day!*

So you're gonna let me bleed to death?

Yep, I type. *Now stop harrassing me. I have work to do.*

My office line rings. Its tone tells me it's an internal call. I pick up. "Bianca Rivers speaking. How can I help you?"

"You can help me by letting me take you out. Give me one night. I promise you, I'll be on my best behavior. Gentleman's honor."

I laugh. "Everett, don't you have work to do?"

"Of course I do," he says. "But right now, trying to get a date with you is more important."

"Then you're a bigger fool than I thought," I say, laughing even harder. "Stop wasting company time trying to fraternize or I'm going to report you to HR."

He chuckles. "I'll take my chances."

"'Bye, Everett," I say, hanging up on his ass, knowing he's not going to give up his quest for some of this good pussy easily.

Thankfully, the rest of my day at the office is uneventful until Nahdirah stops by with another round of foolishness. "Hey, girl," she says in singsong, sticking her head in my office.

"Oh, hey," I say, looking up from my laptop. "Where you been?" I ask the question, but I honestly don't really care. She walks in and closes the door. "I haven't seen you around in a few days." I watch her as she makes her way across the room.

"Yeah, I had to take a few days off."

"Vacation?"

She sighs, taking a seat in one of the chairs in front of my desk. "Not really."

"Oh," I say, staring at her. I take her in a few seconds longer, then blink.

I blink again, attempting to keep my face from revealing what I'm thinking: *Jake done went upside her head.*

She has what look to be the remnants of a black eye, and a lump on the right side of her forehead. "What happened to your eye?" I inquire, pretending like I don't see the knot on her head.

She shifts in her seat, touching her cheek area. "Oh, I accidentally got hit in the face with a van door."

I tilt my head, giving her my "you-really-don't-think-I'm-believing-that-shit" look.

"Whose van was it?"

"Uh," she says, searching for a lie, "a friend's."

"Really? Hmm. How did it happen?"

I purse my lips as she begins to give me her distorted reality of what happened. She claims she was helping "a friend" move. When she went to open the back doors, they were stuck, so she pulled on the latch, and one of the doors swung open and hit her in the eye.

Now, I don't know a lot about domestic violence, but I know enough to know when someone is getting their ass beat. And this chick's face has definitely met a punk nigga's fist.

As I sit here looking at her, this whole scenario reminds me of an incident that happened almost eight months ago down the street from my house. Early in the morning, I had walked out of my front door trying to leave for work, and I spotted this young girl a few houses down from me fighting with her baby's daddy. Dude had his hands wrapped around her neck, strangling her while she tried to claw him and fight him off. The crazy thing was, there were other niggas outside watching this mess and not one of them sorry-ass punks did anything to help her. I guess they weren't 'bout to get caught up in someone else's drama, then have it flipped on them. 'Cause I've seen that happen too. You go to help someone who appears to be in distress, then they turn around and jump on your ass for trying to save them. Well, fuck what you heard. I called the police on his ass any damn way. Let them handle it. And that's exactly what they did.

You want to fight, keep that shit behind closed doors. Don't bring that mess outside where I have to see it, especially first thing in the damn morning, and definitely don't do that shit in front of your child. He was actually beating the mother of his child right in front of the poor thing. I couldn't believe it. *Oh, no the hell you won't!* I thought. *Not on my watch.* The little boy was in his car seat screaming and crying at the top of his little lungs. I slowly drove by while the cops were arresting his ass, and taking her too. Go figure!

Long story short, she ended up right back with him, and has the nerve to be pregnant by him again. Now her ass will really be stuck. But someone pleeeeeeeease help me understand how the hell a man can put his hands on a woman, then come out of his face talking 'bout he loves her. No, nigga, you love trying to control her. That shit ain't love, not healthy love, any damn way. Then what drives me wild is the fact that she continues to take his disrespectful ass back. Talking 'bout he didn't mean it. Come again, bitch? So, tell me, when he stomps you into a coma, or kills you, will he mean it then? Ugh! I will never be able to wrap my mind around that craziness. I don't care how many times someone tries to rationalize it, or psychoanalyze it, I will *never* accept it.

I stare at Nahdirah long and hard, look her dead in the eyes, and say, "You don't deserve to be hit."

"Hit?" she repeats, letting out a nervous chuckle. "Ain't nobody hit me. I told you what happened. I got hit with the door."

I look at her and think, *Sweetie, you don't have to lie to me 'cause I already know how you got your goddamn eye knocked.* She forgets I remember her coming to work last year with her face lumped up, and that time her excuse was that she tripped and hit her face on the edge of the table. I think to remind her of her stories to cover up what is really going on in her household, but I keep my mouth shut, and listen to the poor thing rattle on about how her man would never do anything to hurt her. Unfortunately, I know she's desperately trying to convince herself more so than me. Whatever!

"Jake loves me too much to ever want to hurt me.

Sure he gets a little mad sometimes, but who doesn't?"

I sigh. "Um, Nahdirah, there's no such thing as being a little mad. Either you are or you aren't. And you're right, we all get mad. But it doesn't give us the right to put our hands on someone else." I pause, studying her, hoping what I say sinks in. Already knowing the answer, I ask, "Has Jake ever hit you?"

She shifts in her seat. "Of course not," she answers quickly. "I mean, he's pushed or shoved me around a few times when I wouldn't stop nagging him about something, but other than that, he would never beat me."

No, just blacken your damn eyes. I will myself not to roll my own eyes. Uh, duh, ho…pushing and shoving is physical contact, and a form of hitting someone. Anyway, I am absolutely speechless. I want to snatch her by her damn arms and shake her ass like a rag doll. But, what do I know. When she gets sick and tired of being sick and tired, and realizes she deserves better than having someone go upside her head, she'll find the strength and courage to get out of it. I hope.

All I know is it wouldn't be me. The first time would be the last time, 'cause after I finished gouging his ass up with my fingernails, then punching him dead in his throat, I'd blow a hole in his chest without blinking an eye. I hear the lyrics to Jazmine Sullivan's song "Call Me Guilty" playing in my head. *Get that Glock and take his life. Hospitals and bloody noses, this would end all that I suppose…*

It sure the hell would, I think, shifting in my seat. I feel myself getting pissed off. I'm sorry, but, *no* man should be putting his hands on any woman. And that goes for women as well. I've heard of a few chicks that have no problem stepping up in a man's face and putting her hands up. That's a no-no, period!

Oh my God, I'm telling you. A motherfucker can try it if he wants. He'll be pushing up daisies before dawn. That's a promise!

I get up from my seat and walk around my desk. I sit in the chair next to Nahdirah, then reach for her hand. I clasp both of my hands around it. "If there's anything you ever want to talk about," I offer sincerely, "I'm here for you." Like I've said many times before, she'll never be someone I'll embrace as a friend, but I would never turn my back on her in a time of need.

She stares at me, her eyes glistening. I think I see pain, fear, perhaps relief. She opens her mouth to say something, maybe confess, but stops herself. "Girl, I appreciate that. But I'm good. Like I told you, I got hit in the eye by the door. So, please don't make this out to be something more than it is." She quickly gets up. "Listen, I gotta go."

I watch her, dumbfounded, as she hastily dashes out of my office, closing the door behind her, leaving me with the memory of her black and blue, swollen face. I shake my head, thinking: *Silly bitch!*

CHAPTER
FOURTEEN

I t's Friday, and I am glad to be out of that damn office and in my car, driving home. I am so preoccupied with sex, and dick, and having my guts dug out that I almost run a red light. I slam on my brakes, clutching my chest. I can smell burning rubber.

"Whew, that shit was close," I say aloud, wondering which one of my sex charms I want to come through to fuck me tonight. I already know I'm not in the mood for Mitchell's drunk ass. Besides, he's on the verge of being terminated early from his pussy and ass-eating duties for coming to my house unannounced the other night. I don't feel like seeing Wade or Jamil. And I'm not up for Garrett or Ian either—particularly not Ian.

I think for a minute, then decide to call Nelson, a dude I met a few months ago at Livingston Mall. He's a six-foot-four, two-hundred-twenty-five-pound, milk-chocolate man with a wide nose, thick neck, and big, round brown eyes. He's not officially one of my sex charms since I haven't fucked him yet, but I promise you, if he performs as good as he looks, he will be before daybreak.

He picks up on the third ring. "Hello?"

"Hello, Nelson?" I ask, not sure if the voice on the

other end is his or not since this is my first time calling him. My phone number flashes as private, so he will not know who I am. I never allow a man to have my phone number until after I ride his dick at least once—and then, only if I decide to fuck him again.

"Speaking," he answers. "Who's this?"

"It's Janaye…"

Don't give me that look. I know *that's* not my name, geesh! I'll explain later. But, for now, simply go with the flow. Oh, alright, already! Janaye is my middle name, and one of my aliases. So, depending on the nigga I'm fucking at the time, it may be Janaye or Briana, another alias. That's who I am to them. Please. Why would I give any of them my real name, especially when I know they're creeping? Now when a chick does try to check for me, she's looking for either one of the two, not Bianca, trust me. The ones who claim to be unattached, well, I take my chances and give 'em my real name. And that depends on whether or not I think they're trying to run game on me.

"…I'm not sure if you remember me," I continue, "but we met at the mall a few months ago."

"Oh, yeah," he says, sounding excited. "I know who you are. You were the one talking real slick that day. Had my dick all hard 'n shit. What's good with you? I didn't think you were gonna call."

"I misplaced your number," I lie. Hell, men do it all the time. "I was cleaning my car out this morning and found it stuck on the side of my passenger seat so I decided to hit you up to see what you been up to."

"Oh, that's wassup. For a minute there I thought you mighta got scared or something."

I laugh. "No, baby, I'm a grown woman. I don't scare easy."

"Don't start talking too fast. I don't wanna have you running from me."

"And I don't run easy. You got me confused, big daddy."

"Oh, yeah…is that so? So, what you getting into tonight?"

"The question is: What do I *want* getting into *me* tonight."

"Oh, it's like that? I can dig it. So tell me, then. What do you want in you tonight?"

"A stiff dick," I say, getting right down to business. I have no time to waste going around in circles. Either you want to fuck or you don't. "Can you handle that?"

"Oh, word? That's what it is. You think you ready for me?"

"Neeegro," I say, laughing. "I was born ready."

"Yeah, right," he replies, laughing with me. "I betcha can't take no dick."

"Think what you like, baby. You'll have to get up a little earlier to get me to fall into that mind trap. Not gonna happen. Make no mistake, I'm skilled at what I do," I tell him, veering off onto Route 280 west. "You can savor on that for a minute, then decide in what area you believe I'm talking about."

"Yeah, okay," he responds. "So when you tryna get this stiff dick?"

"Tonight," I answer, smiling to myself. For some reason, tonight I'm in the mood to role play. I want to pretend I am having an anonymous pump and dump session with a thick, chocolate dick. I want this faceless man to walk in and find me naked on my bed, on my knees, face down, all wet and ready. There'll be no words exchanged. In my fantasy, he comes in, drops his pants, rubs his dick up and down the crack of my ass, then slides it into my hot hole and fucks me. He pounds and pumps away until he dumps his thick load of cum deep inside me. Then he gets up, zips up, and leaves me with his nut dripping out of my aching pussy without me ever seeing his face. But in reality, he will pull his dick out of me, remove his condom and toss it on the side of the bed next to me, then walk out.

I tell Nelson this, and it gets quiet on the other end. For a moment, I think he's hung up on me. "Hello, you still there?"

"Yeah, I'm still here. I'm taking it all in 'cause you really fucked me up with that. Whew! I ain't never heard no shit like that before. I see you a real freak."

I grin, imagining him squeezing and pulling at his dick. "You got a problem with that?" I ask coyly.

"Nah, baby. Not at all." He pauses, I'm sure to think

over what I have said. I allow him his moment. "So, let me get this straight," he says, making sure he has heard me clearly. "You want me to walk up in your spot and take the pussy from the back without saying shit to you, then bounce."

"Exactly."

He chuckles. "Damn, you're really something else."

"And there'll be a face mask on the glass table next to the door for you to put on. Now tell me. Exactly how much dick you holding?"

He laughs. "Eight and three quarter inches."

"Is it thick?"

"Most definitely," he states.

"Mmmm," I moan softly. "And are these *real* or imagined inches?"

"I'm real with mine, baby."

"We'll see," I say, speeding past a confused-assed driver who seems to enjoy riding the brakes. I hate that shit!

"Are you cut? And do you know how to use it?"

"No doubt."

"To which question?"

"Both," he says, laughing again. "Damn you ask a lot of questions. Are you taking a survey or something?"

"That's right, I ask questions. Inquiring minds want to know. And if a man can't answer them honestly, then I ain't beat to fuck with him. So if you can't get with that, then you can't get any of this tight pussy. You dig?"

"I can dig it," he quickly says. "Ask all the questions you want, baby."

"Good. So…are you down with role-playing with me or what?"

"Yeah, it's all good. So that pussy's tight, huh?"

"Yep; clamps around a cock like a vise."

"Oh word? What time you want me to come through?"

"At exactly nine-thirty. Not, nine-thirty-one; not nine-forty. Nine-thirty on the dot. If not, then forget about coming. I'm not the kind of chick who waits on a man or his dick, so if you can't be on time, then let me know now."

"Nah, nine-thirty is cool. Let me know where you rest at."

After I give him further instructions, and the directions, I hang up.

On the rest of my ride home, I anticipate tonight's adventure. The whole idea of role-playing causes me to twitch in my seat and my pussy to overheat. As I stop at another light, I start to fantasize about being gang banged; screwed every which way until my hot cunt is sore and tore open. Until my asshole aches and burns. Until my lips are chafed, jaws locked, and my throat is raw and overflowing with cum. Yes, I am being driven and ridden like the Orient Express. I find myself going from one extreme to the other. Then my fantasy turns to having a man on his knees with his dick and balls hanging, and I have his dick in my hand stroking it while I'm licking the crack of his ass. Not that I'd really do it, 'cause some men don't know how to wipe their asses right. But at this very moment, my overactive imagination takes me there. I close my eyes, bringing the act into clear view. There's something about licking a man's ass from the back while stroking his dick that gets me off every time.

A blue Acura in back of me blows its horn, snapping me away from my thoughts. I speed off, visualizing myself walking up to a complete stranger (well, hell, I do that now). Anyway, I walk up to him and beg him to let me suck his sweet, black dick. When he says I can, I grab him by the crotch, rubbing and kneading the front of his pants, feeling him stiffen. Then I drop to my knees, unzip his pants with my teeth, and pull out his dick, sucking and licking and kissing all over it right in the middle of Times Square while other men surround us, pulling their dicks out and jerking off, watching and lusting, for a feel of this deep, pulsating throat. And as I'm gulping down my stranger's dick and swallowing his thick nut, they all cum in unison, spraying their man cream all over the sidewalk. I get up off my knees and strut off, swinging my hips and licking my lips, with a beautiful smile on my face.

The sound of my ringing cell startles me and snatches me from my series of fantasies.

"Hello," I say into the receiver.

"Hey, beautiful, how's my favorite sis doing?"

The voice has me grinning from ear to ear. It's my oldest brother, Terrance, calling from San Diego. Terrance is an eighteen-year veteran with the San Diego Police Department. He's forty-one, married, and has three children. "Fool, I'm your only sis," I say, laughing.

"Well, I'm glad you realize that. I was starting to wonder if I even had a sister. Now why haven't we heard from you?"

Oh my God. I realized it's been over a month since I've spoken to him. I've been so busy with work and getting my back knocked out that I've completely forgotten to reach out to him. Of all my brothers, I'm the closest to him. To me, Terrance is—next to my father—the epitome of what a man should be. He is hardworking, compassionate, and deeply devoted to his wife and children. Interestingly, they say a woman can always tell how a man will treat her by watching how he treats his mother and sisters. Well, I agree that may be the case to some extent. However, that doesn't always mean shit. My six brothers all treat me and my mother like queens and will do anything in the world for us. But when it comes to women in the streets, three of 'em (Tyrell, Lamont, and Trent) treat women any kind of way, cursing them out, putting them out on the highway, sleeping with their friends, doing all types of crazy shit to 'em. And these dumb chicks come back for more. Humph.

Then there are Terrance and Tyler, who are happily

married and give their wives the utmost respect. My youngest brother, Thomas, who's thirty-one, has four kids with three different baby mamas (who all have men) and he's still sleeping with all three of them. They've let him know he can hit it anytime he wants it, no matter who they're with. And on top of that he has a chick whom he lives with. Now what kind of shit is that?

Basically, I have four brothers who have some serious issues when it comes to women and commitments. So you can't always go by what you see, believe that. But Terrance is definitely an example to the rule.

"I'm so sorry. I've been meaning to call you, but things at work have been keeping me busy, and I keep getting sidetracked. How have you been? How are my nieces and nephew doing?"

"We're all doing good, thanks for asking. How 'bout you? What's been up with you? I don't need to fly out there to choke anyone up, do I?"

I laugh, knowing he'd be out here in a heartbeat if he thought some man was trying to disrespect, or God forbid, hurt me. If my father didn't kill him first, Terrance would be next in line to put him out of his misery. Followed by my brother Tyler, who's the second oldest. He's a New Jersey state trooper, which is how I met Garrett.

Anyway, growing up in a house with all boys definitely had its advantages. Not only did they spoil me, but they were extremely protective of me. Sometimes it was suffocating, but I know it was all out of love for me.

And the beauty of growing up with brothers is that you get to listen, learn, and experience the inner workings of a man firsthand. See, my brothers taught me very early how a man is supposed to treat a woman, and how he shouldn't. There are some things that they instilled in me that have stuck with me through life, such as: Never let a man put his hands on you, never let him disrespect you, never let him lay up on you, never fuck with a man you have to clean up, and if he's a liar or cheater, get rid of his ass. And I live by that.

The disadvantage of having them around growing up was that they were always cock-blocking me. A sista couldn't even get her fuck on. At one time, I had two brothers in college, three in high school, and one in junior high, so I couldn't get away with shit. If a dude even thought about looking at me, they'd yoke him up and beat him down. So dudes weren't trying to check for a chick with six overprotective brothers. And the ones who were bold enough to try 'n holla, I had to sneak in through my bedroom window, then hide in my closet or under my bed until it was safe to fuck. The crazy thing is the first guy who split this pussy open was my brother Lamont's best friend, Derek.

Every night around eleven, I'd open my window so he could climb through it. He'd come in, take off all his clothes, and fuck me with his long, fat, black dick. He was eighteen, and I was fourteen. Yes, I was hot in the ass. I had been fingering and rubbing my pussy for almost two years and knew what it was like to experience an orgasm. But the first time he spread open my legs and kissed the inner part of my smooth brown thighs, then pulled apart my slick pussy lips and softly blew inside of me, forcing warm currents to flow throughout my body, I knew I'd never be the same. He slid two long, thick fingers inside my tight pussy, twisting and stroking the inside of my walls, causing a fire to ignite within me, preparing me for his entry before climbing between my legs and pushing the head of his thick dick between the hungry, wet, shivering lips of my pussy. He entered me, stretched me—forced himself into my tightness, inch by inch, introducing me to a pleasantly intense, painfully sweet, more satisfying orgasmic experience than I ever knew was possible.

Over a two year period, everything sexual I had witnessed down in my basement watching my brothers, I performed and practiced with him. It was there on my canopy bed that I experienced the rites of passage into freakhood. And I've been chasing dick ever since.

"No, I'm good," I say, pulling up into my garage, getting out of the car, then gathering my things. I open the door leading into the kitchen, then deactivate the alarm. "Just working, and keeping the peace. How's the weather out there?" I drop my keys and purse on the granite island, then remove my heels. My damn feet are throbbing. I let out a sigh.

"It's beautiful. Eighty-degrees with deep blue skies. What's the weather like there?"

For October it's been seasonably warm, almost like spring. And I'm glad 'cause I can't stand it when it's too hot, and hate it even more when it's cold. "Gorgeous. It was sixty-five degrees today."

He laughs. "Yeah, well too bad it's not year round."

"Yeah, yeah, yeah," I snap playfully, "rub it in my face, show off."

"Well, whenever you ready to trade in that cold weather for beautiful San Diego, you know we'd love to have you. And you know Mom and Dad would be thrilled."

I smile, knowing they'd love nothing more than if I packed up and moved out there. I miss my parents, dearly, but I know I'd miss the east coast even more. There's nothing like that east cock.

"I know ya'll would. But you know I'd be bored out of my mind way out there. I need to be able to have access to the hustle and bustle of the city life," I state, going upstairs to my bedroom, then removing my clothes. I'm hoping to take a quick nap before Nelson gets here and digs my guts out. I glance at the clock. It's already quarter to six. "Besides, if I moved out there, you'd have no reason to miss me."

"I'd always miss you, baby. And you being here would give me more reason to spend time with you."

"Awwww," I say, smiling. "I love you."

"I love you, too."

"So, how's life as a detective?" I ask, running water into the tub, then pouring in bath crystals. I can't wait to put on my Conya Doss CD, lie back in the tub and relax.

"It's great. I couldn't have asked for a more rewarding experience. But, I'm looking forward to retiring in two more years. I've been thinking about teaching a criminal justice course at San Diego State."

"And you'd be great at it," I say. "I'm so proud of you."

"I'm proud of you too. You know Cherelle asked about you the other day," he says, causing the hairs on the back of my neck to stand up. I cringe at the sound of his wife's name. "She wanted to know if I had heard from you." *Yeah, I'll bet she did*, I think, rolling my eyes. *Fucking bitch!*

When Terrance and Cherelle first got married, I really thought she was the one for him. And on the surface she was. She appeared really grounded and into my brother, but everything isn't always what it seems. 'Cause that bitch showed me who she really is. And the one thing I learned in life is that when somebody shows you who they are, that is exactly who the fuck they are.

And, last year while I was in San Diego visiting my family, that ho did exactly that. She dragged me out to a male revue down in the Gas Lamp district at one of the many dance spots on the strip. Anyway, I'm not really into watching male dancers, strippers or whatever else you wanna call them. But she is, so whatever floats her boat. So, we're in this club, and she's drinking and drinking and getting looser by the moment; then somehow, she gets pulled up on the stage and allows this dancer to practically fuck her on the floor, and when he lifted her up and acted like he was fucking her standing up, she had the audacity to lick his damn face. I was too damn through! But I kept my cool, 'cause I'm thinking, "Okay, she's simply letting her hair down a bit. No biggie." The whole time something told me to take a damn picture of her ass, but against my better judgment, I didn't.

Finally, around midnight, we leave that spot and go to another place to dance. Well, this trick starts grinding and kissing all over this dude whom she apparently knew. Or maybe she didn't; who knows? The one thing I did know is that he had his hands all over her ass and she was fucking disrespecting my brother behind his back and all up in my face, and I didn't like it one bit. And when it was time to go, the bitch said she was going to ride with dude. I snapped! Drinks or no damn drinks, this went waaaay beyond letting your hair down as far as I was concerned. I snatched her ass and dragged her to the car, and reminded her drunk ass, that she was a fucking married woman.

Long story short, we get back in her car, and she's too drunk to drive so that means I'm doing the driving. Well, lo and behold, this heifer starts feeling on my titties and trying to stick her hands between my legs, almost causing me to swerve off the damn road. I had to actually fight this bitch off of me while trying to keep my eyes on the road and one hand on the steering wheel at the same time. I couldn't believe her ass. This freaky bitch was saying shit like, "Let me eat your pussy… I bet you got some good pussy…You need to let me rock your box…I won't tell if you won't…c'mon, let me taste that sweet pussy…"

Needless to say, I was shocked, appalled and too fucking through. The problem is, I never told my brother about it. And it has been killing me 'cause I know how much he loves her. He's a damn good husband and father. And he worships the ground this nasty trick walks on. But since that incident, I can't stand her ass. And she knows it. Terrance has asked me several times why my attitude towards Cherelle has changed. And I tell him that I'm not feeling her anymore. I want so bad to tell him the real reason, but I don't know how to without hurting him. I love him and my nieces and nephew too much to see any of them get hurt. The last time I was in San Diego, I decided to pull her to the side and confront her. And do you want to know what she had the nerve to tell me?

The bitch told me to stay out of her marriage. Then she had the fucking nerve to ask me if I wanted to be the one responsible for causing problems in her home or breaking up her family. I actually slapped her damn face, which only pissed my brother off because the only thing he saw was me assaulting her. The only saving grace in this whole mess is that I was smart enough to take pictures of her ass all over that dude she was slow-fucking on the dance floor. The problem is, what do I do with them?

I mean, if I break down and tell Terrance and he leaves her, then the kids suffer and he's hurt. But at least he knows the truth. However, if he stays with her and it backfires in my face, then I'll be the one looking like the meddling fool. This shit has been eating away at me. My loyalty is to my brother. But, I'm so fucking confused. Every time I talk to him, my stomach knots. And, at the end of this month, I'll be out there again for another family adventure. I really hate being around her phony ass. Smiling and kissing all over my brother like they're a picture-perfect couple when I know what time it is with her slutty ass. I'm so fucked up over this. I thought about telling my mother, but I don't want to get her all caught up in it.

It's a damn shame that some of these chicks out here are just as lowdown and trifling as some men are (including my sneaky ass sister-in-law, bitch!). And these are the first ones to say/ complain that there are no good men in the world. Hell, I guess not. Dumb-ass bitches like her have fucked 'em all over to the point of no return. They'll go as far as punching holes in condoms to trap a man (now what kind of shit is that?), will fuck his boys, and anyone else she can give her pussy to behind his back. It's sickening.

There are some chicks who have really good men (and I do believe there are some out there, no matter how close they are to extinction). They'll have hard-working men who are committed to their families. They don't run the streets, don't blow their money on bullshit, and don't cheat. They cook, clean, help with the kids, have never raised a hand to their wives, have never lied to them, and will try to do anything to make and keep them happy. Yet, nothing the man ever does is right. His woman will nag and nitpick about every little thing. She's always looking for shit that doesn't exist. Complaining about and accusing him of everything under the fucking sun. Then she got the nerve to want to ration the pussy. Now, tell. What does this mountain coon think is going to eventually happen? Humph.

My advice to these silly, grimy-assed women: How 'bout you learn to shut the fuck up, appreciate what you have before a ho like me comes around, and gives him what a nagging-ass bitch like you won't. Some steady pussy, a good dick suck, and some damn peace of mind.

So when he ends up in some other woman's arms (and, more than likely, between her legs) you'll have no one else but yourself to blame. Granted, a man is going do what he wants regardless, but if you aren't treating him right at home, what the hell you think is going to happen? Duh, he's going to bounce (or creep) on your ditsy ass. So, play your position, and knock off the bullshit. Now, don't say you haven't been warned.

"...I told her I thought you might be kidnapped or something 'cause you would never abandon your big bro, or let weeks go by without calling me. Speaking of which, you *are* still coming out here for Thanksgiving, right?"

"You know, I apologize. I promise to not let so much time go by. And, yes, I plan on being there for Thanksgiving. Unless I get a better offer," I say half-jokingly. Between you and me, I love San Diego. The weather is beautiful and I enjoy the scenery, but outside of that, it is boring; on top of the fact that my father and brothers watch me like a damn hawk. You would think I was still twelve or something. I swear I wish I could get a hotel room whenever I'm out there 'cause being up under my family the whole time, there's no fucking or sucking going on—whatsoever, which is why I only stay a few days at a time, then flee back to the comforts of my own home, and bed, where I can suck, fuck and be merry.

He laughs. "Don't have me send the S.W.A.T team out on you."

I chuckle. "You know I wouldn't let anything keep me from being there. It's the only time we all get a chance to spend time together."

"Good. Now, let me get back to work. I love you."

"I love you too. Give the kids big hugs for me."

"I will. And make sure you call Mom and Dad, too. They miss you."

"I will," I say before hanging up. I lie down for a quick nap before I begin my preparations for Nelson's arrival.

An hour later, I awake, feeling refreshed and ready to get this party started. I take my bath. Then when I'm done, I use scented oil to moisturize my body. I slip into a black-laced teddy. I light the candles and incense that are situated around the bedroom. The music is playing. The stage is set. Now all I need is Nelson's thick tongue lapping my asshole and the back of my pussy, before he slides his dick into me.

I know leaving my front door unlocked and inviting an unknown man into my home is extremely risky hell, it's downright dangerous. The thought of being beaten and raped, robbed or—worse, crosses my mind for a fleeting moment. Yet it has not made any lasting impression on my decision. I enjoy living on the edge. Sometimes fucking in places that I might get caught makes my pussy hot. Like the time I fucked this dude in a park. It was like eleven at night, and I was out on dick patrol when I pulled up alongside his black Volvo. I blew my horn, and immediately knew the minute he rolled his window down that I had found my prey for the night. I gave him a seductive smile, then asked him if he would mind pulling over. He was more than willing to. We talked for about fifteen minutes, exchanging basic information. Finally, I got right down to business and told him what I wanted. I pulled two condoms out of my designer jacket for effect.

At first, he was shocked. Then he declined. But the way I was talking, real freaky and nasty, had turned him on. So he changed his mind, which is what most of 'em do. Twenty minutes later, he was following behind me with a brick hard dick to a nearby park. We stripped down, got butt naked, I pulled my ruler out of my bag, measured his dick, smiled, then rolled the condom on, and mounted his eight-and-a-half inch thickness. I rode his ass bronco style on a blanket under the stars. The thought of being caught had my pussy juice oozing out, dripping down his dick, wetting up his hairy balls. When we finished, he went his way, and I went mine. And yes, I had an ass full of mosquito bites.

Another time, while on a seven day Southern Caribbean cruise, I fucked this dude I had met a few days prior outside on the Lido Deck of the ship. It was like two in the morning. I leaned over the railing, hiked up my skirt, directed him to slide his dick inside of me, then used my pussy muscles to milk his dick until he filled the condom with his man juice. And the whole time I knew there was a white man sitting on a bench a few feet away watching us. Oooh, just knowing the old pervert was there made me want to scream out at the top of my lungs in ecstasy.

Basically, the thrill of the unknown turns me on. I know danger is always lurking in corners, waiting to strike, particularly since there are so many psychos out here in the world. But the excitement of it all is far greater for me than worrying about what may or may not be lying in wait. So I fuck, and I fuck, and I fuck.

But as I wait, and think, and consider, I decide that tonight isn't the time to trust a complete stranger with walking up into my home without being properly supervised. So I will greet my guest at the door, lock it behind him, then escort him upstairs. Then when he's done, I will walk him downstairs, and escort his ass out the door, locking it behind him. The only person I can honestly say I'd trust to walk in and serve me the dick the way I initially requested is Garrett. Don't ask why. I'm not sure if it's because he's a State Trooper, or because I have some strange connection to him that makes me feel safe with him.

Whatever it is—no matter how much I enjoy taking risks, I'm not chancing having this man I only met once come up in here with some of his boys and doing me in. And yes, getting killed…now that has crossed my mind on more than one occasion.

Granted, if I invite a man into my home, it is usually with the sole intent to get at his dick. The only thing I'm interested in at that moment is how well he can work this pussy over. So if he's in my home, he's going to get fucked. And that's the bottom line. But, I know there are some psychos out there, and you can never be too careful. Oh, trust me. I know every time I let a man into my home, I am increasing my chances of being put in harm's way. What can I say? I enjoy gambling and riding a stiff dick at the same time. And knowing me, I will continue dancing along the edges of fate. Yes, I am aware that playing Russian roulette with my life, and men, is a very dangerous game. Well, so is driving or walking through certain towns or cities. At least I control what risks I take. So I'll keep rolling the dick, I mean, dice, and take my chances.

But not tonight. So I am sitting downstairs on my sofa with my right leg draped over its arm, rubbing my clit and playing in my pussy, imagining him coming in and finding me upstairs blindfolded with my ass up in the air waiting for him to stab my hole from the back.

CHAPTER
FIFTEEN

I am so deep into pleasing myself that I don't hear him pull up in my driveway. I am snapped out of my sex-induced trance by the sound of someone trying to open my door. I glance at the Lenox crystal clock on the end table, and smile. It's exactly nine-thirty.

Because I have changed plans on him, he's smart enough to know to ring the doorbell. I get up from the sofa and open the door, quickly placing my index finger up to my lips, then to his, indicating for him to not say a word. He grins, playing along while walking in. I shut the door and lock it, then hand him his mask. It's a simple black mask, and makes him look like a chocolate Zorro when he places it on his face. I stand and watch him strip off his clothes. Mmmm, oh my goodness! Between his legs is the blackest, prettiest dick I've ever seen. It's thick, shiny and almost the color of tar. My mouth waters and I can already feel the dew from my ripe and ready pussy dripping.

I am almost shaking with anticipation. Between you and me, there's nothing like being on your knees with your head down on a pillow, ass up, cheeks spread open, waiting in anticipation. Pussy lips slick with excitement as you feel the warmth of his breath approaching. His tongue glides across your pussy, from the bottom to the top, then darts in and out while rubbing your clit. Mmm. His tongue is hypnotic. Each lap, each stab of his tongue, gets you wetter and hotter than the stroke before. You twist, and thrust your body to meet his lips. Your moans deepen. You feel yourself getting lost in pleasure. And you beg. And beg. And beg…until he feeds your eager, overheated snatch with deep, fast strokes. Mmmm.

I grab Nelson by his fat cock, slowly stroke it, then lead him up the stairs, pulling him by it. I am surprised, and relieved, that he follows instructions, keeps his mouth shut and says nothing.

Once upstairs, I walk over to the bed, climb up in the center of it, then tie a black silk scarf over my eyes. I snap my ass up and outward, arching my back. This is his cue. He already knows my pussy is wet, and what I expect. I wait for him as he rolls his condom over his deep, dark chocolate log. I silently pray he knows how to use it.

I pull open my ass, give him a peek at my glistening lips, and wet hole that awaits him. "Fuck me," I whisper. "Feed my hungry pussy."

"Oh, shit," he says, forgetting the rules. "You a real live freak."

I want to put him out for fucking up my fantasy, but my pussy is eager to devour his cock. I clench my teeth.

"You're not supposed to open your mouth, just beat this pussy up."

"Sorry," he says, grabbing me by the hips. "But, god-damn…you're something else."

Before I can open my mouth to tell him to shut the fuck up, the head of his dick is knocking at the opening of my hole, preparing for entry. I brace myself as he pushes in. I moan. He pushes more in, then pulls it out to the tip, then back in again. I moan again. He does this three more times, teases my pussy and gets it begging for the dick, then plunges every last inch in and serves me the way I want it: fast, deep and furious.

"Uh…oh, yes…fuck this pussy…"

He grunts. "Ah, shit, you throwing that ass up on this dick."

"No talking," I snap over my shoulder. "Only fucking."

"Sorry," he apologizes, slamming in and out of me. "Oh, shit…you got some good pussy. And you keep grabbing this dick with it. Fuck…uh…Damn…"

I suck my teeth, realizing that perhaps expecting him to keep quiet the whole time might have been asking a bit much since my love snatch has been known to bring a man to his knees. "Slap my ass," I demand, winding and pumping my hips. "Instead of all this talking, you should be using your energy to put that dick to me. Is that all you got? I thought you could fuck," I taunt, squeezing his dick with my muscles. He grunts. His sweat drips onto my back. "I can hear you, but my pussy can't feel you. Where's the dick at?" He picks up speed. His hips crash into my ass, causing me to jerk forward. Yeah, he's banging up against my walls, filling me with deep, urgent thrusts. My sweet cat cries out in unadulterated pleasure. "Yeah, there you go…yeah, uh…mmmph…like that…beat that pussy up."

With his dick still in me, and him fucking me doggie-style, I lift up on my knees, then get into the leap frog position, squatting like a frog. Without saying anything, Nelson places his hands up under my thighs for support, and continues slamming his dick in and out of me. I'm bouncing up and down on his dick, matching his thrusts.

"Fuck this pussy…Yeah, uh…let me wet that black dick up. You want me to come all over that dick?"

"Aaah, shit, yeah…oh, fuck…I'm getting ready to bust this nut."

"Yeah, nigga, bust that nut up in this pussy. Give me that hot cream, nigga."

"Aaah…aaah…uh…uh…here it comes…oh, shit…"

His body starts shaking as if he'd going into convulsions. I can feel his already fat dick swelling and twitching inside of me as I clamp down and around it to milk his nut out. I am cumming. He is cumming. We are both panting and grunting. And sweaty. And out of breath.

After Nelson nuts, his dick stays hard and he continues stroking my pussy until I am having another wave of orgasms. I moan. And grind my ass up on his groin. Ten minutes later, he is nutting again. And I am impressed. He continues a slow grind inside of me for several more minutes, then pulls his dick out and removes the condom, tossing it on the bed beside me as he had been instructed on the phone. I feel its wetness against my arm and smile, removing my blindfold. I get up off the bed.

"Thanks for the dick," I say, glancing down at his shiny pole, slick from his juices. The cum-gulping, fuck-suck freak in me wants to drop down low and slurp up his cock cream, but I don't.

"You got a towel, or something I can wipe myself with?" he asks, holding his dick up. His balls hang like two perfectly round chocolate eggs, and my mouth waters for a taste. Before I know it, I am up on him, then down on my knees with his sticky balls in my mouth, sucking them clean. "Oh, shit," he moans. "Damn you a freak…" I grab his dick from out of his hand and stroke it while ball-gargling him. After a few more minutes of sucking his balls, I get up and walk into the bathroom to bring him a wet rag. "Damn, girl, you 'bout to make a nigga keep coming back."

I smile. "That's if I keep inviting you back," I state. "You can't seem to follow instructions so I don't know if you deserve a second round of this grade-A pussy."

He laughs, wiping his dick. "Oh, word. You funny as hell. How you expect me to be up in that pussy and its feeling good and not say shit? That's crazy."

"Well, if you want there to be a next time, then I

suggest you try a little harder," I say, taking the rag from him and tossing it into the sink. I glance at the digital clock. It's already going on eleven o'clock. "Well, I've enjoyed your company, but it's time to go, big daddy."

"I can dig it," he states, following me down the stairs. I hand him his clothes. "Damn, you don't waste no time putting a nigga out, huh?"

Let me make something perfectly clear before I put Nelson out. If I'm on the phone talking all dirty 'n shit to a man about how I want to get at his dick, and then I invite him over, trust me, it ain't for coffee and conversation. So, if he's sitting down, it better be to remove his damn shoes and socks. And if he is trying to hold a conversation, it better be about how good he's going to ram his dick in me, and fuck the life out of me. Or else, within ten minutes of entering my home, I expect to hear his belt unclicking, his zipper unzipping, and his pants dropping around his damn ankles. And if he doesn't wear underwear, cool. But if he does, then I'm expecting to see his dick hanging out of the slit of his boxers and him stroking it with his hand. Otherwise, I'm looking at the clock, and showing his ass to the door. See ya!

Hell, if he's looking for a chat 'n chew somewhere, then he should take his ass down to the nearest Borders Café. And that's the same way I feel about a man who wants to sit around to get better acquainted after I've finished waxing his dick. No-strings sex means exactly what it is, sex without any damn attachments. So, don't expect nothing, don't look for nothing—'cause you ain't getting nothing.

Oh, and another thing when it comes to no-strings sex, there really is no need for extended phone calls or endless emails unless we're talking about fucking. I'm not interested in a bunch of idle conversation, or heavy breathing in my ear unless we're having phone sex. Other than that, don't call me to talk. Trust me. We have nothing to talk about. Period! So, no boo, you can't get to know me outside of the bedroom. But what you can know is if I fuck you again, riding your cock will always be on my terms. So, again, we have absolutely nothing—and I do mean *nothing*—to discuss.

I tilt my head. Then it dawns on me that he hasn't been given the memo, so I decide to enlighten him. "I didn't invite you here for a social call. This was strictly about the dick—nothing more, nothing less. Everything that needed to be said has been said in the bedroom. So, there's nothing else we need to talk about."

"Damn, that's cold. But I gotta respect it. So, can a nigga at least get a number to get at you so we can at least stay in touch?"

"Nope," I say, smiling. "If and *when* I wanna ride that dick again, I'll call you. And if you can follow instructions, then—and only then—will you get the digits. Until then, you enjoy the rest of your night." I open the door and wait for him to leave.

He laughs. "You a real raw chick, but I dig your style."

"You got a chick?" I ask, taking in the veins that run along his magnificent biceps.

"Nah, baby," he says, stepping into his crisp white Air Force Ones. "I'm riding solo at the moment."

"Then that's even better," I state, walking over to him all slow 'n sexy-like. I pull him into me, then grab him by the back of the neck and place my lips flush to his ear. "I can slow fuck you all night, and not have to worry about sending you home too drained to fuck wifey." I lick his earlobe, pressing my still wet pussy up against his thigh. "Squeeze my ass." His hands slide down my back, rest on my ass, then squeeze a chunk of my ass.

"Yo, you getting my dick hard again; you know that, right?"

I pull away from him. "Have a good night," I say.

"So," he says, licking his lips, "what happens if I happen to be in the neighborhood and stop by?"

"You don't get in unless I invite you, so I wouldn't waste time and gas making the trip if I were you."

He smiles, shaking his head. "Your way or the highway, is that right?"

"Absolutely."

"You have a good night, beautiful," he says, finally walking out the door. I stand in the doorway and watch him get into his silver Grand Cherokee Jeep. Once he backs out the driveway, I close the door and lock it.

I saunter into the kitchen, famished. I heat up some leftover chicken lo mein, then sit at the table, wondering how many men and women actually know the difference between sensuality and sexuality. How many people do you think confuse the two? Does knowing the difference make them better lovers? Does not knowing make them terrible lovers? I ask these questions in my head as I eat.

Hmmm…I wonder. I know I appreciate and understand my own sexuality. I have learned to satisfy it without fear or guilt. And, tonight, I have finished indulging my carnal desires, and I will go to bed with my pussy well-fucked inside out. A smile forms across my face as I reflect on my night with Nelson, and all the others before him—and all the ones that will be after him.

The thought of placing an imaginary ad for sex takes up space in my head. It reads:

> *This is for all of the unknown men I'm going to eventually fuck: How big is your dick, daddy? Is it cut and thick? Do you have big balls? Mmmm…I love being on my knees sucking thick, black dick and big hairy balls filled with sweet, thick cream. So tell me. Are you up for a pair of soft, full lips wrapped around your dick and a warm tongue lapping at your balls? Are you ready for a hot, juicy pussy locked around your cock? If the answer is YES, then you might want to come see me this morning. I'm sucking and fucking 'til noon. Signed, sealed & ready for delivery!*
>
> *Fuckfully yours,*
> *The Man Handler!*

The idea alone has me laughing out loud, hysterically. I shut off all the lights, and make my way upstairs with thoughts of all the endless possibilities of living, loving and learning all there is about life—exploring my sexual desires and expanding my freaky pleasures.

CHAPTER
SIXTEEN

Again, I awake sweating, panting and wetter than the Nile. I've had another dream. And this time, the strangest thing happens. A man old enough to be my father comes to me, pulls me into his embrace, kisses my lips, then slides his tongue into my mouth. He strokes my titties gently, kneading and kissing and licking and pulling on them as if he is trying to milk each one. Instantly, my pussy quivers and juices. His hand slides up my silk nightgown, and he lightly brushes his fingers along the slit of my wet pussy. He slips one, then two, of his big fingers inside of me. Finger-fucks me until my pussy bubbles and boils over. Oh my GAWD! I need him, want him. I reach for his crotch. Grab and stroke him. Feel his cock swell and lengthen between the fabric of his pants and underwear. He grabs and palms my ass, gently pulling open my cheeks. Mmmm.

The whole time in my dream, his face is a blur, but everything else about him is vivid and clear. I tug at his belt, unzipping him. I dig my hand down into his boxers, then pull his big dick out, and cup his heavy balls. I don't have a ruler, but my mental ruler stamps his cock in at nine inches. It is thick, with big veins running along the top and on the right side of it. I drop to my knees, take him in my mouth, and suck him until my pussy screams and throbs and begs to be fucked.

He tells me to get up and to lie back on the bed so he can pound my snatch with his cock. "Ooooh," I moan, doing as I am told. I am turned on by his authority. He is demanding and forceful, and it causes blood to rush to the tip of my clit. He pushes his dick inside of me, plunges deep into my honey well and fills me with excruciating pleasure. My pussy muscles wrap around his dick and grip him with each thrust. He moans. I moan. We moan together. Groan together. And, then we cum together.

When we finish, I lean back on my elbows, thighs wide apart, and pull open my wet, sticky pussy so that he can see the pinkness of my well-fucked hole.

"I love how your curly hair is plastered down and stuck together over and around them thick pussy lips."

Droplets of his thick, creamy nut oozes out of my tight hole, and my faceless daddy buries his face between my legs and licks the center of my pussy, sucking on my clit, shoveling his long tongue deep into me and slurping up his nut. I almost faint. This old thick dick, mack daddy eats his cum out of me! Oh, it turns me the fuck on, and I cum again and again, and again!

Damn him! Damn this dream! I want me a cum-eating, freaky assed man with a big, old-seasoned cock to fuck me, then eat his nut out of me, just like dude does in my dream. Oh, I'm so fucking horny! I'm going to close my eyes again, and hope I can summon him up in another dream. So…here's to good dick and sweet cum!

My pussy is wet, and I am tossing and turning in bed with two fingers pressed on my clit in an attempt to bust a nut. You would think that having been fucked by Nelson earlier in the evening would have been enough. Well, it's not. The problem is, my dream has me so worked up, that I need more. And these fingers are not going to cut it, nor will a damn dildo. I need to be fucked with a dick attached to a man. I want to feel a dick up in my guts. No chit chat. Just straight up rough, sweaty fucking. I mean. I want a man with his dick hanging out of his boxers (and a pair of Timbs strapped on his feet) to walk up in here bare chested, throw me down on the bed, beat this pussy up, fuck me cross-eyed, then walk the hell out. Is there anything wrong with that? Hell, no…not a damn thing!

I glance at the digital clock glowing on the nightstand. It reads: 1:27 a.m. *Who can I call this time of night?* I think, flicking on the crystal lamp.

I flip through my mental Rolodex, getting out of bed to retrieve my cell so I can scroll down the fifty or so names to see who—being single, that is—might be able to come through to scratch this itch. I start going through the alphabet. Aaron, nope; Andrew, nope; Anthony, nope; Brent, nope; Bronson, hell no, not with that lazy dick!

I delete his number. Charles, nope; Curtis, nope; David, nope…I continue scrolling. Frankie, nope; Fred, hell fucking no! He cums too quick! I delete his number. Gary, nope; Gerald, nope; Greg, nope…I sigh, getting frustrated. Harold, hell no! Henry, nope…I purse my lips, continuing my manhunt for good dick. All of sudden, Wade pops into my head, causing me to smile. I haven't invited him over for any pussy in over three weeks, and I purposefully haven't been taking his calls. Sometimes you got to keep a man guessing, keep him wondering. And that's what I do. I never make myself too available too much of the time. But, I have to say, Wade is always good for those last minute, emergency tune-ups. I scroll down to his name, then press dial.

"Hello," he answers after the fourth ring.

"Hello, Wade?"

"Yeah, what's good, baby?" he says in his deep, sexy voice. "I was wondering when I was gonna hear from you. I thought you ditched a brotha or something."

Between you and me, I really hate the idea of dismissing Wade from dick duty, but his three month cycle is almost up. And, as with so many good things, everything must one day come to an end.

"No," I say, lightly pinching and pulling my nipples. "You haven't been ditched, yet."

"Oh," he chuckles, "not yet. Gee, thanks…I guess."

I decide to fuck with him, brushing off his remark, "Wade, don't play, big daddy. You already know why I'm calling."

"Oh, what? You miss this big dick?"

I smile, moaning. "Mmmm…yesssss, Daddy. My pussy is nice and tight. And sooooo wet. I'm rubbing my clit wishing it was your long, thick tongue stroking it. This fat, hot pussy misses you, baby. It's yours to do whatever you want to with it."

"I'll be right over," he says, hanging up. I smile, jumping out of bed and racing to the shower to freshen up before he gets here to rock my insides out.

Fifteen minutes later, he is ringing my bell, looking sexy as hell with a big grin on his face, and a brick hard dick. I answer the door topless, wearing a leopard print loincloth, and matching spool-heeled mules. The minute he walks through the door, he scoops me up in his arms, showers me with deep, passionate kisses, and shows me how badly he wants me, if only for the night.

As soon as I get him upstairs, I turn on the stereo, and press play for the CD player. Mario's "Music for Love" blares through the speakers as I begin to light the candles around the room. I can feel Wade's eyes on me, taking in the sway of my hips as I move about the bedroom to the beat of the music. I pretend not to notice his burning gaze as I lay across my king-sized bed, spread open my legs and massage my pussy.

"Strip for me," I say, pulling open my excited pussy lips, revealing the pink, creamy center that awaits his thrust. He smiles, then licks his lips as I watch him slowly get undressed. He keeps his eye on my opened pussy, removing one piece of clothing at a time, winding his body in sync with the music. Winking his eye at me, licking his lips, and grabbing at his crotch. He is teasing me, and he knows it. But I am teasing him as well. And we are both enjoying it.

By the time he gets over to the bed, I am lying in a puddle of boiling pussy juice. He licks and kisses between my thighs, then sticks his bald head (it's as smooth as a baby's bottom) in between my legs, and rubs the top of his head all up in my pussy, pressing on my clit, massaging my slippery slit. I never knew having someone's head on my pussy could feel so damn good. After about five minutes, he replaces his head with his tongue, dipping in and out of me. Flicking and blowing on my clit, lapping the juices that seep from my overheated lips.

Finally, I have enough of this tongue dance with my clit. I want the dick. He makes me beg for it. And, trust. I ain't too proud to beg. I whine and plead for him to give me that fat dick until he sticks the head of it in, going in and out at first, then plunging all the way in. Slowly pulling back out, then slamming it back in. He does this for almost five minutes. Then he long strokes me. Short strokes me. Reaches up under me, palms and squeezes my ass while sucking on my titties. The nigga is killing me softly with a nice, slow fuck.

He dicks me down for seventy-three minutes and twenty-six seconds (I know because I timed it) before he finally fills the Durex with a hot, thick nut. I am still lying on my back with my legs spread apart, rubbing the space that has entertained Wade's dick. I can still feel him inside of me, and I want more.

"I want some more of that dick," I tell him.

He grins, shaking it from side-to-side. He pulls off his condom and it looks like the skin of a long, thick Italian sausage that has been stretched, and is overflowing with its juices. His dick is slick from marinating in his own cream. The cum-slut in me wants to crawl to him, take his cock in my mouth and slurp down his wet dick. I fight the urge, watching him as he walks into the bathroom, tosses the condom in the trash, then returns with another condom in his hand. I watch as he tears it open, then rolls it onto his slick dick. I pull my legs up to my chest, preparing for him to return to bed and enter me all over again.

"Mmmm," I moan as he climbs into bed, then gets between my legs. He grabs me by the hips and pulls me up, sliding his dick back in. "Oh, yes, Wade...fuck this pussy, baby...make my pussy cream all over your fat cock..."

He strokes me deep and purposefully, then quickens his thrusts. I moan, grabbing his ass. "Let me get on my stomach," I say, panting. I want to get fucked from the back. Want him to straddle my hips and ride up on top of this fat ass. He pulls his dick out, waits for me to turn over and pull open my ass cheeks, then slams his steel-hard cock back in. "Uh...oh, yes..."

A few minutes later, he pulls out again, and we are changing positions. I get on my stomach, open my legs spread eagle. He gets on top of me with his legs between mine; then he slides his dick deep into my quivering pussy, soaked in excitement. Once we get into a real nice groove, I suck on his fingers while he pumps in and out of me. I gyrate my hips, move my pelvis back and forth, around and around, matching his thrusts. Then I close my legs so he can place his legs over mine to dig in deep. Mmmm. Hitting my G-spot exactly the way I like it.

"Oh, yes…Oh, yes…" I moan in delight.

"Yeah, baby," he moans in my ear, "it's 'bout time you called me to get up in this pussy again. I missed fucking this wet pussy." He slams in and out of me, knocking my love basket upside down, then tossing it around. Oooh his dick feels like a heavy log being tossed up on my fire.

A moan catches in the back of my throat. I push it out, and it sounds like a growl. "Aaaaaah, yes…then fuck this pussy like you mean it."

"Aaaah shit, baby…I'm getting ready to bust this nut."

He lifts up and I thrust my hips upward to greet his cock.

"Give me that nut, daddy…give me that nut…mmmm… nut in this pussy."

"Uh," he grunts. And just before he is about to nut, this mofo breaks the #1 cardinal rule. He fucking says,

"I love you, baby." That's what the fuck he says. *HE LOVES ME!!* I scream in my head. Can you believe this shit?! This dries my pussy right on up, and jacks up my mood. It feels like someone has dumped a truck load of sand inside of me, that's how dry my ocean of lust has become. Damn him! I knew I should have weaned him off this clit sooner. But noooooooooo! I have to be greedy and hold onto him. Now, there's really no other recourse. This nigga has to go!

I blink, blink again, hoping my ears are playing tricks on me. I wasn't planning to give up his ever-ready cock, yet, but I will…and I am if it isn't some Freudian slip or some shit. "What did you just say to me?" I ask, twisting myself from up underneath him, and rolling him off of me. He collapses on the bed beside me, trying to catch his breath. I shoot him a look, then glance at his still hard dick. He pulls off the condom, then strokes it. Now under different circumstances I would have a mouthful of his balls as he jerked off, but…

"I said I love you," he repeats. He stops jerking his "fucking" stick, and looks at me. "I didn't mean anything by it. The pussy was feeling so good that it slipped out."

I sit up in the bed. "So you didn't mean love as in you *love* me, but as in you *love* this pussy, right?" I ask, giving him an opportunity to redeem himself since I know that while in the throes of sweaty, toe-curling passion we all are known to say shit we don't really mean.

"Yeah, as in I love how my dick feels in your pussy," he says, unconvincingly, getting out of the bed. He shoots me a look. "But, what if I did *love* you?"

I take a deep breath. "Then I'd tell you you're a damn fool."

"And why would I have to be a fool to love you?"

I tilt my head, stare him in his beautiful face. There's an innocence in his brown eyes that I find endearing. I scan his perfectly chiseled chest that sweeps down into a narrow waist, then flows around rippling, washboard abs. I take in his muscular thighs that part to accommodate a beautifully thick, chocolate dick and two mouthwatering balls. If I could only wrap him and Garrett and Maurice up into one man, then I think I would have the perfect man. But, since I can't, there's no need to settle on one man, especially on one I know I will never—can never—give my heart to.

Now in the back of my mind, I'm thinking I should fuck him real good one more time, drop down on my knees suck him off, then give him his pink slip, but…I keep my gaze on his cock for few seconds longer, then look him in the eyes.

"Because," I finally say, getting up from the bed. I walk up to him and touch the side of his smooth face, "I'm not capable of loving you back."

He stares at me. "Incapable or unwilling to?" he asks, removing my hand from his face. He holds it in his, then kisses my palm. I can feel him searching for something I am unwilling to help him find.

I pull away. "Both. And after tonight, I think it is best we end this situation we got going on."

He frowns, repeats what I've said. "Why's that?"

I slip on my robe. "Because the arrangement was we fuck, we suck, but we don't catch feelings. And you've reneged on the agreement."

"Oh, okay," he says, slipping on his jeans, "so I'm good enough to come through to climb up on your back, but not good enough to love, is that what you're saying? As long as I fuck you on demand it's all good, right? But feeling some kind of way about you, or for you, means this situation is over because you say so, right?"

"Basically," I say, brushing my hair, then pulling it back into a ponytail. My pussy still aches for another round of dick. I glance at the clock. It is already four-thirty in the morning. In a matter of hours, the sun will be rising, and I will have to be getting ready for work. I fake a yawn. "Listen, it's late, I need for you to hurry up and go."

He hurriedly pulls his white tee over his head, then puts on his pinstriped button-up. "Yeah, you right. I gotta get outta here," he says, snatching up his Timbs. "You on some real bullshit at the moment. You act like there's something wrong with a muhfucka diggin' you. But it's all gravy. Do you, ma." I can hear the hurt in his voice.

He walks out the room and heads downstairs. I follow behind.

I stare at him. He looks let down, but what can he

say, or do. Not a damn thing. "Listen," I offer, "I've had a great time with you, but this journey was bound to run its course anyway. It's best that we end it sooner, rather than later."

He turns and shoots me a look, sucking his teeth. "*We* aren't doing anything. *You* are. But like I said, it's all good. No biggie. You right, it was good while it lasted. So, I guess I should thank you for wetting my dick."

"That's not really necessary. Like I said, I enjoyed the time we've spent together."

"Yeah, as long as I don't use words like *love* around you. And you know what's really got me bugging? I almost feel used."

"*Used?*" I repeat, frowning. "Wade, let's not exaggerate here. I would hardly say you were being used. We both benefited from this. I wanted to fuck, and so did you. It was something we *both* mutually agreed on. So, please, don't go there."

"Yeah, but that's not all I want…I mean, wanted from you. I told you I was digging you. I wanted to get to know you. Go out. Do some shit other than fuck all the time."

"Well, that's all I wanted from you—to fuck. And I told you from the door those extras were things that weren't available to you, which is why I stressed 'no-strings-attached,' because I do not want to be attached to anyone. Not right now, anyway."

"Then when? When you get tired of having different

muhfuckas run up in you," he says, shocking me. "Yeah, I know you like getting your fuck on. But, c'mon, at some point you need to stop playing yourself, and let love in so it can do what it do."

I tilt my head, placing my hand on my hip. "And what would that be, huh, Wade?"

He walks up on me, pulls me into him, then kisses me forcibly. I feel myself getting caught up in his storm, and being pulled into its winds. He pulls away before I get swept away. "Love you," he says, gazing at me. I knew then he really had feelings for me. Humph. I almost feel sorry for him, standing here looking all pitiful and whatnot. Poor thing. But he knew the rules. Now, I'll admit. Good dick is my weakness. But, it's something I'll never be a fool over. And my mind is made up. There will (can) be no more fucking between us. *Damn him!*

"That's not what I'm looking for."

"Well, that's too bad," he says, walking towards the door. He looks at me over his shoulder. "'Cause I am."

"Then you were looking in the wrong place, and definitely in the wrong face."

He grimaces as if I've said something hurtful. As if I've tossed a bucket of hot shit in his face. He gives me a painful stare, then says, "I guess I was." And with that said, boyfriend walks out the door, and closes it behind him. *Easy cum, easy go*, I think, walking over to lock my door. Two down, and one more to go.

CHAPTER
SEVENTEEN

L et me share a little something with you. See. I believe there are women who spend their lives wishing and praying for a knight in sparkling, shining armor—or a handsome prince charming galloping up on a white horse to sweep them off their feet. And, interestingly, I believe that many of these women are actually fortunate enough to snag such a catch. However, there are also, I believe, women who sit home night after night, alone and lonely, praying and crying for someone—*anyone*—to rescue them from their miserable situations. Even some of them are lucky enough to meet their saviors. Then there are women who, sadly, even after finding whom they believed to be their perfect "fairytale" man, they find themselves still sitting around wishing and wondering and praying and crying, hoping for shit that will never come true. So they go through life turning a blind eye to the naked truths that the men they have given their hearts to have fucked them over. Humph!

Then there are women who aimlessly sit at the feet of their men, who come to them by command and not by choice, forced to be slaves to the men's egotistical, self-centered, selfish whims; to be prisoners of lies and mind games. Many of these women are aware of this, and yet they stay, making excuses and justifying their men's actions. There are still others who are stuck in deep-rooted denial, blinded by the illusion of love, and will willingly ignore and/or pretend, making choices that keep allowing their men to violate and disrespect them. And that's their business. But, make no mistake, it'll be a cold day in hell before *I* ever allow myself to be lured into believing that I have to idly sit, and take whatever bullshit a man feels compelled to dish out. I'm sorry, boo-boo, I know women have their reasons for why they do what they do—even if it appears out of desperation, but I cannot sympathize with any of 'em. And I damn sure can't wrap my mind around why they'd compromise themselves or allow themselves to be victimized. Fuck that! I will never allow myself to stay in a fucked-up, miserable situation with a man, hurting, just for the sake of saying he's mine.

Trust and believe. I'd rather keep rotating dick and have peace of mind, than have a piece of a man and have to put up with a bunch of his bullshit and be stressed the fuck out, losing mad weight with my hair falling out and bags under my eyes. No, no, no…not gonna happen, trust! 'Cause at the end of the day, when it's all said and done, with all of his cheating and lying and manipulating, is the motherfucker really yours? Better yet, is he *really* worth all the damn trouble? And if you're going to answer, let's be perfectly real about the shit. Unfortunately, most of you know like I do that many of you won't be able to keep it funky with the truth because your dumb asses are so damn stuck in denial, and blinded by your own emotional neediness. But I'm not one to gossip.

Anyway, when I bring a man into my bed, at least I already know who the hell I'm sleeping with. And, most times, it's somebody else's man. Someone I would never consider keeping in my life. And I accept it for what it is: a stiff dick and a wet tongue to be used at *my* discretion. So, the question is, do you really know who's in your bed? Now, you don't have to answer that with me, but it's definitely something to think about.

My cell phone rings, interrupting my thoughts. I walk over to the dining room table to get it. Now, I don't know about you, but I don't usually answer calls that come up on my caller ID as blocked, restricted or private, and I'm not exactly sure what compels me to start today, but I do. I press the green phone button and accept the call, walking back over to the sofa. I plop down.

"Hello," I answer.

"Bitch, how long you been sucking my man's dick?"

"Excuse you? Who's this?"

"Your worst fucking nightmare," the voice on the other end snaps. "And trust me. When I find out who the fuck you are, I'm gonna beat your slutty ass, bitch!"

See. This is the only downfall about fucking another woman's man. You have to expect shit like this to happen from time to time. Some dick whipped bitch, talking out the side of her neck about what she's going to do to me when she catches me. Sometimes I entertain the calls; other times, I hang up. But, today's this chick's lucky day. I feel like playing. What cracks me the hell up is that some of these women really think they done snatched up the door prize. The shit is hilarious to me, and, at times, down- right sad.

I shake my head, and say, "Is that a promise or a threat?"

"Both, bitch!" she snarls.

I laugh, which only incites this crazed woman more.

"Bitch, what the fuck is so funny, hunh? Let's see how funny you think shit is when I got you picking up your damn dick-sucking jaws, you trifling bitch!"

"My, my, my…aren't we mighty hostile," I say, taunting her.

"Hostile my ass!" she snaps. "Answer the question, bitch. How long you been fucking my man?"

I sigh, shaking my head. I clear my throat. "Um, 'scuse me, boo, but would you be so kind as to tell me what man has you so stressed out, calling my home making ridiculous threats, and accusing me of fucking him?"

"Don't fucking worry about all that," she snaps. "Just stay the fuck away from *my* man. He's mine, so go out and find yourself your own, and leave mine the *FUCK* alone, bitch!"

I laugh again, sitting back on the sofa. "Oh, trust, sweetie, the last thing I'm worried about is a man, especially yours. And maybe you should learn how not to as well."

"It's bitches like you," she huffs, "that make it easy for men to cheat."

"Wrong answer, sweetie," I say, crossing my legs. "It's bitches like *you* that make it easy for men to cheat by constantly taking their cheating-asses back, denying that shit in your relationships ain't right, and for always blaming everyone else but the men you dumb-ass bitches keep letting fuck you over. So, don't call me with your bullshit, bitch. I'm not your problem. Your mother-fucking man is."

"You fucking, slutty-ass ho, who the fuck do you think you talking to?"

In my mind's eye, I can see this bitch foaming at the mouth like a pit bull. I must have really struck a nerve.

"You, you dizzy bitch," I snap, getting bored with this little phone game I'm playing with this chick. Although I'm really not mad at her, I'll be damned if I'm going to let a bitch call me talking shit and I don't check her ass. I don't give a fuck if she does think I'm fucking her man. If she wanted to confront me about him, she should have come at me some other way. All this extra shit is uncalled for. And now that I'm thinking about it, I should hang up on her retarded ass. But, I won't. "You called me with your fucking sob story," I continue. "So obviously I'm talking to your dumb ass. Now, what is it you want from me again?"

"I want you to stay away from my man," she states.

It almost sounds like the bitch is begging. "If he calls you, hang up. If he comes by, don't let him in."

"Oh, okay. And how is it you know that it's me he's fucking?"

"'Cause I know."

I roll my eyes. "Bitch, you don't know shit. You think you know; that's what the fuck it is. So, let me tell you what I think. I think he has a slew of numbers in his phone and has probably cheated on you more times than you can keep count, and you keep taking his ass back. And now, once again, you think he's creeping on your ass. I bet your miserable ass went through his phone, checking his messages and calling up and confronting chicks, to catch him out. But, I wasn't one of the bitches who left him a message. You just happened to stumble upon my number in his address book, so your jealous ass thought you would reach out and touch. Bitch, please!"

Silence.

I continue, "So, let me ask. How many chicks confirmed they were fucking him?"

"Bitch, what the fuck you all worried about that for? How many times *you* fuck him?"

"Sweetie, you're delusional if you think I'm worried about who your so-called man sticks his dick in. The fact of the matter is you're the one stressing about it. You're the one calling up chicks, practically begging—"

"I ain't begging no bitch about shit," she snaps, cutting me off. "I'm warning them, including you."

I give her an exaggerated laugh. "Whew, you one funny chick," I say. "But, girlfriend, don't get it twisted. You're not warning *me* about shit. You can ask me, and if I choose to respect your relationship, then I will. But, make no mistake. You're definitely not going to make me do nothing with threats. 'Cause at the end of the day, you stupid bitch, I'm gonna fuck who the hell I want, including your man—if I so choose to. I don't love him, and I damn sure don't admire him. I'm fucking him. I don't want him, sweetie. You do. So, you can make all the threats you want. He's your headache, not mine. And that's exactly how I like to keep it."

Silence again.

For a moment, I think I hear sniffling, but I can't be sure with the noise in the background. *Why the fuck am I even entertaining this nutty-bitch?* I think, shaking my head. *Who's crazier? Her for being so damn stupid, or me for sitting here, listening to her dumb ass? And I still don't know who the fuck she's accusing me of fucking!*

"So, who is it again, you think I'm fucking?" I decide to ask, becoming increasingly disgusted with this shit.

"Seth, bitch," she finally says. "Don't play stupid. You knew who the fuck I was calling about."

Seth, I think, sifting through my mental Rolodex. In my head I scream, "Bitch do you know how many men I have fucked and sucked, and you expect me to remember a motherfucking *Seth?!*"

It takes me a minute to remember who the hell she's

talking about. But then it comes to me. Six-feet, three inches, one-hundred-and ninety-eight pounds of thick, seven-inch, dark-chocolate dick, complete with big, smooth balls filled with thick, white cream. Yes, Seth. I met him almost two years ago. Fucked him four times, then sent him on his merry way. *What the fuck is he still doing with my number in his phone? Dumb ass!*

"Are you fucking serious?" I snap. "You mean to tell me, you're calling my motherfucking house about some dick I fucked over a year ago. You stupid bitch! You could have saved yourself the dime."

"Who the fuck you calling stupid, ho?"

"You," I say, "calling me with this bullshit. If you were calling me about some current dick, then your ass might have had a legitimate reason to be calling here. But to be calling me about some shit that's old news. Bitch, get a life!"

I hang up.

The bitch calls back. And I only pick up to fuck with her one last time.

"Yes, dumb-ass," I say.

"You know what?!" she yells at the top of her lungs. "I don't give a *fuck* if it is old news. The fact that you *fucked* him is still news to me. And trust me. I'm going to beat the shit out of your cum-sucking ass if I ever catch you!"

I let her scream on and on and on about what she's going to do to me. "You don't know who the fuck I am...I'm gonna smash your windows out...I'ma slash your motherfucking tires..." Blah, blah, blah. The true signs of a dick-crazy bitch.

Humph. I really feel sorry for pathetic women like her. Constantly fighting over some man. Poor thing! I wonder how many other women she's had to call and threaten, and beg for them to leave her precious man alone; the one who she lives and breathes and shits for. For some reason, that female group MoKenStef's "He's Mine" starts playing in my head. I start humming. *He's mine...you may of had him once, but I got him all the time...*

"Bitch," she continues, "do you hear me talking to you? What the fuck you humming for?"

"I'm humming 'cause he may be yours, but I've had him, and more than once. And I bet when he's with your nutty ass, he's somewhere still thinking about me, which is probably why he kept my number in his phone. While he's fucking you, I'll bet it's me he still craves, remembering how this tight, wet pussy wrapped around his dick, how he loved eating out my sweet ass, and smearing my pussy juice all over his cheating-ass face before coming home to your dizzy ass. But, make no mistake. I'm not the other woman, and I'm damn sure not trying to fuck him into loving me enough to leave you, or break up your happy little home. Good night, sweetie."

I hang up, singing, *"Never fall in loooooove with a man who don't love you..."* *Stupid bitch*, I think.

My phone rings again. I glance at the caller ID. This time, I let it go into voicemail. When it beeps, I know the miserable bitch has left me a message. Ten minutes later, I receive a text message:

What's good? Listen. My girl is spazin' the fuck out. She's been going through my phone calling up chicks like crazy. Shit's real hectic right now. If she hits you up with the BS, tell her she got the wrong number.

Too late, I text back. *You need to put a muzzle and a leash on her ass.*

I hope you didn't tell her no crazy shit.

I stare at the screen before responding back, shaking my head. This dumb fuck can't possibly think I would cover for his ass. *Yeah, I did.*

Damn! He replies back. *Now she's gonna be tryna put my ass out.*

Oh, well. That's what the fuck you get for having my number in your damn phone. Why the fuck do you still have my number in your phone anyway? It's not like I plan on giving you any more of this good pussy. I hope she fucks you up for being so damn stupid, nigga!

Three minutes go by, no response back; ten minutes pass, still no response. *She's probably fucking him up,* I think as I go upstairs to my bedroom. *I hope her dumb ass cuts her losses and figures out how to move on with her life.* I walk into the master bathroom, turn the water on, then pour in bath crystals. I strip off my clothes, and when the water has filled the tub, I step in, then slowly lower my body down into the steamy bubbles. *Ian really did a number on my ass*, I think, leaning my head back and closing my eyes, clenching my asshole muscles. *Oh my God, my hole is still burning*.

I hear the sound of my cell ringing. But I think I am dreaming. It is not until it starts ringing again that I realize that I have fallen asleep in the tub. I open my eyes, looking around my marble bathroom before jumping out of the water that has now turned cold.

My nipples harden from the assault of cool air that whips around them. I wrap my wet body in a plush white towel, then quickly step out of the tub, tracking the floor with water into my bedroom. I glance at the clock. It's eleven-fifteen.

I pick up my cell off the nightstand, noticing I have six missed calls, and three voice messages. *Damn, I was really knocked out*, I think as I listen to them. One is from Ian; the second one is from Jamil; and, the third is from Mitchell—all three wanting some pussy.

I roll my eyes, shaking my head. When I am prompted to save or delete, I erase them. I'm not interested in fucking any of them—not tonight anyway. I go back into my bathroom, grab my Vaseline cocoa butter body oil, pour some into my hand, oil my body up, then slip into a white silk teddy. I shut off all the lights and climb my silky-smooth body into my bed, drifting off to sleep.

The morning comes—fast. It's five a.m. And I awake feeling surprisingly refreshed, and horny; ready to serve my pussy up on a platter to someone looking for a breakfast treat without wanting me to wet his dick, unless I absolutely have to. Otherwise, I only want to lay back, spread open my legs and watch a nigga feast on my cunt juice.

A smile forms on my face as I flip open my cell and press the speed dial for Nelson's number. Oh, so what. I know it's early, but oh well. The nigga said he was riding solo so there shouldn't be any problem. He picks up on the fifth ring.

"Yo, speak," he snaps into the phone, sounding groggy. "Who's this?"

"It's Janaye," I say in a sweet, seductive voice.

"Oh, hey," he says, softening his tone. "What's good? I was hoping I would hear from you since a nigga can't get at you."

"Well, today is your lucky day, big daddy."

"Oh, word?"

"Mmm-hmmm," I purr into the phone. "My pussy wants to feel your tongue in it."

"Oh, yeah? Is that all your pussy wants?"

"For now," I say, slipping my hand between my legs, then squeezing my thighs shut. I move my hips in a nice, slow grind. "Come through and eat my sweet pussy for me."

"And what you gonna do for this stiff dick in my

hand if I come through there?" he asks, sounding wide awake now.

"Well, I'm not looking to fuck" I tell him, not wanting to get his hopes up. "I only wanna feel those soft, juicy, pussy-eating lips all over my clit and that long, thick tongue deep in my pussy."

"Nah, baby. If you ain't tryna fuck, then you gonna have to suck on this dick or something 'cause I'ma wanna bust this big nut."

Damn him, I think, pursing my lips. *Who the fuck is he to tell me what I'm gonna have to do in order to get my pussy sucked?*

"Wrong answer, boo. I suck dick only when I'm in the mood to stretch my neck. And today ain't the day. This morning I want my pussy ate; that's it."

"C'mon, ma," he whines. "You gonna have all that fat pussy up in my face, and I'm gonna be eatin' the hell out of it…" He sighs. "Yo, you killin' me, baby. I have no problem with helping you get that nut, but I wanna get mine, too."

Humph. I roll my eyes. Take a deep breath. Consider hanging up on him. But, I compromise instead. "I tell you what," I offer. "Come over, let me straddle your face, and I'll wet that dick up nice, and slow for you." *With a nice hand job*, after *I plant my nut on your tongue.*

"Yeah, baby. Now you talking," he says, sounding all excited and whatnot. "What time you want me to come through?"

I glance at the clock. 5:37 a.m. I have to be at work by nine today, nine-thirty the latest. "How fast can you get here?"

"Give me like an hour."

"An hour?" *Nigga, please*, I think. "Oh, no, big boy… no can do. I want to feed this pussy to you *now*. Not in an hour. I want you here with your face in between my legs and your tongue lapping my clit in less than thirty minutes. And if you eat this pussy right, I might change my mind and let you fuck it."

"Oh, word?" he says, chuckling. "I tell you what. I'm on my way."

"I hope you plan on showering first."

"No doubt," he says. "I ain't no slouch, baby. I keeps it fresh all day, every day."

"Just making sure. See you when you get here."

I hang up. Although I showered before going to bed last night, I still jump out of bed, then race into the bathroom to rinse off last night's dust.

Thirty minutes later, I am grinding my pussy down on Nelson's lips, fucking his face, and nutting in his mouth. I let out a loud moan, arching my back and squeezing my titties before pulling them together and alternately licking my own nipples.

"Oh, yes, eat that pussy. Yeah, nigga…Just like that…" He laps at the back of my pussy, then mounts his mouth over it and ferociously sucks before burying his tongue deep inside my slippery walls. He probes around in my pussy, stirring my juices with his long tongue. I can feel his tongue flapping back and forth inside of me and it causes me to cum. I buck my hips. "Aaah, shit. Oh, yes…oh, yes…" I lean forward and cup his balls, taking his dick in my hand at the base, then jerking him with deep, long, strokes that start off slow, but become rapid when I feel myself about to nut all over again.

"Ah, shit," he says, bucking his hips up. "Damn, I ain't never had a bitch jerk my dick and yank my balls like this before." I lightly twist his balls, then yank again. "Ah, shit. What the fuck you doing, baby?" I spit all over his dick, then rapidly twist my hand up and around the head of his dick until it swells and leaks precum. My mouth waters as I watch the clear, sticky fluid drizzle out. I swallow hard, force myself to not swirl my tongue over and around his dick, to not lick its slit.

"Come on baby, suck that dick," he says. "Stop playing with it. Wrap them pretty-ass lips around my dick so I can bust this nut in your mouth, and watch you swallow it. You wanna eat daddy's cum?"

I furrow my brows. *What did this nigga just say to me?* I crane my neck over my shoulder and shoot him a look. He is looking back at me; his lips wet and shiny from my pussy juice.

"You down there teasing it," he says. "You gonna suck that dick for me or what?"

Now I am not annoyed that he wants me to suck down his dick. But, right now, what I am is disgusted that this nigga actually thinks I would let him crack his nut in my mouth. And fucking swallow! What the fuck?! I don't care how much dick I take. I don't know this nigga like that. A ho, yes. But, a smut, never that! Just because he doesn't have a problem letting me nut in his mouth, that doesn't mean I'm going to reciprocate.

"Umm, boo," I say, climbing up off of him, "you are out of your fucking mind if you think you're nutting in my mouth, and I'm swallowing. It ain't that type of party. Now you need to get up and get out 'cause you done ruined the mood."

He lifts up on his forearms, wide-eyed and sweaty. "You joking, right?" He glances down at his rock-hard cock.

I place my hand on my hip. "Does it look like I'm joking? What made you think I'd let you nut in my mouth or swallow it?"

"Damn, baby, I didn't mean no harm by it," he answers, trying to back pedal his way out of getting tossed out. "I'm saying, baby. It was in the heat of the moment. I know you open-minded 'n shit, so I thought anything goes with you."

My eyes lock on his big-ass dick, all black and juicy and thick with bulging veins, throbbing for release. I know he wasn't trying to disrespect me. Hell, I do love sucking the nut out of a dick, but…this nigga has no business assuming shit about me. I walk back over to the bed, and sit on its edge. "Let me explain something to you, big daddy. If you want to remain on the team, then you need to understand a few ground rules. Number one, I don't suck any nigga's dick raw, nor do I swallow—unless you're my man…" Okay, okay, that's not completely true, but he doesn't know that. "And since I'm not looking for one, its not gonna happen."

"I can dig it," he says.

"Number two, if I call you with a specific request then that's all I'm looking for. No extras. If you can't provide the service, let me know upfront, and I will find somebody who can. Otherwise, please don't waste my time, and I won't waste yours. I told you before. It's my pussy…my way."

I glance down at his dick, and lick my lips. *I'ma fuck this nigga one time for the road.* I squeeze the head of his dick. He shakes his head, grinning. "I hear you, ma. I like how you put it out there."

"That's the only way I can be."

"More chicks should be like you," he says. "Keep shit real."

"Shoulda, coulda, woulda, but there'll never be another me," I say, opening up the dresser drawer, then pulling out a condom and unwrapping it.

His smile widens, showing a mouthful of big, white teeth and red gums. I didn't notice it before, but looking him in his mouth almost reminds me of a horse. I try not to frown. "So, you're letting me get up in that pussy?"

"Yeah," I say, pushing him back on the bed, then grabbing his dick, "I changed my mind. No sense letting all this dick go to waste." I roll the condom down on his dick, then straddle him. "I'm gonna feed this pussy." I reach up underneath me and guide his dick into me. "Wet up your dick and fuck you down into the mattress, then put your ass out."

He moans, licking his lips. "Do you, baby. Do you... aaah, shit. Yeah, fuck that dick." And for the next forty-five minutes, I do exactly that.

CHAPTER
EIGHTEEN

The week has come and gone, and Friday is here. Crazy thing is, I don't know why I'm sitting here thinking about my life. Maybe it's because I finished reading this book, *The Sweetest Taboo* by this freaky author chick named Risque. OhmyGod, do you know there was a time in my life when I actually entertained the thought of writing about my many sexual adventures in a journal, or perhaps in a diary? For some reason, I had this grand notion that I could one day turn my entries into a book. And sell millions. Oh my God! That shit is so funny to me. I can't believe I actually considered that mess. Thank goodness I came to my damn senses and quickly dismissed that notion, fearing that what I wrote would end up in the wrong hands. And, baaaaaby, trust…the last thing I want is to risk having the personal and very private details of my sexual life exposed for all to see. Oh, no. Not cute!

I mean, some things are better left unsaid, or unread in this case. Wouldn't you agree? Then again, I do believe revealing a ho's innermost secrets could prove to be quite an interesting and stimulating read, to say the least. But on the flipside, exposing the comings and goings of a ho could also disrupt the lives of those who embrace their ho-ish ways like I do. Needless to say, I think allowing men (and some women) access to too much information on the inner workings of a ho, is an absolute no-no. The less he/she knows about how we manipulate and maneuver our way into a man's boxers, and onto his dick, the better. This is solely my opinion, of course. So, because of that, I refuse to write in anything that could be potentially damaging, or used against me.

My cell rings again, disrupting my thoughts.

I glance at the screen, taking a long, deep, breathe.

"Hello."

"Hey," he says.

It's Wade.

"Hey," I say back, wondering why he's calling.

"How you been?" he asks.

"I've been doing great. And you?"

"I can't complain." He pauses. And in that brief moment, images of his glistening naked body, his thick, shiny dick swinging between his thighs flash through my mind, causing me to shiver as I imagine my head hanging off the bed and him slowly sliding his cock down in my throat, swelling to full capacity, shutting off my airway as he stretches my throat. With each push, I swallow, taking more of him in. He grinds his pelvis nice and slow, then begins to face-fuck me, causing me to gag; forcing tears to escape from my eyes; his heavy balls slapping up against my forehead until they unleash a thick, hot cream.

I swallow hard, gulping down my fantasy.

"So, whatchu been up to?" he asks, shutting off the remainder of my lust-driven thoughts.

"Nothing much," I offer.

"I've been thinking about you."

"Is that so?" I question, slipping my hand between my legs, cupping my pussy. "And what have you been thinking?"

"How much I miss—"

"Please, Wade, let's not go there," I warn, cutting him off.

"Go where?"

I suck my teeth, removing my hand from between my legs. "C'mon, let's not play games here. You know what I'm talking about."

"I'm not playing games. I'm keeping shit real. And if you had let me finish what I was getting ready to say, you'd know that…"

Silence.

"You still there?"

"Yeah, I'm still here," I say, sighing. "I'm listening."

"Now, like I was saying, I was thinking about how much I miss sticking this dick up in you and fucking the shit outta you. You made it very clear that you're not looking for love or no shit like that. And I can dig it. I'm not gonna front and act like I wasn't feelin' some type of way about it, but I'm a man, baby. And I can rock with the best of 'em. So, if all you want is the dick, then fuck it. Let's let it do what it do."

I feel my pussy heating. Subconsciously, I shut my legs tight, and fight the urge to press down on my clit. "So what are you saying, Wade?" I shift the phone to my left ear.

"I'm saying I still wanna at least be fuck buddies."

"And what if I don't wanna fuck you anymore?"

"Then I'm hoping we can at least still be friends…"

Friends? Is he serious? I have never been friends with any man I used to fuck. Never had any interest before, and I damn sure don't now. Does he really think we can be friends? Now, if I had never sucked down his dick, or he had never had his tongue shoved up in my ass, then, yes, we could definitely be friends. But a man I've fucked? That's always been a no-no for me.

The notion causes me to remember a conversation I had with a "friend"—again I use that word loosely— I used to work with before allowing Nahdirah into my personal space. The chick was babbling on and on about this male friend she had who she was "falling" for because he was everything she wanted in a man. I could almost hear the violins playing in the background as she spoke about how great a catch he was, how fine he was, how wonderful of a man he was, how special he made her feel, how she wanted to be in a relationship with him… blah, blah, blah. OhmyGod, it was sickening!

Anyway, girlfriend didn't know what to do about her feelings for him. So, being the *friend* that I am, I suggested she keep her romantic feelings for him to herself, and strictly focus on keeping him around as a friend. But, nooooooooooo, this hyena decides—which was definitely her prerogative—to pour her heart out to him. And…well, are you ready for the grand finale?

Drum roll, *please*…The chick fucks him. And of course he dug her back out lovely. But, then she didn't hear from him again for two weeks. He didn't return any of her phone calls, or respond to any of her emails. Then, finally, he decided to call and tell her he didn't want a relationship, nor was he looking for one. That she wasn't his type because she was too clingy and needy. And the bitch had the nerve to be distraught over it. It took every ounce of my strength not to laugh in her damn face.

Of course, my question to her dumb ass was: Did you ever ask him what he wanted or was looking for? No, of course not! That would have made too much sense. Duh! So, there she was all bent out of shape because she felt like he played her.

I checked her real quick and said, "Trick, you played yourself by opening up your damn legs to him without asking questions. He fucked you, and kept it moving. So get over it!"

Unfortunately, girlfriend couldn't grasp what I had said. So, I asked her if the dick was good. She was like, "Yes…the best I've ever had, and I actually had an orgasm, something I've never had before with any man. I really don't think I could ever go back to being only his friend. I'm really in love with him and it would hurt me to see him with someone else."

Baaaaaaby, listen. I had to blink, then blink again. 'Cause I thought I was looking at a three-headed ho. *What the fuck!?!* I had thought. *So, the ho's "in love" with her friend, whom she fucked without any conversation about what it would mean after all was said and done; and dude doesn't want her ass romantically.*

He fucked her ass one good time, and the bitch was hooked on the dick because she busted her first nut. And he wasn't beat for her ass. Poor thing! Well, I was like, "Honey, charge that shit to the game, and chalk it up as an experience. Accept it for what it was: a damn good fuck. And move the hell on. Geesh!"

She had the nerve to say, "That's easier said than done. I really don't think I can simply get over it, or him. I love him. But, I'm hurt at how he dissed me. We were friends. Never in a million years would I think he'd do me like he does all those other chicks."

Well, that was it for me. She *knew* his track record and pattern with women, and still tried to pursue a relationship outside of friendship with him. I gave her my "Bitch-are-you-fucking-serious" look, shaking my head.

"Well, what made you think he was going to treat you any different?" I had asked, trying not to sound too judgmental, although I *was*. "Did you think you were going to fuck him into wanting to be with you?"

"No," she had replied. "But I thought he had mad love for me."

Yeah, trick, as your friend*!* I remember thinking.

Right then and there, I knew that bitch was a nut. And from that point on, I looked at her ass sideways. Moral of the story: someone who's your friend isn't always supposed to be more than that.

Anyway, now that I've digressed, let's get back to the situation at hand—Wade. Oh, wait a minute. Before we do that, let me ask you this: Do *you* think a man and a woman can be strictly platonic friends without ever trying to cross the line?

Well, I think if opportunity presented itself and it wouldn't complicate the friendship, I'd bet my six-hundred dollar heels that somebody's gonna be fucking before it's all said and done. Hmmm…they say that best friends make the best lovers. I don't know if I can agree with that completely. What about you? Do you think friends can become lovers? But what happens when shit falls apart? Now you've done lost your lover, and ruined what was once a great friendship. Humph, is the gamble really worth the risks?

And, as far as Wade is concerned—after all the fuck-ing we've done, there's no way I can entertain being friends with him. It's better to cut all ties and be done with it rather than try to hold onto something that wasn't based on—or built on—friendship in the first place.

"...Listen. I dig you, baby," Wade continues. "I can't even front. But, I respect your feelings. It is what it is, and I'm down for whatever with you. If you don't wanna fuck, cool. But, if you still with it, then I got a big, stiff dick with your name on it, waiting to put some work in."

A sly grin forms my lips. I think for a moment, consider his offer. A part of me knew he would acquiesce—or should I say, come to his senses. Whatever chick, or chicks, he's been fucking doesn't have anything on me when it comes to handling a dick. Wade, Wade, Wade... what's a girl to do?

Fuck it, I think, glancing at my timepiece. It's 7:15 p.m.

I know, I know...I said I wasn't fucking with him the last time I was with him; that he'd never get any more of this pussy. And I know I probably should leave well enough alone, but damn...I can't let an opportunity to ride that dick one last time slip away!

Against my better judgment, I say, "I can't promise friendship. But if you can get here within the next thirty minutes, I can definitely guarantee you some of this good pussy."

"I'm on my way," he says, sounding all excited and whatnot.

"If you're anything over five minutes late," I state, "don't bother. And I'm not in the mood for a bunch of chit chat. Just come in, fuck me and go."

"Oh, word, damn," he says, pausing.

"Is there a problem?"

"Nah," he finally says. "I got you, babe. See you in a bit."

We hang up, and I jump up from the sofa, shaking and popping my hips on my way up the stairs to freshen up when my doorbell rings.

Now who in the hell is this? I think, peeking through the peephole. *OhmyGod, nooooo, this pencil dick nigga didn't just pop up at my fucking doorstep.* I squint my left eye almost shut, pressing my damn right eyeball up against the little hole in disbelief. It's Jarrod. A damn mistake, and a wasted nut, to say the least! I fucked him once—and let him eat my pussy twice, the last time being eight months ago, after meeting him at an outdoor concert at NJPAC, the New Jersey Performing Arts Center, in Newark last summer.

OhmyGod, he was pumping and humping up and down in me like he was in a race to get to an imaginary finish line, jabbing and stabbing up my insides. His only saving grace was the fact that he knew how to stroke the hell out of my clit—causing magnificent waves of orgasms—with his dick while poking me up. Other than that, it felt like he was fucking me to death with an ice-pick. But, being the gracious, dick-loving host that I am, I grinned and beared it, allowing him to continue gouging up my uterus, suffering in sweet agony.

Finally, after twenty-minutes—yes, twenty long, torturous-ass minutes—of him sweating all over me, grunting like a wounded bear, he pulled out his pogo stick and started jerking it over me. I laid there, staring at him, racking my brain trying to figure out whether or not he had pulled his condom off. I knew I had seen him roll one on, remembered seeing him open the familiar wrapper. But there he was kneeling over me with his skinny dick in his thick hand and, for the life of me, I couldn't recall if he had removed it—and, if he had, where the hell he had put the damn thing.

I think for minute. Do I ignore the bell and get myself ready for my sexual interlude with Wade, or do I curse his retarded-ass out? The answer comes when he presses down on my bell like he's being chased by a pack of rabid dogs. I fling open the door, frowning. "Um, excuse me…What. Are. *You*. Doing here?" I ask through clenched teeth, glaring at him. My hand is defiantly planted on my hip.

"Damn, baby, I guess that means you're happy to see me," he says, grinning.

I suck my teeth, rolling my eyes up in my head. "Guess again. Now why are you here?"

"Damn," he huffs, clearly disappointed that I am not welcoming him with open arms. "Can I at least get a hello, before you start snapping?"

I tap my foot. Count to ten. "Jarrod, I'm going to ask you one more time. Why the hell are you at my door without being invited here?"

He leans up against the frame of the door. "I was in the neighborhood and thought I'd drop by. It's been a minute since we chilled so—"

"So you *thought* you would drop by for some pussy," I say, cutting him off. "Humph, wrong answer, sweetie. I'm not running a whorehouse."

"Oh, yeah." He smirks. "Well, I can't tell."

"Nigga," I snap. "Unless you've miraculously gotten some extra meat on your dick, I'm not interested."

He twists his lip, scrunches his face up. "Say what?" I repeat myself.

"Oh word? But you wasn't saying all that when I had you twisted up like a pretzel, banging your guts out."

I laugh. "Nigga, get a grip. The only thing you did was poke around in my pussy."

"You a real bitch, you know that?"

"Yep, I sure am," I say, smiling. "But I got some good pussy. And your silly ass will never feel the inside of it again. Now get the fuck away from my door before I call the cops on your delusional ass." I slam the door in his face.

"Fucking bitch," I hear him say before, punching my door with his fist.

I sigh, shaking my head. It never ceases to amaze me how some niggas act like bratty, little boys when they don't get their way, pouting and stomping off, having oversized tantrums.

Now, I'm the last person who likes a bunch of mess in her personal space, and making a scene is an absolute no-no. But this fool has lost his damn mind. I snatch my house phone from off the coffee table, racing towards the door. I swing it open and rush outside, catching him before he gets into his Benz. "Nigga, bang on my mother-fucking door like that again, and see what happens."

"Or what?" he snaps, walking back towards me.

Oh shit, I think. The last thing I want is some nigga beating, no, change that—*trying* to beat—my ass out here, but I know—well, at least I *think*—he isn't crazy enough to put his hands on me. The last thing he wants is to have his spot blown up when he has a woman at home. But a nigga with a bruised ego is likely to do almost anything.

"I know you are not trying to come at me," I say, pressing the first number for 9-1-1. He stops in his tracks, putting his hands up in mock surrender.

"You know what, take your ass back inside," he snaps, walking back to his car. "I ain't beat for your dumb ass."

I silently let out a relieved sigh. "Good. And make sure you don't bring your pencil-dick ass around here again 'cause if you do, you're going to find your ass locked the hell up."

"Whatever," he snaps, slamming his car door and starting his engine. "I should have never fucked with your ho-ass in the first place." He starts backing out of my driveway, then screeches off down the street like a raving lunatic.

I don't know what the hell is wrong with these niggas out

here. I look up into the sky, searching for a full moon. And what do you know? There it is, as bright as day. *I shoulda known*, I think, heading back into the house. *You always got motherfuckers tripping*.

Wait a minute. I know what some of you are thinking. You think I could have handled that better; that I shouldn't have come out of my face like that with him. And you're right. I could have. But I didn't. So what! Bottom line, every man I fuck knows from gate that if he ever comes to my house uninvited, he runs the risk of being cursed the hell out. So he had better proceed with caution.

Now before you open your mouth to say something sideways—like he should have punched my grill in; like someone is going to beat my ass; or some other crazy-shit like that. Let's be clear: I don't give a damn about any man who can't follow instructions, especially a cheating-ass one. I'm not going to sugarcoat shit when it comes to my house rules. It's my home, my pussy, and my damn way! And if a nigga doesn't like it, he can carry his happy-go-lucky-creeping-ass back the fuck where he came from. And that's what it is.

Now if you'll excuse me, I have some dick to prepare for. I need to make sure the cat box is fresh for tonight's suck-and-fuck festivities. So, toodles!

CHAPTER
NINETEEN

Two hours later, a sweet, funky scent of hot, sticky, sweaty fucking fills the air. My hair is saturated and plastered around my face. Beads of sweat are rolling down my back, sliding into the crack of my ass. Wade and I have been fucking nonstop, like two wild beasts in heat. I am riding his thick pole, my pussy churning as I crash down onto his dick. I fuck him as if my life depends on it, as if his does. Ride him as if there is no tomorrow, as if there are no cares. And for the moment, there are none.

There are no words spoken between us. Just grunts and groans and moans of passion. I lean over, press my hardened nipples against his hard chest and allow him to slip his wet tongue into my hungry mouth. I suck on it as if it were his dick, feeling heat and ecstasy rising up within me. In unspoken words, we are both aware that this will be the last time we ever share in this sexual bliss.

I slowly, seductively, grind my pussy up, then down, the length of his dick. Then rotate my hips back up and down it again, milking him one inch at a time.

"Ah fuck! Goddamn, you know how to ride this dick!"

he shouts. His eyes roll up in the back of his head as he grips my waist. A sly grin parts my lips. *'Cause I'm the Man Handler, baby. And I was born to slay the dick.*

"Yeah, you like this pussy, don't you?"

"Ah yes…oh, shit…"

"You like how I wet this big dick, don't you?"

"Hell, yeah, baby…"

"Show me how much you want this pussy," I demand.

I stop moving my hips, and allow him to rapidly thrust his hips upward, deep into my sopping hole, stretching the back of my pussy, smashing against the mouth of my womb. I gasp, choking back a scream.

I tighten my pussy around his dick, grasping and pulling him deeper into my honey-coated, cum-slick abyss.

"Oh, shit," he moans. "Aaaah, fuck. This pussy's good."

"Sssh, no talking unless I speak to you," I warn in between another moan.

"Fuck me…"—he continues slamming his dick up into my pussy—"Mmmm…that's right…like that… fuck this pussy…"

His dick slashes into my hole, pulling open my thick pussy lips, causing a throbbing in my clit. I arch my back, toss my head back and bounce up and down on his cock, matching his thrusts, riding the swell of another orgasm.

Wade leans up on his forearms, his gaze locked on the pleasure painted on my face. I bite down on my bottom lip. Let out another moan. And in one swift motion, he lifts up and rolls me over with his dick still buried inside of me, spreading open my thighs with his legs. He reaches up under me and cups my ass, squeezing each ass cheek while pumping his massive dick in and out, around and around, stirring my pussy, caressing my walls with each stroke.

"Oh, shit," he moans again. "Ah, fuck…this pussy's so wet…"

I wrap my left leg around his waist, then toss my right leg up over his shoulder as he fucks me, giving him access to every nook and corner my pussy has to offer. "Oh, yes…oh yes…fuck me," I moan.

I grab his muscled ass, pull him deeper into me. Our bodies fuse together by a blazing fire ignited by lust. Sweat drips from his face onto my chest as he rises up on his arms, bracing his hands on either side of me, twisting and snapping his hips into me. His face contorts.

"Fuck me," I urge. He slams harder. "That's right, nigga, fuck my pussy. Make my pussy nut…"

"Ah, shit, fuck…yeah…"

I moan.

He moans.

His dick is pulsing. I can feel the heat coursing through the length of him racing to the tip of his engorged head. His rhythm quickens; his thrust become longer and deeper. I smile, knowing he is about to cum. My pussy milks his dick, slurps it in.

"Ah shit…I'm getting ready to nut," he groans, quickly

pulling his dick out of me and yanking off the condom. He slips two fingers into my pussy, finger-fucks me. I bend at the knees and pull my legs up to my chest, giving him my basket of goodness, as he rapidly strokes his cock over me.

"Oh, give me that nut, daddy," I coo, licking my lips. "Let me see that big dick spit that milk, baby."

He scoots back some so he can align his dick with its target. He is aiming for the opening of my purring pussy.

"Yeah, daddy, bust that hot nut all over my wet pussy," I whisper, gazing at him through slits of lust. "Give me that sweet dick milk."

"Ah, fuck…ah fuck…yeah…I'ma spit this nut all over that pretty hole." He grunts, and shakes as he shoots a hot, thick, creamy nut all over the front of my pussy. "Oh, fuck…ah shit…" He continues stroking. "I feel another nut coming," he moans.

I thrust upward. Run my fingers along the slit of my pussy, smearing his sticky treat into my pubic hairs. "That's right, bust that nut, baby."

I keep my eye on the prize. Watch him as he rapidly jerks himself. The head of his dick swells, then white cream oozes out of its eye like molten lava from a volcano before it erupts, ejecting his nut in hot, thick spurts.

I let out a moan.

"Oh, shit…oh, shit…" He continues stroking himself, and another nut squirts out onto my stomach, then titties. His dick continues erupting one nut after the

other, soaking up the neatly trimmed patch of hair sur-
rounding my pussy.

I twirl my hips; rub his load of cum into my skin;
grind my ass down into the mattress as he is smearing
his cum all over my slippery clit, and into my pubic hair.
He is still holding his dick in his left hand, stroking out
another nut. And I am grabbing his greedy fingers,
pulling them, and his hand, into my wetness. I let out
a deep, heavy moan. I am on the brink of another
orgasm. Wade senses this, and begins to flick my clit
with his thumb, then presses down on it. I let out a
deafening scream, and cum in a thunderous roar.

I lie here for a moment, allow myself to savor the
moment, then quickly jump up and out of bed. I don't
wait for him to lie down and roll over on his side.
There is no time for getting comfortable. No time for
drifting off into a peaceful, fuck-induced slumber. I get
out of bed, and turn the lights on, blowing out the
candles that have burned down to almost nothing. He
understands what this means. Get your shit, and go!

"Thanks for the nut," I say, glancing over my shoulder at him, heading towards the bathroom.

"Anytime," he says. "Damn, that pussy felt good."

I smile, grabbing two hand towels from out of the
linen closet. "So was that dick," I say back. I catch my
reflection in the mirror as I wet the rags with hot water
and liquid Dial soap. *You a bad bitch*, I think, smirking.
I turn off the water, and return to where Wade is now

sitting—on the edge of the bed. I hand one of the towels to him.

"I guess this means I can't shower here," he says, looking up at me.

"Basically," I say, sitting down next to him.

"I can dig it. It's all good," he says, wiping his dick and balls clean. I hold my hand out for the towel when he is done, handing him the other one. He wipes his face and neck with it, then gets up and walks towards the bathroom. I listen as he pulls the lid up, hitting the toilet water with heavy streams of piss.

I sigh, glancing over at the digital clock. 10:42 p.m.

He washes his hands, then returns to where I am sitting. He stands in front of me; his shiny dick dangling over his large balls. I shift my eyes, lock them onto his. He leans in and kisses me on the forehead.

"I guess this is it."

I nod. "Yes, it is. What we shared has run its course."

"So, why'd you let me come over?" he asks, studying me.

"Do you want me to keep it real with you?"

He nods. "Most definitely."

"'Cause I wanted to feel that dick inside of me one last time," I admit, standing up to face him.

"It doesn't have to be the last time," he says cautiously, almost pleadingly.

"For me it does." I step into his space and touch the side of his face. "I only wanted you to fuck me."

He grabs his semi-erect dick. "And did I rise to the occasion?" he asks, grinning.

"With flying colors," I state, smiling back at him. I give him a serious look. "Wade, I want you to know that I think you are a great catch. You're handsome. Intelligent. Driven. Ambitious. You have a great body and"—I glance down at his now rock-hard dick—"an amazing dick. One day, I know you'll meet someone who can appreciate all the things you bring to the table."

"But that someone isn't you, right?" he asks, but it is meant as a statement.

I shake my head. "No. And it never will be."

"That's really too bad," he says, shaking his head. "But I have to respect your decision."

I shrug. "Maybe it is. I only know you deserve more than what I can give you."

"Look, baby. I'm cool with only fucking you. It doesn't have to go any further than that. Yeah, I got caught up in my feelings, but I'm cool. Like I said, we can keep it to me strictly sticking this dick in you, then bouncing. No questions asked."

I purse my lips, then part a sly grin as my eyes slowly travel over his nipples, to his abs, his navel and between his thighs, to his beautiful, mouthwatering dick.

"No questions asked?" I ask, looking him in the eyes. "Just fuck and go."

He nods. "No questions asked; just two horny adults fucking," he assures me. I open up the nightstand drawer and pull out another Durex condom, handing it to him. He grins.

"Oh, word?"

I walk over towards my dresser with the mirror, bend over and spread open my ass. I speak to him, looking in the mirror. "This is your test. I want you to yank me by the hair, slap my ass, and fuck me from the back deep and hard."

He rolls the condom over his dick, walking up behind me. "And if I pass?"

"Then maybe you can keep fucking me on demand."

"Baby," he says, slapping my ass. "I have no problem fucking you anyway you want it."

"And when you're ready to cum, I want you to spray your nut all over my ass. Then put your clothes on and get out. Can you handle that?"

"No doubt," he says, dipping at the knees, then rubbing the head of his dick all over the back of my still wet, tingly pussy.

"Fuck me," I urge in a throaty whisper. He wraps a fistful of my hair in his hand and yanks my head back, slamming his dick so hard and deep into me, I think he's going to knock my uterus off the hinges. I moan. "Yes. Yes. Like that. Beat my pussy up, nigga."

He places his left hand on my shoulder, then alternately slaps each ass cheek, purposefully pumping himself in and out of me in deep, rapid succession. I match his rhythm, rotating my pussy, slamming my ass back onto his dick. I can feel every inch of his cock inside of me, stroking and stretching me. My body trembles as an orgasm begins to swirl through my body. Wade grabs me by the waist, his hands gripping tightly on either side of me, and bangs the shit out of me.

"Ah…ah…yessssssss…fuck me!"

"Ah, shit, this is some good pussy."

"Fuck me, fuck me, fuck me," I chant.

Wade grunts, then abruptly pulls his dick out of me. I glance over my shoulder and watch as he snatches the condom off. He frantically pumps his dick in and out of his hand. "Ah, shit…" he moans. "I don't know what the fuck you doing to me…"

"Give me that hot nut, nigga. Yeah, nigga…Bust that nut all over my fat ass."

"Ah, shiiiiiiiiiiiiiiiit," he groans, splattering his nut all over my ass and lower back.

Ten minutes later, Wade is dressed and on his way out the door. There are no good-byes, no thank-yous between us; just the afterglow of a good fuck.

CHAPTER
TWENTY

Today is one those "don't-fuck-with-me-'cause-I-got-too-much-shit-to-do-and-I'm-not-in-the-motherfucking-mood-for-any-bullshit" days. I'm in my office—at my desk, my fingers rapidly moving, clicking, against the keys of my computer. I am diligently trying to stay focused so I can complete my department's end of the month status report. But, for some reason, my mind keeps wandering—to Garrett; to Wade. Two handsome, masculine, hard-working men who enjoy fucking me, but want more than what I'm offering—this sweet, gushy pussy. Two men whom *I* enjoy fucking, but want nothing more than what hangs between their legs—two beautiful, mouthwatering, thick, veiny chocolate cocks, alternately thrusting in and out of my sizzling snatch, consume my thoughts and I don't fucking know why.

Okay, okay, I do know. Because I'm greedy, and I don't think there's anything wrong with wanting to experiment with more than one dick in my bed at the same time, especially when it's with two men who equally know how to slay the pussy. Besides, I know them, and I know how much they crave my wet, sticky, cunt juice all over their cocks.

My preoccupation with fucking them both simultaneously, having both of them filling my holes—stretching them wide and deep to capacity—from one end to the other, causes my walls to tighten. I shift in my seat, and squeeze my legs together, trying to pinch away the throbbing in my pussy. I can feel my panties getting moist as I envision having a ménage à trois—two sets of hands, roaming all over my body; two sets of lips, sucking my nipples; two sets of tongues, licking my pussy and clit; two sets of teeth, nibbling on my ass cheeks; two sets of balls for me to suck on, and gargle; two delicious dicks to rub together and deep throat, to mount and ride with reckless abandon.

Mmmm…oh, yes…I can feel my clit swelling.

My BlackBerry vibrates on my desk, shuddering as if it were having its own mini-orgasm, disrupting my own. A tinge of jealousy sweeps through me at the thought. I let out a long, exaggerated sigh. I pick up the device and remove it from its pink leather case, then lean back in my executive chair.

I have received sixty emails from my various email accounts. But the one that is of the most interest to me at this very moment is from one of my old yahoo accounts: Nutcracker69. It's an email from the screen name DickUdownallnight. I open and read it, slowly scrolling down through its contents.

> *Hey, baby,*
> *What's good with you? Just hitting you up to see*

*if I can come through and dick you down and crack
this nut down your throat like old times, baby.
Hope this is your right email address.*

I frown, then reread the lines, trying to figure out who
the hell this is. I check out the screen name again. It
doesn't ring a bell. I try to think who had this particular
email address. *At least fifty, sixty, niggas*, I think, shaking
my head. But whoever he is, it has to be either someone I met online years ago, or someone I used to date—
before I became anti-dating. And, obviously, it's someone I've fucked—and *fucked* good. I continue reading:

*I tried to hit you on your cell, but it's the wrong
number. And I see you done bounced from your
spot over on Jefferson Ave.*

Jefferson Ave? I think. *I haven't lived there in over four
years.* Hmmm. I close my eyes and try to narrow down
which dudes from my past knew me when I lived in
Elizabeth. I sigh, realizing it's too damn many to try
figuring out. I finish reading:

*We need to talk, baby. Word up. I miss fucking
that throat and pretty ass of yours. It's been a minute, and I'm ready to tongue-fuck that hot pussy,
then bang that fatty out. Holla back!*
Marquise

Marquise? The name's not familiar. And I'm really
not interested in exerting any energy in playing the

guessing game. Obviously, there's a reason why this nigga hasn't been able to get at me—I've moved on. He might have been one of those niggas who my girl Jaguar Wright sings about—a nigga with good dick, but no damn common sense. Humph.

P.S. in case you might have forgotten who I am, I've attached a picture to help jog your memory. Hopefully, it'll get your sweet juices flowing, and have you ready to wet this dick!

Of course curiosity gets the best of me, and I press the little white ball on my BlackBerry, then scroll down to open attachment, and press. In less than a minute a picture of a chiseled torso pops up on my screen, I scroll down to see the rest of the picture. And almost fall out of my chair. In between a pair of muscled thighs is a long, meaty, reddish-brown, shiny dick with a bright red bow tied around the tip of its thick mushroom-sized head. Immediately, I start drooling. But, unfortunately, I still can't figure out who this mystery nigga with the mouthwatering dick is. So, what do I do? I press the button to reply.

I quickly type: *Beautiful dick, but I still don't know who this is.* Of course, in my head, I'm wondering if he knows how to use it. I finish typing: *A picture of a pretty dick tells me nothing about who you are, boo. So you'll need to try again. And for the record, I'm not sucking dick, but I am serving up a deep dish of this hot pussy to a man with a long, wet tongue. If that's you, then you need to hit me up with a phone number.* I press SEND, then toss the device in my Tumi messenger bag.

If he replies back with a phone number, which I trust he will, I might call—and perhaps *fuck*—him. Then again, I might not. It will all depend on my mood, and what the hell he looks like. 'Cause for me, a nigga with a pretty dick is fine and dandy, but if the shit is attached to someone who looks like a fucking Troll doll or one of the Flying Monkeys, then you might as well keep it moving. I know, I know…we already had this discussion about looks not being everything. And maybe for you they're not.

CHAPTER
TWENTY-ONE

Another week passes. The weekend is almost over. And baby, baby, baby...let me tell you. You don't know how happy I am to report that today is the first day that my asshole doesn't feel like it's engulfed in flames. What a damn relief! Anyway, it's Sunday, and rainy. What is it about the rain that makes some people horny? I mean, it's been raining like cats and dogs all damn day. And I am horny as hell. Basically, any time it rains, it puts me in the mood to be fucked deep, long, and strong. I can't explain it. It also makes me think back on some of my rainy day and night sexapades. Like the time it was thundering and lightning and pouring down, and I was getting fucked deliciously on the hood of an ex's car. Or the time I was in the Bahamas on a private beach with this dude I had met in the middle of a rainstorm, and he ate my pussy, then fucked me until dawn. Mmmmph. Lord knows I love me some rain!

I'm telling you. It really brings the freak out of me. Oh my God! There's nothing sexier than lying up in bed being pressed down into the mattress by a wide-shouldered, strong-backed, dick-slinging man. And, last night—well, early this morning—that is exactly what I had in my bed. Baby, let me tell you. Up until almost five o'clock this morning, I got slayed lovely!

Last night, I made up my mind that it was time to recruit some new dick. So, after lying around the house most of the day, I decided to go out. I showered, put on a cute Baby Phat jean outfit with nothing underneath the jacket, and rocked a pair of four-inch Gucci heels. Sprayed some *Pasha* behind my ears and on my wrists, then gave myself the once-over in my floor-length mirror. I was satisfied with my look. My hair and face were tight, and the frame was right. Between you and me, I knew I'd have no problem getting some dick. Hell, I never do. Especially not with measurements like mine: A curvaceous 36-24-38. Yes, I've been blessed with nice C-cup breasts with large, Hershey Kiss nipples, a small waist, and a fat, soft ass. And being pretty in the face definitely adds to the package. Not bragging, baby; simply sharing.

Anyway, I figured the best spot to find some dick was to go to a titty bar. So I drove to Cinderella's in Elizabeth, paid my money, ordered a shot of Henny, then perched my apple-bottom ass up on a stool at the bar and took in the scene. A few dudes tried to holla at me, but they weren't what I was looking for. So I dismissed them. I mean, I wanted some dick, but a girl still has to be picky. I'm not that pressed to accept any ole thing. I wanted something tall, dark, and fine. The minute I spotted him walking through the door with three of his boys all dipped in jewels, I knew he was the one. I decided I'd have him in my bed before morning came. I eyed him as he walked around to the other side of the bar. I studied him, watched him toss a few dollars up on the stage at one of the dancers.

A smooth, brown-skinned chick with a small waist, wide hips, full breasts, and a face like Herman Munster was up on the stage shaking and bouncing her ass. A skinny chick was at the other end of the bar with her legs pulled all the way back over her head, giving everyone a full view of her pussy. Then there was another chick working extra hard to get a group of brothas to give up their dollars. Seems like the deeper you are in the hood, the uglier and rougher the dancers look. Some of them chicks really have no business being on stage with stretch marks, and razor, cut and knife marks all over their bodies. Ugh.

Anyway, I flagged the bartender and asked him to send my prey a drink on me. When the bartender pointed over in my direction, he raised his glass and nodded. I smiled. He whispered something in one of his man's ears. They glanced over at me, but I pretended not to notice. Five minutes later, he approached me.

"What's good, ma?"

I sized him up, licking my painted, glossy lips. He is five feet, eleven inches (I know this because I asked him) with broad shoulders, long, thick fingers, a wide nose, and big, brown, dreamy eyes. His smooth, flawless skin is the color of milk chocolate. Yes, he was definitely the one. After about ten minutes of small talk, I got right to the point.

"You, and what's hanging between your legs," I answered. Shit, I had no time for dilly-dallying. Like I said, a ho was trying to fuck. I told him straight out what I was looking for. He didn't flinch. Just licked his lips, then parted a sexy, wide smile.

He shifted his weight from one foot the other. I guess he thought I was joking, because he stood there, looking me in my face like he was waiting for the punch line. When he realized there was none, he widened his smile and started rubbing his dimpled chin. Yeah, he was definitely the one. I let him know I was ready and that I had a wet, fat pussy that was throbbing for a stiff dick. You know some men bitch up when a chick like me comes at 'em direct. I was glad he didn't. Hell, life is too damn short to be beating around the bush.

"Oh word? It's like that?"

I nodded. "Sure is. You married?" I asked, looking him in the eyes. If his eyes shifted around the room, then I would know he was lying. They didn't.

"Nah, baby."

"You got a girl?"

"Yeah," he said, placing his arm on the back of my chair. "But we in the middle of some shit right now. You got a problem with that."

"Nope," I answered. "Your problems with her are no problems of mine." Then I continued my interview by asking the rest of my list of questions.

"Damn," he said, laughing. "Am I interviewing for a position?"

I twirled my straw with my tongue, then slowly slid it into my mouth and sipped my drink. I licked my lips, then gazed back up at him. "Yes, you are. It's for a position between these thighs," I responded, swiveling the barstool towards him and opening up my legs for effect. "And the position requires someone who knows how to rock a pussy."

He smiled, nodding his head. "I see."

"Yeah, I bet you do. But do you wanna feel?"

"Hell, yeah," he snapped. "I'm down." He paused, sipping his drink. "Listen, you got condoms? 'Cause I ain't 'bout bringing no shit home, feel me."

I frowned. "I don't fuck raw, baby. I got a whole box, especially for you."

"Oh, word. Then that's what it is."

I smiled. "And so it shall be."

So after another hour of back and forth, and two more rounds of drinks, he walked out behind me, then followed me home in his steel-grey Jag. The crazy thing is, I didn't even know the nigga's name, or give him mine, until after we were done. I simply told him what I wanted, and how I wanted it, and he was more than willing to oblige.

As soon as I got him in the house, I attacked him like a wild, dick-hungry ho-beast. Pushed his ass down on the sofa, unzipped his sagging jeans, fished down in his boxers, then unleashed his big, juicy dick with the reddish brown tip. I'm not going to lie, I was so damn relieved his dick was meaty. A little dick would have only been an appetizer for me, so I was more than happy when I saw he was packing. My mouth watered, and my panties got wet while looking at it. The shit was eight inches soft, and eleven inches hard. I know because I always pull out my ruler and measure the dick to know what I'm *really* working with. I like to jot down their measurements when they leave for future reference.

Anyway, I lowered my pussy onto his face, then leaned down and sucked him silly. It was all good the minute he stuck his tongue in my ass, licked my pussy and sucked on my clit until I couldn't take it any longer. Yeah, dude had a bitch begging him to fuck me. Mmmm. He flipped me over, strapped on a Durex, then dug my insides out like there was no tomorrow, and he did it doggie-style…exactly how I like it.

The dick was soooo damn good. He has rhythm like no other. Whew! The brotha even made his dick pulsate inside my pussy. No joke. I could actually feel his shit jumping inside of me. Now that bugged me the fuck out.

And the minute I started talking dirty—telling him how big his dick felt inside of me, how good it felt; chanting and moaning, telling him to fuck me harder—

his thrusts quickened, and deepened. As soon as he was about ready to nut, I asked him to pull his dick out of me so I could jerk him off. I wanted to see how much he came. I got a thing with seeing all that white, stickiness shooting, spurting or oozing out of the tip of a man's dick. Oh, how that drives me wild.

Of course, my fuck of the night obliged, and I snatched the condom off, jerked him with both hands, and was pleasantly surprised when his dick spurted a big load of thick, hot cream. If I would have known him better I probably would have licked it up, right down to the last damn drop. But there will definitely be a round two. I've decided to give Mr. Majestic five stars, and add him to my "charm" list. He'll be filling someone's spot real soon. Believe that!

Anyway, I am all fucked out from my weekend activities. And, today, I am curled up on the sofa relaxing. I plan to spend the whole day lying around the house and doing absolutely nothing. Well, that's not completely true. In between masturbating, I will finish reading this book *Dangerously in Love* by this chick Allison Hobbs. Talk about a freaky, engaging read. Then I had the nerve to run out to Borders and pick up her other books *Insatiable*, *Pandora's Box*, *A Bona Fide Gold Digger*, and *The Climax*.

I won't go into details about the books, but DAMN her! What a freak! A few times, she had me slipping my fingers into my already cum-soaked snatch. Now this is one kinky chick. I'll bet she's probably a real greedy, dick-rider type chick. I'd love to meet her in person, and pick her freaky brain.

Anyway, let me finish telling you about last night's adventure, and what I figured out by sitting at that strip joint for almost three hours, watching. See. I realize that the strip clubs are a ho's paradise. Okay? Roll your eyes if you want. But trust me. Testosterone is everywhere. A plethora of dick and balls await you. At the bar, at tables, in corners, against the wall, young and old, there are men of all shapes, colors and sizes. Some who are there to have a few drinks, watch some ass shake, be entertained, then take their asses home. Others are there to get their drink on, get a few lap dances, maybe even some back room head, then take their asses home. And then there are the men who are there hoping to fuck. But, no matter what their intentions, at least ninety-eight percent of them are going to leave out of that spot wanting something hot and wet to slide their cocks up in—mouth, pussy, ass, or all three. Trust me, it won't matter. And it's a greedy, man-loving, dick-craving ho like me who's going to be perched up at the bar, batting her eyes, licking her lips and marking her target for the night. Believe that!

Another thing I will say is—knowing what I know now, if my man was tricking up his money in some titty bar every week, I don't know if that would sit well with me, especially since I know what's really popping off inside most of them spots. Besides the dancers, it's hoes like me in those spots, swarming around like vultures ready to swoop down on unsuspecting prey. Hell, I'd let him go with his boys and all, but you best believe I'd be somewhere on the other side of the room, at the other end of the bar, dipped down real low, making sure his ass stayed focused.

I lay my book face down on the sofa and allow my mind to reflect on how good Majestic fucked me. There's something about a man hitting this soft ass from the back, deep, that drives me bananas. Especially when he has a long, thick dick, digging in and out, nice and slow, then grabbing me by the hips or pulling my ass cheeks apart, or sticking his finger in my asshole. I'll arch my back, swing and shake my hair wildly, then tell him to fuck me hard, to slap my ass. Mmmm. I'm telling you, fuck me from the back and watch me turn into a wild, freaky, ho-beast. And this morning, Majestic's sexy-chocolate ass could have fucked me in every damn hole. I can go for another round for sure. But I will wait for him to call me. If he doesn't, two more will. They always do.

My ringing cell snaps me out of my reverie. I glance at the screen. It's Garrett.

"Hello," I answer.

"How are you? I haven't heard from you in a while, so I thought I check in on you to make sure everything's okay."

Didn't I just speak to this nigga a few days ago? I pull in a deep breath. "I'm good," I say.

"I was hoping to see you today."

Hmm, thinking about my night with Majestic on top of the rain does have me wanting to ride a dick. And although my pussy is still aching, the fact still remains. Garrett always aims to please. Like I shared before, every time he's inside of me, he strokes my pussy and clit just right. Not only is he good with his dick and talented with his tongue, he's the kind of man who is obedient. He does exactly what is asked of him without complaint. If I want my pussy in his mouth or his tongue in my ass, he does it and doesn't expect me to reciprocate. Which is why I don't mind sucking down his dick or gargling his cow-like balls because, with him, there's no pressure. No fuss. Even though he's not scheduled—in my head—for another dish of this pussy for a few more weeks, against my better judgment, I think I will invite him over for a treat. Humph…so much for lounging around today doing nothing.

"Hmm. Sounds like you want a dose of this good stuff," I say, jokingly.

He laughs. "Well, when it's good, it's good."

"Unh-huh, and haven't you heard too much of a good thing ain't always good for you?"

"I'll take my chances," he says.

"Well, don't say you haven't been warned," I tease. "So what time you want to come by?"

"Your warning has been duly noted. Let me see," he says. "It's three-thirty now. How 'bout around seven?"

"Seven is good," I state. "You feel up to doing a little role-playing?"

He laughs. "What you have in mind?"

"I've been a naughty girl, Officer," I coo into the phone. "I need to be placed under arrest."

"Is that so," he says, lowering his voice. "And what should I arrest you for?"

"For wanting to swallow your fat dick down in my throat, then feel it deep inside my hot, wet pussy," I answer.

"That doesn't seem like a crime to me," he says, playing along.

"Well, it will be when I fuck you to death."

He laughs. "Sounds like I may need back-up."

"Baby," I coo, "the only thing you need to back you up is this soft, fat ass. So, bring your handcuffs and that thick dick of yours. My tight pussy is wet and ready to be wrapped around your delicious cock."

He pauses. I can tell his dick is hard, and I have him thinking. "Umm, let's make it for six-thirty."

I laugh to myself, telling him that the minute he walks through my door I want him to strip down naked, and come upstairs wearing nothing but his hat and his boots with his gun on his hip and his dick in his hand. "And don't forget the handcuffs," I add, running my hand over my pussy, then stroking my clit with my index and middle fingers. "I'm gonna have this pussy nice and hot for you."

"You always do, baby," he states. I can hear his aching desire for me in his voice. And I know he will come here on a mission. To fuck me deep and slow and purposefully as he always does. Then he will flip me over onto my stomach and fuck me hard and fast. "I'll see you in a bit."

"I'll be waiting," I say before hanging up.

At six-thirty, I hear the alarm chirp alerting me the door has been opened. In less than two minutes, Garrett struts into my bedroom in all of his nakedness, frisks me, squeezing my titties, tweaking my nipples, rubbing my pussy, grabbing and slapping my ass, before placing me under arrest. He reads me my rights, tells me, "You have the right to a stiff dick. You have the right to be fucked any way you want, for as long as you want. Anything you say or do will be the cause of me busting my nut in you. Do you understand?"

I nod, "Ooh, yes, Officer. Are you gonna beat me with that big stick of yours?"

"Put your hands behind your back," he says, twirling me around. "And spread your legs apart."

I stick out my ass. Brush it up against his cock. He slaps me on the ass.

"Keep still," he snaps, "before I have to charge you with resisting arrest."

"Oooh, big daddy, charge me."

He yanks my hands in back of me, then loosely cuffs them behind my back. He throws me onto the bed, sucks all over my nipples, licks and sucks all over my pussy, then rolls me over on my stomach and nibbles and kisses on my ass. Then he pulls open my ass cheeks, slides his dick into my creamy pussy and fucks me so damn good that my twat twitches and throbs. He slaps me on the ass. This time it stings, but feels good as he is pounding inside of me. He slaps my ass again.

"So you like breaking the law, huh?"

"Yeah, Mr. Officer," I say, moaning and winding my hips up and down on the mattress. "I'm a naughty, freak-nasty girl. What you gonna do about it?" He pulls his dick out of me, yanks me up off the bed, and slaps me on both ass cheeks. "Yeah, fucker, smack that fat ass."

"Oh, you like that shit, hunh? You like talking shit, hunh?"

"Fuck me!" I beg, spreading my legs wider. "Slam your fuck-stick in me!"

He bends me over, pushes my face down onto the dresser, then slides his dick into my piping hot pussy, fucking me from the back, slamming his honey-coated club in and out of me while his heavy balls slap up against my pussy.

I let out a ferocious moan. And by the time Garrett finally releases me from his dick pounding custody, I have cum six times. Oooooh, he really put it on me!

Mmmph. And now I'm lying here, basking in all of

my bareness. I inhale. Savor the moment. I swear I love the smell of sex in the air. There's nothing like the aroma of pussy, and sweat lingering around to remind you of how good you've been fucked. The taste of sex, the smell of sweet, musky fucking is all around me. Its scent hovers over me as I watch Garrett walk around the room with a towel wrapped around his waist. I exhale. There are still beads of water from his shower clinging to his strong back. I watch as he removes his towel and dries himself off. His dick slightly swings from side to side as he walks around the room. I close my legs, reliving how he fucked me deliciously. He glances at me, catches me staring at him. He smiles.

"You know," he says, sitting on the edge of the bed next to me. "I've been thinking." He pauses, gauging my reaction. I hold my breath, not liking the sound of this. I keep my eyes on him.

"I'm listening," I say.

"I need to know where this is going."

"Where what is going?" I question, feigning stupidity. I rise up on my forearms.

"This," he says, gesturing with his hands. "You and me, this situation we got going on here."

"What's wrong with what we have going on?"

"Nothing," he says, rubbing his chin, then running his hands over his neatly-trimmed face. "I mean every-thing. It's been three years and it seems like you are okay with us being strictly fuck buddies, and—"

"I am," I say, cutting him off. "I'm very much satisfied with the way things are between us."

"Well, I'm not. I want more."

For some reason, I hear Wade's voice; see his face, but it's not him. It's the exact same song, only a different performer. I purse my lips, think before I speak. The fact that we are having this discussion comes as no surprise to me. My gut was telling me something like this was about to go down between him and me. I hate how it may turn out. "Well, you can't have more," I huff. "You knew the rules going into this, so don't go trying to change them up now. This *thing* we have works."

"This works for who? You? Well, it definitely isn't working for me, anymore. I don't want to just be some side dick you call on."

I sigh, shaking my head. "Garrett, sorry to disappoint you, but I would rather we keep things the way they are. There's no need to try to make shit complicated."

"Babe," he says, caressing the side of my face. He leans and plants a soft kiss on my lips. And strangely, I don't pull back. "It doesn't have to be complicated unless you try to make it that way. I enjoy you, and you can't tell me you don't feel the same way. So I think it's time we try to take this to another level and see where it goes."

"Another level?" I ask indignantly. "Why in the world would you want to do that?"

He stares at me. "To get to know you outside of the

bedroom," he says. "To get to know you with your clothes on, if that's alright with you. Do you realize we've never gone out in public? Why is that? I would like to at least take you out to a movie, to a Broadway show, or something."

"Going out turns into dating; dating turns into relationships. And I'm not interested in dating, and I'm not looking for a relationship."

"Correction," he says, "going out turns into two people getting better acquainted. Dating simply offers the opportunity to spend quality time with someone you enjoy being around. And if it turns into a relationship, then cool. If not, at least we enjoyed each other's company. I think there's so much more outside of fucking that we can offer each other."

Great, I think, taking a deep breath. *First Wade, now his ass! What the fuck?!*

"What's the harm in wanting to get to know you better? Everything doesn't have to be about sex between us. There are times I would rather hold you in my arms, and watch a movie with you." He gets up and paces the floor, then stops in his tracks. He locks his eyes on me as if he's had an epiphany. He sits back down next to me on the edge of the bed. "Bianca, baby, you gonna need to make a decision."

I blink, blink again. I can feel myself about to tell him to go to hell with this bullshit. But, I will myself to stay calm. In my head, I can see me telling him there is no decision to make; telling him to get the fuck out of my face, out of my house, with this shit. The words form on the tip of my tongue, but none come out in the way I think them. And that baffles me.

"Garrett, I think you should go 'cause I'm not interested in having this conversation with you. Not now, not ever. What you've been getting, is what you get. So, don't start looking for more than what I'm willing to give."

He frowns, studies me. Squints his eyes, then gets up from the bed. "Yeah," he says, removing his towel from around his body. "I think you're right. I'd better get going. I'll call you one day next week."

"That's on you," I say, flopping back on the bed and pulling the covers up over me. "Lock the door on your way out." *Men*, I think, rolling my eyes up at the ceiling.

CHAPTER
TWENTY-TWO

I don't care how hard I try to manage my time, there never seem to be enough hours on the weekends to relax before it's time to drag back up in this piece. It always seems like the weekends fly by, but then comes the work week and the shit is dragging. It's bad enough that, on top of the fact that I don't feel like being here today, I'm worn out from getting slayed Friday, Saturday *and* Sunday. I don't know about you, but for me, a good fucking can be so exhilarating and exhausting at the same time. And right about now, I'm both. Three days of back to back fucking is enough to hold me over for a few days, hell, maybe even a week.

Now contrary to what you may think, I don't fuck every day of the week. However, if I do feel like getting my fuck on, that's what I do. Then the following week, I simply chill, and suck a dick or two while my pussy rests, which is exactly what I plan to do this week.

Also, just so you know, if I'm not fucking on any given day, I might only have a dude who likes—no scratch that, *loves*—to eat pussy to come through and pet this sweet kitty with his tongue. This cuts down on the wear and tear, and keeps my pussy from looking like it's been turned inside out. And if it's really urgent that I feel the thrust of a dick, I'll let him screw me in the ass. Please. Like I already told you, there's no shame in my game. I have three holes, and I intend to use them all. So, think what you want, but I will not be denied!

Anyway, I'm sitting at my desk engrossed in my work, typing a monthly report, when Nahdirah knocks on my office door, and pops her head in. "Hey, girl, you busy?" she asks, scanning the room with her eyes.

"No, not really," I say, looking up at her. "What's up?" She walks in, closing the door behind her, then plops down in the leather chair in front of my desk. "Is everything alright?"

"Yeah, I guess."

"Well, either it is, or it isn't."

"You know I'm starting to see why you stay to yourself here."

Humph, I think, propping my elbows up on my desk, and clasping my hands under my chin. *Somebody must have been talking about her, again.* "And what makes you say that?" I ask, knowingly.

"Girl, I'm really starting to see what you mean about some of these chicks here." I raise my brow and give her a look to get to the damn point. She gets the hint. "Saturday night I went out for drinks with Cheryl, Robin and Rachel down in the mailroom…"

Before she even says anything else, I already know that this has something to do with a man 'cause all three of them bitches she was out with are certified man eaters. So, I am so not interested in hearing this shit. Not today. But I allow her to bore me to death with her drama, anyway. She goes on to tell me how much of a good time she was having with these raggedy hoes until Robin has one drink too many and starts dropping hints about Rachel having slept with her man, Jake, then made some comment about how she had to have a tilted uterus to handle his curved dick. She says that's when it turned ugly.

I roll my eyes, but she is oblivious to my disgust.

"…So I asked her flat out how the hell she knew his dick was curved, and if she had been with him. She waved me off, talking 'bout 'I'm not the one you should be asking', then slapped her hand up over her mouth, looking over at Rachel, who looked like a bitch with a handful of cookies in her mouth…"

I keep my elbows planted on my desk, cupping either side of my face in the palms of my hands. I stare at her as she speaks, then subconsciously drum my fingers along the sides of my face. I find myself daydreaming about sucking some dick. And somehow the thought makes me remember back two years ago when I was at the Mall at Short Hills and bumped into this sexy, brown-skinned dude as I was coming out of the Verizon store. Dude had a shaved head, a mustache and goatee, and muscles for days. Yes, I gave him the once-over. Sure did. And didn't care how obvious I made it. He got the hint and started trying to get his mack on. We walked over toward the chairs in front of Bloomingdales and talked.

Now, I'm not exactly sure how the topic of sex came up—well actually, I do. It was right after he asked me what I liked to get in to, and I told him, "Sucking dick." Dude (and for the life of me, I can't remember his name) asked me what it was about dick sucking that I enjoyed the most. I had to think about it for a minute. Then I answered.

"The one thing I enjoy most about sucking dick is the fact that I am in total control of how good I make a man feel. I can lick, flick, nibble, suckle, slob, gobble, jerk, and swallow the dick. Massage his balls with my tongue, mouth and hands. Make him pant with anticipation. Bring him to the edge of ecstasy, then either push him all the way over or pull him back all in one stroke. Every time I take a man's dick in my mouth, I literally have him by the balls. And that to *me* is power."

Then he asked me what thoughts ran through my mind when I was sucking dick. I told him, "When I'm sucking dick, I'm thinking about my throat being my pussy, wet, warm and tight around a man's cock. My only focus is doing whatever it takes to get him off. I like to be face-fucked. And I like for a man to cum as many times as he likes."

By the time I was done talking, dude was licking his lips, drooling. Said I had him wanting his dick in my mouth right then. I looked down at the bulge in his pants, and smiled. Yes, I knew I had his undivided attention. So, me, being who I am, decided to take it a step further. I asked him who he was out there with. When he said he was by himself, I asked him what he was driving.

He said, "An Escalade."

I leaned in, lowered my voice real sexy-like, and asked, "You ever had your dick sucked in a mall parking garage?"

He looked around, then grinned. "No. Can't say that I have."

I smiled. He smiled. I gazed down in his lap, licked my lips and told him I felt like sucking some cock. I could tell I shocked him. He leaned back in the leather seat, opened and closed his muscular legs, probably to pinch the throbbing in his crotch.

I gestured for him to come closer with my index finger, then leaned in his ear and whispered, "Let me wrap my hot mouth and wet tongue all over your fat cock. It is fat, right?"

I wanted some dick, but not one that didn't have any meat on its bone. Like I said before, I'm not a size ho, but if I'm going to suck a dick I don't want to have to do it through a straw. I was relieved when he said it was nice and thick. "Let's go sit in your truck."

"For what?" he asked, trying to act like he didn't know what was up.

"So I can suck down your dick and lick your balls," I said.

He nervously looked around to make sure I was talking to him. I hate when men do that shit. It's all good when they come at a woman, but when the tables are flipped, most of 'em seem to clam up, and start getting all nervous and shit. Why is that?

Anyway, he said, "Sure, why not?"

And of course, I made sure to ask how long his dick was, and if it was cut. When he said it was eight inches and cut, I told him to lead the way to his truck so I could spin his top.

As soon we got inside his truck, I told him to pull it out. Even soft, it was nice and meaty. My mouth drooled as he stroked it. I pulled out my ruler, measured it. Confirmed his exact inches, then rolled a cherry flavored condom over his dick, and sucked him and licked all over his smooth balls until he popped his nut. I wanted so bad to suck his thick dick raw, but knew that was not an option. And neither was seeing him again.

I bring my attention back to Nahdirah. And she is still rambling on about nothing.

"...I can't believe that bitch was implying that Rachel slept with Jake."

"Well, did she deny it?" I ask, not really caring either way.

"Well, no. Not really. But..." she says, pausing.

I sigh, getting annoyed. "But what?"

"I asked Jake about it, and he didn't deny it either."

Because he fucked her ass, you dizzy bitch! I scream in my head.

"Well, did he admit it?" I ask.

"No, he said she was fucking crazy."

Of course he did, my mind snaps. *That's what they all say*.

"Okay," I say, gesturing with my hand for her to hurry the hell up and finish this boring-ass story. "Then what's the problem?"

"The problem is my gut tells me that they did sleep together. And I said something to Cheryl about it this morning and she shifted her eyes like she knew something, then told me to leave it alone."

I glance at my watch. "Listen. Do you think you can speed this up? I have a lot to do today."

"Geesh," she says, acting offended, "who got your panties all in a bunch today?" She folds her arms tightly across her chest, sitting back in her seat.

"No one," I snap. "I'm not in the mood for any of this ghetto-trash drama. And anything that has to do with any of these chicks here is exactly that. I could not care less about which ho in this building slept with your man. I told you from gate to stop telling these f-ing trollops your damn business, but you keep yapping your jaws."

"The only person I tell anything to besides you is Cheryl, and she's never given me a reason not to trust her."

I laugh at her stupidity. "Are you serious?! She's the main one who grins up in your face, then talks about you, and laughs at you behind your back."

"Well, I can't say if that's true or not since nothing's ever gotten back to me."

I shake my head. "Bless your heart. You need to buy a vowel and get a clue, for real. But hey, it's your life, not mine. Humph. I don't know why you have to hang around them birds, anyway. But you do. So I have to wonder about you as well."

She raises her eyebrow. "And *what* is that supposed to mean?"

There's a part of me that likes this chick; but, like I told you before, she could never be any friend of mine. "It means birds of a feather tend to flock together. So, if you're not one of 'em, but choose to hang around 'em, then stupid is what stupid does. And you get what you get. I told you before about fucking with these chicks here. But you keep on grinning up in their faces. So, truthfully, I don't want to hear nothing about what they said, or did, or felt. Now, unless you have something else constructive to talk about, kindly remove yourself from my office, and take this foolishness somewhere else."

She jumps up from her seat, slamming her hands on her hips. "You got a lot of nerve to be judging me," she snaps.

"I'm not judging you," I snap back. *Bitch!* "I'm judging the company you keep. But if the shoe fits, then wear it well."

She swings open my office door, and storms out, leaving a dust of anger behind her. I frown, shaking my head. *Pathetic*, I think, getting up from my seat to close the door. I'm sorry to say this, but some women out here are fucking trifling. And, trust me. It damn sure isn't always a man's fault for some of these women being so damn jacked up.

My cell phone rings. I glance at the number that flashes across the screen. It's Garrett. I sigh, contemplating whether or not I should answer. Against my better judgment, I pick up. Attitude in my tone. "Hello?"

"We need to talk," he says flatly.

"About?"

He sighs. "What we were talking about last night."

"There's nothing else to talk about. You said what you wanted, and I told you what I wasn't going to give you. What more is there to talk about?"

"Listen," he says, sounding frustrated. "I'm not trying to get into this over the phone. What time you getting off from work?"

"Oh, no," I say, getting up from my desk and walking over to the window. I look down onto the street. Watch as the cars go to and fro. "You are not about to come to my house to beat me in the head about something that isn't an option."

"Why isn't it?"

"Garrett," I say, walking back to my desk. I shuffle through a stack of mail. "I'm not having this discussion with you, today, tonight, tomorrow, or any other time.

Good bye." I disconnect the call, plopping down in my high back leather chair.

See, this is the reason why I need to stick to my three month rule. Fuck 'em, rotate 'em, then let 'em go. Out of all my fuck charms, Garrett—aside from Maurice— is the one who has never brought any drama with him. And he's never tried to make our arrangement out to be more than what it's been. Until now! What the fuck has gotten into him? I should not have to remind him of our "agreement," the one I've been guilty of not fol- lowing (with him) the last few weeks, the last several months: Fuck on occasion, once every few months.

Everything between us was fine. Now he wants to fuck on demand. Damn him! Like I said months ago, I've kept him around the longest out of all my fucks for the simple fact that he came with good dick. And he under- stood the rules. Now he's trying to rearrange shit. And I'm not feeling it. I already see where this is going, and I don't like it one damn bit. I swear I don't want to axe him. He feels so damn good inside of me, but I'll seal this pussy shut before I allow him to try to wife me up.

I take a deep breath. I try to list the reasons why I have been riding Garrett's dick off and on for the last two, almost three, years. Try to remind myself of the fact that he's always good, like Wade, for those last minute tune-ups. He aims to service the pussy with no questions asked. And he doesn't come with any damn drama. I try to balance the pros and cons of keeping him on my team. Try to rationalize holding onto him when I don't have any emotional connection to him. Or do I?

"Hell, *no!*" I snap, glancing at the Waterford crystal desk clock. It is twelve-fifteen. "Girl, get over yourself. The nigga has to go!" I get up from my seat and grab my purse, deciding to go to lunch. "And the next time he calls, I'm gonna serve him his discharge papers," I say to myself as I head out of my office and pass the different work areas en route to the elevators. I spot Nahdirah sitting at her desk, talking on the phone. I toss my hair and act as if I don't see her. Make her retarded ass invisible.

On my way to the Olive Garden on Route 22, Ian calls me on my prepaid cell. He says he wants to see me tonight. I decline. I am in no mood for him after the fucking Garrett and Majestic put on me over the weekend. Although I know sliding up in my pussy wasn't on his mind, having him plunging in and out of my asshole isn't an option either; especially not after the way he had my hole sizzling the last time. Thanks, but no thanks! I don't even feel like sucking his dick.

"Can I get a rain check?" I ask, pulling into the restaurant's parking lot. "Tonight's really not a good night." I park next to a burgundy Range Rover, then remove my seatbelt, keeping the car running.

"Damn, baby," he says, practically whining. "I was hoping to see you tonight." I roll my eyes. "What about tomorrow night?"

"Actually," I say, flipping down my visor to check

my eyeliner, "I was thinking more like one day next week."

"Well, how 'bout I come by and we just chill?"

"Umm, that sounds wonderful, but I'm not really in the mood for a man tonight."

"Oh, word? I can dig it," he says, sounding rejected. "How 'bout you hit me up when you ready to get it in then?"

No, nigga, how 'bout I erase you from my list, I think. "I will," I say, flipping up the visor, then shutting off the engine. "Thanks for calling."

"Aiight," he says. "Later."

I hang up and get out of my car, walking towards the entrance. There are about ten people standing outside, which tells me the place is crowded. I go inside and walk up to the podium, and I am greeted with a wide smile. "Hello, Welcome to the Olive Garden."

Hello," I respond. "Can you tell me how long the wait is?" She says it's a fifteen-minute wait. I decide to stay and give her my name. "I'll be outside," I tell her.

"This will light up," she says, handing me a wooden disc, "when your table is ready."

I go outside and sit on one of the benches. I am glad it's warm out, almost like summer. There are three chicks, two black and one white, sitting on a bench not too far from me. I overhear bits and pieces of their conversation, and roll my eyes up in my head as one of them is saying something about being tired of dating broke men. The other two agreed. I literally almost pass out when I hear her say she agreed with her mother that as long as a woman is spreading open her legs, she should never be broke.

I cross my legs, thankful I have my shades on as I roll my eyes again. I get so tired of hearing women talking about needing or wanting a man for his money. That shit is so tired, and played out. I mean, really. Enough already. I want so bad to chime in and tell her to get the fuck over herself and stop looking for handouts.

We are living in the twenty-first century and more women need to learn to be self-sufficient, and self-reliant, and stop playing the damn damsel in distress role. Stop settling for that gold digger mentality. It's really sad, and fucking disturbing, that there are still a lot of women who buy into that archaic way of thinking that a man should take care of her. As long as women hold onto that belief, they will always be dependent on a man. And when shit doesn't work out, she'll be a prisoner of her own choices—trapped, miserable and damn desperate to latch onto another cash cow before day's end.

Hell, my thing is, get your ass up and do something constructive with your life besides breeding a bunch of damn babies, and gold digging. Get an education, pursue a career, and stack your money. 'Cause at the end of the day, if a man ever decides to walk out on you with the next chick, or if he takes ill, you still need to be able to stand. As far as I'm concerned, don't rely on a man to do shit for you, except provide you with some dick, and maybe a little companionship.

Ugh! I am so glad my cell phone rings to give me something to do besides listen in on their pathetic conversation. It's Mitchell. "Hello."

"You ready to see me?" he asks, chewing in my ear.

I pull the phone away from my ear and frown. "What?"

He repeats himself.

Lucky for him the lights start flashing on my wooden puck. "Listen, delete my number." I hang up before he can say another word. *I don't know how the hell, or why, his woman puts up with him,* I think, getting up from my seat to go inside to enjoy an extended lunch. *Poor thing!*

As I follow the hostess to my seat, I decide I will take the rest of the day off. It's too nice to be holed up in somebody's office. I will go home and lounge around, listening to music and watching movies. Then tonight I will give myself a pedicure and a facial, before luxuriating in a hot, steamy bath with candlelight and soft music. I am not in the mood to be bothered with anyone else's man today. But come tomorrow, I'm sure I'll have my sweet, tight pussy wrapped around someone's stiff dick.

TWENTY-THREE

You know, after sitting here giving all of you nasty peeping toms an up-close-and-personal look into my life, confiding in you, sharing all of my deepest thoughts, dreams, my sexapades, freaky fantasies, sex tips, and even some of my fears as if you were my dearest friends, I realize I know nothing about any of you. Other than the fact that most of you like all this nasty shit I'm telling you, ya'll are a bunch of strangers to me. Hell, no! On second thought, a bunch of voyeuristic freaks, that's what ya'll are.

Humph, and what's even more crazy is that this realization reminds me that I don't have one female friend with whom I can laugh and talk and share secrets. And it also reminds me of the reason why. Because, like I said before, most females can't be trusted when it comes to telling them your personal business, especially phony-ass females. Like I mentioned before, they'll smile up in your face, and be plotting on how they can take your spot. I'm not having that. I did it once, and the trick tried to fuck my ex. So, now you know why I hate when a woman runs her damn mouth about her relationship or her man to her so-called friends. I did

that shit once—confided in a bitch about my relationship, and it cost me, dearly. I lost what I thought was a
good friendship, and a relationship with a man who
claimed he loved me. Then again, in hindsight, I really
didn't lose out on shit. If anything, I gained. And finding out the truth about both of their asses saved me a
bunch of drama in the end. Still, the whole ordeal was
painful. To be betrayed by someone whom you thought
you could trust. After all the times I had her back,
bailed her out of situations, gave her a shoulder to cry
on—hell, even lean on, unconditionally loved and cheered
for her, and…still, that wasn't enough. She wanted more.

And when that trick-bitch turned around and tried
to fuck my ex, Vaughn, I knew then I would never, *ever*,
trust another woman with anything personal again. I
started picking up on what she was doing when she
kept popping up over my house, unexpectedly. And it
just so happened to be any time Vaughn's car was in my
driveway. And she'd be prancing in wearing practically
nothing. Making it her business to let him know what
was what with her ass. A few times, I caught her ass
eyeing him, and licking her lips, trying to be sly with
it. No, I didn't say shit at first. See, I learned sometimes you got to know when to sit back and watch what
the fuck is going on around you. And that's exactly
what I did until I got tired of the show. Then I called
her ass on it. And the bitch had the fucking nerve to
say, "Oh, my God, I can't believe you'd ask me some-

thing like that. That shit is nasty, and disrespectful. You know I wouldn't do no shit like that."

"I don't know what the fuck you'd do," I had snapped. "But what I do know is you been coming around here every time Vaughn's car is outside—just popping up, like you were in the neighborhood, knowing damn well your motherfucking ass lives all the way across town. I also know that the last four times you dropped by, you made it your business to sit across from him so that every time you opened and closed your legs, he could get a glimpse of your pussy—"

"Bianca, now c'mon, girl," she urged, slamming her hands on her hips. "You are really starting to bug now. I can't believe you are going to stand here and accuse me of trying to get with your man. That's really stretching it. Please, he is cute and all, but he is not my type. And you should already know that."

I rolled my eyes. "Karen, do me a favor and save that shit for someone else. A pussy has no motherfucking conscience, and you know like I know that a horny bitch will fuck another woman's man without any thought. And I don't care what you say, *you* wanna fuck my man."

Then this bitch had the audacity to go into an Academy Award winning performance and start shedding tears, talking about how hurt she was that I would come at her like that, accusing her of trying to disrespect our friendship and my relationship. Lying bitch!

"You're like a sister to me," she had the fucking nerve

to say. "I don't know what you think you saw or heard, but I'm telling you, I would never do no shit like that."

"And there are plenty of sisters who will fuck her own sister's man, so don't give me that bullshit."

Well, long story short, the bitch would do some shit like that, and she tried. But, she didn't exactly get what she wanted. And when I confronted Vaughn about my suspicions, he readily admitted, which was surprising to me, that she had been saying slick shit to get at him, but he would brush it off. I asked him why he never mentioned it, and he said because it wasn't a big deal. Yeah, okay. I know better. As far as I am concerned, he should have checked her ass, then told me what the hell she was up to. But since he wanted to keep shit on the low, obviously needing and wanting her to feed his already super-sized ego, I dumped his ass. I had to wonder what else he was keeping from me. Call it extreme if you want. But if some chick I'm supposedly cool with is stepping to my man, I expect to know about it, right then. There's no damn way I want a man in my life who keeps secrets. Sorry, boo-boo, you ain't the one for me!

And since then, I haven't allowed another bitch into my personal space. The only bitch I need in my life is me. At least I know what I'm capable of. But another bitch, humph…now, that's a whole 'nother story. I don't trust 'em as far as I can throw 'em. And trust me, there's too many of them slimy hoes for me to be trying to spend my life tossing around, so I choose to not fuck with 'em, period. Hell, as advanced as technology is, you would think someone would have developed a Ho-scanner by now. Some type of device a chick can either carry in her purse to wand a bitch down, or install around her front door, so that when she allows a chick to enter her home or personal space, bells and whistles start going off, alerting her that the company she is keeping has the potential to fuck her man, if given the right opportunity. And then the bitch would have to wear some type of identifying marker, like a damn metal wristband or something so every woman with a man would know who the hell was amongst her. Now, if you ask me, that would cut down on a lot of damn heartache, disappointment and confusion.

Humph. I haven't given Vaughn or that tramp Karen a second thought in almost four years until today. And in all honesty, I need to probably thank her ass because if it hadn't been for that situation, I would probably be still thinking that bitch was my friend.

Anyway, even if Vaughn would have told me what she was up to, I would have still eventually ended it with him. There were some things about our relationship that weren't sitting well with me. Sexually speaking, he often left me unfulfilled. He had a nice nine-inch dick, but the mofo was stingy as hell with it. He couldn't deal with how I liked to fuck all the time. While I wanted it two to three times a day, he was okay with fucking once or twice a week. What kind of shit is that? That's some mess you do when you're in your sixties.

I practically had to beg him for the dick, or wait until he was asleep, then take it. Trust me. That started getting real played. Please tell me. How many men you know who have access to a steady supply of wet, hot pussy turn it down, unless they getting it somewhere else? But he swore up and down there wasn't another woman. Hmmm, okay. Then maybe…ugh! I don't even want to entertain the possibility of him being one of those down-low brothers as an option. But, nowadays, who the hell knows?

Bottom line, there was no regular fucking going on in my own bed. And when he did hit this pussy, he didn't like for me to talk dirty, or make a lot of noise. I felt so damn constricted with him. Couldn't do this, couldn't do that. Hell, he only wanted me to lie there, and listen to him grunt and pant for forty minutes. God forbid if I did let loose, and go into freak mode, he'd cum within ten minutes, and would barely be able to get it up again for another round, or he'd fall into a deep, bear-growling snore.

And through it all, not once in the three years I was with him, did I go out and get some side dick. I thought about it. And as bad as I wanted to, I refused to cheat on him. But, trust and believe, after I broke it off with him, I made myself a promise that I'd never be involved with another man who couldn't keep me satisfied in the sack. I refuse to be deprived (or stifled) sexually ever again. I will never again be with a man who feels the need to ration out the dick. And I mean that!

Ugh! All this "strolling down memory lane" got me thinking about my worst sexual experience. I was in my sophomore year in college and there was this junior, Jonathan, in my human development class that every chick on the campus wanted. If there were two hundred chicks sweating him, best believe he'd already fucked at least sixty of 'em. And on the surface, I could understand why. Besides being the star point guard for our basketball team, he was capital F-I-N-E. six, three, 210 pounds of smooth, honey-coated skin with the prettiest almond-shaped, light brown eyes I have ever seen (to this day) on a man.

Well, long story short, spring semester I gave him some pussy. And it was absolutely horrible! His dick game was so busted it was almost depressing. First, he had a hard time finding my hole, then he finally gets it in and it keeps slipping out because he's too busy trying to long stroke it when he was only working with a short stick, if you know what I mean. And when I say short, I mean measuring in at four-and-a-half very thick inches. I couldn't believe it! Now, I know I basically said a while back that dick size was strictly a matter of preference. And like I said, a big dick can be a nice treat from time to time. But, as I already mentioned, I'd rather have a man with a thick six to eight inches plunging in and out of my pussy on a regular, than nine inches or more. Because the truth is, I don't want my shit stretched open so wide that a man needs an express train to get to the other side, or a damn escalator in order to hit the bottom. That is not cute. But, fucking a man with only four inches of hard dick, now that is a damn travesty! Hell, as far as I'm concerned, that isn't a dick on a grown-ass man, it's a damn butt plug. Ugh, poor thing!

Anyway, back to Jonathan. I had to wrap my legs around him, then dig the heels of my feet into his ass to keep him in me. Ugh!! I laid underneath him, watching his face twist while his eyes were shut, thinking about the calculus exam I had in the morning, that's how boring he was. He had no rhythm and no damn stamina at all, and his only saving grace was the fact that he could kiss and suck a titty like he was nursing. Other than that, forget it! He came in exactly nine minutes and thirty-seven seconds (I know this because I timed it) and then went to sleep with me lying next to him frustrated, agitated, and disgusted with a very wet and very disgruntled pussy.

However, in all fairness to him, I will say that the second go round wasn't as bad as the first, but it still wasn't something to write home about. However, he did last twenty minutes and thirteen seconds before he splattered his nut across my back. And then he had the audacity to ask me, "Was it good?" My answer: "You have got to be kidding me!" Needless to say, I never fucked him again.

Oh, well. While I'm at it, speaking of men and the Almighty King ding-a-ling, most women don't realize that a man's spirit flows through his dick. And every time he ejaculates inside of her, he's injecting pieces of himself. His energy, his matter, his essence take root inside of her, and spread through her. Every time she allows a man to splash off in her, she invites all that he is into her space. Good, bad, and the ugly.

If a man is no good, she's going to allow him to do no good to her, and in return, she'll get nothing good. In my opinion, the reason why so many women can't break away from a no-good mofo is because his negative spirit lives within them, and holds them hostage. His tainted energy will spread through a woman like cancer, if not treated swiftly. Not that I'm an expert in the matter, but, again, in my opinion, the only way to break free from his ass is by having an exorcism done. She'll need to flush her womb, her mind, and her spirit from his; it's the only way to rid herself of his demon seeds. His negative energy and evil spirit will block her blessings and prevent her from ever meeting a man who represents anything that is positive and balanced.

She'll continue to allow his disrespect, his demeaning, lying, doggish-ways, and will allow him to bring her ass down, dragging it through a whole bunch of changes. So, my point is, women need to be very, very careful of whom they open their legs to, and whom they allow to nut up in them; everything that feels good ain't always good. A woman might find herself getting more than what she bargained for. No need to turn this into a debate. It's only something for you to think about. The only thing I'm trying to do is save some of your dumb asses from getting fucked over. So, beware. You've been forewarned.

Oh, please. Here some of you go, rolling your eyes again, looking at me all sideways and whatnot. Thinking, this bitch got a lot of nerve to be talking when she's fucking and sucking almost everything moving. Well, news flash, dear: I already know that this applies to me as well. However, I'm fucking them, not claiming any of 'em as my man, or trying to trap 'em into being something more than what they are, casual fucks. A choice I recognize is full of risks. Let's be realistic. What doesn't come with a set of hazards? Life is full of 'em.

Every man who I am with steps into this knowing that there's nothing but sex between us. I'm not lying or misleading anyone. And I'm not cheating on anyone. Nor am I willingly letting a man stick his dick in me without a condom. I may throw caution to the wind and fuck with reckless abandon, but I'll be dammed if I willingly get fucked raw. And, yes, I know condoms aren't 100% risk free, but it greatly reduces the potential risk. And since abstinence isn't on the menu for me, I'll go with the condoms. Good-day!

I blink.

Garrett is standing before me, leaning up against the frame of my front door. And I am shocked and annoyed, to say the least. What if I had someone else pulling up, or walking out? The fucking nerve of him to show up here unannounced and uninvited!

I take a moment to consider him before I speak. He's wrapped in smooth, cocoa-brown skin with bright, dreamy eyes that seem to sparkle when he smiles. I drink him all in. From his neatly trimmed mustache, gym-chiseled body and slightly bowed legs to the way he pulls in his bottom lip. I can't front, he is looking so damn delicious that I almost forget that I am pissed at him for showing up at my place. My lust for what hangs between his hairy, muscular thighs slowly creeps up on me, causing my mind to play wicked, sex-driven tricks on me.

For a brief second, I silently stare, toying with the mental images of him snatching open my robe, pinning me up against the wall, unzipping his jeans, then pulling out his hard, strong dick and shoving it up in my pussy. In a rhythm that matches the stroke of his powerful cock, I am suspended, moving my hips against his; his balls smashing against the softness of my open, wet, pulsating snatch until I feel the budding of an orgasm. I hear myself moan.

I blink again, feeling flushed.

Garrett is staring back at me. Perplexed look on his face. Unblinking, I know he is wondering why the hell I am standing here looking at him like a deer caught in headlights.

"Are you going to let me?" he asks, slicing into my fantasy.

I inhale, deeply. Take in his freshly-showered scent. *Why the fuck can't he just stick to the damn script?* "What are you doing here?" I finally ask, already knowing the answer. I shift my weight from one foot to the other. Fold my arms across my chest to block his view of my dark, protruding nipples.

"I told you, we need to talk—*tonight*."

"And I told you there's nothing to talk about," I say defiantly.

He squints. His jaw muscles twitch. I can tell he is thinking, pondering a way to get his point across. He pushes his way past me, bum rushes his way into my house, almost knocking me over.

Un*fucking*believable.

"Garrett," I snap, bracing myself up against the door before I fall on my ass. "Have you lost your goddamn mind?!"

"I told you we need to talk, and I'm not going anywhere until we do."

"I want you out of my house, *now*!"

He removes his leather jacket, tossing it across the arm of the chair, then sits his ass down, totally ignoring me.

I huff, slamming the door. "What the fuck is your problem?"

"You," he snaps.

"Then get out. I didn't invite you here, and I don't want you here, especially if you're trying to beat me in the head about shit I am not interested in. You can't simply come over here anytime you want and barge up in here like you got it like that." He continues to ignore me. "Garrett, do you hear me talking to you! I want you to leave."

He turns and faces me. He stares, but says nothing. Leans back in his seat, interlocking his fingers behind his head. For a moment, I think this nigga is crazy. Hell, maybe we're both fucking nuts.

I am now standing in front of him. Hands on my hips, neck rolling in ghetto fashion. "You got some muthafucking nerve! I don't know who the fuck you think you are coming up in here like you own shit. Last time I checked, I didn't have a man, and I don't want one. So, why are you here, huh, Garrett?"

He continues to stare. And it is starting to piss me off even more.

"So you're just going to sit there and stare. I thought you had so much to say."

He rubs his hands together, then leans over and rests his elbows on his knees, clasping his hands together. I can tell he is waiting for me to finish running my mouth. And in all honesty, I don't even know why I am standing here getting myself all riled up, having a one-sided argument with a man who isn't even mine. A man I don't even want. *Or do I?* I shake my head, finally realizing exactly how crazy I must look and sound.

I sit my ass down in the chair across from him, fuming.

"Are you finished?" he calmly asks.

I fold my arms across my chest, trying not to look like a pouting five-year-old. But for some reason, that's exactly how I am feeling. Still, I feel justified in my anger. As far as I am concerned, I have the right to be mad at him. He's here unannounced. He's pretty much barged his way in here. And he has disrespected, and disregarded, my house rules. He knows, like everyone else does, that I like my dick by appointment. Do not come here unannounced, or uninvited.

My cell phone rings. I look at it sitting over on the coffee table in front of him, chiming away. It suddenly stops, then starts up again.

"Aren't you going to answer that?" he asks, pointing at it. "It might be one of your little boyfriends."

He smirks.

I roll my eyes.

It rings again.

"Someone must really want to talk to you. You sure you don't want to see who's calling?"

I pull in a deep breath, slowly blowing out my frustration. "Garrett," I say evenly. "What do you want to talk about?"

"Oh, so now you're ready to listen?"

I tilt my head.

He runs his hands over his face. "What are you afraid of?"

"Excuse me?"

"You heard me. I want to know why you are so afraid."

"What makes you think that I'm afraid?"

"C'mon, don't do this."

"Don't do what?"

"Answer me with a question," he says.

"Well, I wanna know what makes you ask that."

"You act like you're afraid of letting me—hell anyone, get close to you. I'm not interested in hurting you. I want to spend time with you. What's so wrong with that?"

"What's so wrong with keeping things the way they've been?"

"It's not enough," he says, pausing. He pulls in his lips. Takes a deep breath, then continues, "Listen, I knew going into this what you wanted, and didn't want. You made that very clear. But, damn, after almost three years, you still act like you're okay with only fucking."

"I *am* okay with it. And you should be too."

"Well, I'm not. Don't you ever get tired of not having someone special in your life; a man of your own? Someone who's gonna love you, and appreciate you for all that you are instead of bouncing from nigga to nigga?"

"Honestly," I say, "I don't give it much thought. I am very much happy with the way things are in my life. I'm not looking for love."

"Then what are you looking for?"

"A stiff dick from a man who isn't going to stress me out about trying to give him something more than what I am capable of giving him."

"And what's that, Bianca?"

"Me," I state.

"And why not?"

I take a deep breath, prepare for the moment of truth. And the reality is, if I could draw a pension, I'd be on my knees sucking and/or fucking a good dick around the damn clock. There is nothing better than watching a man's toes open and close tight, and him biting his bottom lip as you're giving him that bomb ass head, or while you're galloping up and down on his dick, squeezing your pussy around it, and wetting it with your juices.

"Because I love dick," I finally say, facing him. "And I love *fucking* different dick. And, honestly, I really don't think one man can satisfy me. Not for long. Hell, I know he can't. I like variety too much for him to be able to."

For a split second, my mind drifts. I hear the deep, piercing voice of a faceless man, "Hey, baby, I'm looking for a horny, cock-loving, cum-hungry ho who wants to drain this big-ass dick."

"Sorry big daddy, I'm not fucking tonight."

"I don't want to fuck you," he says, slowly stroking his

dick, "just want you on your knees with your hot, wet mouth between my legs until I shoot my thick cum down your throat."

"Is that so?" I hear myself saying as I drop down on my knees, and slowly slide his dick down into my neck, lapping at his balls as I swab his dick in my throat. He moans.

Another faceless man comes behind me, pulls up my skirt, then yanks my cum-soaked panties down. He slaps my ass with his dick. "Yeah, you horny, freaky bitch, suck that dick. I'm gonna eat your ass, then ram this long dick up in your back." I hear myself moan, as he spreads open my ass cheeks. I can feel his breath approaching the center of my hole, can feel it pucker up in anticipation of his wet tongue gliding around its edges. He moistens my asshole, darts his tongue in and out until it opens—ready and eager, for his cock. He braces himself, grabs either side of my hips, then presses the tip of his dick into my hole. Slowly pushes in. I moan. He pushes further. I moan again. Take in more of his dick in my ass as I swallow and gulp down the other dick. My neck stretches; my asshole widens. Pulsating and gripping. Spasms of illicit pleasure shoot through me. And my body begins to shudder. I am being fucked at both ends. More stroking, more gulping, more moaning until we explode and I take all of their cum, making sure I don't miss a drip, a drop, or a spurting ounce of their creamy loads. I swish one nut around in my mouth, feel and taste its sweet and tangy milk. Then I swallow.

Leave some in my mouth, on my tongue, and paint my lips with it. I pull in the other nut, hold it deep in my asshole, then slowly push it out, allow it to slowly ooze out, and trickle along the back of my burning pussy. A moan catches in the back of my throat.

I blink, blink again. Bring my attention back to Garrett.

"Okay," he says, tilting his head, "so how many niggas you fucking? Tell me, Bianca, baby. How many dicks does it take to satisfy a woman like you?"

A lot, I think in my head. *Hell, countless*. This is the first time Garrett is actually calling me out. It's the first time he inquires about my sexual proclivities. For some reason, I think he wants me to say it—that I'm a ho, so that he doesn't have to. Hell, I never tried to hide that fact. But I know he's thinking it. Know he's wondering it—if my sexual appetite, and love for dick, is the makings of a full-blown sex addict or a nymphomaniac. I've dissected its meaning. As an adjective: Nymphomania is an excessive sexual desire in (and behavior by) a woman. As a noun: it's a woman with abnormal sexual desires. I am neither. And still the question remains: What's so abnormal with loving the way my pussy gets wet and creamy when a dick is being pumped deep inside of me?

"Garrett, I know you've heard the saying, 'you can't turn a ho into a housewife.' So why are you even wasting your time trying?"

He studies me. "Because, as crazy as this may sound, I have feelings for you. And I'd like to get to know you outside of the bed, and eventually, I want you to be my lady in the streets, and my freaky ho in the sheets. I know you're a good woman who's decided to guard her heart, making it hard for anyone to get close to her. I'm not looking to hurt you. I want to be the only man you ever need, or want.

"I know how much you love to fuck. Hell, I love fucking too. But I love fucking you more. The way your pussy feels around my dick; the way it tastes on my tongue; the way it smells when I press my nose up in it. I got it bad for you, baby. And, yeah, I might be playing myself. But there's no way that after three years of fucking me that you are going to sit here and make me believe that you don't feel some kind of way toward me.

"We have sexual chemistry that you can't deny. When we kiss, when I am inside of you, there's something that connects us. I know you feel what I feel. So why are you trying to ignore it?"

My love for dick, his love for pussy, is what connects us—nothing more, nothing less.

I blink, blink again.

Garrett stands up, pulls off his V-neck pullover sweater, kicks off his shoes, strips off his jeans, then steps out of his black knit boxer briefs. He stands before me in all of his naked glory. Beautiful, mesmerizing, sculpted pleasure. I will my pussy to be still; will my eyes from taking in the bulbous head of his semi-hard dick; the massiveness of his running back thighs. Force myself not to stare at his rippled stomach or the curly patch of hair that rests in the center of his defined chest. I can feel my heart beating. My hands are becoming sweaty. This is not how it is supposed to go down. He is not supposed to be in my home taunting me. Not supposed to be standing in front of me with his dick in his hand, slowly stroking it into a thick, throbbing erection.

I swallow hard.

Damn him, for being so fine!

Damn me, for being so horny!

I open my robe. Just that quickly, I forget that a few minutes ago I was fuming at him. Forget that he is trying to make me into something I am not able to be. Forget that I have to stop fucking him before things spiral out of control. I allow myself to forget every one of my rules, all for the sake of riding his dick, one last time.

I spread open my legs, pull open my steamy, wet pussy lips.

"You want this sweet pussy?" I ask in a sultry whisper. I can feel myself shaking from the inside out as he walks up on me.

He pulls me up from out of my seat, presses his thick dick up against me.

My clit jumps.

"Yeah," he says. "I want all that good pussy. And I want to serve you this dick anyway you want it."

CHAPTER
TWENTY-FIVE

My eyes snap open. Jolting up, I scan the room. It takes me a minute to get my bearings as my eyes adjust to my surroundings in the darkness. I am naked. My hair is disheveled, pussy is aching and Garrett is sleeping beside me, lightly snoring. I glance quickly at the digital clock. 3:21 a.m.

Fuck!

I inhale, exhale. Plop back on my pillow. I think about last night. How Garrett snatched me up and practically turned the tables—and manhandled *me*. Literally ripping my panties at the seams—the silk remnants of fabric still hanging around my waist—and sliding his dick in me full force. He took my pussy. Fucked it like he owned it; fucked my pussy, my ass, my throat to shreds. Let me tell you! I don't know what the hell Garrett was on last night, but he dicked me down so damn good that he had me yelping and howling and sounding like a damn hyena. Had me moaning, and saying shit I know I had no damn business saying. Yes, he fucked me deliciously silly.

And right now, I am hoping he was too caught up in trying to knock this pussy out the frame and busting his nut to remember half the stuff that came out of my mouth. 'Cause, baaaaby, last night, I was in rare form.

I replay the scene in my head. "You gonna let me have this pussy, baby?"

"Uh, mmm…oh…yes," I moaned.

He dug deeper, snapping his hips up against mine, hitting my spot.

"Oh, Garrett, I'll never get tired of this big dick… oh, yes… I've been missing this good dick…Oh, damn, Daddy, no one fucks my pussy like you…Harder! Harder!"

"Yeah, you love this dick, don't you?"

"Yes, Garrett, you're making my pussy cum…I love this big dick, baby."

"You want this big dick?" he asked, slamming it in and out of me, pounding the inside of my walls mercilessly. "You wanna make love to this dick?"

"Mmmph. Oh…fuck!"

He slowed his pace, pulled his dick out to the head, tip-drilled my slit, then slammed himself back in me with hard, deep, thrusts.

"Yesssssss…Oh, yesssssssssss…I want this dick in me every night…fuck your pussy, baby…ooooooh, yes…just like that…I don't want you giving this big dick to anyone else, but me…"

Ugh! And there you have it. Last night, I was saying mess like that and a whole bunch of other shit that has no damn value or purpose in the grand scheme of things. I mean, he didn't say anything about it afterwards, but

I know he damn sure was acting like he had hit the jackpot. Damn me! And damn him, for fucking me out of my damn mind!

I glance over at Garrett's naked body, shaking my head. *What the fuck am I doing?* I close my eyes. Try to make sense out of what transpired. But I can not. There's no logical, rational explanation as to why I have this man still lying in my bed. And most, importantly, there's no sensible reason as to why my pussy still feels sopping wet.

I snap up in bed again.

Realization hits me like a lightning bolt.

"Oh my God!" I scream, feeling between my legs. I am struck by panic. Feel myself starting to hyperventilate. "GARRETT!" I yell, frantically shaking him.

He stirs, but does not open his eyes. He moans something inaudible.

I flip on the lamp.

I shake him again. "Garrett!"

"Yeah," he mumbles, finally turning towards me, opening his eyes. He squints, trying to adjust to the brightness of the light. It is on him like a spotlight. "What's the matter?"

"You fucked me without a condom!" I shriek. "And you fucking came in me."

He stretches, and yawns. Scratches the side of his head, then sits up in bed. He is seemingly unfazed by what I've said. "I think we both got caught up in the moment," he offers, nonchalantly.

I jump out of bed, pacing the floor. "Caught up? Caught

up? Are you fucking serious? What were you thinking? I never, *ever*, fuck without a condom. How could you?"

"It's not like you tried to stop me," he snaps back, sitting up with his back up against the headboard. He watches me pace the room like a wounded lioness. "You are just as much at fault, and just as much responsible as I am."

In my head, I know what he says is true. I am totally responsible for what I allow to happen. I could have stopped him. But, I didn't. I allowed myself to get caught up in the heat of the moment. Still, I want to blame him. Want to lash out at him. This kind of shit *never* happens to *me*.

He blinks, the weight of his actions—our actions— finally hitting him. "Oh, shit. You don't have anything, do you?"

I stop in my tracks. In that moment, flashbacks of the first time I really took notice of my pussy runs through my head. I was twelve, sitting on the toilet with my legs spread open, and a mirror in my hand staring at it. It was then that flashes of those moments down in the basement watching my brother and his girlfriend took on a new meaning for me. Replaying their nasty deeds in my head caused an unexplainable yearning to sweep through me. And for the first time, I touched (I mean really touched) and rubbed my pussy, pulling open my thick, hairy lips until my insides got hot and wet, and started to tingle. I watched my finger slide in and out of my slit, wet and slick. I was so amazed and turned on by how it wrapped around my finger that I started to shake. I pressed on my clit, and almost fell off the toilet when a rush of sensations swept through me. In that one moment, I had experienced the joy of masturbation. After that, I spent every day after school locked in the bathroom, exploring new things about the furry little thing between my legs.

Then I think back on my first taste of six, thick inches of cut Indian dick. And let me tell you. Once I got past the smell of curry seeping out of his pores while he sweated, it wasn't a bad fuck. Actually, he was exceptionally long-winded, and a real greedy fuck. Exactly how I like 'em. He'd bust one nut, change the condom and be ready for more. And he ate pussy which got him extra bonus points. Besides, at five-eleven, one hundred ninety pounds, he was fine as hell with a rich, deep, cocoa-brown complexion, smooth skin, big, brown doe-like eyes with amazingly long lashes, and a beautiful set of teeth. And I kept fucking him, serving him this good American grade-A pussy for about two months, until he propositioned me to marry his ass for five thousand dollars so he could obtain his citizenship, then turn around and send for his family. Wrong answer!

I shake the thought, replacing it with a smorgasbord of cum-spurting dick, a kaleidoscope of images of men I have randomly fucked and sucked; assorted faces of men who have sucked and fucked and licked me every which way imaginable. I have had my pussy juices smeared all over so many faces, and wrapped around so many cocks, that I've lost count.

"It's a little too late to be asking that, don't you think?" I ask, indignantly. "But, no, I don't have anything." The nerve of him! "I get checked out every three months. Do *you* have something?"

I hold my breath. Wait for his response.

He frowns, pausing. And this causes a wave of concern to wash over me, pulling me under and tossing me around. I wasn't only worried about contracting HIV or AIDS, the Herpes virus was also rampant, as well as venereal warts. And I didn't want to be on the receiving end of any of them.

I shift my weight from one foot to the other, waiting.

"Well?" I impatiently push, slicing into the deafening silence that has entered the room.

"Hell no!" he finally snaps. "I get regular physicals, and blood work done. Hell, you've seen the results for yourself."

I silently exhale, relieved. He was right. I have seen his recent tests results, and he has seen mine. However, it was still a question that needed to be asked. And it is still a worry, one that doesn't simply go away on words alone. You are only as good as your last test result as far as I'm concerned. And even then, there are no guarantees. I know I fuck a lot, so I have to always be extra-careful not to contract something.

"So, what else you need to be worried about?" he asks, furrowing his brows. "You're on the pill, right?"

I stare at him, searching my mind for when I last took my birth control pills. Anytime I fuck, it's always on my terms. Everything is always planned, always prearranged. I don't do impromptu fucking. Don't ever risk not having a supply of condoms readily available. And I am always armed and ready with my own contraception. And when I haven't gotten my prescription filled, I only suck dick, or get fucked in the ass. Never, ever, do I—or have I—let a man stick his dick in my pussy, condom or not, without taking my pill. But, in a blink of an eye, Garrett has come and disrupted all that. And I have allowed him. I count in my head. One, two, three…Oh my God!

"I haven't taken them in three days," I tell him.

He stares at me, takes in my nude body. "C'mon back to bed," he says, seemingly unbothered by what I've said as he pats the empty space beside him. "There's nothing we can do about it now. Next time we'll be more careful."

Next time? I repeat in my head. *Nigga, there will be no motherfucking next time.* I glance over at the clock. It's now four-thirty in the morning. I have had enough of him for one night. Hell, for many nights. He has fucked out his welcome as far as I am concerned. Though our sexual tryst was consensual, for some reason I feel violated. "Garrett, get up and get out."

He stares at me, shaking his head. Surprisingly, he

doesn't say anything. He quietly gets up, and heads to the bathroom. I watch him as he makes his way across the room. His magnificent dick, swinging like a pendulum, glows in the aftermath of hot sweaty sex. He takes a piss. A long, angry stream hits the water, followed by a loud flush, then the sound of running water.

"You're a real piece of work," he says, walking out of the bedroom. I follow behind him. He moves so fast down the steps I almost think he jumps down them to get to the bottom of the staircase. He picks up his clothes. I watch him slip into his pants, glance at his beautiful dick. He doesn't bother with putting on his boxers. He shoves them in his back pocket, then slips his pullover over his head. "Whatever it is you're looking for I hope you find it before it's too late. 'Cause I'd really hate to find you ten years from now still chasing something you may not ever find."

"Then I guess I'll keep looking," I huff.

"Yeah, you do that," he says, glaring at me. I think I see a hint of pity burning in his eyes. But I do not entertain it. There is nothing pitiful about me wanting to fulfill my sexual desires. As far as I'm concerned, there is nothing shameful in my actions. And I offer no excuses, or apologies. He opens the door, preparing to walk out, then abruptly stops and turns to face me. "And the fucked up thing is I don't even think you know what the hell you want."

I say nothing. Just watch him as he walks out, slamming the door behind him. He leaves me standing in the middle of my living room, shaking my head. *Good riddance!* I think, cutting out the lights, then making my way back up the stairs. *Just like the rest of 'em, he'll be missing this good pussy.*

CHAPTER
TWENTY-SIX

Fuck, I'm so damn horny! I know, I know, after that mess with Garrett a week ago, dick should be the last thing on my mind. But it is, damn it! I want a man inside of me, feeling my walls wrap around his dick as I pull him deep into my pussy. Then I want my wet pussy in his face while I'm sucking his dick, grinding my hole down on his mouth while he has a finger in my tight ass. That's what I want tonight.

I'm telling you, if I were into animals, I could fuck a horse right about now. I swear it's nights like this that having my own man would come in handy. But, then I come to my senses, realizing how much work that would require and get sick to my stomach thinking about having one man crowding my space all the damn time. Ugh! *Oh, well*, I think, scrolling through my cell. *Can't miss what you don't have. But you can damn sure use what you got, to get what you need, so let me see who I can call.* Hmmm…Got dick?

I decide to call Ian.

But just as I am getting ready to dial his number, my phone rings. It's an 860 area code, a number I'm not familiar with. But I answer anyway. "Hello?"

"Hello, can I speak to Janaye?"

"Speaking," I say. "Who is this?"

"It's Q…we met a while back at Studio 9."

I smile. *Lady Luck and the Fuck Gods must be smiling down on me tonight*, I think. "Oh, so you finally got around to calling me; took you long enough."

"I couldn't remember the last two numbers," he offers. "I've been trying to get at you for a minute, ma. I tried every combination of numbers until I got you."

"Well, tonight's your lucky night."

"Yo, that's wassup. How 'bout I come through and scoop you up; you know, take you out to dinner and a movie?"

Dinner and a movie? I think, shaking my head. *Awwww, how cute!* I can't see myself sitting up in a restaurant with this young boy. But, I can definitely see him between my legs rocking this pussy. Of course, I'm not going to waste time telling him my no-dating rule. I glance at my watch. 7:18 p.m.

"How about you come fuck me instead," I say.

I can see him cheesing through the phone. "No doubt, baby. Where you rest at?" I give him the address. "Bet, give me forty-five minutes, and I'm there. You want anything?"

"Yeah," I moan into the phone, "that big dick ramming in and out of my ass."

"Ah, shit. That's what it is. You got my dick hard as hell."

"Just make sure it stays hard," I playfully warn. "I don't wanna have to throw your young ass out."

"Listen, baby girl, check this out. I might be young, but I ain't no chump when it comes to pussy. I've been fucking since I was twelve. And the one thing I can do is fuck all night."

"That's what your mouth says," I tease. "Now let's see if you can follow through."

"Well, I tell you what. I hope you can handle all this young dick 'cause I'm 'bout to come through and put it on you."

I laugh. "Baby, I was born to take dick. So, bring it on."

"I'll be there as soon as I drop my man off at his spot."

We hang up. I close my eyes, stretch my neck back and inhale, then exhale. "Bitch, I can't believe you are really going to fuck that boy; he's barely legal," I say out loud.

And, your point? I say in my head as I walk into my bathroom. I turn on the shower, take off my clothes, then step in. *The nigga's talking like he knows how to put the work in. So, hell yeah, I'm going to let him clock in. It's not like his ass is under eighteen. Shit, he's almost grown. Besides, anyone over the age of eighteen is fair game in my book.*

I step into the shower, grab my Dial Tropical Escape body wash and lather up my body. When I am done, I rinse off, then remove the shower head, place it between my legs and allow the pulsating stream of water to beat against my clit and pussy lips, spreading them open and letting the warmth of the water tease me. I press the shower head up against my hole and wind my hips. I grind my pussy into the water. *Yeah, I'm gonna ride the shit out of that young nigga. Wet that dick up all night.* A moan escapes me as I feel the budding of an orgasm. I press down on my clit, then cum in a thunderous roar.

An hour-and-a-half later, I open the door, wearing a black silk robe and a pair of red stilettos, along with a scowl. The nigga's late, and I'm not pleased. He waltzes his fine-ass in like he's got it like that. I take a deep breath. Think to tell him to go the fuck back where he came from for being so damn late. But the minute he grins and licks his lips, I quickly exhale and decide against it.

"Rule number one," I say, shutting the door behind him. "Be on time, or be turned away."

"Go 'head with that dumb shit, baby," he says, pulling me into him. *Ooh, he's an aggressive motherfucker.*

He's much taller than I thought. I look up at him, raising my brow. "'Go 'head' nothing. You don't show up here late and then be nonchalant about it. I don't know how the chicks you fuck with get down, but you don't have it like that with me."

"Yeah, but I will," he says in a cocky tone, grabbing my ass. "Damn, you got a soft ass."

I don't respond. Instead, I sniff. Sniff again. *This nigga's been smoking weed.* He attempts to kiss me on the lips, but I yank my head back, frowning.

"You been smoking?" I ask, stepping out of his embrace.

"Yeah, why? You got a problem with that?"

"Yeah, I do. I don't smoke. And the smell is offensive, so in the future—if you wanna get invited back, don't do it."

"Oh, aiight. You got that, ma. Anything else?"

"Rule number two—" he grabs me by the arm and pulls me into him again.

"Listen, I'm here to fuck, not get lectured on your house rules. So what's good, we fucking or not?"

Oh no this little young nigga didn't, I think, *shut me down in my own house.* My pussy jumps. "We fucking," I say, sheepishly, taking him by the hand and leading him up the stairs.

"That's what it is," he replies, slapping me on the ass, then palming it. "Yeah, you got a nice, fat ass. All that shit you been talkin' got me wantin' to beat somethin' up."

"I hope you know how to deliver."

"I can show you better than I can tell you."

"We shall see," I say, grinning.

And the minute we step into my bedroom, I push his young ass down onto the bed. He leans up on his forearms. "Don't get up," I say in a sultry whisper as I untie my robe, then let it fall off my shoulders and drop to the floor. I am standing in front of him naked.

"Gotdamn, you got a banging body," he says, licking his lips and pulling at his crotch.

I walk up to him, drop down between his legs, then reach up and unbuckle his belt. I unsnap the button to his jeans, then use my teeth to unzip his pants. He lifts up his hips and allows me to pull his jeans down around his ankles. He kicks off his unlaced Timbs and pulls off his shirt as I remove his pants from around his ankles and toss them over in the corner. He attempts to remove his black Polo boxers to release his already hard dick. Its weight is pressing up against the fabric of his underwear. But I grab his hands and stop him.

"Leave 'em on," I say, burying my face in the center of his crotch. I open my mouth and glide it along the length of his dick over his cotton boxers, wetting them up with my spit. I find the head with my tongue, then suck it over the fabric. His dick is deliciously thick. And its head is large and bulbous. I greedily suck on it.

"Yeah, you want that big dick, don't you?" he asks in a deep moan. I say nothing, just continue wetting up his underwear. "Ah, shit."

My pussy begins to tingle and my clit starts to fill with excitement. Unfortunately, I can still smell the weed, and it's starting to make me sick. I know I'm not putting him out because I want to fuck him all night and taste my cunt juice on his lips and tongue. Yes, I plan on breaking my no-kissing house rule. So what!

I abruptly get up off my knees and walk toward the bathroom. I can feel his eyes on the bounce of my ass. "Yo, why you stop?" he asks.

"I'll be right back." I go into my linen closet and pull out a bath towel set and a bar of soap, along with a new toothbrush, then turn on the shower. I walk back into the bedroom and hand them to him. "Here."

He looks at my hand and frowns. "Yo, what's this for?"

"If you want me to suck your dick and give you some of this pussy, then you need to go brush your teeth and take a shower, first, 'cause I can't stand that damn weed smell. Maybe them young chicks like that shit, but I don't."

He looks at me stunned, but says nothing. He stands up, steps out of his underwear, leaving it in the middle of the floor and walks toward me. I try not to stare, but I am amazed at how defined and muscular his body is. His beautiful dick swings like a pendulum as he walks.

"You getting in with me?" he asks, stepping up into my space.

I shake my head. "No, I'm already showered. I'll be lying right there—" I point to the center of the bed— "with my legs open, waiting for you to put your face in between them."

I laugh at him as he races into the bathroom. Ten minutes later, he steps out smelling like Lever 2000. *Lights…camera…action, let's fuck 'n roll.* I spread open and bend my legs at the knees, then pull them up to my chest. My thick, soft pussy lips immediately open to greet him. "Eat my pussy," I whisper to him.

He crawls up onto the center of the bed, buries his

face between my velvety smooth thighs, gives my pussy a deep passionate kiss, lovingly tonguing it, then opens his mouth and plants it over my pussy lips, darting his tongue in and out, lapping and twirling it around the insides of my pussy. I clench my walls in a greedy attempt to entrap his tongue. He feverishly sucks my cunt inside out. His mouth, his tongue, his fingers, play a sweet melody against my clit, causing a delicious current to rush through my body.

I let out a soft moan.

He replaces his tongue with two fingers, and slowly finger fucks me.

"Oh, yes…"

"You like that, don't you?"

I moan again.

"Yeah, that's right. Wet them fingers up." He pulls them out of me, then slides them into his mouth, one at a time and sucks on them. "Mmmm, you got some sweet-tasting pussy."

He lifts up, looks up at me. His lips shiny from the slick, sloppy wetness of my pussy. I reach for him, pull him up to towards me. Without words, he obliges. Hovers over me, and kisses me. He slips his cum-soaked tongue into my mouth. The scent from my pussy is heavy on his breath. And it is turning me on.

I extend my right arm, feel for one of the condoms that are on the nightstand and grab one, then hand it to him. "I'm ready to feel that dick in me." He tears it open with his teeth, rolls it on, then aims his engorged dick at my eager hole. He pushes in. I feel the stretch, and the heaviness of his dick as he plunges it into me, then quickly draws it back to slam it in again. "Oh, yes... *fuck* me..."

Twenty minutes later, I am on top, straddling his cock, swallowing every inch of him into my overheated, steamy pussy. He licks his lips, closes his eyes, gives into the feeling of being engulfed by flames of desire. "Oh shit," he moans. "You got some good pussy, baby." I smile, knowingly, clamping my muscles around his dick. I bounce up and down on him. Wind and grind down on his shaft.

"You wanna keep fucking this pussy?"

"Hell, yeah...fuck...oh, shit..."

He reaches up underneath me, grips my ass. "That's right, squeeze that ass, nigga. You wanna put your dick up in that, don't you?"

He lets out a deep moan:

"Oh, fuck...you riding the hell outta this dick. Oh, shit..."

I slowly turn my body around on his young, virile dick, then lean in and brace my hands on the shins of his legs. I continue bouncing up and down on him, giving him a back shot view of my pussy slurping in his dick. I ride him fast and hard until his body begins to shudder and he busts his nut.

"Aaaaaah, shiiiiiit...Aaaah...aaaah, fuck..." When he

stops shaking, I lift myself up off of his dick, then climb off the bed. "Damn, that shit was good," he says, catching his breath.

"Oh, the party's just getting started," I coo, opening up the bottom drawer of my nightstand and pulling out a jar of anal lube. "You still got this ass to fuck. And there are still three more condoms to use after that. And you're not leaving up out of here until we use every last one of 'em."

And with that said, Q pulls the wet, sticky condom off of his still rock-hard dick, tossing it on the side other side of the bed and replacing it with a new one. I climb back up on the bed, place the jar of lube next to me, then arch my back and spread my ass cheeks open.

"Stick your tongue in my asshole, first," I say over my shoulder. "Get it nice and wet, then put some of that lube in it. I want you to get it nice and slippery, working that hole open with your fingers, then run that big dick up in it until my pussy nuts."

When he finally gets his dick in my ass, I think I bug him out when I start slamming my hips and bouncing my ass back on his dick, talking real nasty and freaky while cumming from my ass and pussy. We fuck all over the bedroom in every way possible. And by the time I finish draining his dick—five condoms later, it is almost four in the morning.

"Yo, you the truth," he says as he's walking towards the front door. "You know how to handle ya business and take the dick like a real trooper. Word up. I'm tryna come through and hit that shit again real soon, ma."

I smile. "Anything's possible," I say, opening the door.

"You can really make a nigga fall for you, you know that, right?"

"So, I've been told. But I wouldn't let that happen if I were you. It would be your worst mistake."

"Oh, word? Why you say that?"

I don't answer. Don't feel like schooling him on the inner workings of my ho-ism. I yawn, covering my mouth with my hand. "Oh, 'scuse me. Aah. I'm beat. Thanks for the nut."

"No doubt, ma. Thanks for the experience."

"Get home safe."

He walks out with a big ass Happy Meal smile on his face. I wait for him to get into his car, then close the door behind him. I smile, knowing this will be one of his most memorable moments. Trust me. I was his first: his first taste of asshole on his lips and tongue, and his first feel of ass around his dick. It'll be a night he'll never, ever, forget.

'Cause I'm the Man Handler, baby!

CHAPTER
TWENTY-SEVEN

I think I am dreaming when I hear the chiming of my doorbell. But when the bell continues ringing, I drag myself out of bed, and shuffle down the stairs to see who the hell it is at my door at six in the morning. I swing the door open, surprised to see Tyler standing there in the doorway. Immediately my scowl fades into a smile.

"Hey, baby girl," he says in his cheery voice, giving me a big hug the minute I open the door. I step into his embrace, and melt. It feels good being in his strong arms. As a little girl, his hugs always made me feel safe.

I inhale his scent, closing my eyes and smiling.

He kisses me on the forehead. "Sorry for waking you."

"No problem. Is everything okay?" I ask, rubbing sleep from my eyes.

"Everything's fine. How's my favorite sis doing?"

"I'm your only sister, fool," I reply, playfully swatting at him.

He laughs, stepping back and removing his coat, then hanging it on the hall closet door knob. He takes a seat on the sofa. "Okay, then, so how's my beautiful sis doing?"

"That's better," I say, grinning. I sit beside him. "She's doing wonderful, thanks."

"You sure?"

I look at him, tilting my head. "Of course I am, why?"

He shakes his head. "Oh, only asking."

I know Tyler better than anyone. He doesn't simply ask something unless there's a reason behind it. I decide to let it go. "How are you doing?"

"I'm doing good. Your nieces and nephew have been asking about you. You really need to come by for dinner and spend some time with us, soon."

I smile. "I will. I promise. Now, tell me. To what do I owe the pleasure of this early morning visit?"

"Damn, can't a brother just wanna see his baby sister?"

"Of course you can. But, I know you, Tyler. You don't drop by *this* early in the morning unless there's something wrong. Are you sure everything is okay? Are you and Jacki okay?"

"Yeah, we're fine. Couldn't be happier."

"Ohhhkaaaay, so again, what's really your reason for dropping by?"

"Are you and Garrett still kicking it?"

As soon as he says his name, I shift in my seat. I raise my brow, tilting my head. "Why?"

He leans forward, and clasps his hands together, turning his head towards me. "Listen, Sis, you know I love you, and I don't get into your business or anything, but

I saw him the other day, and dude was looking real fucked up. It looked like he hasn't slept in days. I stepped to him on some brotherly type shit to see if he wanted to talk about whatever was going on, but he didn't really want to get into it. Garrett is like a brother to me, and it fucked me up to see him looking so down. My gut told me it had something to do with you, so I thought I'd come here to find out what was going on."

"And what made you think it had something to do with me?"

"'Cause for the last three years since dude met you, all he did was smile. Now he's moping around like he done lost his best friend. Are the two of you beefing or something?"

I sigh, shaking my head. "No, we're not beefing. Honestly, I haven't spoken to or seen Garrett in a few weeks."

"Ya'll still…you know, dating, right?"

"Garrett and I were *never* dating," I state. "He was simply someone I was spending time with."

He sits back in his seat. "The way dude talked, it sounded like it was more than that."

"He wanted it to be," I offer, deciding to be perfectly honest with him. "But I only wanted sex from him."

He playfully covers his ears, shaking his head. "I don't wanna hear all that."

"Oh, boy, quit," I say, laughing. "I'm a grown, sexy, and very single woman with needs."

"I know, I know. But I don't need to have that image of you planted in my head." ·

"Well, what the hell did you think I was doing with him? Playing cards?"

He lets out a hearty laugh. "Yeah, something like that."

"Yeah, okay."

He glances down at his watch. "Looks like ole boy got it bad for you."

"Seems that way," I say, crossing my legs, then flinging my hair. "But can you really blame him? I mean, look at me."

He laughs again. "Not at all. Even with all that sleep in the corner of your eyes, and your hair all wild, you still a beauty."

I laugh, too.

He shifts his body, facing me. "Look, baby girl. I know it's really none of my business as to why things didn't go anywhere between the two of you. But, trust me. Garrett cares a lot about you."

"Did he send you over here to talk to me?"

"No, not at all. He doesn't even know I'm here. Truthfully, he never really talked much about the two of you. He didn't have to. It was all over his face. And I respected him for that. He's really a good dude."

"I know. That's why I kept him around for as long as I did. Tyler, I really wish I could have given him more, but I don't have it in my heart to be in a relationship right now. And I don't want to be in one, just for the sake of being in one. It wouldn't be fair to him, or to me."

"I hear you. So, what exactly did he want from you that you weren't ready to give him?"

"He wanted to date. But, ultimately, he wanted a relationship."

"Would that have been so bad?"

"Not if I wanted him like that."

"But you kept him around for almost three years, why?"

"You want the truth?"

He nods. "Please."

"We had an arrangement. One I thought was working out fine until he wanted to change it up. I was content with the sex, 'cause the man can put it down in the—"

"I get the point," he says, cutting me off.

I spare him the rest of the details and say, "I told him I didn't think we should continue seeing each other."

"Oh, I see," he says, shifting in his seat. "And there was no room for compromise?"

I shake my head. "No, not as far as I was concerned."

He smiles, shaking his head. "Still the same ole Bianca, I see."

"What's that supposed to mean?" I ask, feigning insult.

"Spoiled rotten," he says, laughing. "Still gotta have everything your way."

I fold my arms defiantly across my chest, pretending to be hurt that he would say such a thing. "Well, what's wrong with that? I've always gotten my way. I have a mother and father and six overprotective brothers who have always given me my way."

"That's because none of us wanted to deal with your nonstop tantrums."

I laugh. "Whatever."

He gets up. I stand as well. "Listen, beautiful, I gotta get going. I had really hoped you and Garrett would have hit it off. I wanted him to be the one for you."

"Well, I'm not sure if anyone is the *one* for me."

He studies me, furrowing his brow. "What are you so afraid of?"

Honestly, Tyler's question takes me off guard. I hadn't expected him to ask me that. And I definitely didn't expect to answer it, not in truth, anyway. But I do. I take a deep breath, and say, "Commitment, and getting hurt."

He slowly nods, knowingly. "You gotta face your fears, baby girl. And be willing to take some risks. You won't know love unless you open up your heart and mind to it."

"I'm not ready to."

He gives me another big bear hug, holding onto me for what seems like forever. I don't know why I am becoming so emotional, but as soon as he pulls away, I feel myself tearing up, not wanting to let him go. "I love you, Sis."

I force a smile, fighting back tears. "I love you, too,

Tyler." I open the door for him. "Thanks for stopping by."

"Anytime, baby. You know I'm here for you. Day or night, anytime you feel like talking, about anything, you call me, you hear?"

I nod.

"Good." He kisses me on the forehead. "Now, get back in the house before I have to arrest one of these peeping toms in your neighborhood for staring too hard at you."

I giggle. "Bye, silly."

He starts to walk off, then turns around. "Oh, one more thing, I think you should call him."

"Call who?" I ask, feigning ignorance.

He grins, wagging a finger at me. "You know who, fool. Garrett."

I shrug. "Maybe."

He throws his hands up in the air, walking off, shaking his head. "See you at Mom and Dad's for Thanksgiving," he says over his shoulder.

"Can't wait."

I watch him get into his SUV, and wait until he backs out of the driveway and pulls off before shutting the door.

Thirty minutes later, I am in the bathroom hugging the porcelain bowl with my face inches from the toilet water, violently throwing up my guts. My head feels like it's ready to explode into tiny pieces. A film of sweat forms across my forehead. *Oh God*, I think, heaving, *I'm pregnant.*

I practically crawl up the stairs, and pull myself up in my bed. I reach for the phone, and call out sick from work. Though I don't need anyone to tell me what I already know in my heart, I call my gynecologist's office, anyway, and leave a fierce message for someone to call me back to set up an emergency appointment. Although I ride the pro-choice and pro-life fence, I am very much aware of what I have to do. There's no other recourse. *I can't have this baby*, I think, drifting back off to sleep.

CHAPTER
TWENTY-EIGHT

After three days of being out sick, I'm finally back up in this bitch. Although I'm still not feeling one hundred percent myself, I'm not throwing my guts up as much. And, despite some tossing and turning, I was able to get a few hours of sleep last night.

I'm sure most of my restlessness is due to the fact that my gynecologist did confirm that I am pregnant. A situation I don't feel like thinking about, or discussing, right now. And another contributing cause for my sleeplessness was the dream I had last night. I was being fucked by Derek (of all people!). He was my first dick suck, my first fuck, my first kiss, my first love. And now, after all these years, he was in my dreams, opening and exploring my pussy with a new found appreciation, savoring every inch of me. In my dream, he recognized, and appreciated, the fact that I wasn't that same naïve little girl he had fucked on my twin bed all those years ago. He acknowledged I was a woman with a pussy that devoured dick for breakfast, lunch and dinner. And he fed me his big, thick, black dick that seemed to have grown and had gotten thicker from the days of our youth. He understood I was a woman with needs and wants and desires; a woman who knew her body like the back of her hand; a woman whose pussy ached for and begged for and cried for dick. He sensed this and embraced my womanly curves, adored my full titties and large nipples, kissed my hips, my thighs, the back of my knees, my ankles and feet. He sucked on each of my toes, then dragged his tongue along the center of my thighs until he reached my paradise. Then he mounted his lips around my pussy and clit, and sucked and licked and slurped until my pussy exploded in his mouth.

After that, he crawled up over me, kissed me with his pussy-stained lips, started sucking on my lips, then stuck his tongue into my mouth, twirling his around mine. We became tongues and hands and mouths and lips and bodies colliding against each other. Tasting and touching and wanting and feeling desire until he slid his dick inside of me and stretched my pussy to capacity, hitting its bottom, knocking its sides, causing its walls to expand and contract and erupt into a sea of sweet, sticky juices.

I reached up underneath him, reached for his balls, touching them, stroking them, spreading my legs wider so that he could get lost in my pussy, bury his dick in my pussy, and never want to leave my pussy. I felt for his dick while he humped and pumped and banged and grinded and thrust in and out of me, feeling his hot, thick cum creeping out of my wet pussy, trickling down the center of my ass. Then…I woke up!

Gazing out of my office window, I squeeze my legs shut and wonder why I would dream about Derek—of all people, after all this time. I haven't seen or heard from him in years. Haven't even given him any thought. The last I had heard, he was married with six kids, living somewhere in Houston. *Damn, six kids,* I think, shaking my head, remembering how good he stroked my pussy. I suppose if things had been different between us, if we hadn't grown apart, I would have been the one bogged down with a house full of whining-ass brats. I shudder at the thought. I don't know how some of these women do it. Pop out a bunch of babies like bunny rabbits.

I wonder to myself what's worse, not wanting to have a baby by someone you love or not wanting one by someone you have no emotional connection to. For either scenario, I come up with no logical answer. Is there really a difference?

Someone taps on my door, disrupting my reverie. The door slowly opens before I can invite whoever is on the other side in. Everett peers his head in. "Hey there," he says, smiling. "You busy?"

"No, not at all," I reply, motioning for him to come in. I silently watch him as he shuts the office door, then glides across the room towards me.

Cool.

Calm.

Collected.

His eyes are on mine, and there is a flicker of lust behind his pupils—and mine. But I dare not act on it. I will not. Everett has a confidence in his swagger that borders on cockiness. One that lets me know he's a man who handles his business in and out of the bed. A man who knows what he wants, and goes after it, even if it means taking it. I find it, him, enticing. He sits in one of two leather chairs positioned in front of my desk.

"You're looking *and* smelling good enough to eat, as always," he says, innuendo dripping from his thick lips as he sits back in his chair. He spreads open his legs. I try hard not to look in the center of his crotch. I shift in my chair, twirling a strand of hair. *This delectable motherfucker is asking for trouble*, I think, leaning forward in my chair, then steeple my fingers beneath my chin, taking him in. He looks deliciously fuckable sitting in front of me wearing a crisp, starched pink shirt, a chocolate-brown and pink swirled tie, and chocolate-brown dress slacks. His faded beard is neatly trimmed. Not a hair out of place. I breathe in his cologne. Silently hold it in, then exhale. *Nice*, I think, catching the glint of his one-carat diamond in his left ear.

He smiles, flashing straight, white teeth. Then tilts his head, studying me.

"What?" I ask, fumbling with the diamond pendant hanging around my neck.

"You're glowing."

I nervously shift in my seat. "So, what brings you to

my side of the world?" I ask, dismissing his comment.

You, I hear him say in my head. I shift in my seat.

A mischievous grin forms on his lips as he eyes me seductively. "I don't think you're ready for the answer to that," he says, his grin turning into a wide smile. "So I'm going to give you the politically correct response, and say I was only stopping by to see how life is treating you."

"Yeah, okay," I reply. "You could have called me for that."

"Yeah, you right," he offers, still smiling. "But it wouldn't have been the same as seeing your beautiful face."

Despite myself, I smile, shaking my head. "Everett, you are a mess."

"I'm trying to be your mess, but you keep running from me."

"Okay, here we go with this running foolishness again. Think what you like. But I'm not going to keep having this conversation with you."

He leans forward in his seat, resting his forearms on his thighs, cupping his hands together. His eyes lock on mine. "Why can't two consenting adults who happen to work in the same building spend time together outside of work when they both are obviously attracted to each other?"

I stare at him, consider him without being too obvious. Summa Cum Laude Morehouse graduate; third ranking at Wharton School of Business; chiseled, athletic build, smooth cocoa-colored skin with high cheekbones and almond-shaped eyes; succulent, pussy-eating lips; ruggedly handsome; well-spoken; and impeccably dressed.

"What makes you think I'm attracted to you?" I ask, raising my brow.

"Oh, you're not?" he asks, feigning hurt. He sits back in his seat with his legs gaped open, then breaks into laughter. I stare at him. Count the number of times he fans his legs open and shut in my head. *Eight.* I force myself not to look at his bulging crotch. I shift in my seat, keeping my eyes locked on his.

"Not at all," I lie. "Don't get me wrong. You look good and all, but definitely not my type."

He lets out another hearty laugh.

"I'm glad you find me so amusing."

He gets up from his seat, places the open palms of his hand down on my desk, leaning forward. His face is inches from mine. He stares into my eyes, and I feel myself becoming flushed from the heat of his breath. But I do not blink, do not shift my eyes from his gaze. I refuse to become undone.

"Amusing, you are not," he says, licking his lips, "but beautiful and incredibly sexy you are. So, why don't you stop fronting and let me take you out to show you how a real man treats a woman?"

"Everett, sweetie, sorry to bust your bubble, but there is nothing you can do for me that I can't do for myself. I pamper myself. And I already know how to treat myself the way a woman should be treated without the offerings of a man."

"Is that so?" he asks, smirking. He softly brushes the back of his index and pointer fingers across my cheek. "Then perhaps I can offer you something else."

I sigh, pushing my chair back from my desk and getting up. I walk around my desk to where he stands. He turns and faces me, and I step in front of him—closing the space between us. I look up into his piercing eyes.

"I see how you look at me," I say seductively, pulling on his tie. "The way you undress me with your eyes, licking your lips every time I'm in your space. So, it's no secret that you want me; that you want to run your dick up in me. Want me to wrap my soft lips around your dick and suck it nice, and slow and very wet, then gulp down your nut…"

He grins.

"Yeah, you like that don't you, big daddy? You like it when a woman talks nasty to you. Gets your dick hard, doesn't it?" I move in closer, reaching between his legs, feeling the length of his dick as it thickens. "Yeah, you gotta nice big dick…"

He is up against the edge of the desk. "Why you fucking with me, baby? Don't you know you're looking to get yourself in a heap of trouble?"

I continue stroking his dick. He looks over my shoulder, watching the door. "Oh, trust me. I'm not fucking with you, big daddy. And I'm not scared of trouble.

Isn't this what you want me to have?"—I lick my lips—
"All of this long, juicy dick."

He sits on my desk, allows me to knead and pull at
his dick over the fabric of his pants. OhmyfuckingGod
his dick is big! I feel my panties getting soaked. If I
didn't stand by my rules of never fucking anyone from
the job, I'd pull his dick out of his pants, drop down on
my knees and suck the nut out of his ass.

Everett grabs me by the shoulders, pulls me into him,
and brushes his lips against my left ear. "Let's get out
of here and take an early lunch so we can go somewhere
more private." His voice is low and sexy and full of lust,
but sounds almost pleading. "You got me real fucking
horny now. I'm ready to beat that pussy up, baby."

I smile, pulling away from him. "That won't happen,"
I say, abruptly letting go of his dick. I walk over to the
door, feeling his gaze on my ass. And I throw an extra
shake in my hips. I open the door, turning to face him.
"Thanks for the visit, but I have a lot of work to do. So,
if you don't mind, it's time for you to go."

I walk back over to my desk, and sit down.

He is looking at me with a dumbfounded expression
on his face, glancing down at the massive imprint of
his dick. When he finally realizes what has happened,
he shakes his head, smiling. "Ain't this a bitch?" he
mumbles, getting up and adjusting the front of his pants,
trying to conceal his bulging cock, to no avail. "Give
me a minute," he says, walking over to the window and
looking out.

He is silent for a moment, thinking, searching for a distraction along the busy streets to ease the swelling in his pants.

"Is everything okay?" I ask, grinning.

He shakes his head, bringing his gaze in my direction. He straightens his tie against his shirt. "You have no idea," he replies, walking towards me. He plants his hands down on my desk, leans in and speaks in almost a whisper. "You've awakened the mighty beast, and it will not rest until I finally have you in my arms, and in my bed—where we both know you wanna be. Make no mistake, pretty baby. I will finish what you've started. I just hope you can handle it."

I cock my head to the side. "Is that so? Well, I wouldn't hold my breath if I were you, or your beast."

"Oh, don't worry, beautiful. I'm a very patient man. I'ma have you, if it's the last thing I do. And when I do, I'ma fuck the shit out of you real good, baby. Enjoy the rest of your day." He winks at me, then heads towards the door, gently closing it behind him.

I swivel in my chair, leaning my head back, fanning myself. Replaying what I've done has me heated, and wanting to fuck or—at the very least, suck down a dick. "Bianca, are you nuts? What the fuck did you just do?" I think aloud in my head. "You were actually playing with his dick in here. Anybody could have walked in on your ass."

Well, then they would have caught me with a handful of dick, I muse, breaking out in uncontrollable laughter.

My cell phone *dings*, snapping me out of the moment, alerting me that I have a text-message. I hate being texted!

My BlackBerry vibrates. I ignore it, pulling my phone out of my bag, then reading the message. *When can I slide my dick up in that hot pussy again?*

Ugh! It's Barry. I think to ignore it and delete the shit, but decide against it. Shifting in my chair, I stare at the screen, then reply: *You can't.*

Ten seconds later, he replies back: *Stop frontin'. You know you want me to fuck you.*

I text back: *LOL. Get over yourself.*

He replies: *C'mon, baby. I wanna feel those soft, pretty lips wrapped around this big dick.*

I text back: *Barry, go to hell, nigga!*

My phone rings. It's him. "What part of go…to… hell don't you understand?" I ask.

He whispers into the phone, "Why you fucking with me? You know what it is."

"I don't know shit, nigga. Why are you calling me?"

"I want some pussy."

"Get it from your woman. Mine is no longer available to you."

"Why not?"

"Uh, because I said so; because the last I checked, it was my pussy and I fuck who the hell I want, when I want. And it's not you."

"What, you got some other nigga hitting that shit?"

Oh my God! This nigga has the fucking nerve to sound

jealous. How typical is that? Nigga got a woman at home, and still trying to check for me like I'm his or some shit.

"Listen," I say, sighing. "I'm not doing this with you, okay? I've tried to keep this shit short and sweet, but you are really trying to work my nerves. I done told you once, and now I'm telling you again, Stop calling my motherfucking phone. I already warned you before, if you keep fucking with me I am gonna blow your spot up. Is that what you want? 'Cause if so, you are on your way to getting it."

"You know what," he says, sounding agitated. "On some real shit, fuck you."

I laugh. "And sweet dreams to you too, boo-boo."

He hangs up, fuming I'm sure.

Twenty minutes later, my BlackBerry vibrates again, alerting me that I have received more new emails. I pick up the device, and look at the various email accounts. I scroll over to my Nutcracker69 email address, then press to open. There are six emails, but the one of interest at this moment is the one from Dickudown-allnight. I smile, knowing he'd do precisely what I knew he would. I read the note:

Call me, anytime. 908-555-1313.

Now the question is, do I call him now to squelch my curiosity, or do I make his ass wait a few days. Hmmm. *Never let a nigga think you're too eager, even when you are*, I think in my head. That settles that. He waits.

I glimpse up at the clock hanging on the wall. It's almost noon so I decide to get out and grab lunch. There's nothing worse than staying cooped up in an office building all day. Cold outside or not, I need some fresh air. Just as I'm gathering my things, my cell rings. I glance at the number, rolling my eyes. It's Andre. Another dismissed fuck charm. Now Andre is one handsome dude. I must give him that. He's five-eleven, two hundred ten pounds of mocha-colored man with deep, piercing, hazel eyes and a sexy-ass smile. And it definitely doesn't hurt that the nigga has a thick, seven-inch dick with the biggest set of balls I've ever seen on any man. But the problem with his ass was he lied too damn much for me, just one lie after the other. Why, I could never understand. At first I would entertain the lies, like the time he told me he owned all this property, yet his ass was bouncing from spot to spot, sleeping on floors and sofas.

"Umm, and why aren't you staying in one of the places you own?" I asked him.

"Oh, because they're all rented out," he answered, looking me dead in my face.

"Hmmm, they're all rented out, I see. Well, sounds like you should be sitting on serious paper."

"Yeah, I am. But it's all tied up in investments."

I laughed.

"What, you don't believe me?"

"Actually, I don't. But if you say so."

"Oh, you think I'm lying?"

I *tsked* him. This motherfucker must have gotten the wrong memo to believe I'd believe the shit he was tossing out. I read his ass. "Yeah, nigga, I think you're full of shit. How the hell you gonna own all this property, but you don't have your own shit to live in? How you gonna have all this money, but you running around borrowing other people's cars 'n shit? What kind of shit is that?"

"Yo, fuck it," he snapped. "I don't have to answer to you, or prove anything to your ass. You're just like the rest of these scheming-ass bitches, always tryna get up in a nigga's pockets."

"Oh, you got the wrong one," I snapped. "If I wanted to dig into your pockets, the only thing I'd be pulling out is lint, nigga. So, don't get it twisted. All you do is lie. And I'm sick of it. You're not my man; you are someone I fuck. There's no reason for you to hit me with a bunch of fucking lies. So do me a favor, if you don't know what the truth is, keep your damn mouth shut when you're around me. Hell, the only thing you really should be doing when you come here is eating and fucking this pussy, then getting the fuck out."

Needless to say, I had him eat my pussy. And after I came all over his mouth and tongue, I kindly put him out.

Let me ask you something. Do you think men cheat more than women? Or is it that men simply get caught more often than women? Well, if I had to take an educated guess, I'd say that it's probably sixty/forty. Men cheat more, but women are much better at doing it. See. With women, unless they are a trick off the bat, most are going to be faithful to their men no matter what, but when they start to feel slighted or have had enough of their men's neglectful ways…watch out! A woman might start to look elsewhere, but it won't be with just any ole Tom, Dick or Harry. And she's definitely not going to be impulsive about it. She is going to weigh her options. She'll mediate on it, and may even attempt to communicate her feelings of concern with her mate before she makes her move. But when her cries for attention and affection fall on deaf ears, she'll take matters into her own hands. And when she finally does decide to creep, trust and believe it's going to be a calculated, and well-planned event.

Whereas, a man will jump at the opportunity to have sex with another chick even when there's nothing amiss in his relationship, as long as he thinks he can get away with it. And most men are extremely impulsive when it comes to sex. Get a man's dick hard, and he's ready to fuck on the spot if and when possible. It's the thrill of the chase (or the possibility of getting caught) that gets him off. And it's an ego booster. That's not to say that women don't push their men into another woman's arms with their post menstrual-nitpicking-histrionic-drama-queen bullshit, because they do.

However, I do believe that men and women typically cheat for different reasons. But at the end of the day, no matter what the reasons, men and women (both) want to feel appreciated, needed and significant in their relationships. And when they don't, it makes it a whole lot easier to justify their cheating ass ways.

But, the bottom line for me is, people are going to be who they are. A person who isn't invested in or committed to his partner, who doesn't believe in—or understand the concept of—monogamy, is going to cheat no matter how many times, or how many ways, he is fucked by his partner. He is never going to be satisfied with what he is getting at home, and he is always going to be scheming about how he can get it without getting caught. And, yes, it is really fucked up.

I am not in a relationship—yes, ironic I know, a ho giving relationship advice—go figure. Still, I have fucked enough men to know that in order for any relationship to work, both parties have to listen to each other. And when I say listen to each other, I am not only talking about verbal cues. I mean, listen to each other's breathing, pay attention to their movements. Trust me, it will tell you all you need to know. If a man hits a spot on a woman's body, or licks/sucks her pussy and clit a certain way that makes her ribs rise, and a gasp escapes from the back of her throat, he should remember that spot, make a mental note of it. If a woman is sucking her man's dick, or riding his dick, and he starts to wiggle underneath her, starts moaning, that means he's enjoying how she's giving it to him. That doesn't mean stop what you're doing; keep the rhythm going. When she/he no longer responds, then change up. On that note, I'm moving on…

My cell phone rings. I glance at the number. It's Jamil. My fuck charm, and, of course, another man creeping on his woman; see what I mean? "Hello," I answer, tossing my latest issue of *Ebony* on the coffee table, then placing my bare feet up on top of it.

"Hey, you free tonight?" he asks in a low, monotone voice. He sounds discouraged, perhaps depressed.

"Is everything alright?" I ask, partially concerned.

"Yeah," he replies, sighing. "I want some stress-free pussy tonight."

"Oh what, wifey ain't giving you any this week?"

I chuckle to myself, knowingly. The only time Jamil calls is when his woman is in bitch mode and has shut down the pussy, which seems to be every other week. That's the craziest shit to me. I remember this chick I used to be cool with telling me how she and her man would be beefing and she wouldn't give him any pussy for weeks. I almost choked on my chicken salad. What in the hell?! The way I like to fuck, I could never be the type of chick who withheld pussy from her man. What kind of shit is that? The only person I'd really be punishing is *me*. And, like I've said many times before, I'm not depriving myself of shit. I'm sorry. There's no way, I'd have some dick lying next to me, and I wasn't riding or sucking it. Not going to happen. My thing is, so what if you and your man are beefing. What the hell does one thing have to do with the other? Curse his ass out, fuck him real good, then finish addressing the issue. And if it can't be resolved, either let it go, or move the hell on. Trust me. After a good fuck, you'll see things more clearly. Well, that is, if you're not the type of chick who's weak, and allows a stiff dick to control her. Anyway, go figure. And these chicks got the nerve to wonder why their men creep. Duh! 'Cause your whack ass ain't serving up the pussy.

Don't roll your eyes and suck your teeth at me. Please. That shit is so damned corny to me. As far as I'm concerned, withholding sex is one of the worst things anyone can do in a relationship. It is definitely asking for trouble. I mean, I can understand a few days (*maybe* a week at most). But more than that—weeks, months, years—is pure craziness.

I remember this dude, Cedric, I used to fuck a few

years ago. His wife, well girlfriend at the time, would go months at a time without giving him some pussy. She would talk about how she didn't feel like it. I couldn't believe it. And he had been with her for almost fourteen years. But he had had enough of the begging, and eventually wandered outside looking for someone who would fulfill his needs. And, ooh la-la…lucky him!

See. With me, it was an open invitation. And he truly appreciated being able to have access to some good pussy on a regular. I'd delightfully wet his cock and balls up with no hesitation. Mmmph. Let me tell you. His dick was six and a half inches and thick as sin. And he knew how to work the hell out of it. Oh my God, he was such a damn good and greedy fuck. He would gobble this hot pussy up like there was no tomorrow, then fuck me like his life depended on it. We kept up our little rendezvous for almost eight months, before his dumb-ass wife came to her senses and started fucking him like she had some damn sense. Damn, I miss that dick. Oh, excuse me for digressing. As you can see, I do that from time to time.

"Something like that," he states, bringing me back to the conversation.

"Poor thing," I coo. "I bet that juicy, black dick is aching for some of this wet, sweet, gushy stuff."

"Exactly. So you got me or what?"

I glance at my watch. It's a little after eight p.m. on a Wednesday night. I really don't feel like being bothered with him, and my sex drive still isn't up to par, but—after entertaining thoughts of smearing my creamy nut on his tongue, I decide to allow him to indulge his carnal urgings. And hope I don't get sick in the process. Anyway, I always heard pregnant pussy was the best kind, so until I have my procedure, there's no sense in letting any of it go to waste.

"What time you tryna come by?" I finally ask, forgetting all about the dick fast I'm supposed to be on.

"In like an hour."

"I'll be here," I say, before hanging up.

Humph, I think, shaking my head. *I wonder what his dumb-ass did this time for her to stop wetting his dick.* Now, make no mistake. Like I said, I don't necessarily agree with rationing out the pussy. However, I do believe there may be instances where a woman probably should. Like when her man continues to take her for granted and expects her to keep catering to his whims while he shits all over her. Or when she fucks her man any-and-every which way the wind blows and the greedy mofo still isn't satisfied, still needs to run off and fuck the next chick. Oh, hell no! Now, that's when the shop should shut the hell down—indefinitely. And if you ask me, after that, her ass should be entertaining divorcing herself from his no-good ass. Damn sure not staying.

I'm sorry. I know I fuck other chicks' men, but trust me. If my man was cheating on me, and I found out, there is no other discussion to be had other than when you moving the fuck out—if we live together. Or I'll see you in divorce court—if we're married. I'm not going to want to hear none of that "baby-I'm-sorry-it-was-a-mistake-I-fucked-up-I'll-never-do-it-again-because-I-didn't-mean-for-it-to-happen" bullshit. Lies, I say! You can save that shit for the birds.

I know; I know; that's easier said than done. And that's why there are countless women staying in fucked up situations because they believe it's too damn hard for them to get out of them. Maybe it is; maybe it isn't.

Speaking of which, how many women do you think believe in the saying: How you get him is how you'll keep him, or is that how you lose him? Hmmm…Let's see. I suspect not too many buy into it 'cause if they did, they wouldn't be hard-pressed to jump into a relationship with someone who they already know is capable of cheating, because he was cheating on the ex with her dumb ass.

Now, my next question is: What makes this ho think her pussy and head game is so damn tight that he won't ever get the itch to cheat on her retarded ass with someone else? If he did it once, isn't it possible he'd do it again?

No need to answer now. Let's let it sit and marinate for a while. Jamil will be here in another thirty minutes, and I need to get ready.

Jamil rings my doorbell, and I open the door wearing a loosely-tied, baby blue, silk robe. My cleavage and the scent of lust greets him. My hair is in an upsweep do, but I anticipate it being tossed about by the time he finishes with me; this is what I think—hell, hope for, as he walks through the door and grabs me. I quickly turn my head as he tries to kiss me, causing his dark lips to brush against my neck.

"Oh, you still on that shit?" he says, stepping back, looking at me. "I don't know what the big deal is."

"You know how I feel about kissing," I say. It's not that I dislike it. I actually enjoy it. But I am not letting every man who walks through my door and sticks his dick up in me, kiss me. In my opinion, kissing opens the doorway to the heart, forces emotions to surface. Brings about a certain level of intimacy that should only be reserved for someone you are emotionally connected to. Not someone you only want for fucking. Oh, alright already, with the exception of Garrett, Maurice, and…yes, Wade. And I'm not emotionally connected to any of them. But that's beside the point. "Besides," I continue, "you're not my man; nor will you ever be, so there's no need for your lips to ever touch my lips unless they're the ones neatly folded between my legs."

He laughs, removing his jacket, then pulling off his brown Timberland boots. "You crack me the hell up with all of your little rules."

"Well, that may be so," I say, opening my robe and letting it fall from my frame. "But this is where you chose to be; this is where you wish to be, so my little rules must not be a problem for you."

"Hell, baby," he says, stepping out of his boxers, "you can have as many rules as you want as long as you keep serving up the pussy and wetting this"—he grabs his cock and swings it back and forth—"dick up as good as you do."

His cell phone rings. He lets it go into voice mail.

I roll my eyes. Men are so fucking stupid. I have told him over and over again, when he's with me and his woman calls, answer the damn phone. Continue doing what you do when you're not creeping with me. Don't change up your routine. But, this mofo disregards what I say every time.

"Why didn't you answer?" I ask. But at this point I could really care less.

His phone rings again.

He ignores the question and the call, taking me by the hand and leading the way upstairs. When we finally get up to the bedroom, he sits down on the edge of the bed with his legs spread apart. He rests his elbows on his thighs, clasping his hands together, and sighs. I sit next to him, reach for his semi-hard dick and begin stroking it until it thickens.

"Why can't I get this shit at home?" he asks, turning his gaze on me. "Instead of a bunch of bullshit," he blurts out.

I stare at him, let go of his dick. "If you're not happy with her, why do you stay?"

He looks at me as if what I've asked is incredulous. As if the answer should be obvious. "I love her."

I blink, blink again. If that isn't the weakest, lamest, most overused excuse in the world.

"But you're sitting here."

"What does me loving her have to do with that?"

"Yeah, okay, if you say so. If cheating on your woman is love, then do you, boo. But obviously, you're not happy."

He scowls. "I never said I wasn't happy. I simply can't stand her mood swings and shit, and her being stingy with the sex. Other than that, I'm good."

"So then why are you sitting here again?"

"For some pussy."

"And why is that?"

He sucks his teeth, leaning back on his forearms. "What's this? Twenty fucking questions?" He huffs, looking down at his dick resting on the left side of his stomach. "You gonna take care of this dick or what?"

"Yeah," I say, taking his cock back in my hand. I flick my tongue over the head, plant slow, wet kisses along the back of its shaft, then abruptly stop, letting go of it again, "after you answer my question."

"Are you serious?"

"Absolutely. If you want your dick wet, you'll answer the question."

"I'm here tryna get some pussy, because I ain't getting it at home."

"Hmm...very interesting," I say, getting up from the

edge of the bed. I walk over to one of my walk-in closets and pull a satin robe off one of the brass hooks. I slip it on, then tie it tight across my body.

He frowns. "What you put that on for?"

Now, before I go off on his ass, let me vent for a minute. I already know that, in life, you get what you get, when you do what you do. But, dammit, please tell me what in the hell I ever do to have to listen to a damn man whine and complain about what it is his woman doesn't do. Okay, okay...usually, I'm all ears. But, tonight, at this very instant, I am not in the mood to hear shit except his balls slapping up against the back of my pussy. But he wants to bitch about shit that makes me no never mind, and it has fucked up my mood. It's bad enough I really wasn't up to seeing his ass tonight anyway. But, because I let my pussy talk me into letting him come through, I got to listen to this shit. Sorry, baby...not tonight.

"Because," I say, facing him with my hands on my hips, "obviously you need a relationship therapist; not pussy."

And before he can open his mouth to say anything else, I put him out. Tell him to get his shoes on, stuff his dick back into his boxers, and to get the hell out of my house; and to never, *ever*, ring my goddamn doorbell again unless he's coming here to fuck, not vent. And I mean it. When I say I'm not in the mood for any chitchat, only fucking, that's the hell what I mean. Don't come here with the extras!

CHAPTER
THIRTY

Okay, another question for you—and let's see how many of you can get it right. What is the one thing that a man cherishes, and will die trying to protect; the one thing that will bring him the most drama if he isn't able to be in control of it; the thing that will disrupt his life if not used wisely? Answer: His DICK!

Yes, his most prized possession. The thing he nurtures, and adores, and defines and measures his manhood by. The thing he takes pride in. The cock, the dick, the penis, the pipe, the wood, the schlong, the ding-dong, the ding-a-ling, the Jimmie, the Big Boy, the snake, the bamboo, the bozack, and a slew of other pet names assigned to describe his appendage. Hell, I remember having a man in my bed lying on his back with his legs spread wide, begging me to make his "hotdog" spit. Ugh! That was it for me. Dude had to go. Then there was one who had the nerve to tell me to suck the cream out of his "Twinkie." Maybe it's me, but a grown-ass man referring to his dick as a damn Twinkie has some serious issues, as far as I'm concerned. And I'm not sucking or fucking anything being likened to a damn sponge-cake filled with a bunch of white cream.

Anyway, dick (or whatever cute, little descriptive term used), is made to be sucked, to be fucked, to be pleased. And I have no problem doing what is necessary to take it on the most enjoyably wet, toe-curling ride of its life. I have no problem teasing it, tormenting it, or taming it.

And like I said before, when I'm fucking a man, my mission is to give him a total out-of-body experience. I want to take his breath away, then give it back. Make his damn toes curl, his nipples harden, his balls rattle, and his eyes roll all the way in the back of his head. Then when he's about ready to bust that nut, make his body ripple with an electrical energy that shakes his soul. When I roll off of him, I know the mission is complete when he's looking dazed and confused, then starts drooling and slurring his words, lying there paralyzed. Yep, I've fucked his ass into a stroke.

My phone rings. I am not familiar with the number, but I answer anyway. "Hello?"

"Hey, Beautiful," the smooth, velvety voice says on the other end. "I'm in town for a few days and was hoping you had some time for me."

It's Maurice. He's a cross country truck driver I met three years ago at a party in Brooklyn. He's six-two, two hundred forty pounds of thick, dark-chocolate man meat who calls me whenever he's in the area. The last time we fucked was about six months ago, so I'm down for another round of his nine and three-quarter inch dick with the thick vein running along the shaft. Mmmm.

And of course he calls me, wanting to dip his dick into my sweetness. And, *yes*, he's another man I've tongued down.

I smile. "Of course I do," I say, imagining his pillow-soft lips on my nipples and clit. Mmmph. The thought of his dick up in my love basket sends chills down my spine. I'm telling you, there's nothing like straddling a man's face and cock, and riding his ass down into the mattress. Mmmm. And with Maurice, I can position his dick in me to hit every angle of my pussy and grind my clit against his pelvis to really get off. Oh, yes! The thought of shoving my panties in his mouth while I slam my wet, hot pussy down on his dick has me tingling. In my head, I hear myself telling him to lie back, and enjoy the damn ride. "What time you coming?"

"I'm on my way," he says. "And I'm horny as hell, too."

"Just how I like it," I say, sliding my hands between my legs, then pulling open my lips. "Ooh, daddy," I whisper. "I can't wait to feel your dick in this pussy."

"And this dick can't wait to feel you," he says. "I'll be there in 'bout half an hour."

I glance at the clock. 8:17 p.m. *Oh, shit*, I think, jumping out of the bed and racing to the bathroom. *I have to freshen up this cat box.*

Twenty minutes later, I am showered, and relaxed, and horny as hell. The thought of fucking Maurice has me on fire. I crave body contact, body heat. Humping and grinding. Mmm, I smell temptation in the air. Or is that sex? No, it's Maurice ringing my doorbell.

I rub almond body butter into my smooth skin, then hurriedly pull out the bobbie pins that keep my wrap in place, and comb it out, allowing my hair to form around my face. I shake my hair, admiring its shine and bounce, then add a splash of cherry wine lipstick onto my lips. I slip on my red-lace robe and slide my feet into my black mules. I give myself a once-over in the mirror. I smile. *You a bad bitch*, I think, smiling as I head down the stairs to let in the dick for the night.

When I open the door, Maurice is standing there, smiling and holding a bouquet of flowers that he obviously got from Shoprite. But I am appreciative of the gesture. I smile back at him. "For me?" I ask, feigning surprise. I take the rainbow assortment of roses from him and bring them up to my nose. "Mmm, they smell pretty." Every time he comes through, he brings a different bouquet of flowers. The last time he was here he brought me a bunch of damn, big-ass sunflowers. What the hell! But I graciously accepted them anyway because it was the thought that counted. "You are going to have me spoiled if you keep bringing me flowers every time I see you."

Before he even gets the door closed, he is pulling me into him and prying my lips open with his tongue. I allow his cinnamon-flavored tongue to dance with mine. It is his kissing that gets my already hot juices to stir between my legs. Like Garrett, Maurice is really more than just a fuck for me. I genuinely like him, but unfortunately not enough to have him as my man. However, I like him enough to allow him to kiss me, use my shower, rest, eat whatever food he might bring or order in—'cause I don't do any cooking for a man who isn't mine—and I even allow him to hang around after the sex. He still has to be out of here before the sun comes up. All that waking up in my bed, looking for breakfast or another dish of pussy is out.

"Damn, girl you look good," he says, stepping back from me. "I missed the hell outta you." He grabs his crotch area. "Look how hard you got my dick, baby."

I reach for the lump that has formed down the inner part of his thigh and lightly squeeze. "Oooh," I moan. "I can't wait to feel this fat dick up in me. I hope you ate before you got here 'cause I'ma fuck the shit out you, and I don't want you passing out on me."

He laughs. "Baby, I got two weeks' worth of nut for you. So we can fuck all night if you want. Just let me take a quick shower."

I smile, taking him by the hand and leading him to the stairs. I walk in front of him, seductively swinging my hips as we climb the stairs. My ass cheeks peek out from under the edge of my robe, and he grabs for them, palming a handful of my ass with his big hand.

"Damn, I've missed all that fat ass. Looks like it's gotten fatter since the last time I came through."

I playfully smack his hand away, racing up the stairs. He laughs, following behind me. And as soon as we get into the bedroom, he pounces on me like a sex-starved lion ready to devour its prey. I fall back on the bed and he falls on top of me, kissing me with a passion I never knew he possessed. And this shocks and excites me.

His tongue dances alongside of mine. It is eager and demanding. His kiss is causing electrical waves to jolt through my body. He is sucking on my bottom lip. I am sucking on his top lip, then his bottom lip. My pussy aches for his deep strokes. My clit pulses for his touch. I know I will fuck him right now if he doesn't get off of me and go take his shower.

"Hold up, baby," I say, prying his lips from mine. "Slow down. I'm not going anywhere."

He kisses me again. "I know. I've missed you."

"I can tell," I say, smiling. I lean back on my right forearm, then raise my legs—bending them at the knees—and open them wide, showing him my dripping snatch. "And look how much this pussy missed you."

He leans in and kisses the slit of my pussy, then slides his tongue in and stirs my fire. I let out a soft moan. "Oh, yes…eat that pussy baby. Mmmph…" He flicks my clit, then mounts his mouth over it and sucks on it, causing it to swell. I fall back on the bed, rest my legs up over his shoulders, then press his head deep in between my thighs. I thrust my hips upward. Fuck his face. Grind my pussy onto his soft lips and thick tongue. "Oh, yes…Oh, yes…oh, yes," I chant. An orgasm is crashing against my walls, shaking my uterus. He senses this, and sticks his thick middle finger, then his index finger, inside of me, massaging the roof of my pussy. I twist and moan.

"Yeah, you like that, don't you, baby?"

I moan.

"Yeah, that's right, wet these fingers." His thumb flicks against my clit, teasing it, taunting it, causing my pussy to grab his fingers. "That's right, squeeze them fingers, baby. Bust that nut for daddy."

I am bucking, and moaning, and cumming, and screaming. "Aaah, aaah, aaah…oh, shit. Aaah, aaaah, aaaah…"

He removes his fingers and replaces them with his tongue, digging deep into my treasure chest. My body shakes. The room spins. And I am cumming all over again.

When I am done, Maurice continues licking up my juices. And when he finally comes up for air, his lips are coated with my cream. I reach for him, pull him into me and lick his lips, suck on them. Kissing him, and tasting the sweet-tanginess of my pussy on his lips and tongue throws me into the most powerful orgasm I've had in weeks. We share a long passionate kiss for a few more minutes while I cum before he pulls back from me. "I better go get in the shower before I end up saying fuck it."

I smile, panting. "Yeah, you better, 'cause I don't want to be sucking on your smelly balls."

He plants another kiss on my lips, then gets up. I watch him make his way into the bathroom. The water turns on; then the shower head comes to life. Maurice leaves the door open. It's his unspoken way of inviting me to join him. I smile, knowingly. Oh, what the hell? I get up and remove my robe, then saunter into the bathroom.

I step into the shower behind him. He turns around to face me, smiling. I take the soap from his hand, and lather him up. I massage his dick and hairy balls, rinse him off. He does the same for me, then directs me to sit on the edge of my shower ledge and wrap my legs up over his shoulders so that he can eat and finger my pussy again. I reach for the shower rack, and pull down a string of beads. Maurice takes them from me, licks my clit until I am moaning, then sticks the anal beads into my ass one bead at a time. And when I start to cum, he increases the licking, fingering and pulling the beads out one at a time, driving me wild. I return the favor. I get down on my knees, kiss the tip of his dick, flicking my hot tongue over it, licking up and down his shaft as if it were a chocolate lollipop, then wrapping my lips around the head and sucking him slow and deep until his dick throbs. He dips at the knees, pumps his hips and face-fucks me with slow, long purposeful strokes. And when his balls tighten and dick thickens, I replace my mouth with my hands, jerking him off until a load of thick, white cum erupts from the head of his dick, like hot lava.

By the time we get back into the bedroom, we are so heated and horny from our shower episode that we are all over each other like wild savages, pulling and grabbing at each other. I push him down on the bed, slip on a condom and climb up on his dick. I lean forward, place the palm of my hands flat against his chest, and start licking and sucking on his nipples while he grips my hips, and thrusts his pelvis up and down, stabbing his dick in me. Mmmm. The shit feels so damn good.

I take his fingers into my mouth and slowly suck on them. By the way, did you ever notice how sucking on a man's fingers turns him on? Well, most men that is. Anyway, more women should try it. So, here's my personal tip: When you gently suck on them, love them with your tongue, sliding your lips all the way down to their knuckles, then licking the spaces in between. Trust me. The warmth and wetness of your mouth and the softness of your lips will drive them bananas every time.

Well, that's if you're doing it right. 'Cause if you're sucking on a man's fingers like they're a chicken bone, he'll be turned the hell off, and you'll probably get punched in the eye. Bottom line, some chicks damn sure don't know jack about being sensual. They get to sucking on shit, their stomachs start growling and then they start biting down on the man like he's their last damn meal. Go figure.

Finally I lean back, sit all the way down on Maurice's dick, reach around and start rubbing and massaging his balls and bouncing up and down on him. I lock my pussy around his cock, then fuck him into a seizure. He jerks and shakes underneath me. And by the time I am finished with him, I have ole boy stuttering.

Thirty minutes later, we are fucking again. I love intercrossing my legs with Maurice's, and fucking him scissors-style because I can cup and massage his balls while he's deep in me. And he loves watching his slick dick glide in and out of my smoldering wetness. I snap this pussy around his dick and make him feel like he's floating on warm clouds. His dick always feels so damn good inside of me!

"Oh, aaah, shit," he moans. "Damn, this pussy's good."

"Look how wet you make my pussy," I whisper, watching his dick slide in and out of me. "Mmmm. Oh, this dick is sooooo good." I pull in my bottom lip, close my eyes, and arch my back, slamming my pussy on his dick. We are bucking and moaning and drenched in sweat. We interlock our hands, then grind deep into each other until he is ready to nut. He quickly pulls his dick out, and snatches off his condom. I place my hand between my legs and massage my clit as he towers over me and jerks his dick until he shoots his hot cum all over my stomach and chest. Maurice leans over, kisses me again, then collapses beside me. Three minutes later, he is snoring.

I get up and wipe his nut off of me, then decide to take a quick shower. I turn the water on, and step in. I toss my head back and allow the pulsing water to beat against my body. I close my eyes and find myself having another one of my fantasy moments.

There's an unknown naked man in my room. He's dark chocolate, bald and delicious. His legs are gaped open and his dick and balls are freely hanging between his muscular legs. The sight of him makes my pussy twitch and I salivate as I get on my hands and knees and slowly start crawling towards him, licking my lips. My nameless guest looks down at his dick, then back up at me. He is smiling. He knows what I want. I instinctively know what he wants. And we are both eager to give it to the other. He leans all the way back in his seat, widens his legs as I approach, and waits.

When I finally reach him, I wrap my right hand around his cock and stroke it while I use my left hand to rub my clit. His dick thickens and I flick it with my tongue, then slowly wrap my lips around the head and swirl my tongue over it, cupping his big, smooth balls. The more of his dick I take it my mouth, the harder and longer it gets. I don't bother measuring it with my ruler 'cause I already know from experience that it's exactly ten inches. And I swallow down every inch of it until my lips are around the base. His toes open and close; his eyes roll in the back of his head; he bites on his bottom lip, then moans as I increase the intensity of my sucking and licking while gently juggling and massaging his balls. The fact that I don't gag drives him wild, and he is pumping his hips, pushing his dick deep into my throat. And the minute I press my index finger onto his asshole, I can feel his heart beat in his dick and knows he's ready to explode. And I let him. As his cream shoots down into my throat I slowly pull his dick out and suck ferociously on the head, making popping sounds. His leg shakes as he continues to shoot his man milk. It overflows from the corners of my mouth, then rolls down the shaft of his dick, and I greedily lick his creamy drippings up. When I am done cleaning his dick and balls with my tongue, he bends down and sucks on my lips, then shoves his tongue into my mouth, tasting his sweet, salty nut.

I grab the shower head, place it between my legs, and allow its warm stream to beat against my clit until I am having an orgasm. When I finish cumming, I finish my shower, then wrap myself in a towel. I walk into the bedroom, and notice Maurice has gotten underneath the blankets and has made himself comfortable. I glance at the clock. It's 12:47 a.m. He looks so peaceful in his sleep.

I oil my body, then slip into the bed beside him, deciding to let him sleep. I set the alarm for four-thirty. *This'll give him enough time to get his self together before the sun comes up*, I think, closing my eyes. I am feeling well-fucked and exhilarated. A smile forms across my face as thoughts of sweet dreams and a wet pussy invade my space.

CHAPTER
THIRTY-ONE

I'm lying here in bed wondering where in the hell the time has gone. It dawns on me that Christmas is right around the corner. Can you believe that shit? It feels like I just blinked my eyes and now it's November. Humph. Before you know it, the year will be over, it'll be time for a new supply of dick, and time to sift through another year of new bullshit. Oh, joy! And I still haven't made my appointment to rid myself of this unwanted pregnancy. To be honest with you, I don't know what is keeping me from taking a coat hanger and scraping my insides up myself. I don't think I'm having a change of heart or anything crazy like that. And I know it's not something I can ignore and think it will miraculously disappear. I'm already six weeks so I don't have a lot of time to play with.

Anyway, besides having this abortion, I'm already thinking about doing something different for the upcoming holiday season. I mean, it's always nice to spend the holidays with family, but every damn year? I don't think so! This year, I want to go away. Actually, I *need* to get away. It's been a long time since I've been anywhere. And this year, I think I want to bring the New Year in somewhere else besides here. Somewhere exciting; somewhere exotic; somewhere captivating. I consider this, for a moment, then decide I need to also be someplace secluded, where I can kick back, and chill. Fuck and suck on some unknown dick. Yeah, that'll take the edge off. Some good, thick, foreign dick is exactly what I need to ring in the New Year. The question is, where?

Maybe Hawaii, I think, imagining myself prancing around in a hula-skirt and bikini top, shaking and popping my hips on the beach, dropping down low and sucking down on some Poly-nesian cock. *Or perhaps Tahiti or Bora Bora where I can hopefully fuck all night in a bungalow that overlooks soothing waters. Hmm…I wonder if Polynesian men are circumcised, or if they have a slab of skin flapping over the head of their dicks.* I laugh to myself, shaking my head. "Girl, you a damn trip," I say, giggling. "All you do is sit around thinking about dick."

You got that right, baby, I answer in my head. *Cock does the body damn good.*

My home phone rings, disrupting my musings. I sit up in bed and lean over, glancing at the caller ID. It's my mother.

"Hello, Mom," I say.

"Bianca?" she asks, surprised to hear my voice. "Well, hello to you, too, young lady. Your father and I were wondering when we were going to hear from you."

"I'm sorry. I've been meaning to call you," I state apologetically. "I've been so caught up with work and whatnot."

"Mmm-hmm," she says, half-believing me. "Too busy to pick up the telephone to check in on your aging parents. You know—the parents who worked hard to provide you with a good, decent life; the ones who loved you and spoiled you rotten."

I roll my eyes, wondering why she always feels the need to try to make me feel guilty when it never works. "Mom, you and Dad look wonderful to be retirees, and I'm sure the both of you have enough going on to keep you busy enough to not notice how long it's been since we've spoken."

"Oh, nonsense," she snaps, chuckling. "Flattery will get you nowhere. You're our baby and our only daughter, so naturally we are going to get worried when we don't hear from you in over a month. A month, Bianca? My God!"

"Okay, okay. You made your point. I apologize."

"Well, what has kept you so busy that you can't find the time to pick up a phone to call us? I hope it's a nice young man. It would be wonderful to see you married. And I would love to be around to see my only daughter give birth to her firstborn."

Oh, Lord, I think, shaking my head. *Here we go with this mess again.* For some reason, my mother has been dropping hints about seeing me with a nice man, getting married and bearing children while she's still alive.

"No," I snap. "It's not a man."

"Well," she huffs. "I wish it *was* a man, then I could understand your forgetfulness."

"Mom, it's not, so let's please change the subject."

"Well, are you at least dating?" she asks, ignoring my request.

"No, but I'm pregnant, and fucking everything moving," I hear in my head. I shake the words out of my mind. "No," I answer, getting up from the kitchen table, then climbing the stairs to my bedroom. "I'm not dating. I don't have any interest in all that right now."

I want to tell her I don't like men. Think to tell her that I'm considering sucking clits and tits. Hell, I should tell her I've decided to have three kids by three different men. That will surely throw her into cardiac arrest. But she's my mother, and I love her too much. So, I decide against it, knowing she'd kill me first before she passed out.

"Besides," I continue, removing my bra and panties. "I don't really have the patience for a man, nor do I want one." I stare at myself in the mirror, admiring my beautiful nakedness. I run my hands along the front of my stomach, holding it in, then poking it out, trying to imagine myself with a pregnant belly. I frown at the image.

"You don't want one?" she repeats, almost choking. "Please tell me, my dear child, what would you prefer over a man?"

His dick. "A slow, burning death," I state.

"Bianca," she gasps. "Are you losing your mind?"

"Only joking," I say, laughing. "I mean about the

slow burning death. But I am definitely serious about not having time for a man." *Only what hangs between his legs*, I think, turning around and admiring my firm, plump ass.

"And why is that?"

I sigh. I swear I love my mom. We have a wonderful mother-daughter relationship. One in which we can laugh and share hurts and pains. We are very close, for the most part. Probably not as close as we should be, but close enough for me to know that I can go to her in time of need and she'll always be there without question or reservation; that I can talk to her about anything without judgment, if I chose to. But when it comes to men and love and relationships, she and I will always be at odds.

Though she believes a woman should be financially able to take care of herself, something she instilled in me, she also believes a woman should have a man, a companion, someone to complete her. I, on the other hand, believe a woman doesn't need a man to complete her. She should already be complete. A man should be there to complement her.

"Most of 'em come with too many issues for me."

"Oh, please," she says dismissively. "We all have issues. That doesn't mean that there isn't someone special out there for you. There are some really good men out there. You just have to open your heart and mind to them."

Or in my case—my legs, I think, chuckling as I slip into a burgundy lace teddy.

"What's so funny?" she asks.

"Oh, nothing," I lie. "You never cease to amaze, Mom. And that's why I love you so much. You will stop at nothing until you have me married off."

"Well." She giggles. "Sweetheart, I'm anxious to see you with a good man, someone who will make you as a happy as your father has made me."

I smile. "Mom, what you and Daddy have most people only dream of. I don't think I could ever be so lucky."

"Sure you can. You have to believe. And pray on it."

Oh, trust me, Mom, I think. *I definitely* prey *on it.*

I laugh, realizing there will never be any winning with her. "Mom, if nothing else, I believe you are always praying on it."

She laughs, too. "You know me so well. Now, tell me. What day will you be flying in?" she asks, changing the subject.

"I'll be there Wednesday night, and flying back on Friday," I say.

"Oh," she replies, sounding disappointed. "I thought you'd be staying a little longer than that, since we don't see much of you."

"Mom, I was just there a few months ago."

"And you only stayed two days that time as well. It really doesn't make sense to me for you to fly out all this way and not stay for at least a week."

I laugh. "Mom, if I were staying a week, you'd be saying that wasn't long enough. Then you'd want me to stay a month."

"And what would be so wrong with that?" she asks, laughing.

I think about her question, try to consider my response, remembering my visit for the Fourth of July weekend. My parents were having a big family barbeque and wanted all of us there. And while I was there, everyone doted on me, showering me with love. But the one thing that put a damper on my almost perfect visit was the lack of dick. And, my wonderful, loving brothers—all six of them—made sure that getting any was damn near impossible. So the only fireworks popping off that weekend were the ones going off down at Balboa Park, 'cause there definitely wasn't anything cracking between my legs.

I smile. "Not a thing, Mom," I finally say. "I can't wait to see you."

"I can't wait to see you either, baby. Travel safe, and see you when you get here."

"I will," I say, hanging up. "I love you."

"And your father and I love you more," she says in her sweet, motherly tone. I smile, hanging up, looking forward to feasting with my family.

CHAPTER
THIRTY-TWO

Thanksgiving was beautiful. Although I picked at the food—because I didn't have much of an appetite the whole time I was there and I was afraid I'd start throwing up again if I overate, from what little I did eat, my mother really outdid herself. And, as always, the weather was great. With the exception of having to look in Cherelle's fucking face, I really enjoyed my time with everyone. But, I am so glad to be home. I love my family dearly, I swear I do. However, more than two days with all of my brothers, well, four of 'em, in one room is enough to have me slice my wrists. Terrance and Tyler are the only two who consistently prove that there really are good, decent men still around. It's too damn bad that Terrance is married to a damn trick. Who, by the way, did her very best to keep her distance from me, which was fine by me. I hate that bitch! And it tears me up to see how Terrance has so much love in his eyes for that ho. It is bitches like her that are so undeserving of a good man, but they seem to always be the ones to end up with one. Despite this knowledge, it was really nice to see how Terrance and Tyler interact with their families. It reminds me so much of our father, and how he treated our mother and us growing up, doting over her and his children. Yes, Terrance and Tyler are truly good men.

But the rest of my brothers, forget it! They are womanizers in every sense of the word. Oh my God, I can't get over how cocky and chauvinistic Lamont and Thomas are. Chicks really have them gassed up into believing that they are truly God's gift to women.

"I expect a woman to jump when I speak, and not give me a bunch of backtalk when I tell her to do something," Lamont had said while we were all sitting around the table, talking about relationships while playing spades. "If I tell her to wash my feet, if I tell her to get on her knees and bark like a poodle, I expect her to do what she's told."

I rolled my eyes, sucking my teeth. "And if she doesn't?"

"Then I dismiss her. Next," he said, snapping his finger. "Someone else is filling ya spot. So If you wanna keep ya position, and want me to keep giving you all this good lovin', then you'd better stay on ya job or be ready to get replaced."

Tyler laughed. "Man, I don't know where Mom and Dad found you, but you one sick dude."

"Yeah, whatever, man. You can call it what you want," he snapped back, smirking, "but I'll never be hen-pecked. Like some of you. I promise you that."

"And what's wrong with a man loving his family, and wanting to see his wife happy?" I asked.

"Ain't a thing wrong with it," Lamont stated, "if you like borrrrring."

"So, let me get this right," Terrance asked, rubbing his chin. "A man being devoted to his family and committed to his wife is boring to you?"

"Hey, man, if you like it, I love it. I just know it could never be me. I need variety in my life."

I smirked, knowingly. 'Cause Lord knows I have had an assortment of dick to fill my platter.

"And you will always find yourself bouncing from bed to bed."

"And the problem is?" he asks, raising a brow, laughing. "They don't call me the Panty Slayer for nothing."

"Ugh," I grunted in disgust, studying my cards, "too much information."

"Your go," Trent said to me.

I rolled my eyes, tossing out the queen of hearts. It walked. "And the queen still rules," I said, winking at Terrance and scooping up our books.

"Even the queen needs a pipe layer to bang her back out and keep her in check," Lamont said.

He and Trent gave each other a high-five. Then Trent started his mess about how all women, with the exception of me and our mother, are only good for seeding and breeding.

"Say what?" I asked incredulously. "You have got to be kidding me."

Just as I was about to say something else, Tyrell walked through the kitchen with some chick sporting a bunch of shoulder-length micro-braids and a neck wrapped in a bunch of gold jewelry. She was cute in the face and small in the waist with a set of big double-D titties. And she left no room for the imagination in her little, peach knit sweater and extra tight mini-skirt. Humph, the smartest thing Tyrell has ever done when it comes to a relationship, or women, was to only have one child. 'Cause, baby let me tell you, when it comes to him choosing women, he falls short every time. And on top of that, he seems to have a new one every time I'm there to visit. The last chick he had ended up being a certified psycho, cutting up all his clothes because he didn't come home. Granted, he should have called her, but damn. Cutting up his belongings was a bit extreme, in my opinion. Humph. And then the dumb bitch ended up getting arrested for chasing him down the street in her bra and panties with a knife because he was trying to leave her crazy ass. It was bad enough she had taken one shoe from all his sets of Timbs and sneakers, and threw them out. Poor Tyrell had nothing but mismatched pairs of shoes to put on his feet. Then she had the nerve to cut off one leg of all of his pants, from his sweats to his jeans. How ridiculous is that? When I heard that shit, I had to shake my damn head. Why are some damn women so fucking desperate?

I swear some of these chicks out here are so fucked up, and so damn afraid of rejection that they'd stoop to doing some of the craziest shit to try to keep someone who no longer wants them because they've chased him away with all of their bullshit. Crazy hoes!

Of course Lamont and Trent gawked and drooled at Tyrell's current flavor of the week like two dogs in heat as she stood there popping her chewing gum. If you ask me, they were sniffing ghetto trash.

Anyway, when I brought my attention back to Trent and asked Trent what exempted me and Mom from his beliefs about women being good only for fucking and having babies, he looked at me like I had a dick hanging out of my mouth or something. And truth be told, I wished I did.

He said, "Because that's our mom. She's the one who gave me life. And you, well…you're not hot in the tail, running around chasing down dick like some cum-hungry, gold-digging chick." Then he looked over at Tyrell's chick of the week.

Of course I almost knocked my drink over. If he only knew how much mileage my pussy gets he—along with the rest of my brothers—would be ready to beat me down… It's Ho Central, but they'll never hear that from me.

Anywaaaay, there's nothing like home! Between my mother badgering me about settling down and getting married and my brothers watching me like damn hawks, along with the lack of dick intake, I thought I'd lose my motherfucking mind if I had to stay another day. Besides, I was starting to get real paranoid. My mother kept staring at me and smiling as if she knew my current predicament. They say a mother always knows her child better than anyone else. So, I had to get out of Dodge quick, fast and in a hurry before she started asking a bunch of questions and putting two and two together.

CHAPTER
THIRTY-THREE

At four a.m. I awake to another one of my crazy ass dreams. I dream that I am in this sex store that looks like an old abandoned warehouse from the outside, but inside it is this gigantic space, practically the size of a department store and there are huge, flat-screen TVs throughout the store playing sex videos portraying all types of kinky sex. I'm not sure exactly what town or state this place is located in. But it is a dark, seedy area. The store is sectioned off by ropes and multi-colored doors.

Anyway, I am walking through the store pushing a cart, dressed in black leather from head to toe, wearing a leather crotch-less bikini underneath a full-length, leather trench with knee-high stiletto boots. My hair is tucked under a leather derby and I am holding a leather flogger in my hand. I am going down different aisles tossing all types of flavored gels and lotions, dog collars and leashes, cock rings, clamps and clips, vibrators, butt plugs and dildos in different colors, shapes and sizes into my basket. I even pick out a few wooden spoons and paddles, some smooth and others with ridges to add to my assortment of goodies.

When I am done with my shopping, I go through this security checkpoint; then I'm allowed to enter any door of my choice. Behind each door there are different types of men waiting to be dominated; men who secretly want to submit to a woman. My pussy is drooling with excitement. I open the first door and there are three men in this room sitting on chrome and leather stools: a handsome, well-built white man wearing a pair of red silk boxers; a beautiful, dark chocolate-coated hunk with shoulder-length locks wearing a pair of black silk boxers; and a fine-ass caramel-coated man with hazel eyes, butt-ass naked with a long, juicy dick.

I slam the door, taking off my trench and tossing it on the floor. They jump up, standing at attention. I strut over to Hazel Eyes and scream, "Who the fuck told you to get naked, you nasty dog? Get on your damn knees!" He does what he is told, and I place a leather-spiked collar around his neck, then attach the leash. I yank it. "Sniff my pussy, you bad dog." I spread my legs apart, then take both of my hands and press his face into my crotch. He sniffs and sniffs, and sniffs. I cock one leg up on the barstool. "Lick my pussy, you nasty mutt!" He licks it, but he is lapping it real soft and lovingly. I want it rough and fast and wet. I slap his face. "Wet my pussy, damn you!" I slap his face again. "Yelp, like the nasty lying dog you are!" He starts yelping like a wounded puppy. When he finally gets my pussy nice and wet, I pet him. "That's it, just like that. Good doggie. Mmmm, yes. Wet Momma's pussy."

The other two are still standing like toy soldiers, not daring to look over to see what is going on. I see the curiosity and the uncertainty in their faces. I can smell their excitement in the air as I remove my top and let my titties free. "Spit in your hand and jerk that big dick, you fucking dog!" Again, he does what he is told. "Yeah, that's right, stroke that dick." I slap his face. "Don't you dare stop licking my pussy. Rub your nose in it!" He does. "Lick my clit." He does. This goes on for about fifteen minutes until I am ready to cum. "Make me cum, you dirty dog." I can tell he is getting into it and is about ready to cum himself. I slap his face again. "Nut on my boot, not on the floor or I'm gonna smear your nose in it. And you better howl when you're getting ready to cum."

He strokes his dick, panting and growling. And as soon as he is ready to nut he starts howling. He bursts his nut all over my boot, and then I make him clean it up with his tongue.

Next I walk over to White Hunk. I run my hands over the front of his boxers, then grab his dick in my hand, massaging it over his underwear. I lick his right nipple, then his left. "You'd better not let this dick get hard." I keep stroking him, and feel it start to thicken and grow. "What the fuck did I tell you, you weak-ass fucker?!? I said you'd better not get hard." I slap him with my free hand, while still stroking his dick. I continue licking his nipples, alternately sucking and biting and tugging at them with my teeth. His leg shakes.

"Oh, you like that. You wanna show Momma how big your dick can get, huh? You wanna cum for Momma?" He barks, nodding his head. "Good! Then cum you shall." I tell him to remove his boxers. My Lord, I'm not gonna front, he has a big beautiful dick and big, smooth balls. My mouth starts to water. I walk back over to my bag of goodies and pull out some items. I place a clamp on each of his nipples. He winces. "Don't you dare, you pathetic weakling!" I slap his face again. Then I hand him some sandpaper and order him to wrap it around his dick and masturbate his dry dick with it. His eyes bulge but he obeys the order and does what he is told, like the good little dog he is, and cums in thick, painful spurts.

I walk out of the room, then enter another door. There's a tall Hispanic man with a football player's build sitting on a leather bench. "Get the fuck up, motherfucker," I snarl, "and strip!" He does what he's told. When he is finished undressing, standing before me in his naked splendor, I tie his hands in front of him, then walk over to the wall and press a button that raises his hands up over his head and slowly lifts him up off the floor. His very large feet dangle in the air. He grimaces, pain etched on his face as he hangs in the air by his arms, fearfully waiting for them to pop out of their sockets.

His limp dick, fat and juicy like a plump sausage, hangs before me at eye level. I reach out and brush the back of my fingertips along the shaft, then grab it and violently shake it.

"You nasty fuck-face!" I sneer. "You better not let this fat cock get hard, or I'm gonna bite it off. You understand me, you motherfucking scumbag?"

He growls. I yank his balls, then dig my nails into his flesh and squeeze. He yelps. "Shut the fuck up, you weak-ass fucker!" Beads of sweat start to line his forehead. I let go of his nuts, and walk over to a black leather bag and pull out a leather whip. I crack it to the floor, walking back over to him. "You know what's next, don't you, you sneaky fuck?"

He whimpers, nodding. His eyes bulge as the whip continues to crack and snap against the concrete floor. I walk behind him, and give him ten lashes across his ass. He yells, pleads, as I whip his ass mercilessly. His body jerks. Then when I tire from swinging the whip, I abruptly stop and walk back in front of him. I grab his dick, then gently slip it into my mouth. I slurp it, suck it down, then stop when it begins to thicken. "If you nut, I'm gonna whip your ass again, you horny bastard," I warn, slipping his dick back into my mouth and lovingly nursing it into a full erection.

He moans.

I moan.

Then…damn it—just when the shit was starting to get good, I wake up to a soaking wet pussy. Ugh, I hate this shit!

Hmmm…I never really thought of myself as someone who could get turned on by that whole dominatrix
shit. But the thought of having a man be totally submis-
sive is exciting, and quite entertaining. What would I
do to him? Maybe have him wear a diaper and suck a
pacifier, then get spanked by Momma before being put
to bed, or making him worship my beautiful body, giving me a tongue bath with his thick tongue cleaning
my asshole and pussy out; or make him beg me to sit
on his face and smother him with my pussy, smearing
my juices all over his lips, then making him suck my
bloody Kotex; or maybe, make him lean over a chair
while I whip his bare-ass with a belt until it whelps and
blisters for being naughty, then make him jerk his dick
and eat his own nut; or pinch and twist his nipples, then
squeeze and dig my fingernails into his balls. Oh my
God, the thought has me hysterical. I'd probably torture
the hell out of his ass. I wonder how many men there
are who crave to be dominated, and about the number
of women who seek to dominate them.

I run my hands between my legs and play in my dick-
hungry snatch. The dream has me so fucking horny. I
need a dose of dick, ASAP. I glance at the clock, knowing it is too late to have someone come through to hit
this pussy off. Well, it's not, but I don't want to chance
them not being out of here before the sun rises. So I
opt for plan B. I climb out of bed, go into my closet,
and pull out a wooden box from the top shelf where I

keep my sex trinkets, a large collection of pussy pleasing gadgets to get me off. When I find what I am looking for, I saunter back over to the bed to begin my mechanical stimulation.

Oh, how I enjoy masturbation. I do it daily. At least two to three times a day depending on my schedule. There are even times while I'm at work when I've gotten so horny that I've had to close my office door, put the "do not disturb" on my phone, then handle my business. Other times, I've gone into the ladies' room and done myself just to take the edge off until I was able to get home. When I'm finished, I typically feel so energized, I'm practically racing. So masturbation definitely does the body good. Is there anything wrong with that? Hell no!

But of course some folks might think otherwise. Fuck 'em! Shit, it's safe, and it keeps me in tune with my body. And using sex toys really aids in the process.

Speaking of masturbation, who do you think masturbates more: men or women? I'd suspect men do since they typically have sex on the brain more than most women. But, I do believe that there are a large number of women who enjoy playing in their pussies. Hmm…I wonder how many couples get off watching their partners get themselves off.

I know I personally love watching a man beat his dick. Sometimes, I like to help him out a little by either licking or sucking his balls, licking/sucking on his nipples, sometimes even flicking my tongue across the head of his dick while he's stroking it. Or I'll join in and masturbate with him. Other times, I like to sit across from him or next to him and watch. Truthfully, there's something about hearing and watching a man cum that turns me on. Oh, how I wish there was some dick here tonight. I'd have him laying in the center of the bed, with his legs stretched open, jerking his dick off for me while I lowered my pussy over his face with my back towards him so I can watch him long stroke his cock while he's eating my pussy. My mouth drools at the thought.

I glance over at the clock again. 4:10 a.m. In three more hours, it will be time for me to get up and get ready for work. I let out a sigh. The last thing I want to think about is work. "Fuck," I say out loud as I lay back in bed and spread open my legs.

I don't feel like fucking; but I definitely feel like being on my knees licking some big black balls, running my tongue along the veins on a thick, juicy dick. Hell, I might even let the nigga slap his dick across my lips and face, while I moan and beg him to feed me his cock as I play in my pussy. I want him to run his hands through my hair, pump his throbbing shaft in and out of my mouth, and talk dirty to me, while I deep throat him, gulping down every inch of him, wrapping his dick with my soft lips, burying it down my throat, submitting to him on my knees, sucking, and licking, and slurping, willing and eager to make him feel good until he nuts that sweet dick cream. Oh, shit. Just thinking about it has my pussy aching.

I pull open my pussy lips with my right hand, then take my left hand and slip my index and pointer fingers into my mouth and wet them up, before placing them on my clit. I work my clit, pressing down in slow circular motions, making it swell to an aching knot of flesh. I am rubbing my pussy, winding my hips to a beat that causes my pussy lips to swell with excitement and get slick. When I can no longer take the yearning that is building up inside of me, begging for an escape, I reach for my Ben-Wa egg and slide it inside of me. My pussy greedily slurps it in. Then I take my Mini-Tongue and turn it on high and allow it to lap at my pussy and clit. "Oh, oh, oh…Mmmm… Mmmm…" I moan. It doesn't take long before I can feel a nut roaring inside of me. Between the vibrations of the egg inside of me, and the vibrations of the Tongue on my clit, my hot juices spurt out of my pussy like hot lava from an erupting volcano, spilling down the crack of my ass and onto the sheets. I scream and moan to the high heavens, sweat and cry, and cum a hundred more times until I am practically weak. After my earth-shattering adventure, I pull the egg out of my wetness, suck off my sweet juice, then drift back into a peaceful sleep.

THIRTY-FOUR

Tonight, I'm really not in the mood for this shit. I take a deep breath. Now, when a man breaches the rules of engagement, like continuously coming here unannounced, putting hickeys on my damn body, trying to check for me, catching feelings, or getting sloppy with his creep, then he has to be shut down, quick, fast and in a damn hurry. Bottom line: A careless man is an absolute liability.

I have no time or patience for a raggedy mofo who has the potential to bring me drama. And this is exactly why I like to stick to my ninety day rule of simply fucking 'n dumping them. But, every so often, as you already know, I seem to get swooped up in the funnel of bullshit, like right now.

"Listen, stop buggin'," Jamil says, huffing. His ear is pressed to his cell, and I can hear screaming on the other end—a female's voice, which tells me this conversation is a domestic dispute. Now, normally, when I'm in the mood for some fast, rough, furious fucking, I like it when there's a little trouble in paradise because then the men I'm fucking will try to take their frustrations with their women out on my pussy. But, today, I am not in the mood for having my snatch beat up because shit isn't going right at home. And here lately, Jamil seems to be caught up in a lot of home drama. "I already told you no, so why you keep asking me the same bullshit. Look, I gotta go." He hangs up, tossing his cell on the sofa. I eye him, watching him kick off his boots, then removing his shirt. "Always fucking bitch-ing," he mumbles, stripping off his jeans. He doesn't have on any underwear, so his dick swings freely.

"Is everything all right?" I ask, raising an eyebrow, waiting for him to start his whining. He eyes me. I smile to myself, knowing he doesn't want to have a repeat of what happened a few weeks back when I tossed him up out of here.

"Yeah, I'm good," he says. "Ole girl bitching again. C'mon"— he walks up and grabs me by the hand— "let's go upstairs. I don't feel like talking about it. I really want some pussy without all the extras, feel me?" His cell phone starts ringing again. He ignores it, pulling me by the hand. "I ain't beat."

All of a sudden, my cell starts ringing. My first thought is that it's one of my sex charms, or one of the strays I straddle from time to time. But, the number is restricted, so I don't answer. I let it go into voice-mail. Two seconds later, it rings again. The number is still restricted, but for some reason I pick up thinking maybe it's important.

"Hello?" I say.

All there is on the other end is a bunch of heavy breathing, then silence. I hang up.

"Yo, you tryna wet this dick up or what?" Jamil asks in back of me, clearly annoyed that I am not already naked and pouncing down on his dick. "You standing there bullshitting. I gotta get home in an hour or so. And you know how I like to put work in when I come through."

"Wait a minute," I say, placing a hand on my hip. "I understand you pissed and all, but don't take that shit out on me. You get this pussy on my time, not yours. You don't like it, then get up and take your ass home. Right now, I'm trying to figure out who—"

My cell rings, again. I pick up. "Hello?"

Whoever it is hangs up. I take a deep breath. Now, I don't know much, but one thing I do know is when someone keeps calling your house, or your cell, and hanging up, it's usually the work of some nutty-ass bitch.

My cell rings again. This time the caller is bold enough to reveal their number. "Hello?" I say, getting agitated. Now, I know I could easily ignore the call, but I don't want to. My intuition tells me that it's a woman who is calling me—just like the last time, and I want to know who she is, and which one of the men I'm fucking is the cause behind this foolishness—*again*.

"Bitch, I know you been fucking my man, and when I find out who you are, I'm gonna beat ya motherfuckin'—"

"Um, who is this? And how'd you get my number?"

"I'm Jamil's woman," she snaps into the phone. "That's who da fuck I am, bitch! And I know that mother-fucker's over there. So, put him on the phone."

"Oh, really? Well, that's nice to know."

I cut my eye over at Jamil, who is sprawled out in the center of my bed, playing with his dick and rubbing his balls like he has no care in the world.

"So are you fucking Jamil or not?"

"You said you knew I was. So if you know that already, why you asking? But since you asked, yeah, I am." There was no sense in lying. Please, he's not my man, so what do I care. Besides, they all know if they don't want to get aired out, then don't get sloppy. Apparently, Jamil's retarded ass didn't pay attention to the memo.

"Well, I tell you what. You fucking with the wrong bitch's man, ho. And I'ma serve that ass when I catch you."

Here we go with this "when I catch you" *shit again*, I think, rolling my eyes.

"Listen, sweetie," I calmly say, taking another deep breath, "I don't know how you got my number, but I'm going to ask you nicely not to call me again."

"Or what?! Bitch, I'ma call you as many times as I want. As a matter of fact, I'ma call you every fucking day. And when I find out where you live, it's on, bitch. Believe that! So, if Jamil's there, you need to either put him on the phone, or tell him to bring his sorry ass home before I cut up all of his shit and toss it out on the streets. And he has fifteen minutes to get his ass home."

Getting caught up in a back and forth argument with another chick over, or about, her man isn't serious for me. There's always more dick where his came from, so she can have him. That's my thinking. So, getting all nasty and stressed out by cursing the chick out is usually not necessary. But from time to time, I allow myself to get sucked in, then have to bring it to 'em. And I can already tell this bitch's the type that's going to keep pushing the envelope and force me to eventually serve her.

"Well, I appreciate the warning," I state sarcastically. "And after I'm finished with him, I'll be sure to pass the message along and send him on his way. You have a wonderful night."

I hang up, then turn the phone off.

"Who was that?" Jamil asks.

No, this motherfucker did not just part his lips and ask me no shit like that. Now, normally, I would simply throw a mofo out, but I want my pussy ate, and I want it done by Jamil. So that when I do throw him up out of here, he goes home with my nut on his breath. I shake my head and remove my silk robe, prancing my naked ass over to the bed. I climb in, ignoring his question.

"It's 'bout damn time," he says, leaning up on his forearms. "You so worried about who the fuck's calling you when you got a nigga in ya bed with a hard-ass dick ready to clock in."

I smile, taking a bottle of lotion from off of my night-stand and pouring a glob of it into my hand. I grab the base of his dick. I squeeze it, then glide my hand up and around the head of his dick while working his balls with my other hand. I decide to give him a nice hand job. I lean in and swirl my tongue around his nipple, then lightly pull it with my teeth until it hardens.

"Oh, shit," he moans, reaching between my legs and rubbing my pussy lips. "Damn, I want some of this." I ignore him. I continue jacking him off with deep, fast strokes. "Ah, shit, you 'bout to make me cum." He tries to pull my hand off his dick, but I tighten my grip. I bring him to the edge of pleasure, then I abruptly stop. I lap around his balls with my tongue a few times, while slowly stroking his cock. "Damn, baby, why you fucking with me? C'mon and put them pretty lips on this dick, and stop playing."

"You want me to wet this dick up?" I ask, gliding my lips along his shaft, then replacing my lips with my hand, stroking it.

"Yeah," he grunts, pumping his hips, "but you fucking playing 'n shit. C'mon and get up on this dick, girl."

I lower my voice to a sensual whisper, "Your dick feels so big in my hand, Daddy. I can't wait for you to ram this hot cock all the way up in me. I want you to make me scream, baby. Can you do that for me, big daddy?"

"Yeah," he says, panting. "I'ma fuck you good." I

deepen my strokes on his dick. I press up into the fleshy part between his balls and ass and massage the area. His breathing becomes raspy and quick. "Ah, shit…"

"You wanna feel how wet you make this pussy?"

"Yeah, baby…I'm ready to fuck…"

"Put your tongue in my pussy, first," I say, swinging my legs around over his body, then straddling him with my back facing him while still jerking him off. I lower my pussy down on his face. He sticks his tongue in, and I commence to riding it like it's a runaway train. He's lapping and licking all around my pussy, then he mounts his mouth onto my clit and sucks on it like it's one of the sweetest, juiciest peaches he's ever eaten. "Oh, yes," I moan. "That's right, eat this pussy all up, Daddy." *Munch, munch, nigga! 'Cause as soon as I nut in your motherfucking mouth, I'm putting you the fuck out!*

Between you and me, I wish I were on my period 'cause I'd serve Jamil a nice bloody treat without giving it a second thought just for being so fucking stupid. Trust me. I would serve this nasty, no-good mofo the red rag special all night.

Jamil pulls open my ass cheeks and devours my whole pussy. My clit throbs, and I can feel the beginnings of a nut building up inside of me. *That's right, gobble that shit up you stupid-ass fuck 'cause it'll be the last time you get it.*

"Uh, uh, uh…Oh…oh…Mmmm…" Jamil's long tongue is giving my pussy and clit a good licking, and it is causing me to hyperventilate. I grind down on his

mouth and rock my hips back and forth. "Oh, yes...
Oh, yes...like that...keep sucking on my pussy," I
whisper, squirting warm juice onto his tongue, rolling
my eyes up into my head. He obliges and slurps it all
up. I lean forward and brace myself on his legs so that
I don't topple over onto the bed. I steady my breathing, then lift myself from off his face, getting off the
bed. His cock is rock-hard. And I ignore its bouncing
want for attention. I slip into my robe, then stand in
front of the mirror and brush my hair.

"Where you going?" he asks, raising his body up on
his forearms.

"I'm not going anywhere," I answer, looking at him
in the mirror as I speak. "You are."

"What's that supposed to mean?"

"Uh, duh, it means get up and get out, that's what."

"Oh, hell no!" he huffs. "Not this shit again."

"What shit is that, Jamil? Me putting your black-ass
out again?"

"I ain't going nowhere," he sulks, defiantly flopping
back on the bed as if he's about to have a tantrum. "Fuck
that. I done ate your pussy and you got my dick hard as
hell. Hell, no! I want some pussy, some head, something."

I turn to face him. His dick is pointing upwards
awaiting a long, wet ride. I decline. In all honesty, I
hadn't give much thought beyond getting my pussy
eaten by this long-tongued idiot. I really didn't factor
in what might happen after I toss him out, since this is

the first time I've had to actually deal with a chick calling me when her man's ass is actually here while I'm trying to get it in with him. *Please don't make me have to pull out my chrome on your ass*, I think, pulling in a deep, exaggerated breath.

"Well, I'm sure you do want some of this tight pussy, or this wet throat. But you're not getting it here, especially after your chick called my cell talking shit. Yeah, that's who I was talking to earlier. So, take your happy ass on home to wifey before she cuts up your shit. Her words, not mine."

"Oh, so what…That's it? You get yours and it's fuck me? Is that how you doin' it?"

"Yep," I state, leaning up against the dresser and folding my arms across my chest. I stare at him for a few seconds, then walk out the room and go downstairs where I wait for him to bring his silly ass down to get his clothes on—and get the hell out! I glance at them strewn on the floor near the door, and roll my eyes.

Now don't ask me what the hell is taking him so long to come down the stairs 'cause your guess is as good as mine. But five minutes have passed, and that's five minutes too damn long.

"Jamil, what the hell are you doing up there?" I yell up the stairs at him. No response. "Jamil?!"

"What? I was using the bathroom," he says, finally bringing his ass down the stairs. He glares at me. "Damn, you really buggin'."

"Bugging? No, you got it wrong, baby. I ain't bugging. I'm done with you—big difference."

He sucks his teeth, picking up his jeans, then slipping them on. "Yeah, whatever," he huffs as he stuffs his dick down in them, then zips them up. I'm standing by the door waiting to open it to let him out. He takes his time putting on his shirt. But, it's fine with me. I have all night. I fold my arms and wait.

"So, just like that you gonna flip the script, is that what you saying?"

"Jamil," I say, sighing. "I told you from gate I don't play that shit with women calling me about their men, and that I expect any man I'm fucking to keep his shit tight. You failed to do that. So, yeah, I'm done. Now, hurry up; get the rest of your clothes on and get up out of here."

He is staring at me like he's clueless. "Yo, ma, I don't know what the hell you're talking about, for real."

I roll my eyes and snort. "Oh, really? Well, answer me this: how the fuck did your girl get my phone number, Jamil?"

"Fuck if I know," he says nonchalantly, slipping his size eleven feet into his Timbs. "Yo, this is some fucked up shit. Word up. You get my dick harder than a muh-fucka, and you just gonna up and put me out."

"Yep. Take that dick back home to that crazy-ass chick of yours 'cause it's obvious she needs it more than I do. Now, tell me. How the hell she get my number 'cause I know I didn't give it to her?"

"Well, don't look at me. I didn't give it to her. She probably went through my damn phone again."

I blink, blink again. *She probably went through my phone again*, I repeat in my head. I raise my brow. Now, I've always known most men were real stupid when it comes to women. They are damn good liars, but when it comes to cheating they are about as dumb as they come. Hell, Forrest Gump has better sense, and we all know he wasn't the brightest light. And Jamil is a prime example of what stupid looks like. Why the hell would this silly mofo have my number programmed into his phone? And now his damn chick has all the incriminating evidence against his dumb-ass, which is why she was on the phone beefing with his ass earlier. Now what kind of shit is that? What a fucking idiot! And I'm telling you, if by some strange chance she comes here ringing my fucking doorbell, Jamil is seriously going to need plastic surgery 'cause I'm going to gut his brainless ass.

I swing open the door. "Jamil, get the fuck out of my house." He snatches up his keys, then steps up in my space. I tilt my head and stare him down. "Is there something you wanna say to me?"

The muscles in his jaws are twitching.

"You really fucking up a good thing over nothing," he says.

I laugh in his face. "*A good thing?* Nigga, please. Get out, Jamil. And take that bullshit back to your woman 'cause I'm not the one. Good day."

"Yeah, aiight," he says, walking out the door. I slam and lock it.

· "Good riddance!"

Now help me understand why in the hell would an already involved man have another chick's number programmed in his phone or be saving emails (in the first place) when nine times out of ten, he's fucking with some nutty, insecure · chick whose going to go snooping through his cell, start prying through his email file cabinet, or rummaging through his wallet looking for any signs of infidelity. Don't these fools know that most women (who are already one pill away from crazy, and seriously dick whipped) have nothing but time on their hands, and will spend all day trying to figure out phone codes and email passwords? Unless he simply doesn't give a fuck, only a nigga sucking on paint chips would be retarded enough to leave a trail of evidence. Of course, this is only my opinion.

I turn my phone back on, then head for the shower. When I finish my shower and return to my bedroom, I check my phone. The flashing envelope alerts me there are messages. I retrieve them, and laugh. There are three from Jamil's dizzy-ass chick. Message one: "Bitch!" Message two: "You better hope I don't catch you, fucking ho!" Third message: She's playing Monica's song "Sideline Ho" in the background. Interestingly, I really like the song. It definitely doesn't apply to me. But Jamil's little wifey seems to think so, so it is what it is. She blasts the song into my phone, then lowers the volume and speaks, "That's right, bitch, you a side-line ho. Get your own man, and leave mine the fuck alone 'cause he don't want ya dumb ass. He was only using you." This is the message I find the most amusing. "He was using me; oh really?" I laugh out loud. "Girlfriend, if you only knew."

Now, like I said, I love that Monica joint. I mean, I think the song is really *cute*, and really gives you something to think about. But Miss Thing has me fucked up with someone else 'cause ain't no way a man can use me for shit. I wet a mofo's dick because I want to, not because he sweet-talked his way into my drawers. And I'm definitely not fucking him because I'm lining his pockets with my money, so he can bring it back home to his chick. So, how am I being used?

Anyway, I laugh at her assumption that I'm sidelining for her man. Girlfriend has me twisted up with one of them brand-new fools on the block. I'll be damned if I'm standing on the side of anything, waiting, hoping for a man to come through and do anything for me. I don't want to know shit about his family, finances, or future. I don't give a fuck where he goes when he walks out this door, and I don't want him whispering shit in my ear, except how good my pussy is. All that other mess, he can save for the chick at home wringing her hands, wondering where the hell his ass is.

I'm going to let you in on a secret: See. When it comes

to a cheating-ass man, I know where he is when he's not with her ass. He's in my bed, eating my pussy, and giving me the dick the way I want it. And when he's not with me, I still know where he is. At home with her ass, thinking about me, wondering how he can get out of the house to come back for some more of this good pussy.

While she's cooking, and cleaning, and taking care of his kids, playing the happy wife and mother, he's sneaking into the bathroom, or basement to call me to complain about her ass, telling me how bad he wants to feel my lips wrapped around his dick again or have his tongue in my ass. So, hell no! I'm not a sideline ho, a crack ho, a project ho, a groupie ho, or a damned gold digging ho. I'm a ho who loves dick.

Now, answer me this: who's the real fool in the room?

Forty minutes later, my cell phone rings. I look at the number on the screen and see that it's this crazy bitch again. And I know good and well Jamil took his simple ass home. Instead of letting the call go into voice-mail, I decide to indulge her one last time.

"Yes, Sweetie?" I say, fucking with her.

"Stay the fuck away from my man," she warns. "Jamil came home and told me everything. He told me how he fucked you one time and you been bugging ever since. You keep tryna get at him, begging him to come fuck you again. Bitch, you mean to tell me that you that hard-pressed to be sweating another woman's man?

I know my man got some good dick, but, bitch, you need to check ya'self quick. Find your own fucking man, and leave mine the hell alone. So, I'm telling you now to back the fuck off."

I can't believe what I am hearing. That punk-ass mofo twists the shit up to make him look good, trying to make it seem like I'm riding his jock. And it's obvious she believes it. I laugh. Not that what she says is funny, but the fact that she is actually saying it is what I find entertaining. I am convinced that the two of them deserve each other for her to be as stupid as his ass is. And for some reason, I almost feel sorry for her.

"What the fuck is so funny?" she asks.

"You are, boo," I say, still laughing. At this point, I'm laughing so hard at this bitch that tears are streaming down my face. "Whew, I see Jamil has you all fucked up in the head. Better you than me, sweetie. That's for sure. But since you wanna talk about your man, let's. But, be very clear, bitch, I don't want him. Never have, never will. *Your* man sweats me. Your man begs *me* for this pussy. Your man comes to *me* and complains about how fat and lazy your ass is. Your man tells me how all you do is complain about shit. I'm *not* your problem, boo-boo. *Your* man is. So make no mistake. I don't want him. I only borrowed him, but he can gladly be returned 'cause I have no more use for him. You can surely keep him and his bullshit, 'cause the dick ain't really all that to be stressing over…"

I laugh again.

"Boo-boo, you're calling here like you done snatched yourself the brass ring. Baby girl, please, what you need to be doing is getting your mind right, instead of calling here harassing me."

What I say throws her over the edge and she starts cursing and screaming into the phone like a raving lunatic. For a minute, I think I'm listening to Linda Blair. In my mind's eye I see the bitch's head spinning around, and her spitting out green shit all over the place. "Bitch, I'ma bust you in your motherfucking face when I catch your ass. Who the fuck is you, telling somebody what they need to do, when you the one fucking someone else's man? Get your own man, bitch! And stay the fuck away from mine!"

I sigh, pull the phone away from my ear, and shake my head. Jamil's dumb ass came with more drama than dick, anyway. So she can keep his clown ass. *Poor thing*, I think, tossing the phone down on the bed while I go into my walk-in closet to get my shit ready for work in the morning. Yeah, I could hang up on her, but it's obvious she's hurt, and she wants to blame me for her relationship being fucked up, so out of kindness, I allow her to vent. Oh, ohhhkaaaay, maybe I shouldn't have told her all those things Jamil's fucked-up ass said about her, but, hell—she needed to know. Of course she sees me as the problem. Truth be told, I'm not her damn enemy. The dumb bitch is sleeping with him.

My home phone rings, I pick up the cordless off the nightstand and see that it's my mother calling. I let it go into voice-mail, and pick up the cell.

"...Do you hear me talking to you, bitch?!"

"Umm, 'scuse me, what were you saying, Sweetie?" I ask, plopping down on the bed, then lying back.

"I asked you how long you been fucking Jamil?"

"That's something you should be asking him."

"Bitch, I already asked him. Now I'm asking you."

"And obviously you either didn't like his answer, or you don't believe him. So, maybe you should make some decisions about your relationship—"

"Why the fuck you wanna fuck another woman's man?"

I'm thinking to myself that the answer should be obvious, but apparently it's not. "Because I can," I state. "And trust me, if it wasn't me fucking him, it'd be somebody else because your man ain't satisfied with only you. There you have it. So, again, sounds like you need to make some decisions."

"Bitch, I already made my decision. I'ma fuck your nasty-trick- ass up when I see you. Jamil ain't going nowhere and neither am I."

I roll my eyes, shaking my head. It kills me how women want to lash out at the other chick. My fucking another woman's man isn't personal. I don't even know these women, nor do I want to. I can't tell you what they look like or how the hell they're living. But what I do know is, a woman stuck in denial, or blinded by fear, or desperation, or some type of pathological love will never be able to wrap her mind around that idea that she's in a fucked up situation. And that's exactly why men keep doing the shit they do because some women are always stroking a man's ego, stepping out of character, acting all indignant, playing themselves over their trifling asses. That shit ain't cute. Sometimes I just want to snap on these dumb ass birds.

"Bitch," I snap before I realize it. "Wake the fuck up! You can call and threaten me all the hell you want, but when all is said and done, your man is still going to cheat on your dumb-ass. I'm not the fucking problem—"

"And you fucking my man ain't the solution either, bitch. If bitches like you didn't make it so easy for a man to cheat, maybe he wouldn't be so pressed to do it."

. I take a deep breath. *She needs to catch it hard*, I think. "I'ma tell you this one more time. I don't want your fucking man, Sweetie. Never have, never will. Yes, I fucked him. Not once, not twice, but any fucking time *I* felt like riding his dick, or having his tongue stuffed up in my ass. See, dear, while I'm fucking your man, you're the one looking like the damn fool. Because you keep taking him back. And that's your prerogative.

"But I'ma give it to you like this: If I don't fuck him, there's always another chick in line who will. So either check your man, or step to the back of the bus, and shut the hell up! And yes, *your* man, the one you're so hard-pressed to hold onto, has had my pussy smeared all up over his face on more than one occasion, and then came home crawling up in your bed. So, tell me… how does my pussy taste?"

"Bitch, I swear on my four kids, I'ma fuck you up."

"Okay, and how many times are you gonna keep saying that? Do what you need to do. Bottom line, your man is a fucking cheater. And the person you need to be directing your energy and attention on is him, not me. But since you have nothing better to do than calling me with this shit, I'm gonna enlighten you 'cause it's obvious you're young, and dumb, and don't really know any better." I pause, taking a deep breath. I really don't want to go in on her, but she's bold enough to keep calling my house, so guess what? She's got to get it. She was the one who stopped taking care of herself; she's the one who does nothing to look good for herself, or her man. Just sits around stuffing herself with slabs of chocolate and tubs of ice cream, then wonders why she can no longer touch her toes, and needs more than one roll of tissue to wipe her elephant ass. Duh… 'cause you fat and nasty!

And her and the rest of these women who have the nerve to go to bed wearing frumpy nightgowns or oversized nightshirts and raggedy ass head rags, and big-ass drawers, got the nerve to question why their men don't want to fuck them anymore. Uh, duh…'cause you all are hot, sloppy messes! So what, you have kids now. So what, you have to manage the house. So what, you have to work. That has nothing to do with keeping yourself together. Pamper yourself. Push back from the table. Pull out some sexy lingerie, if not for your man, then dammit, for you! I mean…what the fuck?! Be sexy for *you!* If not, it's going to be a fly-chick like me who's going to give your man something to think about, and something to remember. So, sleep if you want, but once again, you've been warned.

Humph. If everything is so damn solid at home, why the hell are these silly-ass bitches calling around trying to track their man's whereabouts? Why the hell are they making excuses and blaming someone else for their fucked up relationships? What they need to do is get the hell off of Fantasy Island, take the damn blinders off, pull the dick from out of their asses and see the shit for what it is. Not for what the hell they want it to be.

And if the dumb bitch is really that invested in being (or staying) in a crazy, fucked up relationship, then she needs to do herself a favor and not call the side chick's fucking house, or mine. Instead, get herself some side dick, and go get her fuck on. Hell, if he can do it, then, dammit, why can't she?

These chicks might view me as the bitch on the side, or the grimy, homewrecking ho, (and that's all fine and dandy) but I'm not the one stressing over a nigga, sniffing his boxers, and running his pockets every time he comes home. I'm not the one crying and begging for him to stop his doggish ways. I'm not the one playing

Dick Tracy, trying to crack codes and find missing clues that will lead to where her man is at one, two, three o'clock in the damn morning, this time.

I decide telling her all this is not going to make any difference, so I let it go. "I feel sorry for you," I finally say. "And I almost feel sad for you."

"Ho, don't feel sorry or sad for me. I'm good. Jamil ain't going nowhere and neither am I. So like I said, back-up off my man 'cause he ain't leaving me for you."

I laugh at how crazy she sounds. One thing you need to know about me—I don't think, or feel, or believe that I'll eventually fuck her man, or anyone else's, into loving me enough to leave his family for me. Like I said before, I'm not looking for love, and I'm damn sure not expecting it from some mofo who can't keep his dick in his pants. A man like that has no damn integrity, if you ask me. So why the hell would I want him? Only a delusional bitch would entertain that mess. As far as I'm concerned, there's nothing a damn cheater can do for me, except fuck me as needed, on my terms—period.

So, it's crystal clear to me that this chick hasn't heard a word I said. I'm done. And I've had enough of going around in circles with her. I purposefully yawn in her ear.

"Well good for the both of you. There's really no need to continue with this utterly ridiculous conversation."

"Bitch, who the fuck is you calling ridiculous?"

"I said *this* is ridiculous, but now I see that you are

too. I've entertained you long enough. Toodles!" I hang up.

Now I may be many things, but stupid, or crazy, isn't one of them. You don't actually think I'd give all these mofos I fuck my *real* cell or home numbers, do you? Oh, hell no! I'm always prepared for shit like this because I know it comes with the territory. That's why I give them all the prepaid jump-off, and keeps it moving 'cause I know right off the bat that there are some dumb mofos like Jamil—and that stupid ass Seth—who will get caught out there. Please, I have no intentions of making it easy for any chick to track me down, which is why I haven't been too pressed about Jamil or Seth's chick's idle threats about trying to get at me. That's the least of my worries. Unless a chick is squatting in the dark, following her man with her headlights off, driving in an unmarked car—or worse, her man points me out—she is going to have a very difficult time trying to figure out who I am. Believe that.

CHAPTER
THIRTY-FIVE

Due to the fact that I didn't get a lick of sleep last night, I feel like shit today. I am cramping like hell, and it feels like someone is poking my uterus with a thousand damn needles. I decide to call out from work, and lie in bed and pop Motrin all day, listening to music. The sadistic part of me is hoping I am having a miscarriage, but I know that would be too simple. In some strange way, it would be letting me off the hook, making it easier for me to not have this abortion. For a fleeting moment, guilt finds me.

"I can't keep this baby," I say to myself, sitting up in bed.

One more day, I think, reaching for the remote for my Sony stereo. *All I have to do is get through one more day of this, then it will be all over*. I press play and wait for Lauryn Hill's *MTV Unplugged* CD, disc one, to play, then fluff my pillows up in back of me when she starts singing "Mr. Intentional." I close my eyes and move my head from side to side to the beat. The words of the song take up space in my head, and I start wondering if some of the fucked up shit most—being the operative word—people do to the ones they claim to love is intentional. Maybe it is, maybe it isn't. Who the fuck knows?

But what I do know is that this pregnancy was *not* intentional. Not on my part, and I definitely hope not on Garrett's part either. I think for a minute, then dismiss that notion as silly. There's no way he would stoop to that level. Then again, stranger things have been known to happen. Anyway, like I said, being pregnant was not my intent. But fucking someone else's man is. Though my intention isn't to disrupt someone else's home, it damn sure is my objective to satisfy my sexual needs. And if the nigga who creeps on his woman is willing to risk getting caught—or worse, losing his family behind a piece of ass, then that's on him. His ignorance is my sweet bliss.

I lean back and close my eyes, allowing Lauryn's philosophical soul to drift through the room. Ohmy-God, I am so exhausted. I can barely keep my eyes open. We'll finish up later. Until then…here's to thick dick, soft lips and a bottomless throat!

When I awaken, it is four o'clock in the morning. I can't believe I actually slept a whole day away. I stretch and yawn, then get up and head for the bathroom. I relieve myself, then turn on the shower and wait for the stall to steam up. I step in. When I am finished showering, I oil my damp body with coconut body butter, then wrap myself in a white towel. It's only four-thirty. I set my alarm to wake me up at seven-thirty, then lie back down. But sleep doesn't find me. Instead, I toss and turn. I find myself thinking about some of the niggas I've met and dismissed, and the ones I've fucked, shaking my head. Thinking back, I can't help but laugh at how pathetic some of them were. Like Marco. We never fucked, just spent a lot of time talking on the phone about sex, and a few times having phone sex.

One particular night, we were having one of our sex talks when he told me he fantasized about me sucking his big, black dick nice and slow. He said he liked for a woman to be on her knees, worshipping his dick and sucking it and loving it, with long, slow swallows from his head to his balls. Well, it all sounded good until he told me he expected (yes, EXPECTED!!) me to drink his cum. I thought I had heard him wrong until he repeated himself. Now, I know he was out of his rodeo-do-si-do-rabbit-ass mind with that shit. And I told him that. Then he said, "Well, maybe we can compromise. Don't swallow." Whaaat?!! I was too through. I told him, "I got a better one for ya." When he asked, "What's that?" I said, "This!" Then hung up on his ass. The nerve of him to think I'd let him bust off in my damn mouth. I'm a ho. Not some dirty whore who willingly gulps down buckets of cum. Not that I haven't done it before, but only with my damn man. Not some fucking nigga I'm simply fucking. Don't get it twisted!

Then there was Edwin, my first—and *last*, blind date. Dude wasn't bad looking, and I was contemplating making a move on his ass so I could taste the goods. But his damn breath stunk so bad, I thought I would throw up everything I had eaten right in his damn face. It was more than simply bacteria around his teeth and gums that caused his bad breath. I am convinced the smell of sewage wafted relentlessly from the back of his throat, and clung to the grooves of his tonsils because he was a shit eater. There was no other logical explanation for it. He even had the nerve to be all up in my face, crowding my space and burning the hairs in my nose, trying to get his rap on. The whole time he spoke, I held my breath. I was getting lightheaded, trying to be cordial and keep a straight face. But this man was literally making me sick. I tried to back away just enough to suck in some fresh air before I passed out. Finally, I had had enough. Without being too nasty, I got up, and said, "Don't call me; I'll call you."

Then there was Dexter. Damn him! And damn me! That's what the hell I got for going out on the prowl. I never, ever, bring a man home without running my hands across the front of his pants first. And this particular night was no different. I grabbed a handful of his crotch area and thought I felt (and saw) a lump in his pants, which is why he got through my damn front door. But obviously, the nigga stuffed a pair of sweat socks, or something, down in his shorts. Because when he got here, what I felt, is not what the fuck I saw. When I measured him with my ruler, I had to do it again to make sure that the measurements and my eyes weren't playing tricks on me.

Here he was six-six, two hundred forty pounds; chiseled from head to damn toe, with big hands, a big nose, size fourteen feet, and a teenie-weenie Oscar Meyer Weiner. What kind of shit is that? All I can say is that another thick, strapping nigga dispelled the myth. And, yes. I was more than disappointed. I was downright disgusted to say the least. Humph.

The minute he stepped out of his boxers, my over-heated pussy immediately began to lose its steam. The fool was trying his damnedest to seduce me. And as fine as he was, I didn't have the heart to throw his ass out. So, I did what any decent ho would do. I gave him a pity-fuck. I let the nigga crawl up on me, stick what felt like his thumb in me, then, after about six pumps, he had the fucking audacity to ask me if it felt good. He had the gall to be pumping me like Humpty Dumpty, then wanted to know if it felt good.

I wanted to ask, "Does what feel good?" But, instead, I humored him, and screamed and moaned like he was ripping my insides out. And every chance I got, I silently rolled my eyes up in my head, chuckling to myself. He was sweating and grunting, working overtime. I grabbed and pulled at his dick. Yet, no matter how hard he stroked, the nigga couldn't even fill my basket.

Anyway, he pulled out of me, then climbed up over my chest, slid his dicklet (my term for his little assed dick) between my titties, pressed them together, then pumped and pumped as if he was really doing something spectacular. He was panting, and huffing away. Just a choo-chooing his little heart out. I engaged him in some dirty talk. Lied about how good he made my pussy feel. Gassed him up to no end about him being the best fuck I'd had in months. I "oooh-baby-babied," "yes-big daddy-daddied" him until he cracked a nut as thick as oatmeal. And the crazy thing is, that little assed dick shot like a damn cannon. He blasted his nut all over the place. I'm certain the nigga tried to bust in my face. It's a good thing I turned my head when I did; otherwise, the shit would have hit me in my damn eye, instead of hitting the headboard. You can rest assured, he never saw the inside of these walls again!

Forty minutes pass and I am still up, sifting through my "miserable fucks" list. I squeeze my eyes shut tight, then concentrate on my breathing. In that moment, a thought comes to mind. I jump up and race to my PC. I know exactly where I want to spend the holidays. I wait for my computer to boot, then to go online and book a ten-day trip to Egypt. Yes, the Motherland, that's where I want to bring in the New Year. I've always wanted to see the Pyramids, visit the Valley of the Kings, and go to the museums. *I hope I'll be able to experience all that Egypt has to offer, including some African dick*, I think, getting back in bed and finally falling to sleep.

When I awaken at six a.m., I quickly jump in the shower, then rush around the house trying to get dressed. And now it's nine-fifteen, and I am on my way to my OB-GYN appointment. My stomach is in knots. And

I feel the beginnings of a headache emerging. *Ho, I know you ain't getting cold feet. As much as you like to fuck, you don't need to be thinking about being hogged down with no crying-ass baby.* "Hell, no," I snap, veering off the Garden State Parkway ramp towards South Orange Avenue. "I'm almost eight weeks. The sooner I get this over with, the better off I'll be. I'll be able to get on with my life."

Bitch, please. You shouldn't be in this mess in the first place. Your ho-ass is supposed to always be on point.

"Mistakes happen," I rationalize.

Yeah, ho, and mistakes kill. Next time, before you let your hot ass get caught up in the moment, make sure you strap the nigga up or you're gonna end up with something you can't scrape outta ya ass. A reckless ho is a dangerous ho.

I make a right turn onto Old Short Hills Road, then follow the road until I reach my doctor's office. I find a parking space, then go toward the posh brick and glass building.

When I enter my doctor's office, I give the receptionist my name, then take a seat and wait to be called. While I am waiting to see the doctor, I pick up a few brochures off the wooden coffee table and read some information about STD's, and HIV.

OhmyGod, the statistics are really scary. Every time I read that AIDS is now the leading cause of death for African-American women between the ages of 25 and 34, I get sick to my stomach. And when I read that out of the 166 estimated numbers of babies born with HIV each year, 104 of them are African-American; then to read that non Hispanic blacks between the ages of 19 and 24 were 20 times more likely to be infected than any other racial group, really had my stomach in knots.

Yeah, ho, just like I said, mistakes kill. Sex is glorified and glamorized by the media, in music and books. And your ho-ass don't make it any better. Morning cum, afternoon cum, evening cum, you need it. Want it. Love it. And you know you could use a hot dose of dick cream down your cum-loving throat to get your day started. All you think about is sex, sex, sex. And no matter how responsible or safe you've tried to be, look at your dumb ass now. Knocked up.

Oh, please. There's nothing wrong with loving, or enjoying, sex. There's nothing wrong with being uninhibited. The key is (and will always be) to be totally responsible for your choices. And to be completely honest with yourself and your partners about what your needs are. You are always going to need, want and crave sex. I'm sorry, boo, but you love dick!

I sigh. A full-fledge headache is pounding in the center of my forehead as I try to fight off the voices in my head. I pick up another pamphlet. This one provides information on the different stages of an abortion: Manual Aspiration, four or five weeks from last menstrual; Vacuum aspiration, seven to fifteen weeks from last menstrual; Dilation and Evacuation, fifteen to twenty-four weeks from last menstrual. As I continue reading the procedural process of each type, it is clear to me the longer you wait, the more complicated the method. *Oh my God,* I think, *who in the world would deliberately have an abortion at six months of pregnancy?* I don't think I could do it. I take a deep sigh, thankful I am still in the early stages of pregnancy.

So what you gonna do, kill an innocent child now because your ho-ass done fucked up? That's a life growing inside of you. How can you be so fucking selfish?

Ho, please. Selfish my ass. You doin' the right thing. Your ass ain't ready to be no damn mother. You too busy chasing dick to be tied down to a child you don't want. Hell, you the type of bitch who would probably get all depressed 'n shit, then try to kill the little fucker in its sleep. So, fuck all that dumb shit; get the little crumb-snatching bastard scraped out, sucked out, or whatever! And keep it movin'.

Nonsense, you can still get your fuck on, and be the ho-freak you are and still be a decent mother. You'd just have to be able to balance the two. And be very careful who you let in and out of your house, and bed. You'd have to cut back on fucking a bunch of stray niggas. Find one or two steady dicks and stick with fucking them, instead of being so damn greedy.

Please, ho, you know you'd be bored with the same ole dicks; get real. I bet you if a man pulled out his dick right now, you'd drop down and take the head of his cock in your throat while your tongue lapped every inch of his shaft, slipping a finger or two into his ass, working his hole and sucking his dick until he couldn't take it any longer, until his body shook and he exploded a thick nut over your tongue, down your throat, over your lips and onto your chin. Then you'd continue to suck and lick him until you got every drop of his sweet, sticky dick milk. 'Cause that's exactly what a messy, cock-sucking ho like you does.

Oh, give me a fucking break. That's still not a reason to have an abortion.

"I'm going through with it," I whisper, looking up at the ceiling. "The last thing I want to be is some man's baby momma." I close my eyes, pulling in a deep, exasperated breath.

That's right; good answer. You won't be able to use your pussy for a while, but come tomorrow, you'll be back sucking dick and taking it in the ass like the greedy, dick-loving ho you are.

OhmyGod, you selfish bitch! And you don't think Garrett should have a say in all of this? He is the child's father. He has a right to know.

Please, you stupid ho, only if you are keeping it. Other than that, you don't have to tell him shit. It's your body. You don't want him or that little thing growing inside of you, anyway, so let it go.

All this back and forth dialogue is starting to make my head spin. "I don't need this shit right now, so will you please shut the fuck up!" I scream in my head. "I'm getting rid of it and that's all there is to it."

"Bianca Rivers," the nurse calls out. I let out a bittersweet sigh of relief, standing up. She smiles. "Right this way. Doctor Krishna is ready for you."

CHAPTER
THIRTY-SIX

"**M**y pussy aches for some of that fat, black dick," I bluntly state into the phone, lying across my bed with my hand between my legs, lightly brushing my fingers across my clit. It's been two weeks since my last dose of dick, and a ho is more than ready to get fucked *down*.

"Damn, baby. You making my dick hard."

"Come fuck me, Majestic."

"When?"

I glance at the clock. 7:49 p.m.

"Nooooooow," I purr into his ear. "Mmmm…I need your dick deep inside me, now, big daddy!"

"Damn, baby. You want me to come make love to you?"

I frown. "What?!" I snap. "Make love? No, nigga, I said I want you to fuck me! Fuck my pussy 'til it is raw and torn inside out."

"Awww, shit. That's what I'm talking 'bout. I'll be over in a minute to beat that shit up."

"Good," I say delighted, disconnecting the call.

I scroll through my address book, then press the call button. "Yo, speak," the voice says.

"Hello, Nelson," I say.

"Who's this?"

"It's Janaye, big daddy."

"Oh, damn. What's good, baby?"

"You, and that sweet black dick," I state. "You feel like getting it wet tonight?"

"Hell yeah," he says excitedly. "When?"

"Tonight, around eleven-thirty."

"I'll be there."

"Perfect," I say, disconnecting the call.

Yes, it's exactly what it looks like. After my little ordeal at the doctor's office three weeks ago, I am feeling real greedy tonight. And I'm in the mood for a double-dose of dick. And, yes, I'm going to have a two for one fuckfest tonight. The last two days, my libido has been off the damn charts. All I want to do is fuck. It's like a switch has clicked on, and I am in nonstop fuck mode.

Twenty minutes later, my doorbell rings. I open the door, and let Majestic in. He's looking good in a beautiful, brown leather bomber with a chocolate brown scully over his head. He removes his coat and hat and hands them to me. He's wearing Thierry Mugler's "Angel Men." It's one of my favorites on a man, and it smells irresistibly delicious on him.

Unfortunately, once he gets inside and takes off his clothes, I am surprisingly unmoved. When I was on the phone talking to him and before he got here, I wanted to be fucked senseless, wanted to fuck the skin off his dick. Hearing his voice had me moist. But, now that he's here, standing in front of me, in all of his scrumptious nakedness, I am not the least bit inter-ested in having him sweating all over me, jabbing up my pussy. Just like that. I want him out of my house.

I sigh. I try to focus on how good his dick will feel inside of me. Try to conjure up sweet images of having toe-curling orgasms. But nothing happens. And I know it really has nothing to do with him, per se, 'cause he's fine as hell, and can fuck his ass off. Oh, how I wanted to be slayed, but I don't have that tingly feeling I nor-mally get when I see a stiff dick attached to a muscular man.

"I can't wait to get up in that pussy, again," he says, pulling in his bottom lip. "My dick felt good as hell in that shit, real talk. You take dick better than my girl."

I smile. "That's because I take pride in what I do, baby," I say, forcing myself to get in the mood. There's a part of me that really doesn't want to send him on his way without at least trying to get in the mood. "Dick is my specialty."

He grins, stroking his dick. "That's wassup, baby. And I got a whole lot of it for you to put to use tonight."

I open my mouth to tell him that I've changed my mind, that tonight's not a good night, but the voice in my head gets to me first. *Ho, snap out of it. If you let all that dick walk up outta here without fucking it first, I'ma revoke your gotdamn ho card. You know we don't let nothing that good go to waste. You better represent.*

And with that, nothing else needs to be said. I take him by the hand and silently say, "Oh, sweet pussy, please don't fail me now," as I am leading him up the stairs.

Once we are inside my bedroom, he starts kissing me softly on my neck. Untying my robe, he places his hands on either side of my hips, then pulls me into him. "You sexy as hell," he says, gazing into my eyes. "You could really fuck a weak nigga's head up." He plants more wet kisses along my neck, and over my shoulders.

"Oh, so you're not weak," I ask playfully.

"I'm weak for good pussy," he says in between his kisses, "but I'm definitely not weak-minded." His hands find their way to my ass. "You got a nice, big ass."

"Tell me something I don't already know," I tease, reaching for his dick and stroking it. Although mentally I am still not into it, my body responds to his touch and his kisses. He slips his left hand between my legs and begins playing with my clit while his right hand kneads my breasts. He grabs my left one and twirls his tongue around its nipple before placing it in his mouth. His warm, wet mouth and tongue causes an electric current to shoot through me. My nipples have always been sensitive, but tonight they are on extra high.

Despite myself, a moan escapes me as he lowers himself down onto his knees and begins leaving a trail of wet kisses along my stomach, dipping his tongue into my navel. He has two fingers inside of me, moving them in a nice, steady rhythm, causing my knees to buck. I begin fucking his hand.

"That's right, wet my fingers up. I want you to cum all over my hand." When his face reaches the neat triangular patch of hair between my legs, I spread my legs apart and allow him to mount his mouth over my clit. I grab him by the back of the head and fuck his mouth. Before I know it, I toss my right leg up over his shoulder and start grinding my pelvis into his mouth.

"Ah, yes, suck that clit...oh, oh, oh, yes..." An intense orgasm was building up inside of me. I can feel it in my stomach, shooting through my back, coursing throughout my body, making its way toward my clit, ready to explode out of my pussy in any minute. "Ah, ah, ah...gobble that pussy up, nigga. Oh, yes..."

"Yeah, you like that shit," he whispers, glancing up at me while jerking his dick. He places his mouth back on my clit, and continues finger-fucking me. "That's right, baby, nut for me." I buck my hips. Moan again, and again, and again until I drench his hand with my sweet cream. He removes his hand, and I watch as cum drips between his fingers. He slips them into his mouth, licking and sucking them clean. "Daaaaaamn, your pussy tastes good. That shit's nice and wet; now I'm ready to fuck."

I reach for him as he gets up off his knees. As wet as

my pussy is, and as good as he has made me feel, I still don't feel like being fucked. Truth be told, now that I've cum, I feel like putting him out. I try to shake the feeling off.

"It's my turn," I say, pushing him back towards the bed. "Lie back on the bed and let me wet your dick nice and slow for you." I drop down to my knees, and take his dick in my mouth.

"Yeah, that's what it is," he moans, leaning back on his forearms, looking down at me as I swirl my tongue over the head of his dick, then slip it back into my mouth. "Ah, shit. That's right, suck that dick…fuck…"

Then when his cock is nice and slippery from my spit, I lift up and put his dick in the middle of my chest, press my plump breasts together and give him a nice, wet, titty fuck until he nuts all over me, smearing his cum around my nipples. And the crazy shit is: I really want to lick his dick cream off my damn nipples. That is the only time my pussy twitches. Seeing his dick milk spurt out of his dick and onto my titties turns me on.

"Damn, that was good," he says, sitting up, then wiping himself off. He reaches for my titties and lightly pulls my nipples, then rolls them between his fingers. I moan. His dick is still hard. "I want some head, baby; then I wanna get up in that pussy."

I take him back into my mouth and slowly suck him again, gliding my mouth down the back of his shaft and flicking my tongue over his balls every so often before devouring all of his dick.

"Yeah, that's what I'm talkin' 'bout...suck that shit, baby..."

Once I get my groove, I greedily suck his dick like it's a Charms lollipop. Slobbering and spitting all over it, cupping his balls and slowly licking and pulling them into my mouth one at a time. And when I finally have him all the way down in my throat, causing him to buck his hips and open and close his toes, I break a major dick-sucking rule. I throw up all over his dick.

And of course he storms up out of here pissed off, but who gives a fuck. I strip and change my sheets, then race back into the bathroom, throwing up again. When I am finished, I wash my face and brush my teeth, then get ready to climb into bed when my doorbell rings. I glance at the clock. 11:30 p.m. It's Nelson.

"Shit," I say out loud, pulling the comforter up over me and turning off my night lamp. "I forgot to call him and cancel." I sigh. *Oh well, fuck him*. He rings the doorbell three more times before giving up. I close my eyes, deciding to delete his number.

CHAPTER
THIRTY-SEVEN

"Hey, Sis, how's it going?" Tyler asks.

"Hey to you, too. Everything's fine, thanks. How are you and the family?"

"We're all fine. Haven't spoken to you since Thanksgiving so I wanted to give you a ring to see how you were doing."

"Awww," I say, smiling. "That's real sweet of you."

He chuckles. "Well, I kinda figured it beats dropping by early in the morning."

"Well, big bro, for the record, you can drop by any time you like. But don't get too excited," I tease, "'cause that doesn't mean I'm gonna always open the door to let you in."

"Hey, hey," he says, laughing. "I'm an officer of the law. I have ways of still getting in."

"Yeah, yeah, come kick the door in and arrest me."

"How 'bout a hug instead?"

I smile. "Any time."

"You talk to Garrett yet?"

"Nope," I say, lying across my sofa, rubbing my stomach. "He hasn't called me, and I haven't called him."

"I see. Don't you think you should reach out to him?"

"For what?" I ask, hoping to not sound too callous. But, what the fuck?! "He's not my man."

"Yeah, maybe he wasn't, but after three years, I'd think you'd have, if nothing else, a fondness for him. I'd hate to see you let a good man slip away."

Yeah, I did. I was fond of that thick, cut, juicy-ass dick. "It's probably for the best."

"For who?"

"For him."

"Why, don't you think you deserve to have a good man in your life?"

"Of course I do."

"So then, what's the problem?"

I think, consider, his question; contemplate telling him that the only thing good I want from a man is his dick, that I am easily bored with men; that I am very freaky and nasty. That I love being face-fucked and sucking dick, edging a man for hours, wrapping my lips around the underside of the rim of his dickhead and working it with my warm, wet lips, taking him to the brink again, and again, and again, each time more intense 'til he plunges into a shattering orgasm. I wonder how he would respond to all of this, then decide it probably wouldn't go so well.

"I'd rather not discuss it," I state, "so, let's change the subject, please."

"Okay, you got that. I know when to back up, and mind my own business."

"Thank you."

"So what are your plans for the holidays? Jacki wanted me to invite you over to spend Christmas Eve with us. She's cooking a big dinner, and we'll be lighting the tree. We're expecting about twenty-five people."

"I wish I could. It sounds like it will be fun. But, I'm going to be away."

"Away? Where?"

"Egypt."

"Egypt?" he asks, sounding surprised. "When did you decide to go there?"

"A few weeks ago."

"Wow, how long is the flight?"

"Eleven, twelve hours, I think. It's six or seven hours to Frankfurt, then another five or so hours to Cairo."

"Sounds exciting. When are you leaving? And how long are you going to be over there?"

"Yeah, I'm excited. I'm leaving on the twenty-third."

"Cool. How long will you be gone?"

"I'll be there for ten days."

"Well, you make sure you stay safe.

"I definitely will."

"Who you going with?"

"Myself," I say.

"Wait a minute. You're going to a foreign country by yourself? Are you serious?"

"Tyler, I'm a big girl. I'll be fine."

"The hell you will!" he snaps. "I'm not comfortable

with you flying across the ocean alone. You need me to come along as security."

I laugh. "Boy, you silly. I promise you, I'm gonna be fine. The adventure will do me some good."

"Well, you make sure you leave your hotel info, and check in every night so that I know you're okay."

I shake my head. "Yes, Dad. Anything else?"

"Yeah, I love you."

"I love you more."

"Call me before you leave."

"I will. Give everyone a hug for me."

The minute I hang up from him, my BlackBerry vibrates, alerting me that I have new emails. I pick up the device off of the kitchen counter, then scroll over to my Nutcracker69 address. There are two emails, one from Dickudownallnight and the other from Jamil. *Nigga, please,* I think, deleting Jamil's without opening it. I open Dickudown's: *What's good, baby? I'm still waiting to hear from you. Hit me back, Marquise.*

I sigh. As tempting as his dick looked in that pic he sent, there's a reason why I don't recall who he is, and I'm sure an even better reason why I stopped fucking him. I have no interest in trying to figure it all out. *No going back to dismissed dick*, I think, hitting the reply button. *I've broken enough rules already.* '*Sorry, boo, thanks for the offer. But, I'm not interested.*' I press SEND, then delete his message.

My cell rings. I pick it up and glance at the number

flashing across the screen. It's Wendell. I'm not in the mood for him, either. As matter of fact, I haven't been in the mood for much of anything, particularly any-thing that has to do with a man. The only thing I am interested in at this moment is catching my plane in a few days. I press decline, then toss the phone on the sofa, deciding to go through my phonebook before the new year comes in, and delete useless numbers.

I go into the kitchen, pour myself a glass of ginger ale, then sit at the kitchen table, glancing up at the wooden wall clock. It's almost seven o'clock in the evening. I hold my glass to my lips, pursing my lips before taking a slow, deliberate sip. I sigh. I will need to make some major changes in my life for the New Year. Of course, giving up dick definitely isn't one of the things I plan on changing—or giving up. But, maybe, the number of men I'm fucking at one time does need changing. *For now, at least*, I think, getting up from the table, placing my half-empty glass in the sink, then heading upstairs to lie down. I stifle a yawn, realizing I'm extremely exhausted. I climb up into my bed with my clothes still on, then slowly drift off to sleep.

Two days later, I am running through the house like a raving lunatic, tossing shit into my suitcase, making sure I don't forget anything, before zipping it up and placing it near the front door. My limo will be here in an hour. I run back upstairs to finish putting last minute items into my carry-on, then bring it downstairs and place it beside my suitcase. My doorbell rings, and I think it is my driver to take me to the airport. I glance at my timepiece. It's only one-thirty. My flight doesn't leave until five. "You're early," I say, swinging the door open. "I—"

My jaw drops. "Garrett? What are you doing here?"

"Can I come in?"

I take him in. He looks tired, and as if he's lost some weight. But he is still as fine as ever. A part of me wants to slam the door in his face, curse him out for coming to my home unannounced, but, in all honesty, he hasn't done anything, other than trying to wife me up, to warrant such disrespect. My thoughts temporarily slip back to the last time we were together, how he fucked me deliciously. Better than all the other times. How his dick fit perfectly inside of me; how my pussy saturated his dick with its love juices, causing pellets of lust to rapidly burst through me with every stroke. Then I remember, how being fucked down by him— without a damn condom—got me into all this mess in the first place, and shake the images out of my head.

I step back and allow him to enter. "What brings you here?"

"I was thinking about you," he says as he walks through the door. He glances over at my luggage. "Going somewhere?"

I glance at my watch. "Actually, I am. I thought you were the limo driver when you rang the doorbell. You could have called."

"You mind if I have a seat?" I extend my hand toward the sofa, gesturing for him to sit. He sits, and I find myself taking a seat on the other end of the sofa, keeping a safe distance between us. "Yeah, you're right. I could have called, but I wanted to see you before the holidays."

I smile. "That was thoughtful of you." I remember what Tyler told me, and decide to ask, "How have you been?"

"I've had better days, but nothing I can't shake."

For some reason, him sitting here making small talk feels strange, and makes me uncomfortable. I shift in my seat, deciding to skip all the niceties. "Listen, Garrett, why are you *really* here?"

He raises his brow. "I told you, I wanted to see you."

"Okay, that sounds good, but…"

"I've been having trouble sleeping," he says, leaning forward, resting his forearms on his knees.

"Ohkaaay. And what do I have to do with that?"

He stares at me. The intensity in his eyes feels hot against my flesh. *Oh my God, he knows.*

Nonsense, I reason. "Why are you looking at me like that?"

"You look different."

"Yeah?"

"Yeah, you have this glow about you." *He knows, ho.* He squints, forces himself to look deeper, then tilts his head. "I had a dream you were pregnant."

"Whaat?!" I ask, letting out a nervous chuckle. "Pregnant, me? OhmyGod, what made you dream of something like that?"

I know what some of you bitches are thinking, "Well, you *were*, ho." Well, so what? The fact, whether I was or wasn't, isn't up for discussion with him, not right now at least.

He shrugs, shaking his head. "I don't know. I've had the same dream for the last two weeks. I've been real tired, lately, almost drained. I was talking to my sister about it the other day, and she jokingly asked me if I had gotten someone pregnant. At first I laughed it off, but later on I started wondering if…" he pauses, and allows the silence to fill the space around us. It is at this very moment, I wish I could blink him and what happened between us away. Wish I could rewind the clock and go back to the night he fucked me without a condom, and simply erase it from out of my life. I hold my breath. "You'd tell me if you were pregnant, wouldn't you?"

Okay, now comes the moment of truth. I slowly exhale. "I probably wouldn't. I don't know."

"You don't think I would have the right to know."

I slowly shake my head, diverting my eyes from his. "Not if I wasn't going to keep it. But, that's neither here nor there."

"But would you keep it, if you were?"

"I'm not in love with you, so why would I?"

"Because I'm in love with you, and it would be a life we created."

"Not by choice. And definitely not out of mutual love." He looks as if he's hurt by what I've said. He glances back over at my bags.

"You spending the holidays in San Diego with your family?"

I shake my head. "No, not this year. I'm going to Egypt."

He slowly nods. "I see," he says, pausing. He stares at me. "Always the adventurous one."

"Something like that," I state, glancing at my watch again. *Where is this damn driver?* I think, hoping he'd hurry the hell up and get here.

He keeps his gaze on me, tilting his head. "What will it take?"

"For what? I'm not sure what you're asking."

"For you to let someone love you?"

"I'm not looking for love."

"At some point, we all need and want to be loved."

"Maybe."

"Do you even know what you want? I mean, what are you looking for in a man?"

"You really wanna know, Garrett?" I ask, sighing.

He nods. "Yes, talk to me."

I get up, glancing at my watch, again, pacing the floor. "If I were looking for a man, I would want to meet someone who was as freaky as me. A man who wasn't afraid of pleasing me whenever, however, wherever, without any hang-ups; a man who was comfortable enough in his skin, and in his sexuality, to simply go with the flow and not get caught up in what he thinks I might think after we're done. He wouldn't have to keep going and going, and going, like me. I mean, if the dick was good, I'd be willing to work with him. I would want a man who understood the power of fore-play, and was skilled at delivering the best damn orgasms possible, causing waves of electrifying heat to course through me every time he dipped his tongue in my pussy, or someone who stroked me into an unconscious state every time he slid his dick up in me. That's the kind of man I would want."

He raises his brow. "So, you mean to tell me, getting fucked good is the only thing you'd want out of a man? Well, if that's all that you require, I can give you that. Hell, for the last three years, that's all the hell I've been giving you. Aren't you ever gonna get tired of just being fucked?"

Oh, alright, good dick isn't really the only thing I'd want from a man. In all honesty, I'd want him to not be afraid to love me, or let me love him. I'd want a man who understood the concept of fidelity and trust and commitment, a man with integrity and ambition and patience and compassion. I'd want a man who'd respect me as woman and appreciate my individuality, my sensuality, my sexuality. One who would not deprive me, or deny me. And, yes, damn it…have good dick.

I look Garrett in the eyes and tell him all of this. He stares back at me.

"How can a man with flaws, an imperfect man, love a woman who sees the world through rose-colored lenses?"

I shift my weight from one foot to the other. I shrug. "I'm not sure. However, if I were looking for a man, I wouldn't be looking for perfect. But, is there anything wrong with wanting something or someone close to it?"

Okay, okay. I know nothing in life is perfect, that it's an illusion of what and how we want things to be in the perfect world we create in our minds.

Garrett gets up from his seat and walks over to me. "Bianca, you're a beautiful woman. Have you ever thought that maybe you might really have a problem?"

I frown. "A problem? What kind of problem are you talking about?"

"With sex."

I scoff at his absurdity. "I don't have a problem with sex. I love it."

"Yeah, maybe a little too much."

I place my hand on my hip. "And what exactly is a little too much, Garrett?"

"I think your love for sex might be more of an addiction?"

"An addiction?" I ask indignantly. "Are you serious?"

"Yeah."

"Garrett, now you're really reaching. I enjoy having sex, and lots of it, but that doesn't mean I'm addicted to it. I don't live and breathe sex."

He looks at me disbelievingly.

"I can stop fucking at any time," I huff, wondering if what I say is to convince him or myself. "But why should I? I'm single, and I don't have to answer to anyone, so I can fuck whomever I want, whenever I want."

"But what about having someone to love you?"

Here he goes with this love shit again. "If I were looking for that, then maybe. But, right now, I only wanna fuck."

He shakes his head. "Well, then, let me be the one to keep fucking you."

"Honestly, Garrett, no offense. But I'd become very bored with one man, one dick."

"Maybe you haven't let the right man prove you wrong. Maybe if you were with someone who was open to letting you fuck other cats, as long as they were able to participate and/or watch. Maybe explore the swingers set with you, you wouldn't feel that way."

I try not to show my surprise at what he says, but in my head, I'm thinking: *Swingers? Watching me get fucked? OhmyGod, now he's talking my kind of language, but why now?*

"It's something I've been wanting to talk to you about for over a year," he answers, reading my mind.

"So, you're saying to me, you would be down with threesomes, and you'd be cool with watching me get fucked by someone else."

He nods. "Yeah, as long as I can either get my dick sucked while he's hitting it from the back, or we can both fuck you. And it would have to be a situation that is discreet and mutually comfortable for both of us…"

I cannot believe what I am hearing. Then again, I can. I think back to the first time I let Garrett fuck me in all three holes. He said he wanted to try something different, so he asked to see my toy collection. I got out of bed and walked him into my closet, opened up my secret chest full of sex goodies and gadgets, and watched him rummage through it. He pulled out my anal rocket and leather gag, then took me by the hand and pulled me back to the bed. To say the least, I was shocked, but so fucking turned on. He tied the gag around my mouth, told me to get on my knees and to spread open my ass cheeks. Then he ran his tongue along the crack of my ass before sticking his tongue in my hole while fingering my pussy. After he got my ass nice and wet, he slowly pushed the anal rocket in, then slid his dick inside my pussy, flipping the rocket on. Oh, my God, I came so damn fast and hard. By the time he finished with me, I was seeing stars. And that's when I started breaking every fucking rule in my damn ho book with him.

"There are several swingers groups in Jersey and in the New York area we can check out, and a club in Charlotte, North Carolina I'd like to take you to."

I blink, bringing my attention back to Garrett. I stare at him in disbelief. It is all sounding too good to be true. Fucking him and Wade, together, immediately pops into my mind. I feel myself starting to salivate, and hyperventilate all at once. And this is the first time in weeks my pussy starts to twitch and tingle and marinate in its juices.

"But what if I wanted you to just sit back and jerk off, watching the show?"

"Then I'd be cool with that as well. I'm open to a lot of things, when it comes to you. All I'm asking you to do is step outside of your box for a while, and let's explore sex together. We can take it slow."

"Garrett, listen—" the doorbell rings. "I can't have this discussion right now." I open the door, and I'm relieved that it's my driver. I point to my bags, then tell him I will be out shortly as he carries them out to the car. Garrett gets up from his seat. He watches me as I put on my coat. His eyes lock on mine, then travel to my stomach. He's slowly undressing me. I quickly button my coat. He walks up into my space.

"No pressures. No strings. Just straight fucking, however, wherever, whenever you want this dick." I open my mouth to speak. Prepare to tell him that I can't make him any promises, but he places his finger to my lips. "Sshh, don't answer now."

"Garrett—"

He presses his lips against mine, shutting me up. When he pulls back, I am stunned. "You can't stop me from loving you," he states. "But, you can stop me from seeing you. However, I don't think that's something you really want. I know you feel what I feel. But you need to figure that out. Go out, fuck who you want. Do you, baby. But know that when you're ready, there's a good man willing and ready to love you."

I pull in my bottom lip, taking a deep breath. "I gotta go," I say. "But we *really* need to talk about some things when I return."

He kisses me again. "I'll be here waiting."

Tell him. He deserves to know.

"Um, Garrett, I—I—"

"Yes, what is it?"

Tell him.

"Um, enjoy your holidays."

He smiles. "Enjoy yours as well. Be safe over there."

"Thanks, I will." I look around the house one last time to make sure I have turned everything off, then set the alarm.

Garrett walks out with me. "I'll be thinking about you."

I offer him a smile as he opens the limo door. He closes it once I am in, then stands in my driveway and watches as we drive away before getting into his car. I take another deep breath, then slowly exhale. *I hope I haven't made a mistake*, I think, laying my head back, rubbing my stomach.

Ho, you did what was in your heart. It was what you had to do.

Humph, I guess. As far as I'm concerned, all the ho had to do was make sure the nigga had a condom on. Now look at your ass. So much for bragging about never being pregnant.

Well, you've had a good run. Maybe this is a sign for you to stop chasing Mr. Goodbars, and think about giving Garrett a chance. Hell, he's fine, the dick's good, and he fucks like a stallion. And now he's talking about swinging 'n shit. Ho, that gives you an open invitation to feast on an assortment of dicks, and still have a man of your own. It can't get any better than that. And if shit works out between the two of you, cool. If it doesn't, then you can always take your ass back out on the ho-stroll.

I shake my head, staring out of the window, lost in thought all the way to the airport.

"We are now ready to board Lufthansa flight 403 from Newark to Frankfurt," the attendant says over the intercom. "Passengers flying business and first class can now board." I gather my things, and move towards the line. When I finally get to my seat, I buckle up, then lean my head back and sigh, closing my eyes.

When the flight reaches flying altitude, I peer out into the clouds. Allow myself to get lost in the peacefulness of their fluffy whiteness. The sound of a suction machine cuts into the quietness, and instinctively, I clutch my stomach. I remember hearing somewhere that it's better to regret having done something, than to regret not having done it at all, or something like that. I think back on that afternoon in Dr. Krishna's office, pulling in my bottom lip. I fight back tears. Then I do something I haven't done in years, I find myself wondering about my life beyond a stiff dick. I decide to use this getaway to reflect, consider making some changes in my life. That's not to say I'm dismissing the idea of fucking some exotic-looking, authentic African dick while I'm over in Egypt.

Ho, the only thing you're gonna end up with is some exotic shit your ass can't get rid of, so if I were you I'd think about keeping your legs shut. Get your mind right, and put fucking to the side for a minute. You have more pressing shit to tend to.

I sigh, "Yeah, you're probably right."

"Excuse me, did you say something?" a very handsome, very sexy, distinguished-looking Italian man asks, looking over at me.

"Oh, no," I say, meeting his gaze. *Damn this man is sexy.* "I was thinking out loud."

He smiles, knowingly, then goes back to his Sudoku puzzle.

Garrett's voice plays in my head. *You can't stop me from loving you…Have you ever thought that maybe you might have an addiction? But know that when you're ready, there's a good man willing and ready to love you.*

Damn you, Garrett! I shift in my seat, then out of nowhere, I get this crazy idea, wondering what a woman would say to her pussy if she had to write it a letter. The thought makes me laugh. I reach for my bag underneath the seat in front of me. I pull out a notepad and pen, then write:

Dear Pussy,

Some may say that over the years I have misused you, and even abused you. That I have taken you for granted, that I have been disrespectful to you. But the truth is I love you, dear pussy. I love all things you represent: womanhood, femininity, strength, the valley that brings life into the world. I love the way you feel, the way you purr when you are being stroked just right, the way you roar in delight when you're being fucked. I love the sweet, musky scent you emit when you become overly excited from gripping and slurping in a thick dick. I love the way your walls shiver, the way your lips swell, the way your clit tingles when you are on the brink of an orgasm. I love the way your juices slosh and splash along the sides of a dick as it's being thrust in and out of you, deeply and purposefully. The way you greedily milk the dick, causing a man to scream out in ecstasy. Oh, yes, my beautiful pussy, there's nothing more magnificent than you. You have the power to make a man's eyes roll up in the back of his head, make his toes curl, have him forget his name. It is you who can bring a man to his knees, have him losing his mind over you. It is you they beg for, and crave for.

Some may say I hate you for the number of men I have allowed to enjoy you, even when they were not deserving of your goodness. But you see, my precious pussy, I heard your whispers in the still of the night, felt your aching, for a beautiful black dick. I listened to your sweet pleas for pleasure. And I took heed, not caring if he was worthy of you or not. His worth wasn't, and isn't, important to me. What hangs between his legs is. And his ability to feed your hunger, to quench your thirst. For a good dick and a good fucking is all I care about. And with each man I have invited inside of you, to be engulfed by your warmth and wetness, I have relished your moans of satisfaction.

Why would I forsake you? You have been good to me. You, my precious pussy, are the keeper of joy and pleasure and pain; the receiver of a man's spirit. And when you open your floodgates, all things good and bad flow from the center of you in abundance, allowing you to cleanse.

Carelessly, I have allowed one man to plant his spirit in you, and now his seed has taken root, and will bring forth a child, my child. One I am ambivalent about having. But I couldn't go through with that abortion. I just couldn't. So, I don't know what this will mean for me, or for you. I can't

-promise you that I won't continue to fuck while I am pregnant, but I will promise, no, no…I'll try, not to fuck with wild abandon for a while. I can't make any guarantees. 'Cause I love to fuck. And I love how fucking makes you feel. You are very special to me. I appreciate you. I adore you. We are connected. I am my pussy. And my pussy is me.

Love always,

Bianca

I reread it, then chuckled to myself, shaking my head. *What a hot damn mess*, I think, neatly folding it then slipping it inside my purse. I'm not only a dick-loving ho, but now I'm a pregnant one. Isn't that some shit?

I purse my lips, thinking about this pregnancy. *There's nothing you can do about it now. Everything happens for a reason. Be thankful that out of all the dicks you've fucked you didn't end up with something deadly. Be thankful it was Garrett who bust up in you raw, and got you pregnant. He'll be a good father.*

I take a deep breath, deciding to tell Garrett that I am carrying his child the minute I return from my trip; that I am open to exploring the swingers' scene with him; that I want to have a threesome with him and Wade. I will tell him that I will give him a chance, but the minute he starts smothering me, or stressing me, or getting on my damn nerves, all bets are off.

I glance over at the handsome passenger sitting next to me and catch him eyeing me. He is no longer working on his puzzle. Instead, he is sipping on a glass of champagne. By the look in his eyes, he's had more than one glass. I take in his clean-shaven face. Admire his tanned skin, dark eyes and chiseled features. I don't see any ring on his thick finger.

"Are you married?" I decide to ask.

"Divorced," he answers. "And you?"

I glance down in his crotch. "Extremely horny," I say in a whisper, slowly licking my lips.

He gives me a mischievous smirk, taking a long gulp from his flute.

"You know, I was staring at you earlier. You are a very beautiful woman."

"Thank you." I lean into his ear again and whisper. "Have you ever slipped your dick into a black woman?"

"I love all women, Beautiful," he says. "I don't discriminate. Will you be staying in Frankfurt?"

"No, I'm catching a connecting flight to Cairo," I share.

"That's too bad. I would have loved to continue this discussion, and perhaps further explore each other's passions, in a more private setting."

I look around the spacious cabin. There is only a sprinkle of people flying first class. "Well, it'll be dark soon. And we still have several hours before we land." I pause, giving him time to absorb what I am offering.

I reach for my purse and discreetly pull out a box of condoms. He nods, knowingly. "Perhaps," I continue, lightly touching his knee, "I can entice you to some slow, wet head, then a little dose of sweet pussy."

He lifts his flute, grinning. "Perhaps you can." He squeezes his legs shut, allowing me to see the meaty bulge that has formed in his lap. I fight the urge to touch it, to stroke it against the fabric of his slacks.

"In another hour, I will slip into the bathroom. Wait five minutes, to make sure no one is paying attention, then come in behind me."

He finishes his drink, licking his lips. This time he leans over towards me and whispers in my ear, "And I'm going to fuck that sweet black pussy like no other man has."

I lean my head back, and smile. The thought of giving a stranger some of this juicy pregnant pussy excites me and is making my panties wet. Oh, don't look at me like that. Why should I pass up this opportunity to get fucked on a plane? Oh, alright, if it'd make some of you judgmental hoes feel better, how 'bout I let him fuck me in the ass, depending on how fat his dick is, instead of giving him some pussy? Would that make you feel better? Geesh. Then again, I don't give a hot shit what the hell any of you think. I'm a grown ass woman! My slick cunt muscles constrict. *Oh, yes*, I think, shifting in my seat. *I'm gonna suck and fuck the shit out of this fine-ass man.* Hell, I'm knocked up, not disabled. Besides, I'm the Man Handler, baby. And I love to fuck!

ABOUT THE AUTHOR

Cairo resides in New Jersey. His next literary creation is *Deep Throat Diva*. His travels to Egypt are what inspired his pen name. You can visit the author at www.myspace.com/Cairo2u, www.blackplanet.com/Cairo2u, or email the author at cairo2u@verizon.net.

DADDY LONG STROKE

ONE

Damn, I love eatin' pussy. 'Specially when a broad got that sweet 'n tangy, saucy-type pussy that sticks on the tip of my tongue. Or that juicy, gushy-type pussy that squirts into my mouth, then drips down my chin as I slurp it all up. Man, listen... there's nuthin' like havin' a chick squattin' up over my face, sittin' her pussy down on this long tongue, or havin' her on her back wit' her legs up over my shoulders and my face buried deep between them smooth thighs while I'm tongue-drillin' her, or havin' her bent over a chair wit' her ass spread open and my tongue deep-strokin' her from her asshole to the back of her slit— while I'm beatin' my dick, or got her throatin' it.

Mmmph, mmmph, mmph...I love the way it tastes, and smells—well, provided the ho isn't a walkin' fish market, smellin' like sewage, or leakin' a buncha shit that looks like snot or cottage cheese, feel me? A smelly bitch, forget it…no tongue, no dick, nada—it's a muthafuckin' wrap! But a chick who keeps that box right…mmmph, man, listen…finger lickin' good! There's nuthin' more intoxicatin' than the savorin' scent of a clean, excited pussy oozin' wit' hot, sticky juices. Gotdaaaaamn, talkin' 'bout gobblin' up a pussy got my dick bricked like a muhfucka, word up. And, on some real shit, I love eatin' it almost as much as I love fuckin' it.

I also like to kiss on the pussy. From soft, gentle kisses to deep, tongue-probin' French-kissin', I love havin' my tongue and lips all up on it, and in it. Sometimes, I lay my tongue flat up against it, then flap it up and down, draggin' it along the front and back of her slit. I use my mouth and tongue to stimulate all the sensitive areas of a bitch's pussy and clit, circlin' my tongue all over and 'round it. I listen to what makes a broad moan, and know when to change it up to give her that ultimate tongue experience.

Fuck what ya heard. Tongue-fuckin' is sumthin' a muhfucka should take pride in when doin' it. Just like I expect a broad to handle this dick like she loves it, I expect the same shit from myself when it comes to eatin' her pussy. I make love to that shit wit' my mouth, lips, and tongue, eatin' it like there's a chocolate-covered cherry stuck dead in the center of her pussy. And the only way to get to that sweet muhfucka is by mountin' ya wet mouth 'round it, then plungin' ya tongue deep in it, lickin', lappin' stickin', and flickin' that hole 'til she starts buckin' them hips up. See. A nigga like me is a greedy pussy eater, real talk. I ain't tryna stop 'til a bitch's walls start to shake, her asshole starts to ache, and she's chantin' to a higher power. That's when I slowly slip these big-ass fingers in her, swirlin' 'em 'round the inside of her cunt, pressin' up on that G-spot while I'm suckin' on her clit. I don't care how long it takes, I'ma make sure she gets hers. And when her breath quickens, her body quivers, and her moans escalate, I start wildin' out on the pussy—suckin' and lickin' her clit like a frantic, crazed-ass muhfucka 'til she nuts all over my tongue, hard. Then I ease up over top of her, slip my tongue in her mouth so she can taste her creamy juice on it, while I'm slidin' this dick up in her. And by the time I'm done slayin' her wit' this wood, nine-times-outta ten, the bitch done forgot her name and address, done tossed me the keys to her whip, or done begged me to move in.

So, to my nigga's who eat pussy: keep ya tongues wet, playas. And to those lame cats who act like they scared to taste the pussy, or who can't eat no pussy: You'se some wack-ass muhfuckas, word up! Get ya minds right, my niggas, and step ya tongue game up 'fore another muhfucka takes ya spot, real talk.

Nah, hol' up! I ain't sayin' e'ery ho deserves to have her pussy eaten 'cause some of these broads out here are straight nasty. That's why a muhfucka gotta use some discretion. But for the ones who keep that pussy lookin' right and feelin' right, a muhfucka gotta learn to let it do what it do, feel me? 'Cause trust me. I've had plenty of bitches drop major paper, or lace a muhfucka wit' some wears, after I done served 'em a night of tongue lickin', followed up wit' a pussy beatdown wit' this long-ass dick.

Like this trick I got holed up in my room right now. Shakeeta's her name, a brown-skinned cutie from Irvington—wit' a lil' waist and one hundred and forty pounds of ass 'n titties. And, of course, she's a ho I met offa Myspace. We been fuckin' off and on for 'bout two months now, and she's already sucked down my dick and swallowed my nut 'bout eight times. And I've fucked her 'bout three. Now, she's actin' like she's in love wit' a muhfucka. But tonight's the first time I'm givin' her this tongue treatment. And the only reason she's gettin' it *now* is 'cause she laced a muhfucka wit' four pairs of 7 For All Mankind jeans and two pair of Gucci loafers for my birthday. Well, it ain't my actual born day, but she doesn't know that shit. Yo, relax. Sit tight. I'll explain later.

Shit, hol' up…let me introduce myself to ya'll, first, before I start suckin' the nut outta this broad's fuck-box. Aiight, check it. I'ma six-foot-four, 215 pound—lean and solid, for the record—slightly bow-legged cat with dark-brown eyes, thick full lips, a chiseled chest, strong muscular back, and big hands. My government name is

Alexander Maples. But my mans 'n 'em call me Alley Cat, 'cause a nigga like me is always prowlin' 'round for some new pussy. However, on some real shit, I shoulda been named Hershey 'cause I'ma dark chocolate nigga that melts in ya mouth and all up in ya guts. Yeah, that's right. I'm ya sweetest, most dangerous addiction. And I'm here to feed ya cravin's—one stroke, one slurp, at a muthafuckin' time.

So I'ma let you know from the gate. I'm the type a cat who loves to fuck—all day, e'eryday. Just like the U.S. Postal Service, I'm always ready to deliver. Rain, snow or sleet, I don't care if it's in ya face, ya mouth, or ya muthafuckin' ass, I'm ready to skeet. That's not to say that e'ery chick I get at is willin' to give up the pussy after seein' all this beef hangin'. 'Cause eight outta ten times, the ho's gonna run scared. But, for the hoes who do try, it definitely doesn't mean that they can actually handle all this dick. It only means they done bit off more dick than they can chew—or fuck, I should say. So they usually grin 'n bear, beg 'n pray, or cry 'n scream, hopin' their well-fucked, over stretched pussies snap back for them average dicked niggas they fuck wit'.

However, for those ambitious freaks wit' them bottom-less, unlatchable pussies, the ones who take e'ery inch of this dick, they call me Daddy Long Stroke 'cause I gotta long, thick, chocolate stick that heats up and beats up the pussy. Nice 'n slow, long 'n deep, fast 'n hard, all muthafuckin' night long—anyway, anywhere, anyhow you want it, I give it. Ya heard? You want it rough, you want it rugged. I'ma slay ya muthafuckin' ass 'til ya shit-hole starts to smoke. You want it slow, you want it gentle. I'ma rock ya box 'til ya eyes cross, real talk. Fuck wit' this dick if ya want, a nigga like me'll have ya ass crawlin' 'round tryna find ya way home. Have ya soakin' ya swollen pussy lips overnight. So, I'ma tell ya some real shit. Fuck at ya own risk. And be prepared to get rocked inside out 'cause I'ma slam it, grind it, and wind it, all up in ya. Deeply, savagely, tenderly—whatever, this dick is made for stretchin' that sweet, tight, wet pussy to the limit. And there you have it.

Anyway, back to the bitch I got in front of me. I have her legs up over my shoulders, my face is buried between her thighs, and I'm tongue-fuckin' the shit outta her pussy, alternatin' between eatin' her pussy and lickin' her asshole while jerkin' my dick. I got her wrigglin' and squirmin' and moanin'. "Oh, yes…ah… ah…oh, yes… ohmyGod, you gonna make me cum…aaaah…aaaaah… oh, shit…I'm cuuuuu—" Now guess what the fuck she does while she's creamin' on my muthafuckin' tongue?

This nasty bitch lets out a loud, hot-ass fart! And it's one of them rotten-ass, lingerin' kind. Now I don't know 'bout you, but this kinda shit ain't acceptable. Keepin' shit real, a few times I've had a chick fart while suckin' on my dick. But, I have never—and I mean mutha-fuckin' *never*— had no shit like this happen. It feels and tastes like I've just sucked in a mouthful of horse shit.

This bitch is lucky I'm not into smackin' up a chick, 'cause if I was... man, listen, I'd peel her muthafuckin' skull back. I can tell she's embarrassed. But I. Don't. Give. A. Fuck. I'm sorry, it's a wrap. Game over! This bitch has to go!

"Yo, what the fuck?!" I snap, yankin' my head back and jumpin' up. "You'se one nasty ass bitch for real, yo. How you gonna bust off in my muthafuckin' face like that?"

"I'm so sorry," she says, apologetically. "Sometimes I cum real hard and, when I do, I pass gas unexpectedly. I tried to hold it in, but it crept out. You had me feeling so good. I really didn't mean for it to happen."

Crept out? Nah, fuck that. Who the fuck she think she's talkin' to? I done fucked her pussy inside out, makin' her nut 'til she shakes. And not once did this bitch ever bust outta her ass. But, okay, maybe she does cum hard and farts at the same time from time to time. Yeah, whatever! If that's the case, then why the fuck didn't the slut warn a muhfucka? Crept out, my ass! This bitch is literally full of shit—word up. The way that fart roared the fuck out, the bitch pushed it out purposefully, feel me?

"Well, why the fuck didn't you tell me to move outta the way, or somethin', instead of havin' a nigga's face all pressed up in your ass like that, suckin' in ya funky-ass fumes?"

"I got caught up in the moment," she offers, sittin' up. "And wasn't thinkin'."

"You wasn't thinkin'?" I repeat. She tries to keep from laughin'. But, a muhfucka like me don't find shit amusin' 'bout someone bustin' they ass in ya muthafuckin' grill. Stupid bitch! "Well, guess what? You not thinkin' done got ya funky ass put the fuck out. So, get ya shit on, and get ta steppin'."

She looks at me like I have boogers 'n snot hangin' outta my nose or some shit. But fuck what ya heard. I ain't the one. She frowns. "Are you serious? I said it was an accident."

"Yo, I'm dead-ass. Get the fuck out." I walk over and start pickin' up her clothes and tossin' 'em at her.

She gets up offa the bed and starts snatchin' her shit up. "That's real fucked up. You know that, right?"

"Bitch, I don't give a fuck," I hear myself sayin' in my head. But I igg the ho instead; stare at her as she puts back on her bra. I pick up my cell, scroll through my address book 'til I get to Carla's number. I hit the call button, then wait for her to pick up.

"Hey, boo," she answers. "You finally got around to calling me."

"Hey, baby, what's good?"

"You," she coos.

I cut my eye over at Shakeeta. She got the nerve to be ice-grillin' me while gettin' dressed. I keep my eyes locked on hers. Stare her down. Stupid bitch! Who the fuck names their child Shakeeta any damn way? Fuckin' ghetto-ass bird.